nickelodeon

THE LOUD HOUSE

PAPERCUTZ

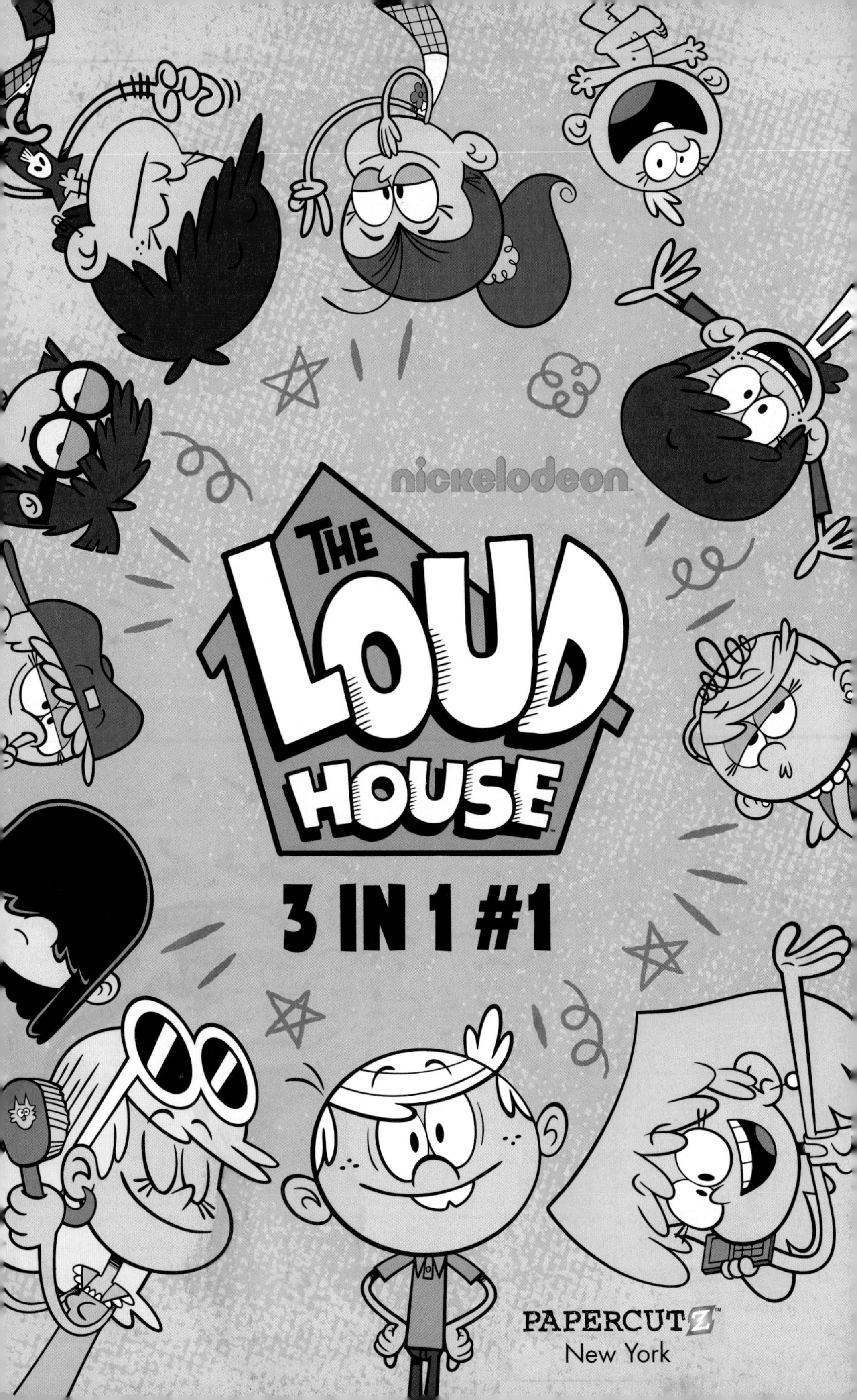

nickelodeon

THE LOUD HOUSE

3 IN 1 #1

PAPERCUTZ
New York

LENI
LORI
LUNA
LUAN
LYNN

LINCOLN

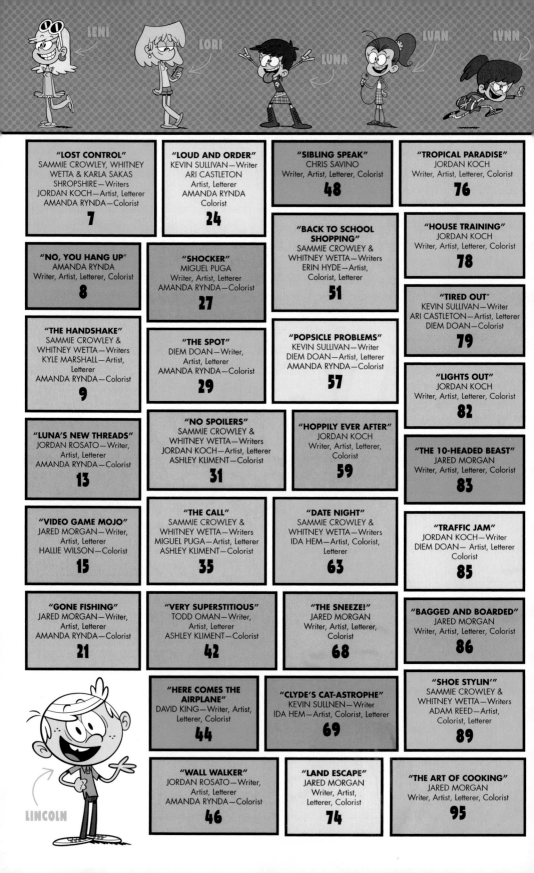

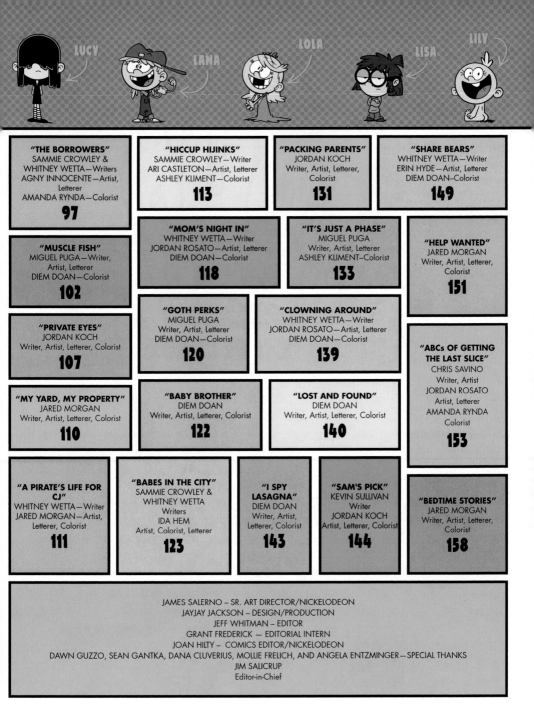

LUCY LANA LOLA LISA LILY

JAMES SALERNO – SR. ART DIRECTOR/NICKELODEON
JAYJAY JACKSON – DESIGN/PRODUCTION
JEFF WHITMAN – EDITOR
GRANT FREDERICK — EDITORIAL INTERN
JOAN HILTY – COMICS EDITOR/NICKELODEON
DAWN GUZZO, SEAN GANTKA, DANA CLUVERIUS, MOLLIE FRELICH, AND ANGELA ENTZMINGER—SPECIAL THANKS
JIM SALICRUP
Editor-in-Chief

ISBN: 978-1-5458-0530-5

Printed in China
January 2019

Distributed by Macmillan
First Printing

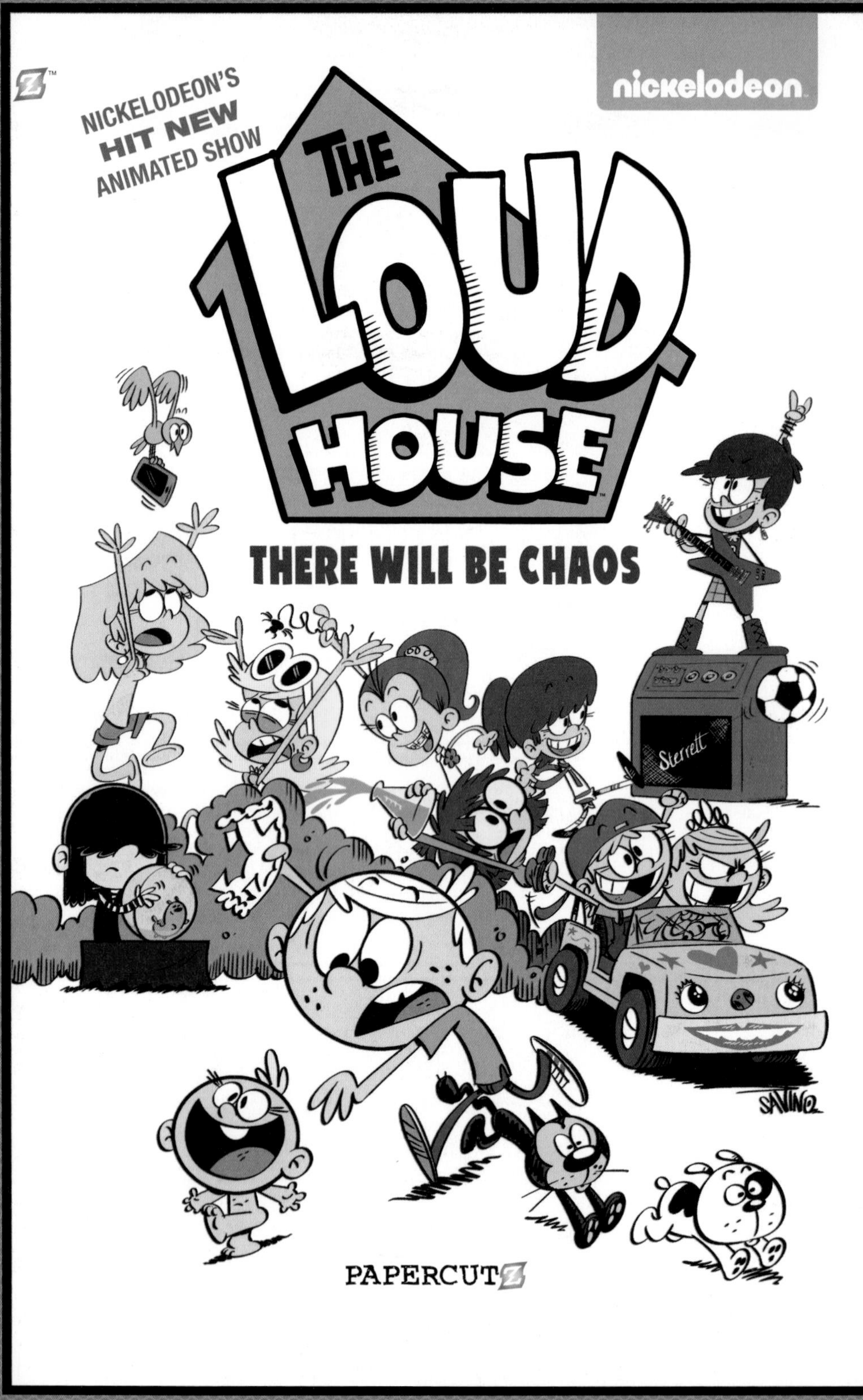
nickelodeon
NICKELODEON'S
HIT NEW
ANIMATED SHOW
THE LOUD HOUSE
THERE WILL BE CHAOS
Sterrett
SAVINO
PAPERCUT

THE LOUD HOUSE #1 Cover by Chris Savino

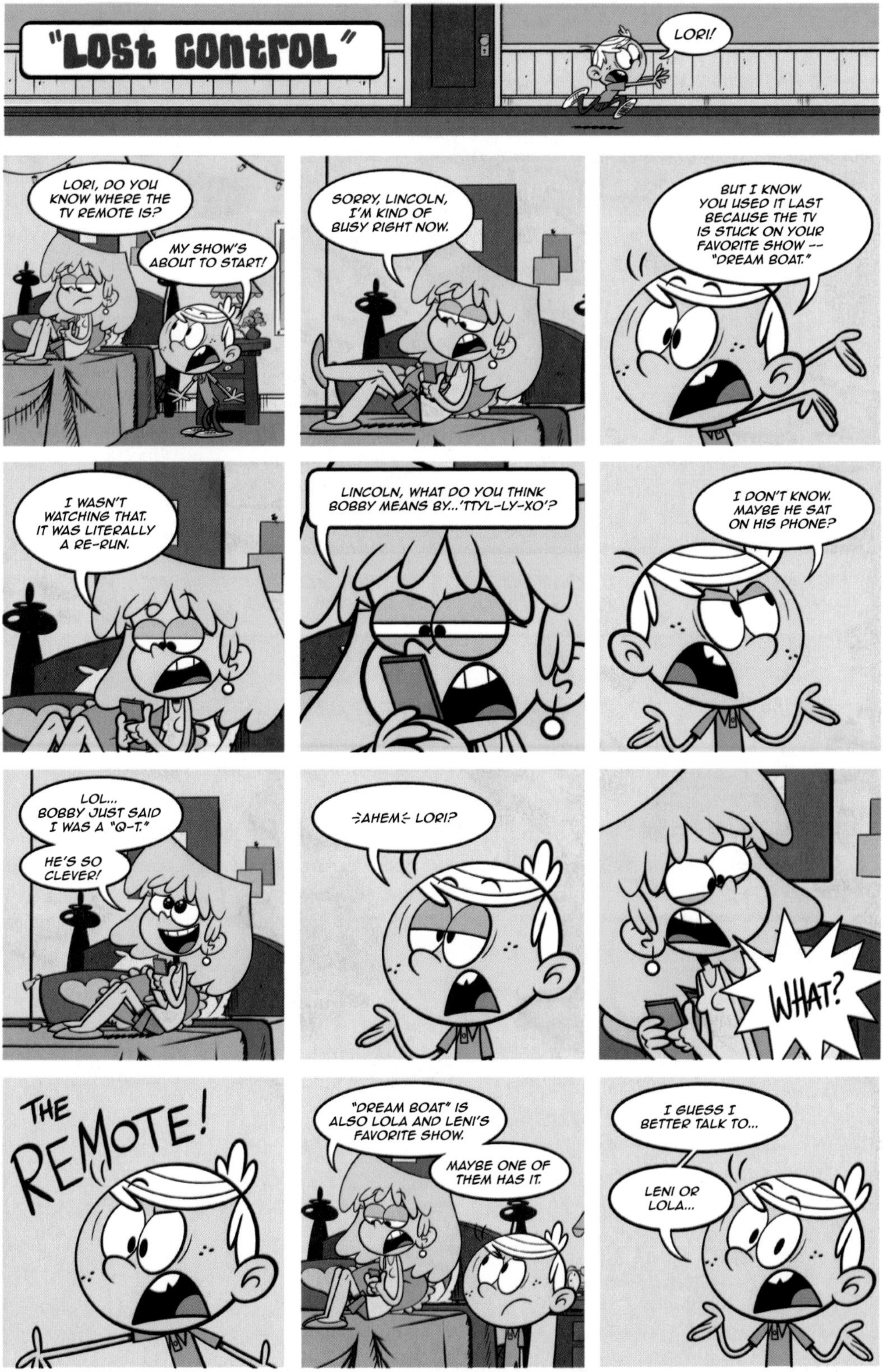
"LOST CONTROL"
LORI!
LORI, DO YOU KNOW WHERE THE TV REMOTE IS?
MY SHOW'S ABOUT TO START!
SORRY, LINCOLN, I'M KIND OF BUSY RIGHT NOW.
BUT I KNOW YOU USED IT LAST BECAUSE THE TV IS STUCK ON YOUR FAVORITE SHOW -- "DREAM BOAT."
I WASN'T WATCHING THAT. IT WAS LITERALLY A RE-RUN.
LINCOLN, WHAT DO YOU THINK BOBBY MEANS BY...'TTYL-LY-XO'?
I DON'T KNOW. MAYBE HE SAT ON HIS PHONE?
LOL... BOBBY JUST SAID I WAS A "Q-T."
HE'S SO CLEVER!
AHEM LORI?
WHAT?
THE REMOTE!
"DREAM BOAT" IS ALSO LOLA AND LENI'S FAVORITE SHOW.
MAYBE ONE OF THEM HAS IT.
I GUESS I BETTER TALK TO...
LENI OR LOLA...

TO TALK TO LENI, GO TO PAGE 138. TO TALK TO LOLA, GO TO PAGE 49.

"NO, YOU HANG UP"

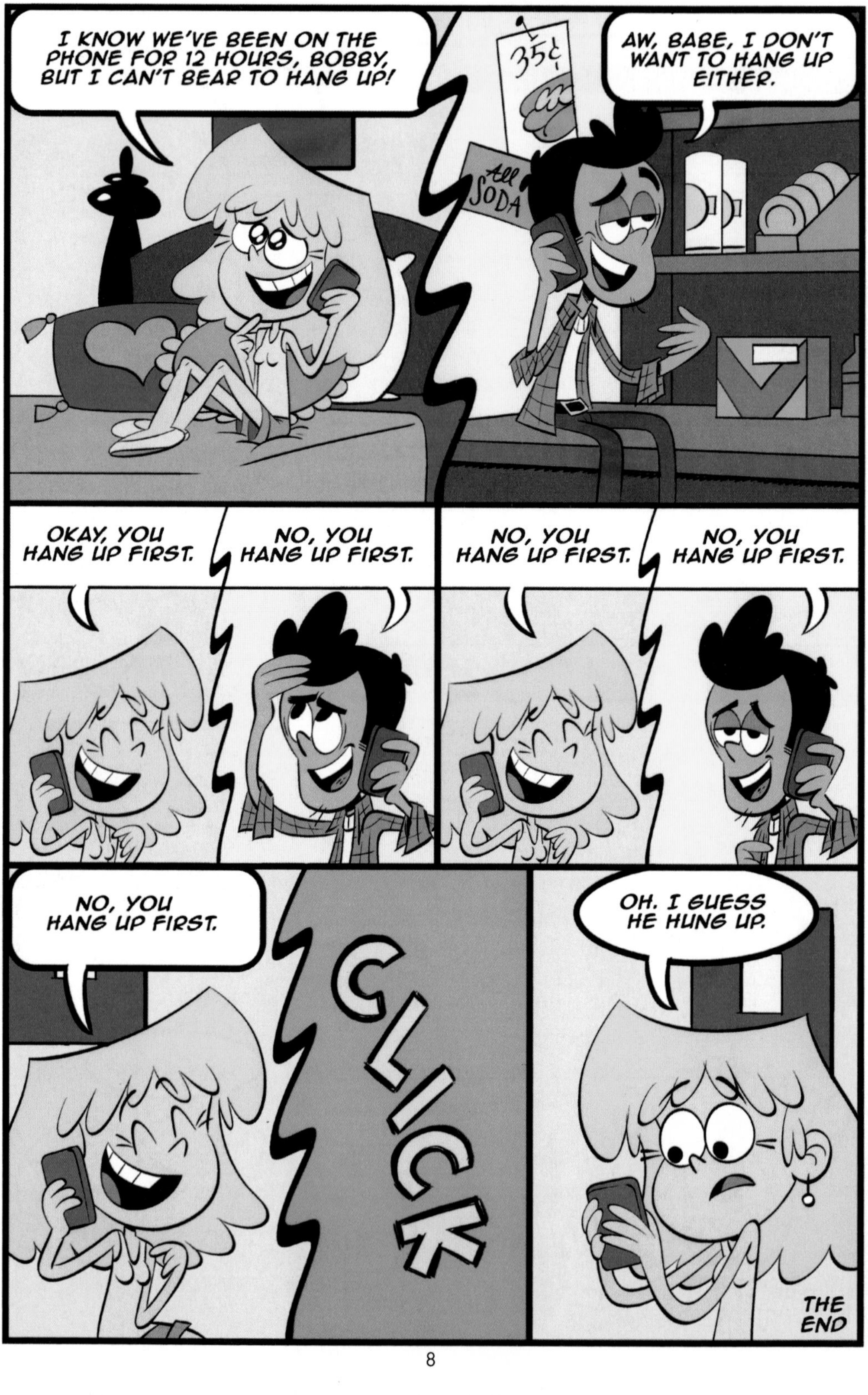
I KNOW WE'VE BEEN ON THE PHONE FOR 12 HOURS, BOBBY, BUT I CAN'T BEAR TO HANG UP!
AW, BABE, I DON'T WANT TO HANG UP EITHER.
35¢
All SODA
OKAY, YOU HANG UP FIRST.
NO, YOU HANG UP FIRST.
NO, YOU HANG UP FIRST.
NO, YOU HANG UP FIRST.
NO, YOU HANG UP FIRST.
CLICK
OH. I GUESS HE HUNG UP.
THE END

"THE HANDSHAKE"

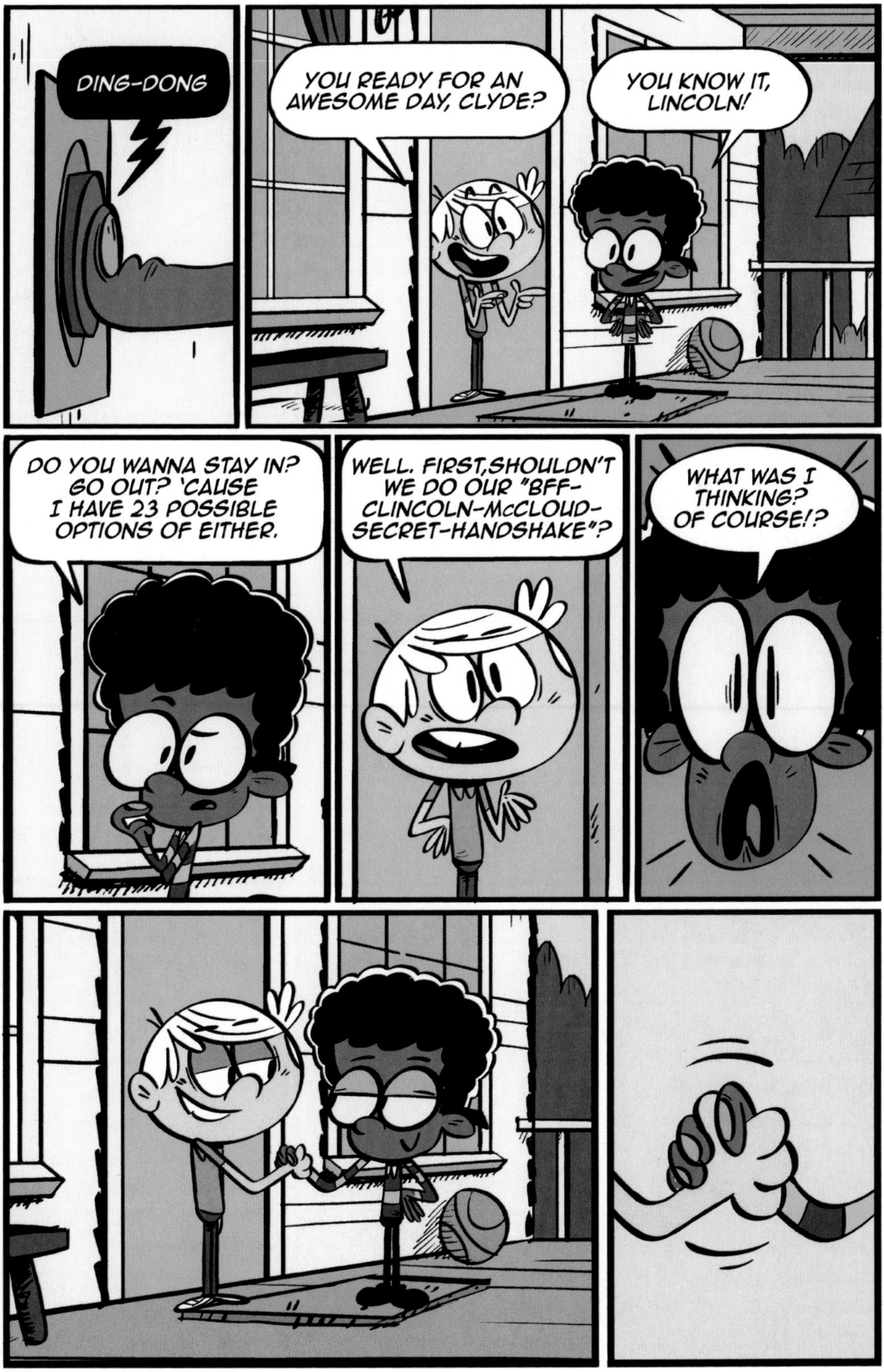
DING-DONG
YOU READY FOR AN AWESOME DAY, CLYDE?
YOU KNOW IT, LINCOLN!
DO YOU WANNA STAY IN? GO OUT? 'CAUSE I HAVE 23 POSSIBLE OPTIONS OF EITHER.
WELL. FIRST,SHOULDN'T WE DO OUR "BFF-CLINCOLN-McCLOUD-SECRET-HANDSHAKE"?
WHAT WAS I THINKING? OF COURSE!?

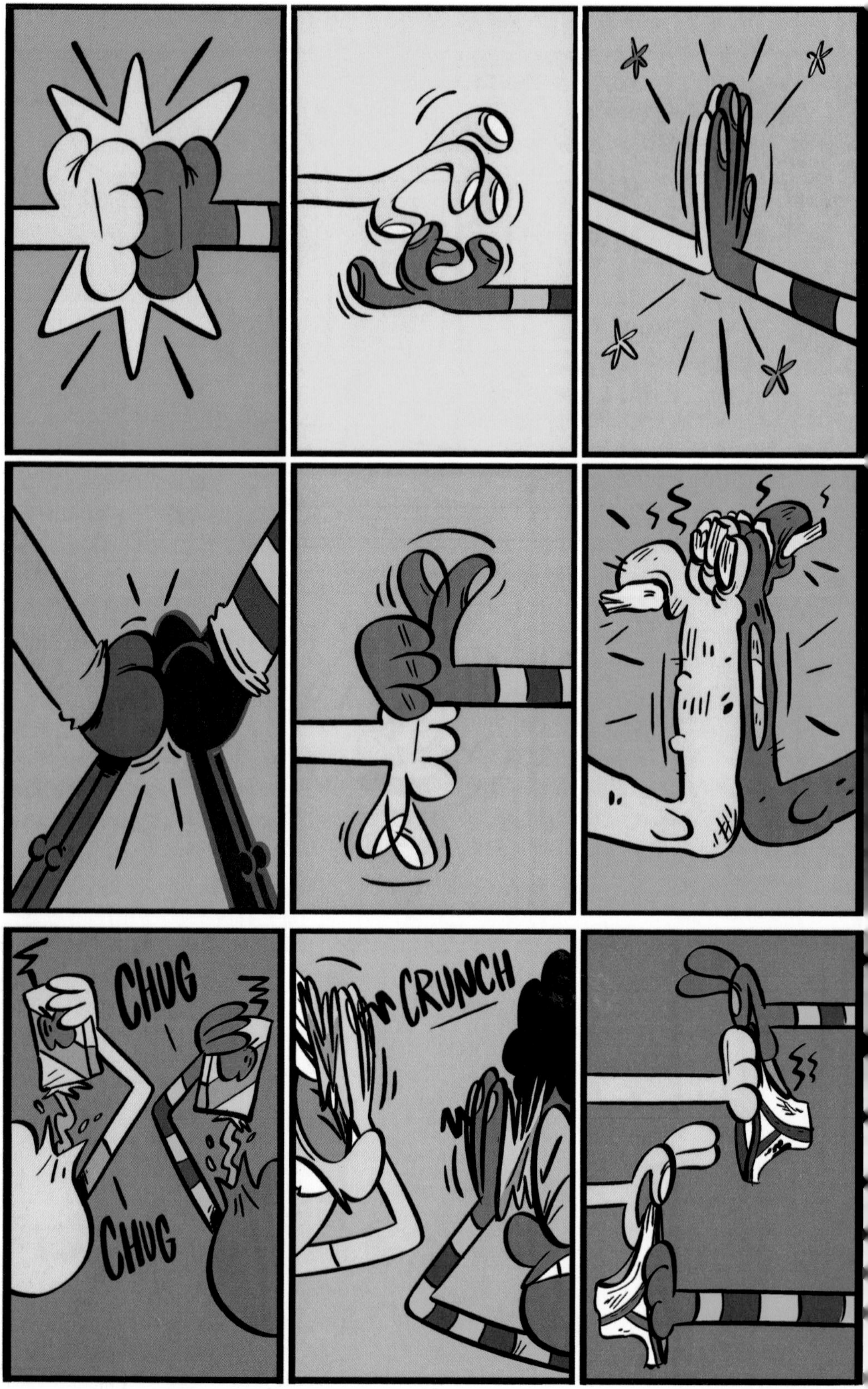
CHUG
CHUG
CRUNCH

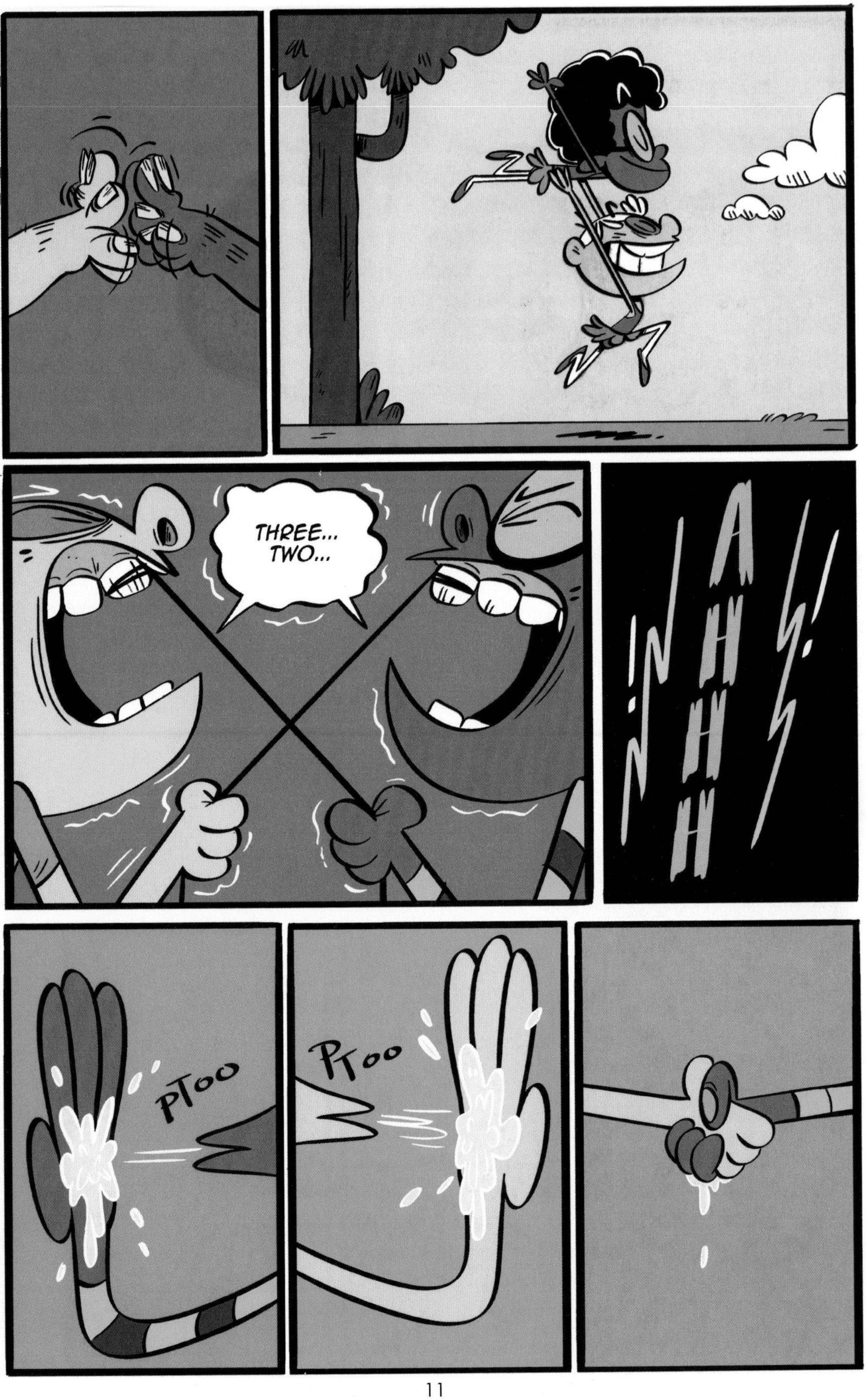
THREE... TWO...
AHHH!
PTOO
PTOO

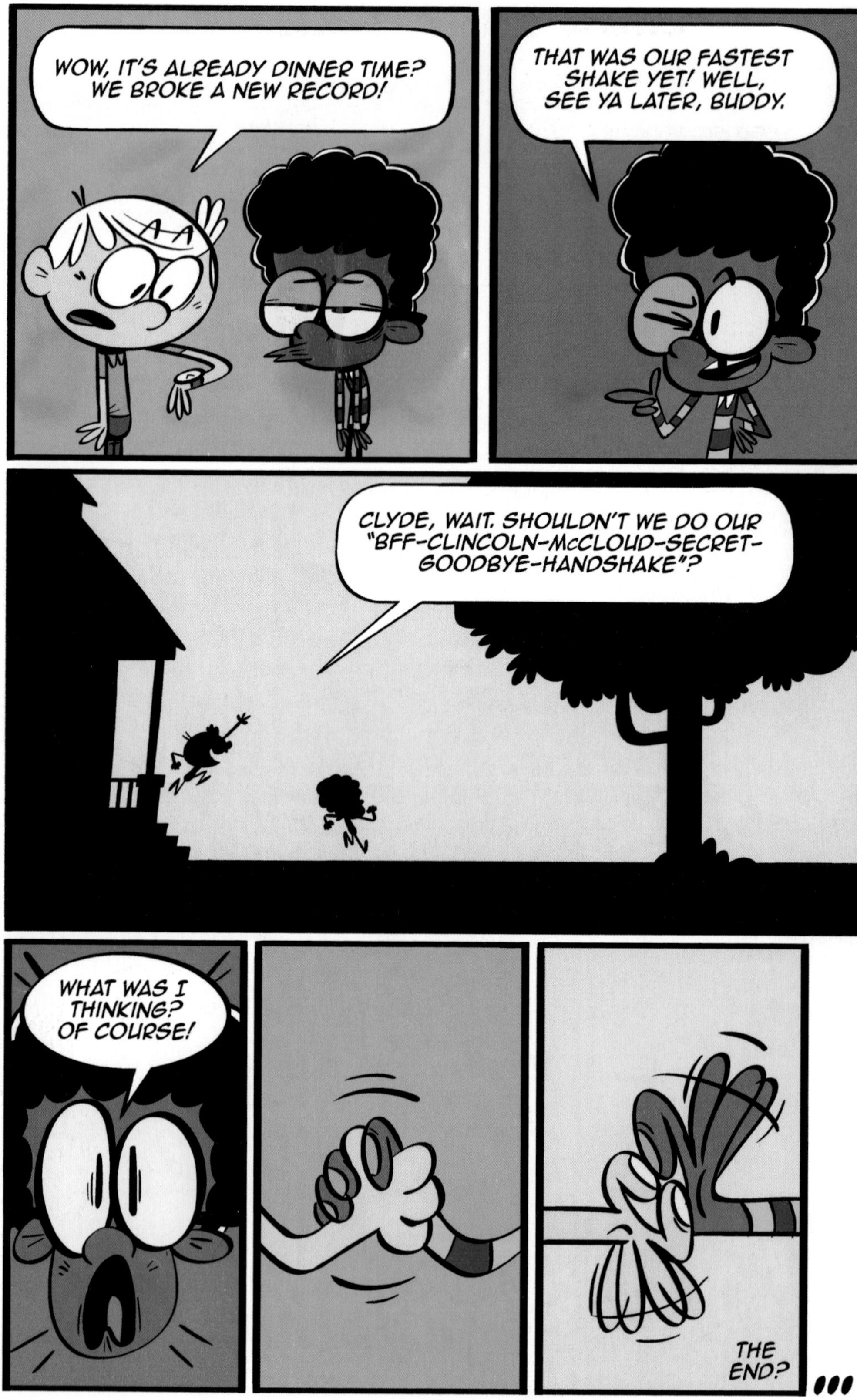
WOW, IT'S ALREADY DINNER TIME? WE BROKE A NEW RECORD!
THAT WAS OUR FASTEST SHAKE YET! WELL, SEE YA LATER, BUDDY.
CLYDE, WAIT. SHOULDN'T WE DO OUR "BFF-CLINCOLN-McCLOUD-SECRET-GOODBYE-HANDSHAKE"?
WHAT WAS I THINKING? OF COURSE!
THE END?

"LUNA'S NEW THREADS"

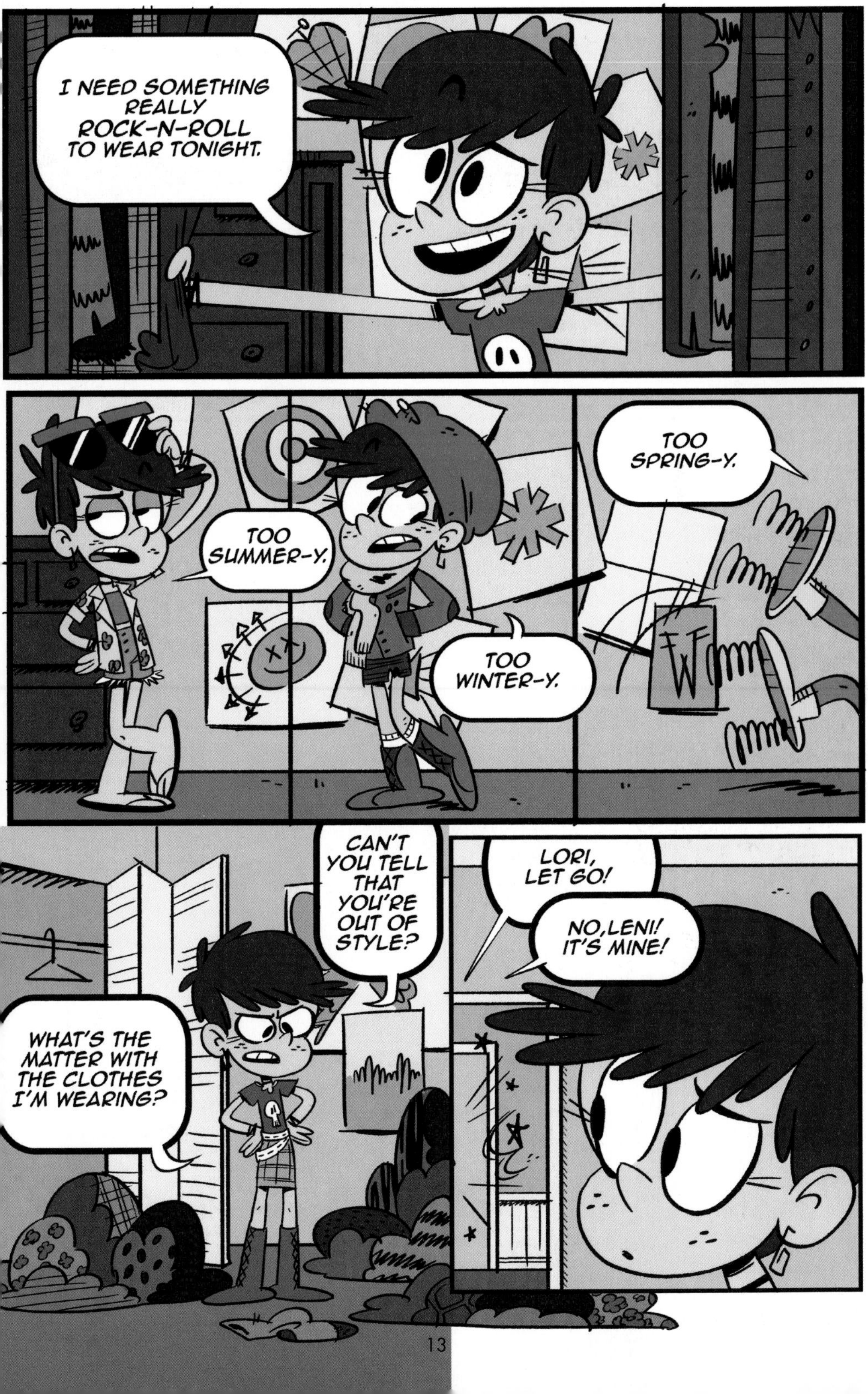
I NEED SOMETHING REALLY ROCK-N-ROLL TO WEAR TONIGHT.
TOO SUMMER-Y.
TOO WINTER-Y.
TOO SPRING-Y.
WHAT'S THE MATTER WITH THE CLOTHES I'M WEARING?
CAN'T YOU TELL THAT YOU'RE OUT OF STYLE?
LORI, LET GO!
NO, LENI! IT'S MINE!

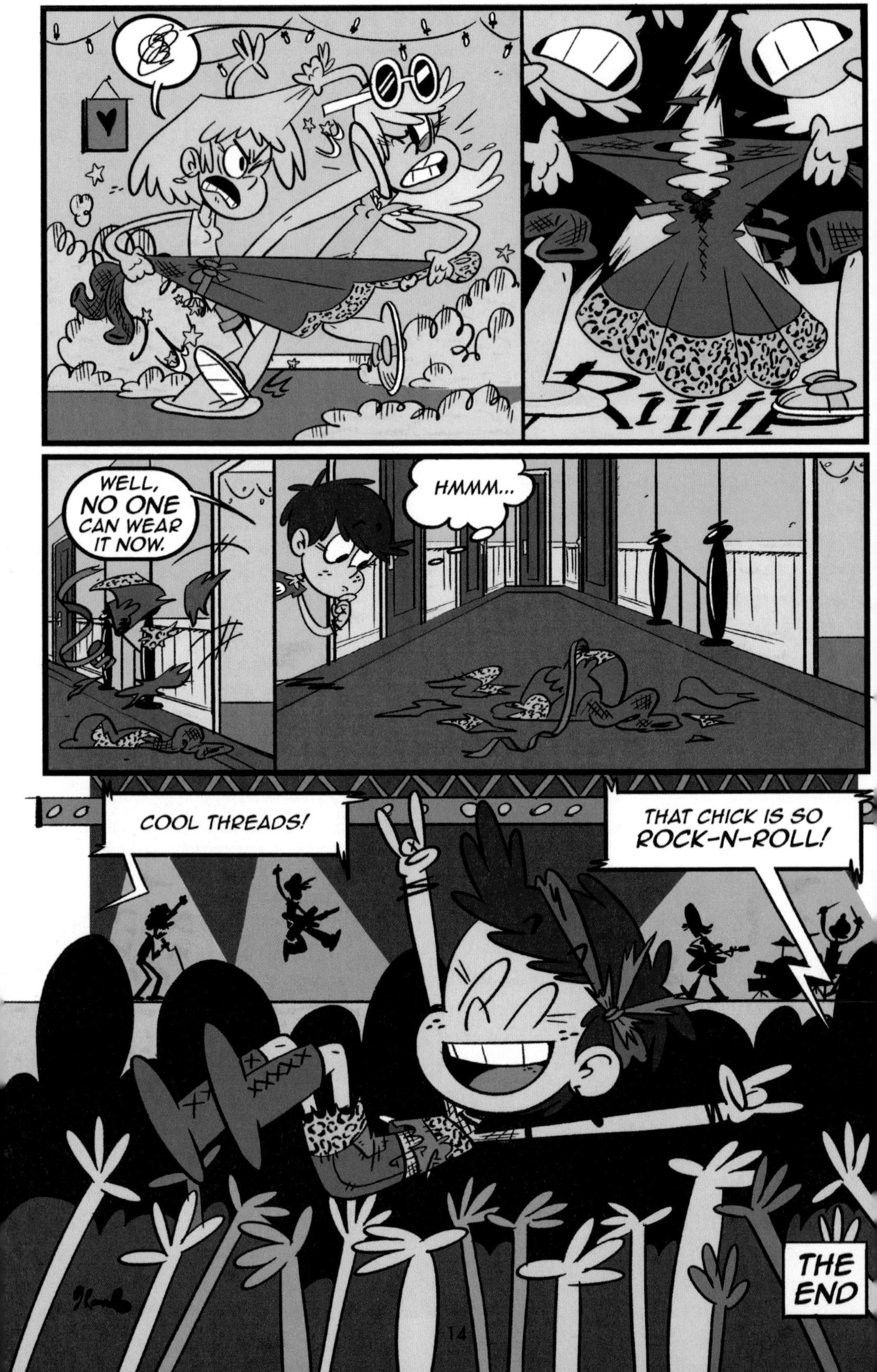

RIIIIIP
WELL, NO ONE CAN WEAR IT NOW.
HMMM...
COOL THREADS!
THAT CHICK IS SO ROCK-N-ROLL!
THE END

"VIDEO GAME MOJO"

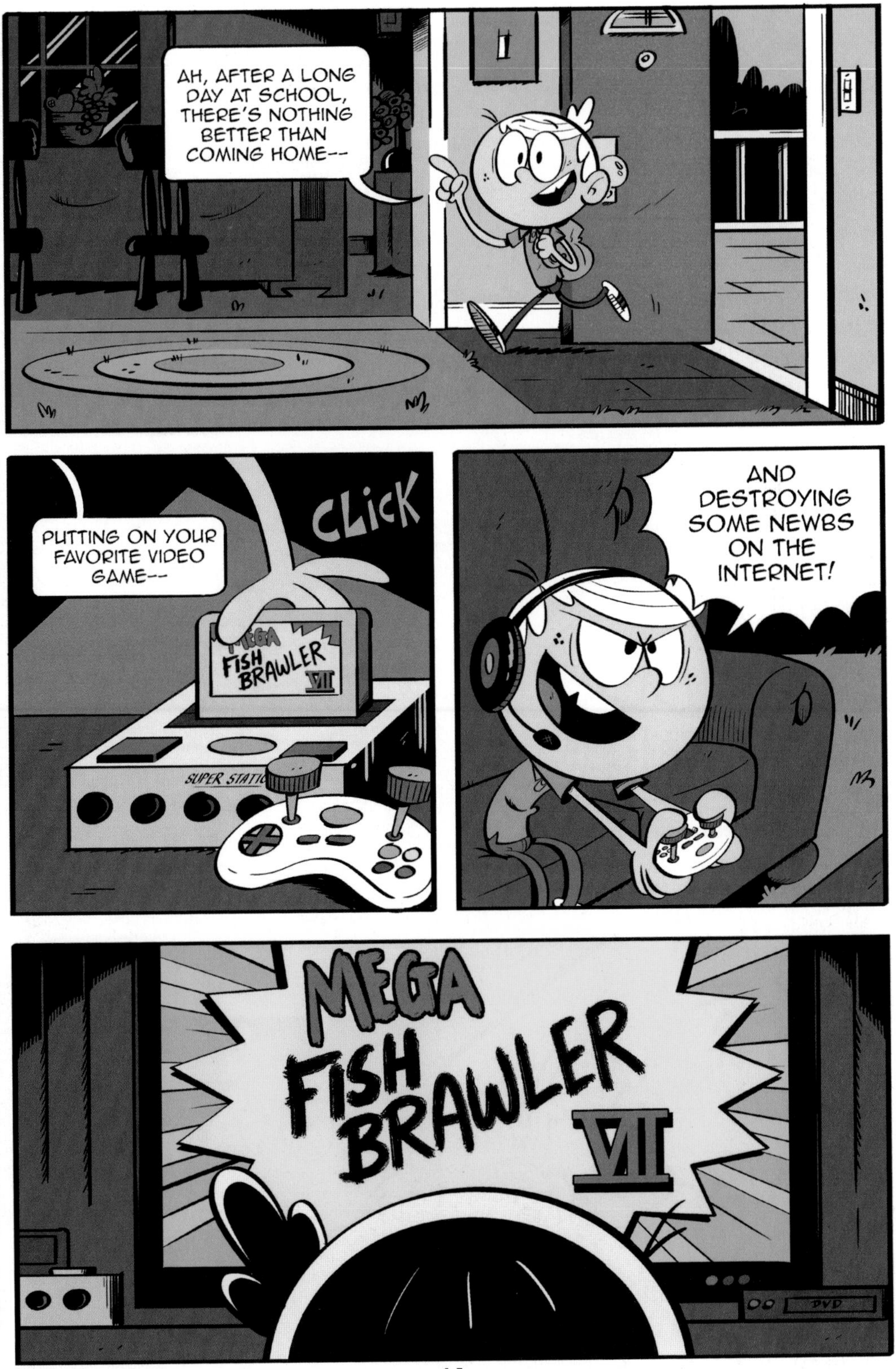
AH, AFTER A LONG DAY AT SCHOOL, THERE'S NOTHING BETTER THAN COMING HOME--
PUTTING ON YOUR FAVORITE VIDEO GAME--
CLICK
MEGA FISH BRAWLER VII
SUPER STATIO
AND DESTROYING SOME NEWBS ON THE INTERNET!
MEGA FISH BRAWLER VII
DVD

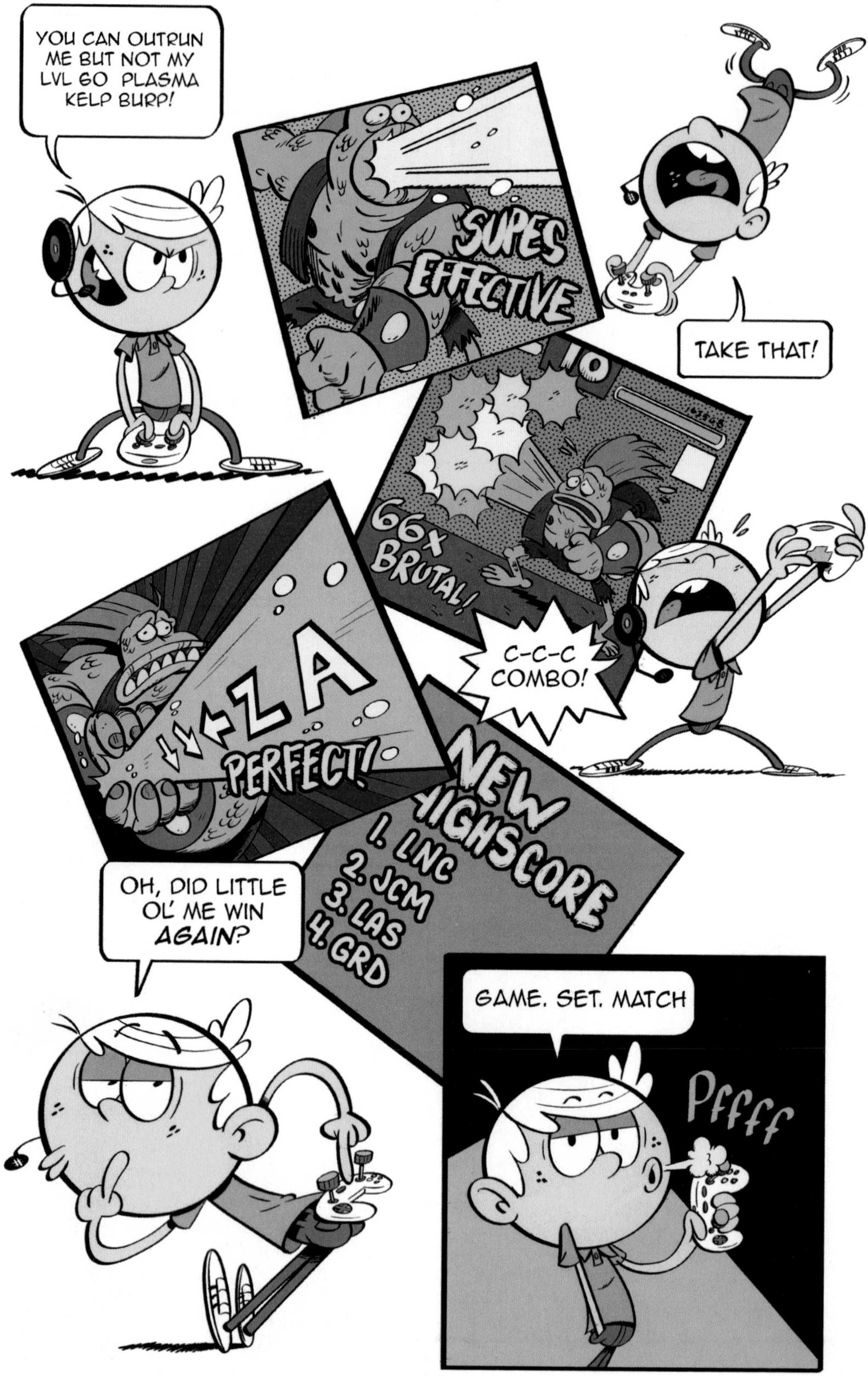
YOU CAN OUTRUN ME BUT NOT MY LVL 60 PLASMA KELP BURP!
SUPES EFFECTIVE
TAKE THAT!
10
66x BRUTAL!
C-C-C COMBO!
ZA
PERFECT!
NEW HIGHSCORE
1. LNC
2. JCM
3. LAS
4. GRD
OH, DID LITTLE OL' ME WIN AGAIN?
GAME. SET. MATCH
Pffff

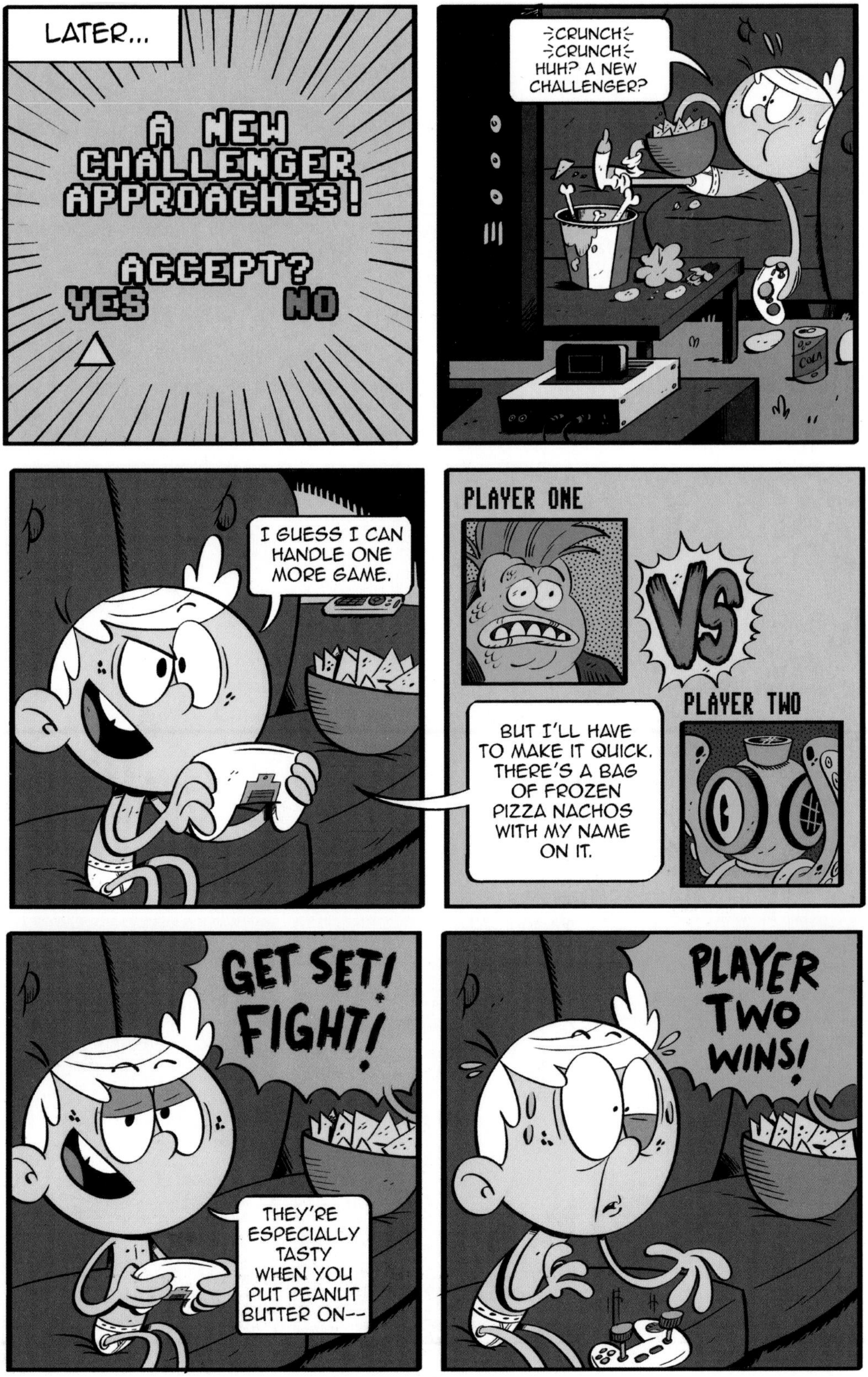
LATER...
A NEW CHALLENGER APPROACHES!
ACCEPT?
YES
NO
CRUNCH
CRUNCH
HUH? A NEW CHALLENGER?
I GUESS I CAN HANDLE ONE MORE GAME.
PLAYER ONE
VS
PLAYER TWO
BUT I'LL HAVE TO MAKE IT QUICK. THERE'S A BAG OF FROZEN PIZZA NACHOS WITH MY NAME ON IT.
GET SET! FIGHT!
THEY'RE ESPECIALLY TASTY WHEN YOU PUT PEANUT BUTTER ON--
PLAYER TWO WINS!

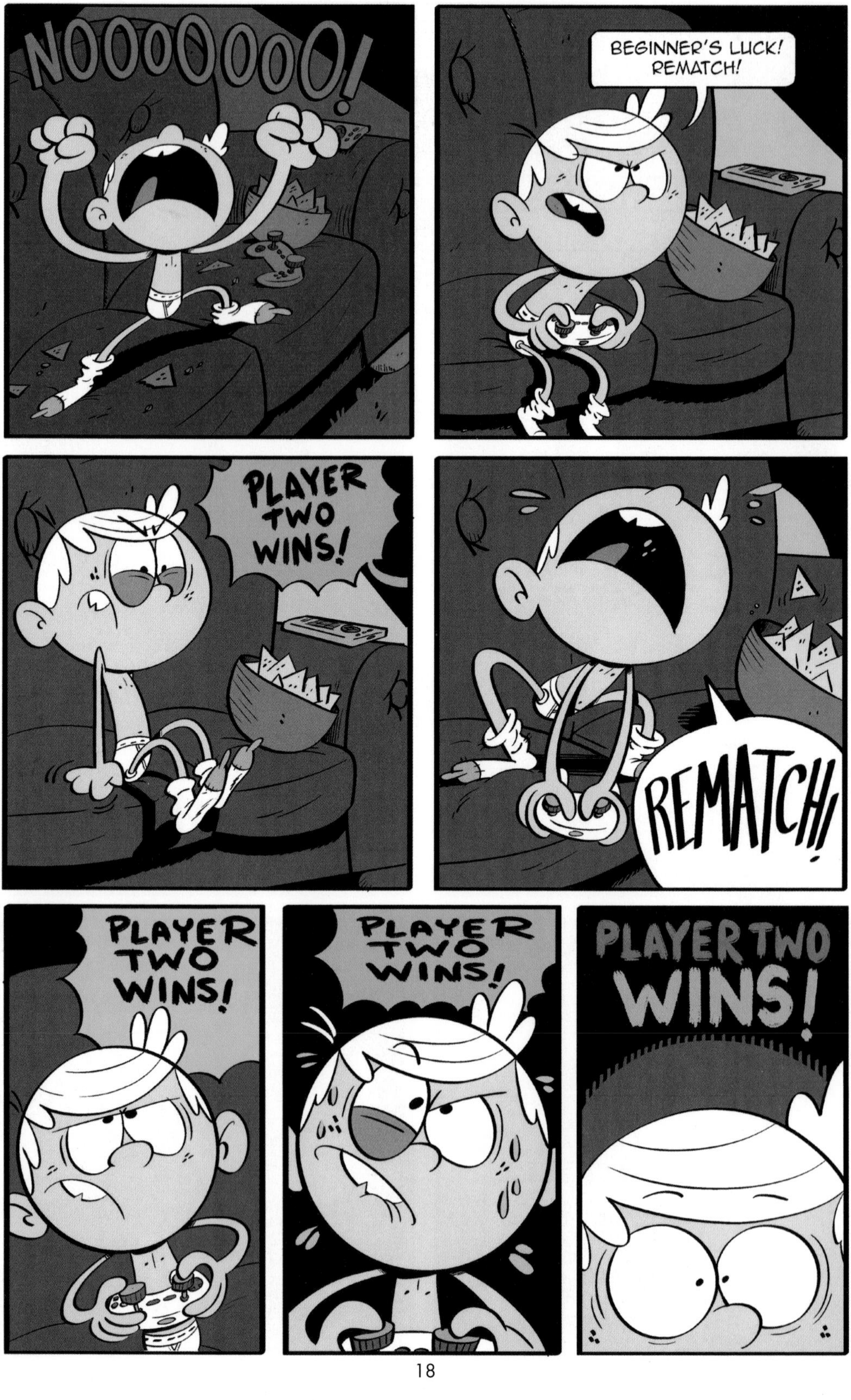
NOOOOOOO!
BEGINNER'S LUCK! REMATCH!
PLAYER TWO WINS!
REMATCH!
PLAYER TWO WINS!
PLAYER TWO WINS!
PLAYER TWO WINS!

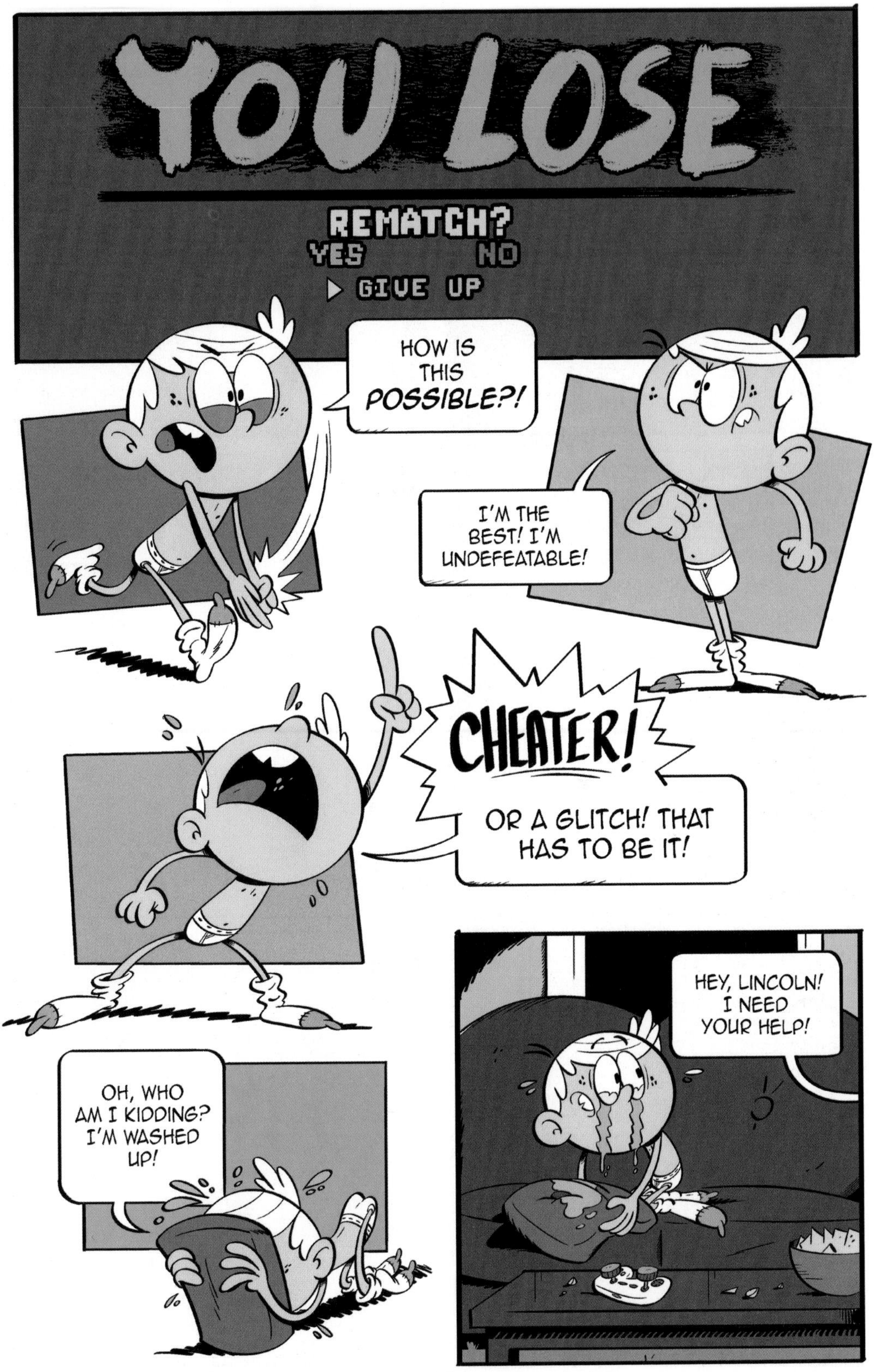
YOU LOSE
REMATCH?
YES
NO
GIVE UP
HOW IS THIS POSSIBLE?!
I'M THE BEST! I'M UNDEFEATABLE!
CHEATER!
OR A GLITCH! THAT HAS TO BE IT!
OH, WHO AM I KIDDING? I'M WASHED UP!
HEY, LINCOLN! I NEED YOUR HELP!

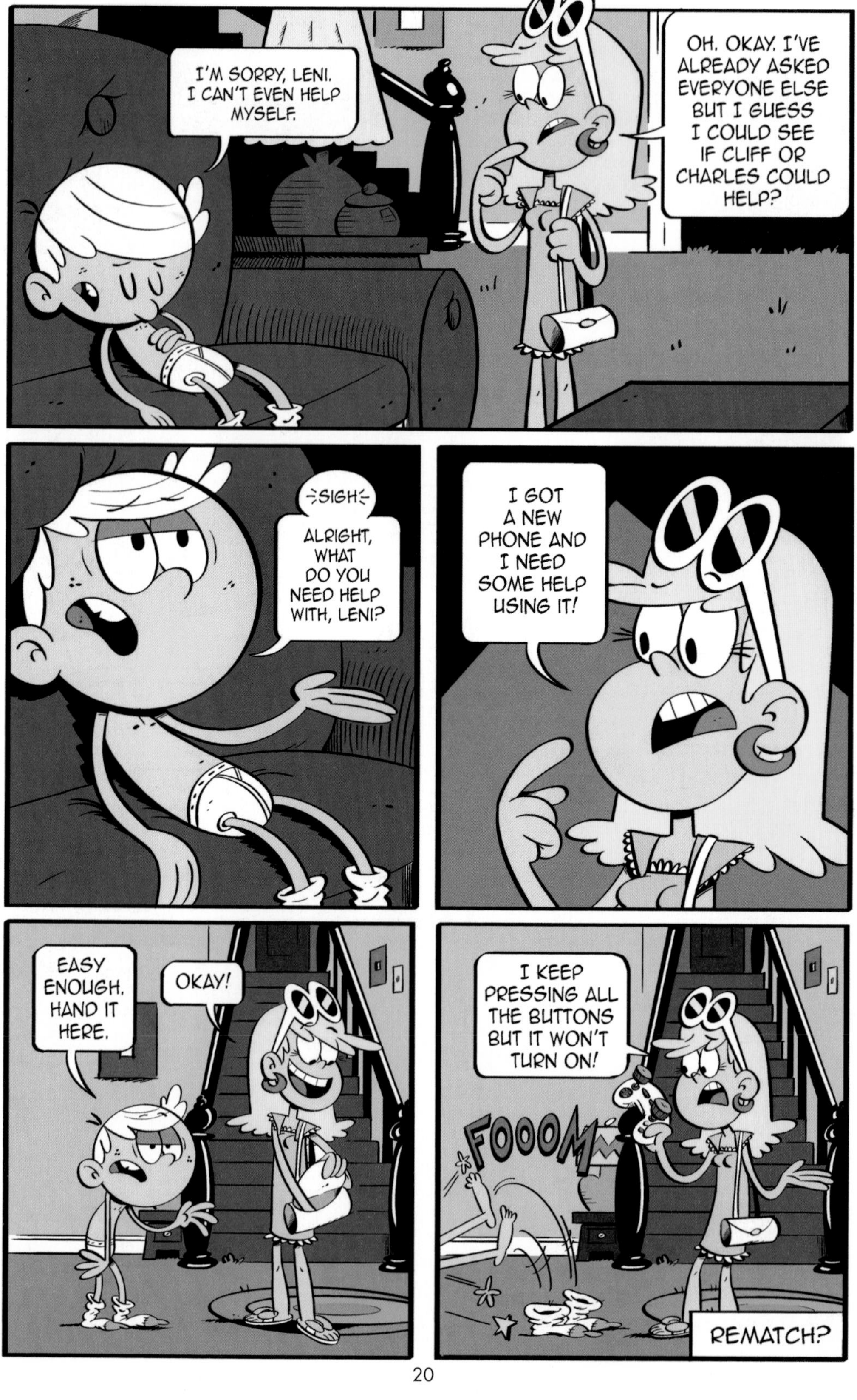
I'M SORRY, LENI. I CAN'T EVEN HELP MYSELF.
OH. OKAY. I'VE ALREADY ASKED EVERYONE ELSE BUT I GUESS I COULD SEE IF CLIFF OR CHARLES COULD HELP?
SIGH
ALRIGHT, WHAT DO YOU NEED HELP WITH, LENI?
I GOT A NEW PHONE AND I NEED SOME HELP USING IT!
EASY ENOUGH. HAND IT HERE.
OKAY!
I KEEP PRESSING ALL THE BUTTONS BUT IT WON'T TURN ON!
FOOOM
REMATCH?

"GONE FISHING"

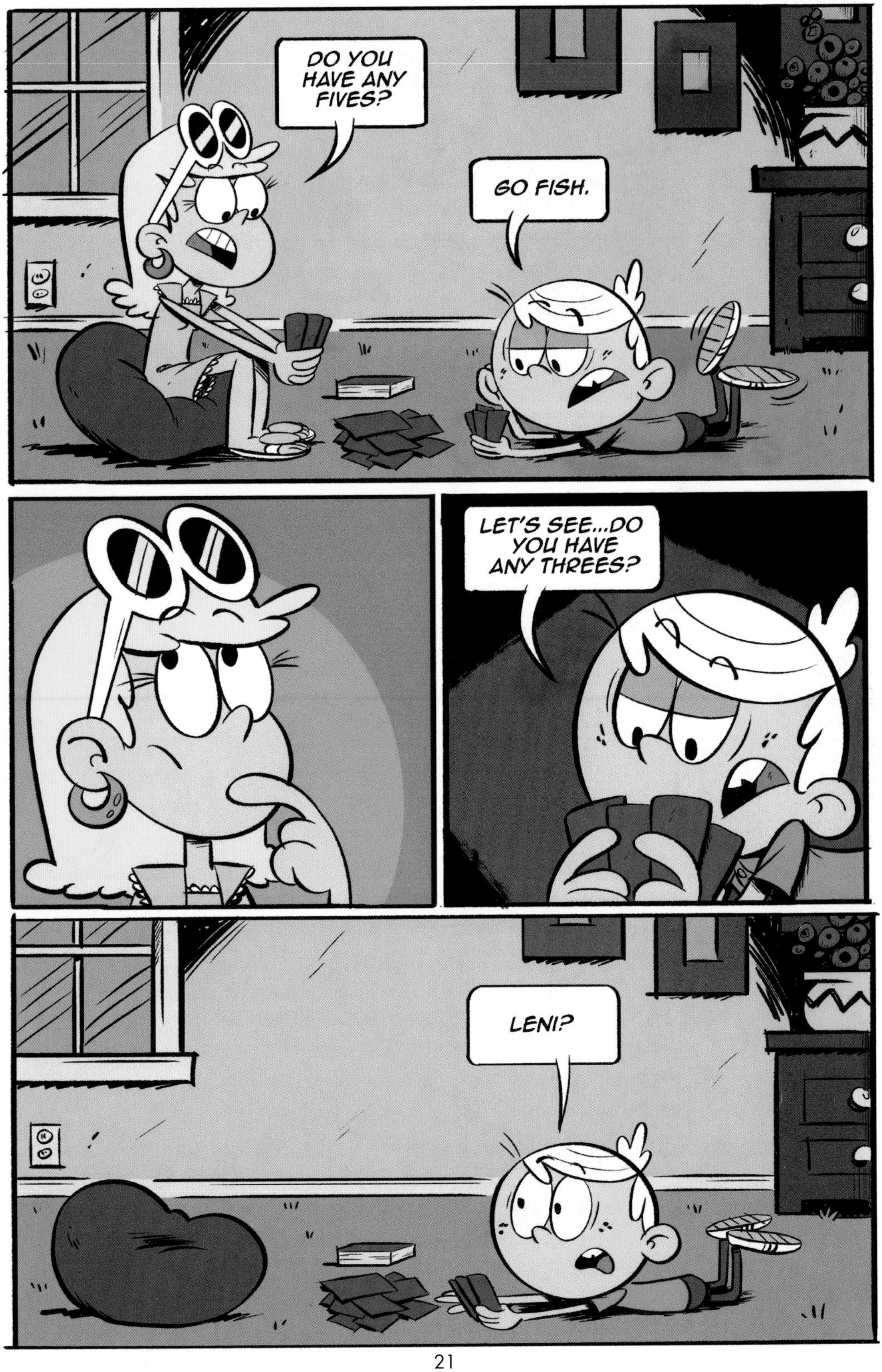
DO YOU HAVE ANY FIVES?
GO FISH.
LET'S SEE...DO YOU HAVE ANY THREES?
LENI?

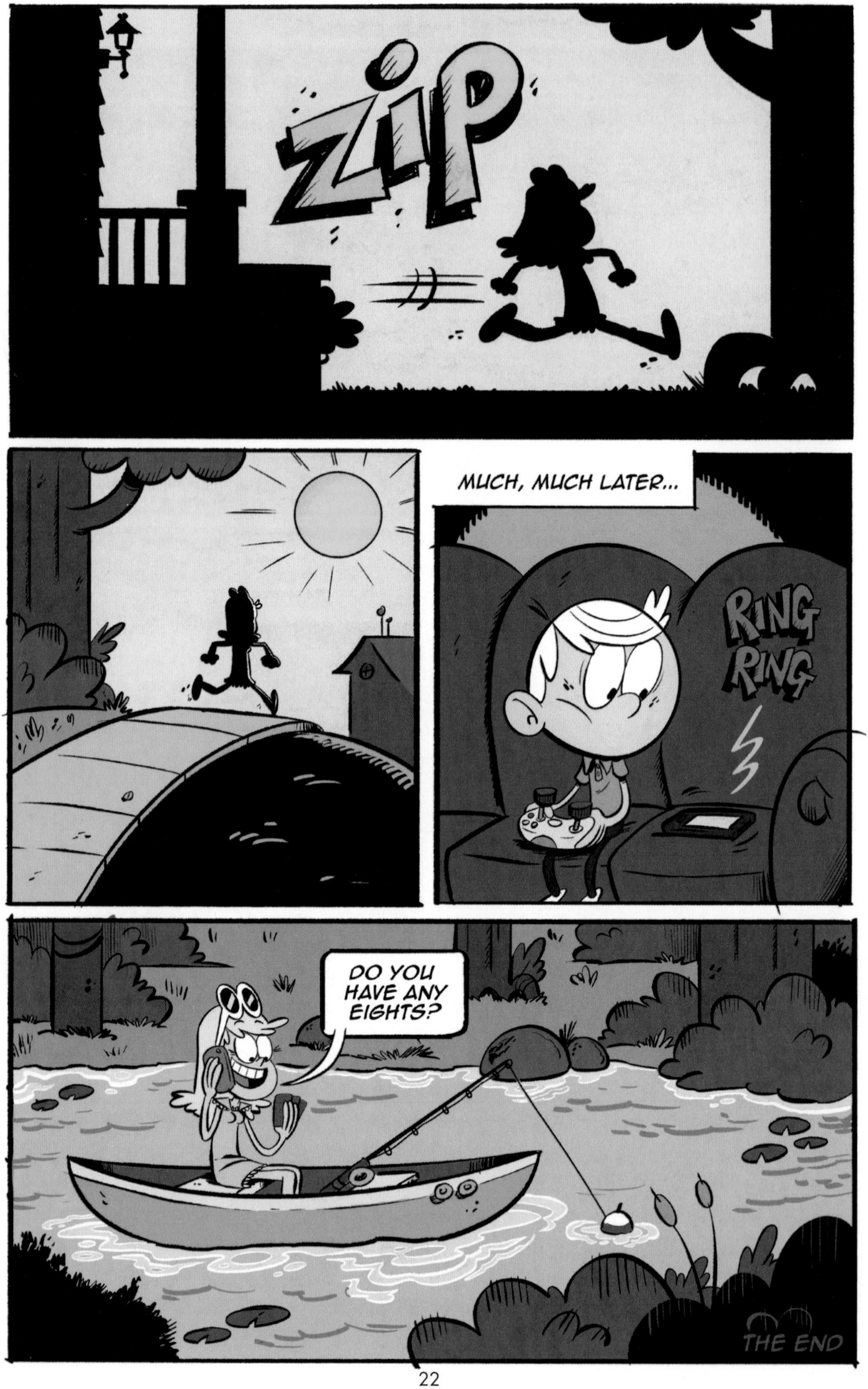
ZIP
MUCH, MUCH LATER...
RING RING
DO YOU HAVE ANY EIGHTS?
THE END

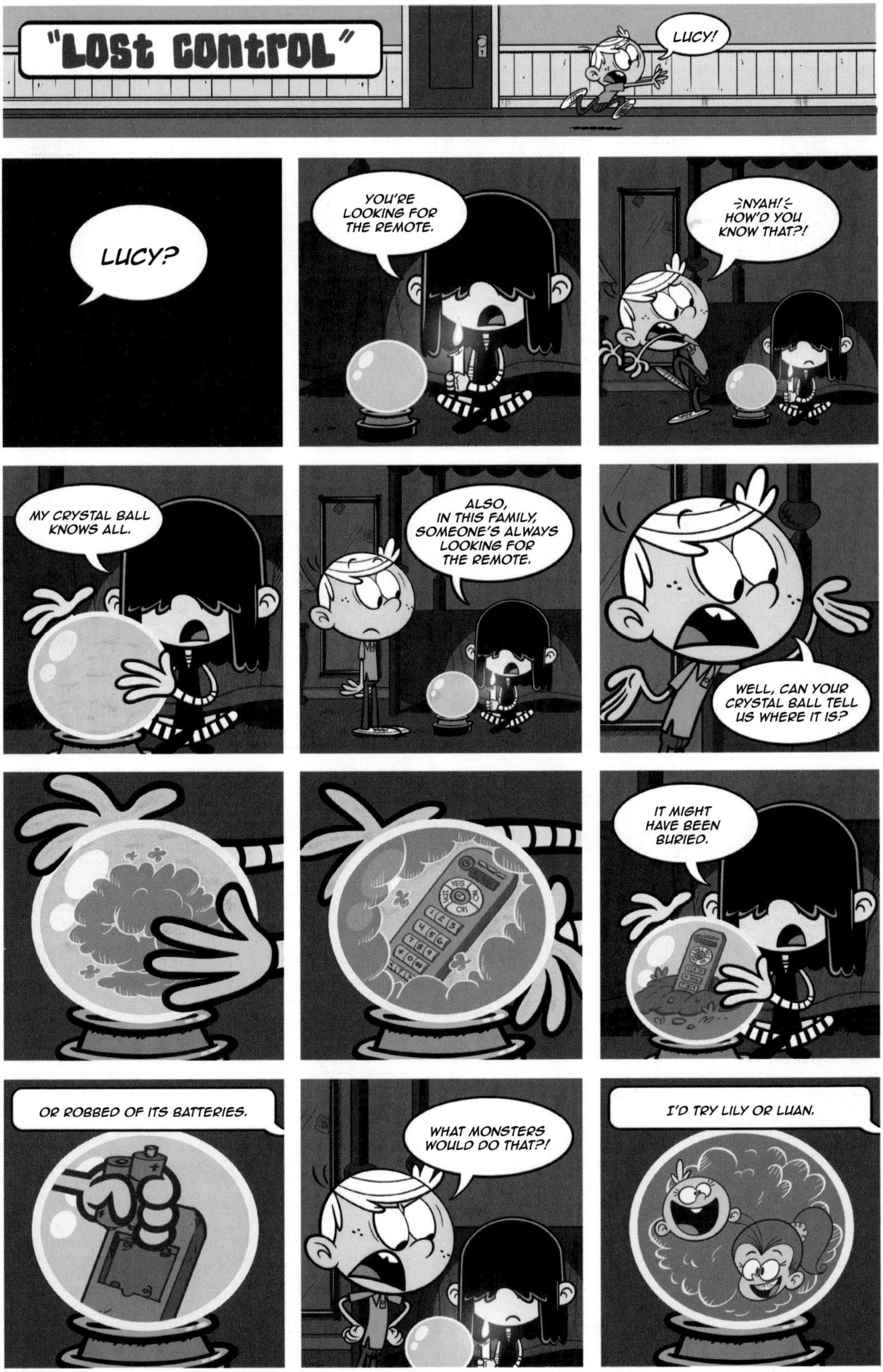
"LOST CONTROL"
LUCY!
LUCY?
YOU'RE LOOKING FOR THE REMOTE.
NYAH! HOW'D YOU KNOW THAT?!
MY CRYSTAL BALL KNOWS ALL.
ALSO, IN THIS FAMILY, SOMEONE'S ALWAYS LOOKING FOR THE REMOTE.
WELL, CAN YOUR CRYSTAL BALL TELL US WHERE IT IS?
IT MIGHT HAVE BEEN BURIED.
OR ROBBED OF ITS BATTERIES.
WHAT MONSTERS WOULD DO THAT?!
I'D TRY LILY OR LUAN.

TO TALK TO LILY, GO TO PAGE 30. TO TALK TO LUAN, GO TO PAGE 41.

"LOUD AND ORDER"

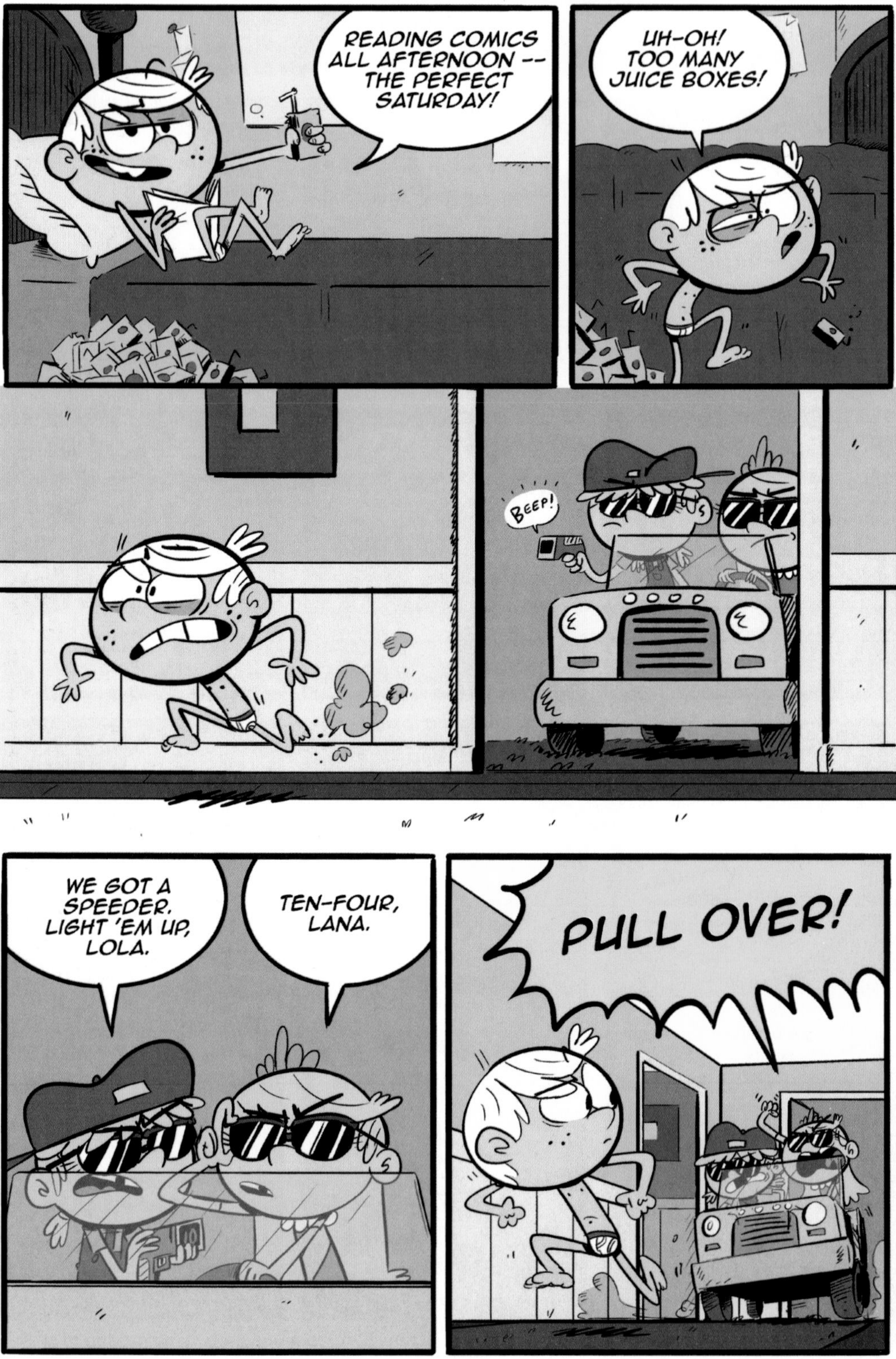

READING COMICS ALL AFTERNOON -- THE PERFECT SATURDAY!
UH-OH! TOO MANY JUICE BOXES!
BEEP!
WE GOT A SPEEDER. LIGHT 'EM UP, LOLA.
TEN-FOUR, LANA.
PULL OVER!

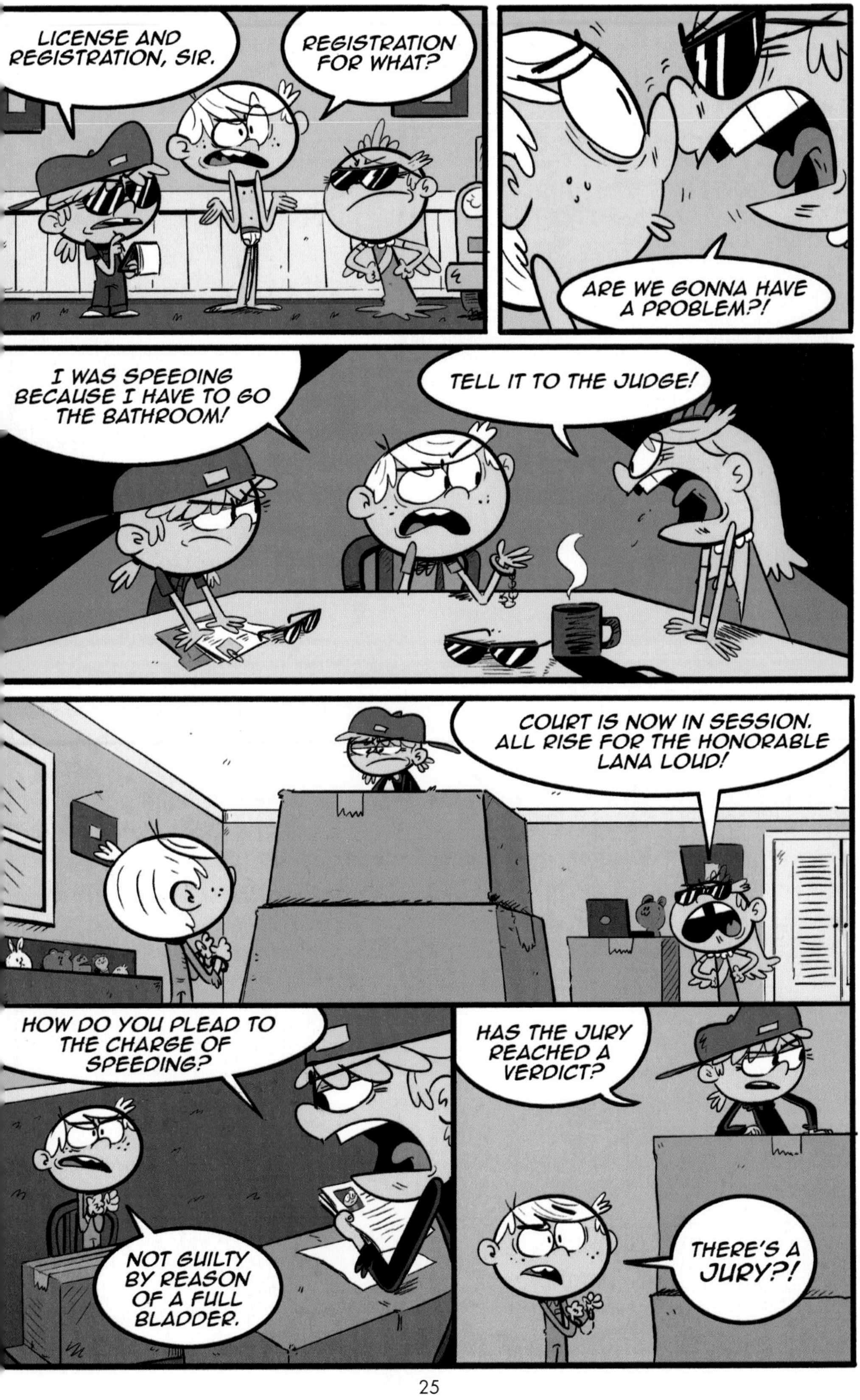
LICENSE AND REGISTRATION, SIR.
REGISTRATION FOR WHAT?
ARE WE GONNA HAVE A PROBLEM?!
I WAS SPEEDING BECAUSE I HAVE TO GO THE BATHROOM!
TELL IT TO THE JUDGE!
COURT IS NOW IN SESSION. ALL RISE FOR THE HONORABLE LANA LOUD!
HOW DO YOU PLEAD TO THE CHARGE OF SPEEDING?
NOT GUILTY BY REASON OF A FULL BLADDER.
HAS THE JURY REACHED A VERDICT?
THERE'S A JURY?!

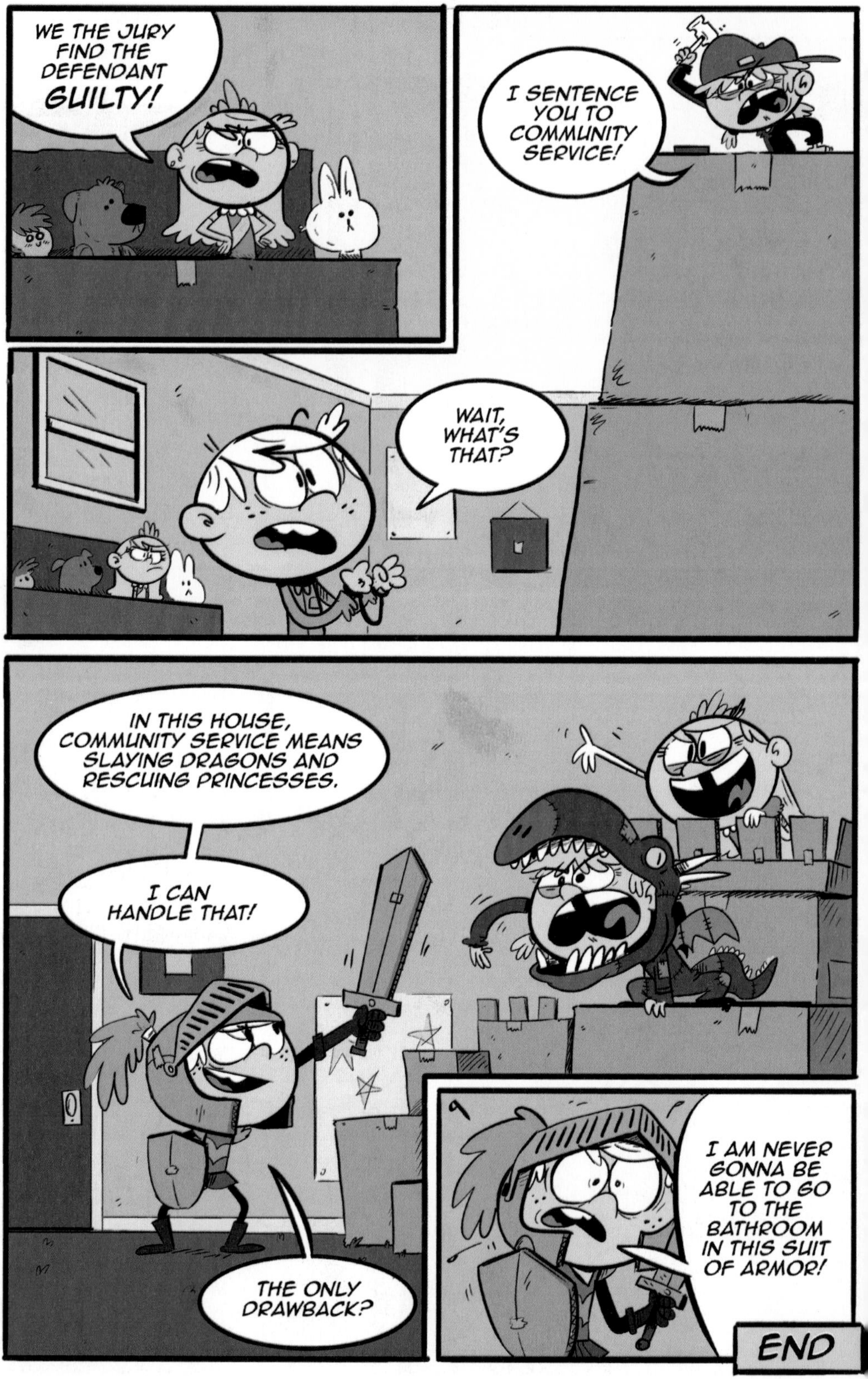
WE THE JURY FIND THE DEFENDANT GUILTY!
I SENTENCE YOU TO COMMUNITY SERVICE!
WAIT, WHAT'S THAT?
IN THIS HOUSE, COMMUNITY SERVICE MEANS SLAYING DRAGONS AND RESCUING PRINCESSES.
I CAN HANDLE THAT!
THE ONLY DRAWBACK?
I AM NEVER GONNA BE ABLE TO GO TO THE BATHROOM IN THIS SUIT OF ARMOR!
END

"SHOCKER"

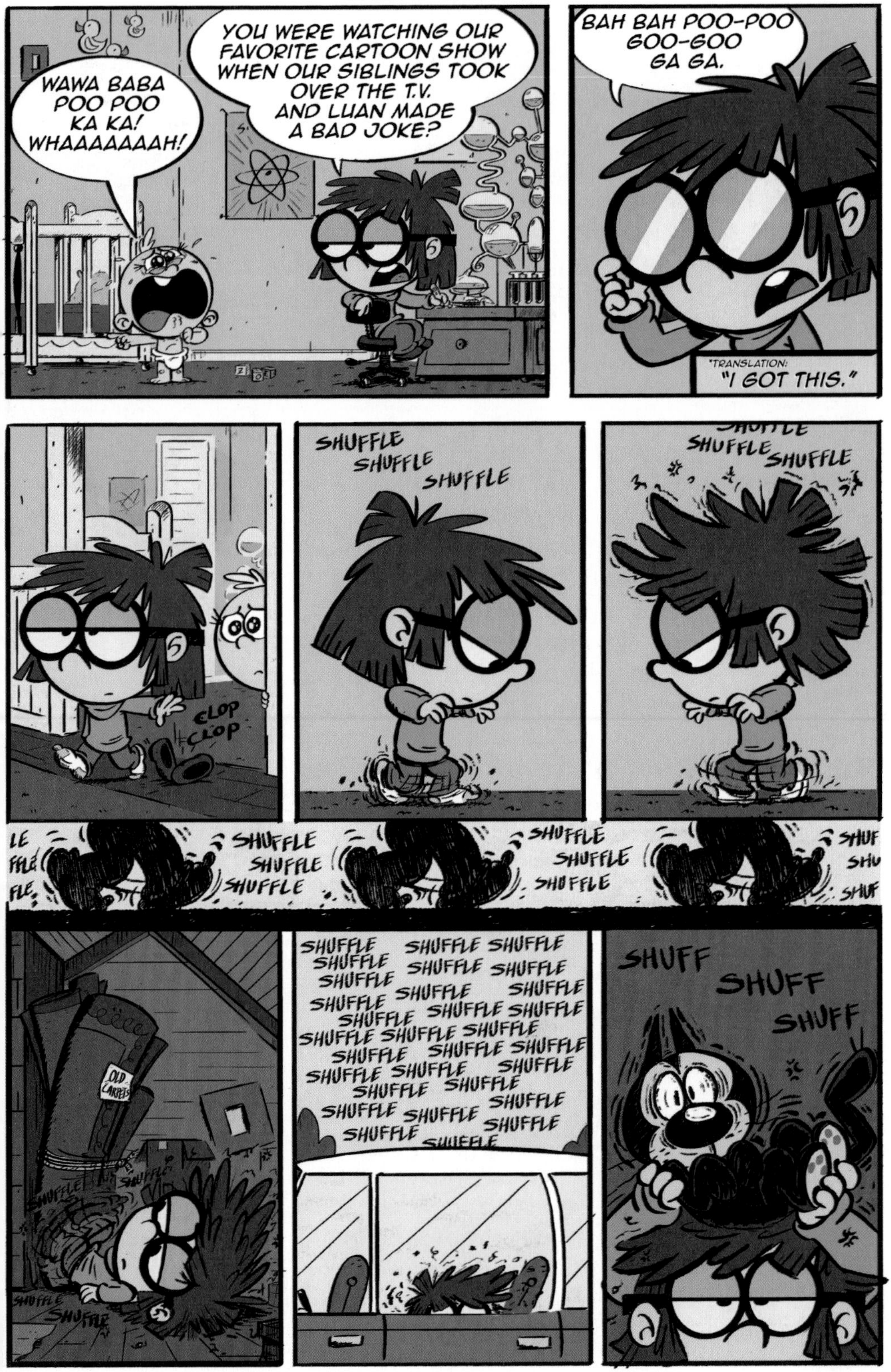
YOU WERE WATCHING OUR FAVORITE CARTOON SHOW WHEN OUR SIBLINGS TOOK OVER THE T.V. AND LUAN MADE A BAD JOKE?
WAWA BABA POO POO KA KA! WHAAAAAAAH!
BAH BAH POO-POO GOO-GOO GA GA.
*TRANSLATION: "I GOT THIS."
CLOP CLOP
SHUFFLE SHUFFLE SHUFFLE
SHUFFLE SHUFFLE SHUFFLE
SHUFFLE SHUFFLE SHUFFLE
SHUFFLE SHUFFLE SHUFFLE
OLD CARPETS
SHUFFLE SHUFFLE
SHUFF SHUFF SHUFF

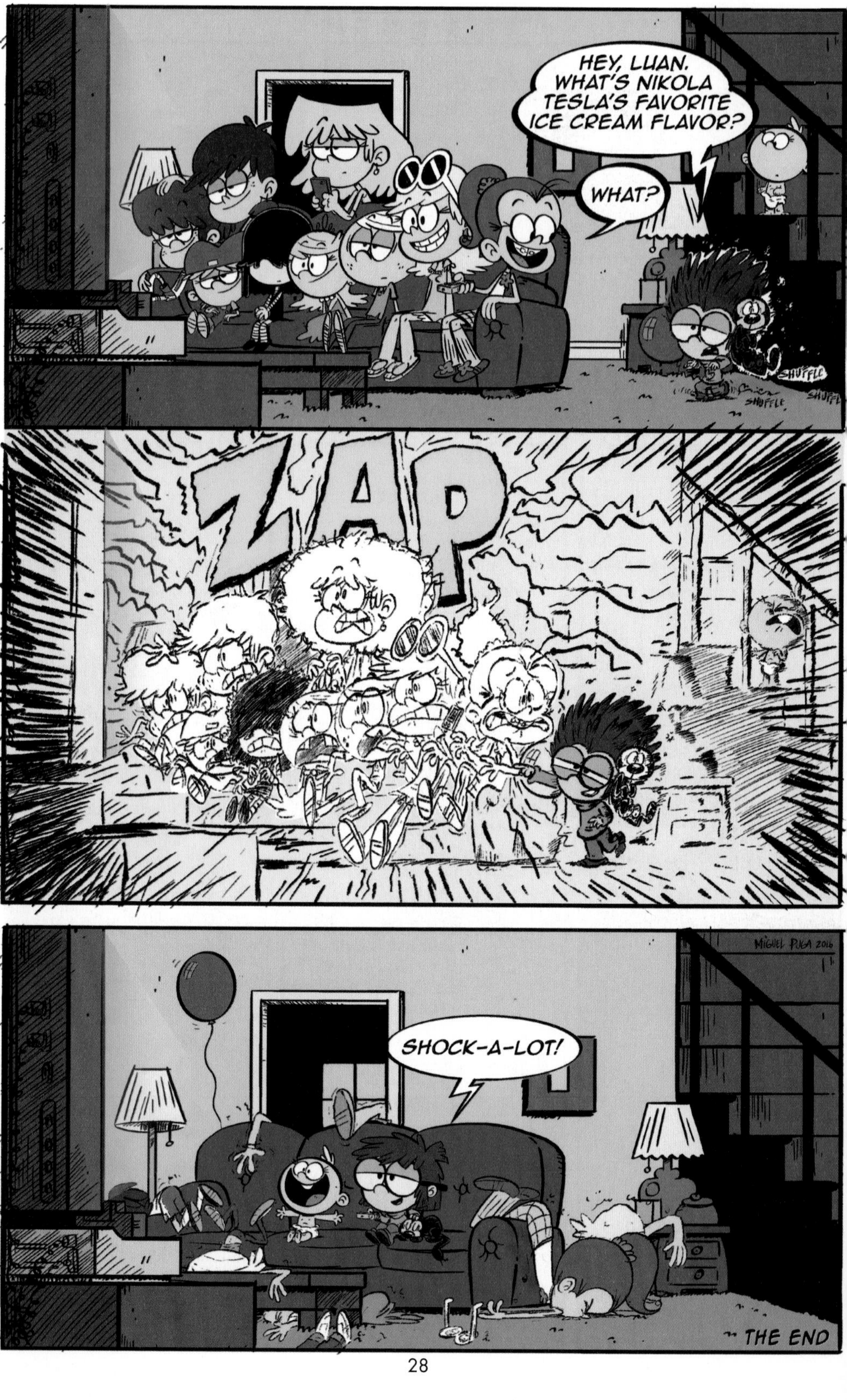
HEY, LUAN. WHAT'S NIKOLA TESLA'S FAVORITE ICE CREAM FLAVOR?
WHAT?
SHUFFLE
SHUFFLE
SHUFFLE
ZAP
MIGUEL PUGA 2016
SHOCK-A-LOT!
THE END

"THE SPOT"

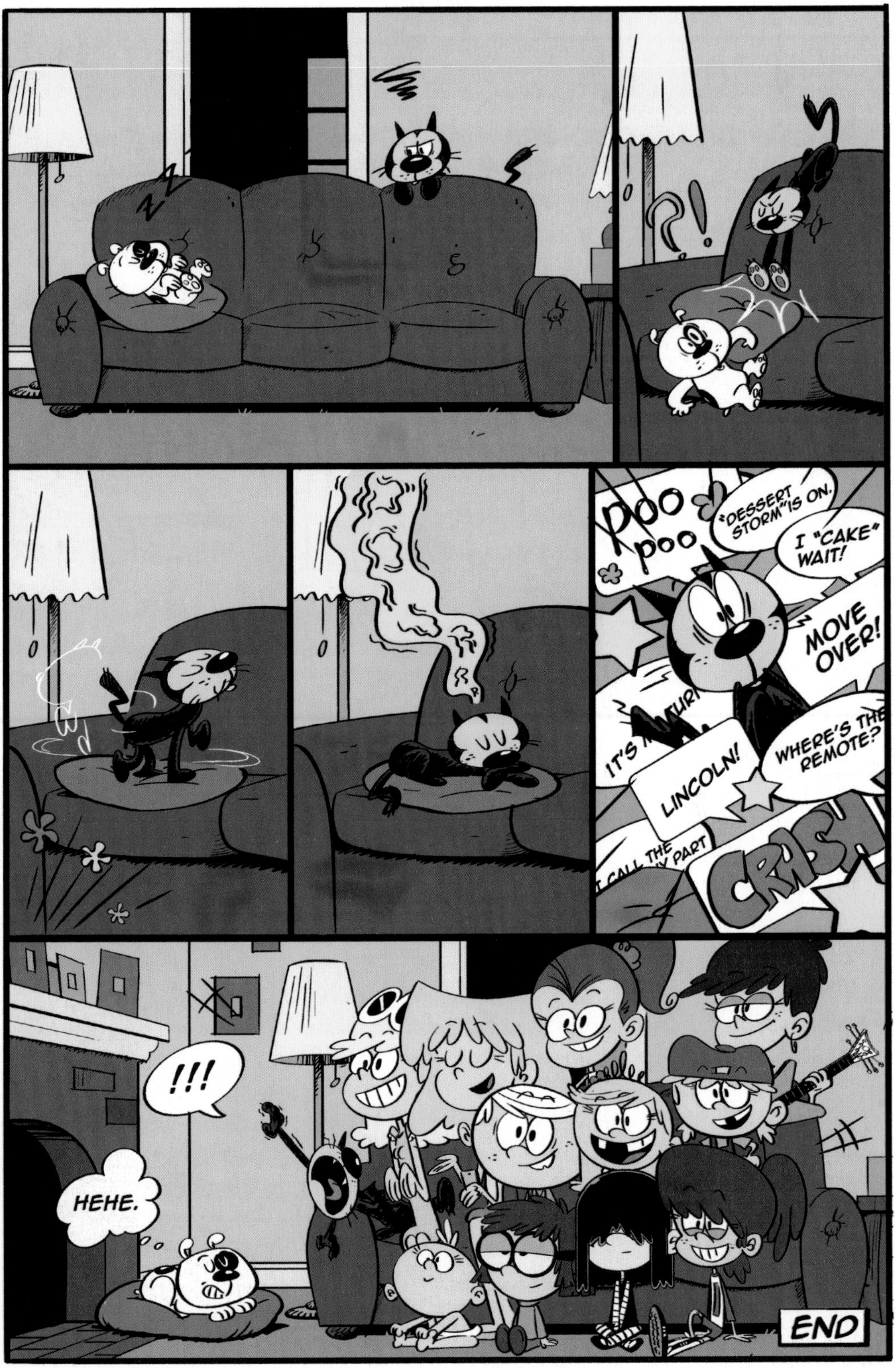

?!
POO
poo
"DESSERT STORM" IS ON.
I "CAKE" WAIT!
MOVE OVER!
LINCOLN!
WHERE'S THE REMOTE?
!!!
HEHE.
END

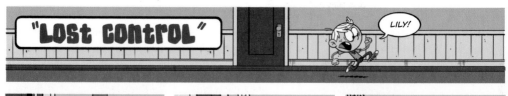

"LOST CONTROL"

LILY!

THE JIG IS UP, LILY! I KNOW YOU HAVE THE REMOTE!

BA LA BA LA BA LA LA BA BA BA BA BA LA LA LA LA BA LA

I'M SORRY, YOU'RE RIGHT. I DON'T HAVE ANY EVIDENCE.

BA LA GA BA LA BABBLE GAGA LA BA LA GA LA

WAIT...WHAT WOULD CLIFF WANT WITH THE REMOTE?

GA BA LAGGLE LA GA BABBLE LABBLE GA BA

FAIR POINT.

BABBLE LA GA BA GA LABBLE AGA LA GA BA GA

OR LANA?

BA BABBLE GA LABBLE LA GA LA LA BA LA BA LA GA BA

MAKES SENSE. I GUESS I SHOULD TRY TALKING TO CLIFF OR LANA.

TO TALK TO CLIFF, GO TO PAGE 121. TO TALK TO LANA, GO TO PAGE 104.

"NO SPOILERS"

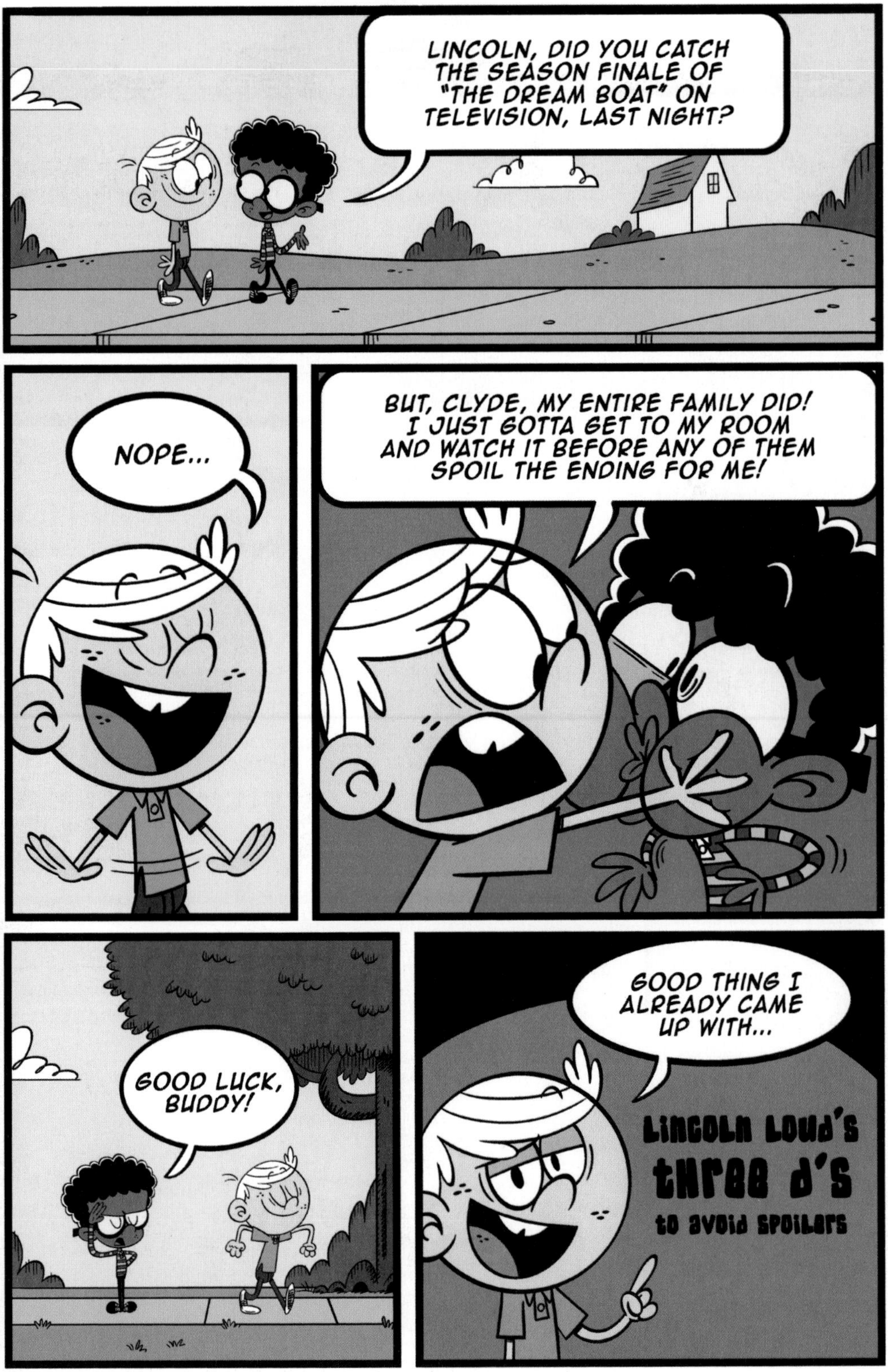
LINCOLN, DID YOU CATCH THE SEASON FINALE OF "THE DREAM BOAT" ON TELEVISION, LAST NIGHT?
NOPE...
BUT, CLYDE, MY ENTIRE FAMILY DID! I JUST GOTTA GET TO MY ROOM AND WATCH IT BEFORE ANY OF THEM SPOIL THE ENDING FOR ME!
GOOD LUCK, BUDDY!
GOOD THING I ALREADY CAME UP WITH...
Lincoln Loud's
three d's
to avoid spoilers

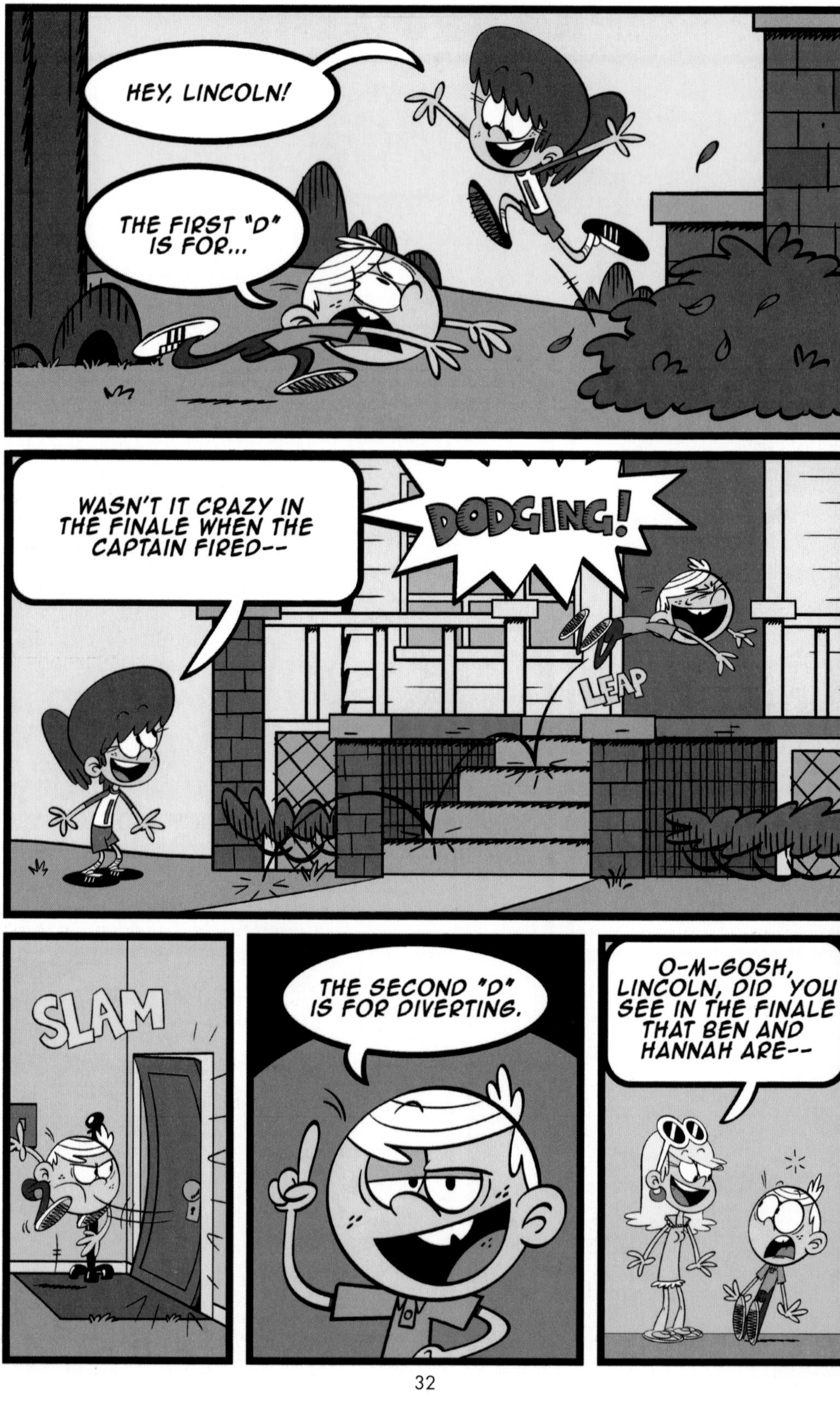
HEY, LINCOLN!
THE FIRST "D" IS FOR...
WASN'T IT CRAZY IN THE FINALE WHEN THE CAPTAIN FIRED--
DODGING!
LEAP
SLAM
THE SECOND "D" IS FOR DIVERTING.
O-M-GOSH, LINCOLN, DID YOU SEE IN THE FINALE THAT BEN AND HANNAH ARE--

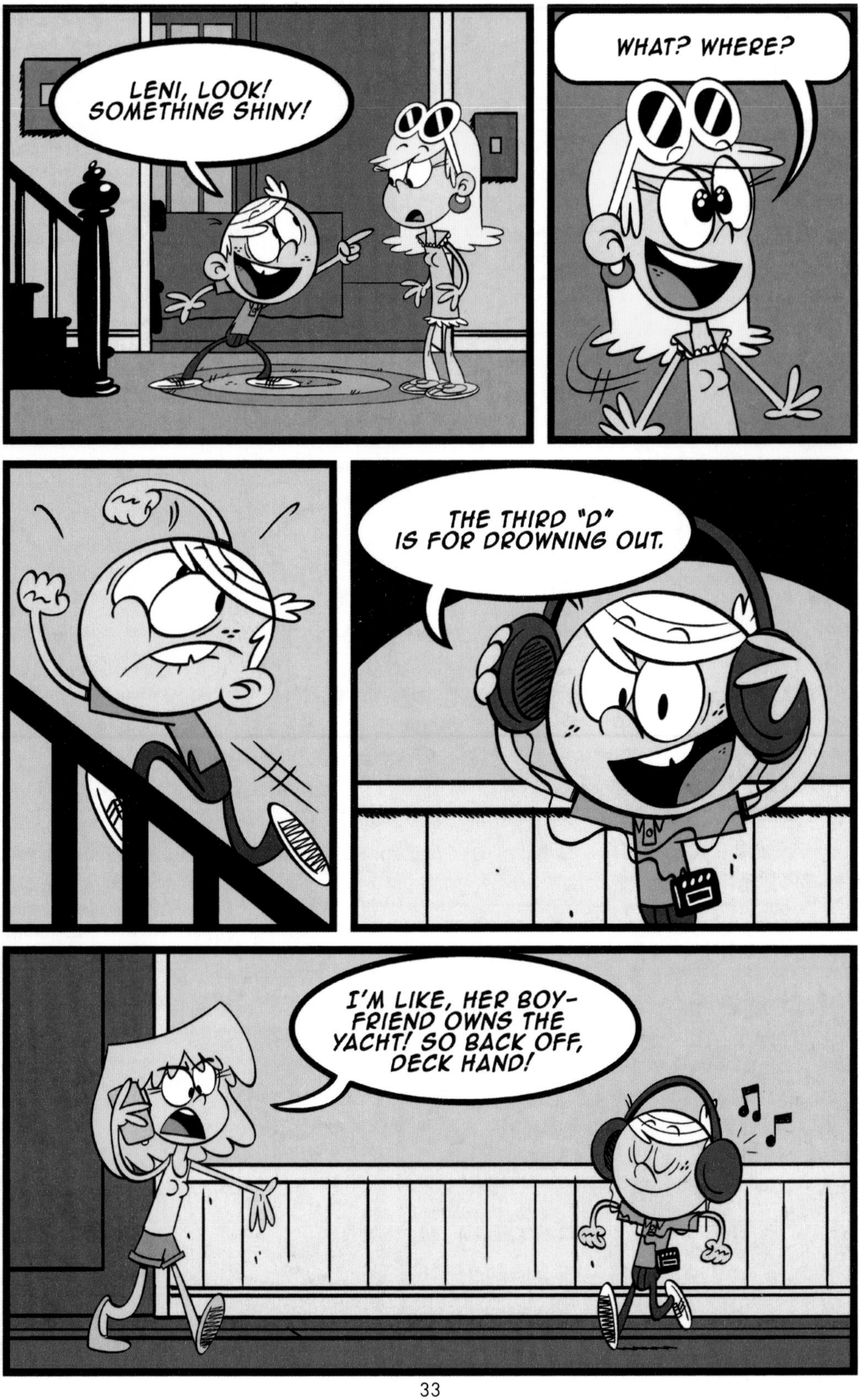
LENI, LOOK! SOMETHING SHINY!
WHAT? WHERE?
THE THIRD "D" IS FOR DROWNING OUT.
I'M LIKE, HER BOY-FRIEND OWNS THE YACHT! SO BACK OFF, DECK HAND!

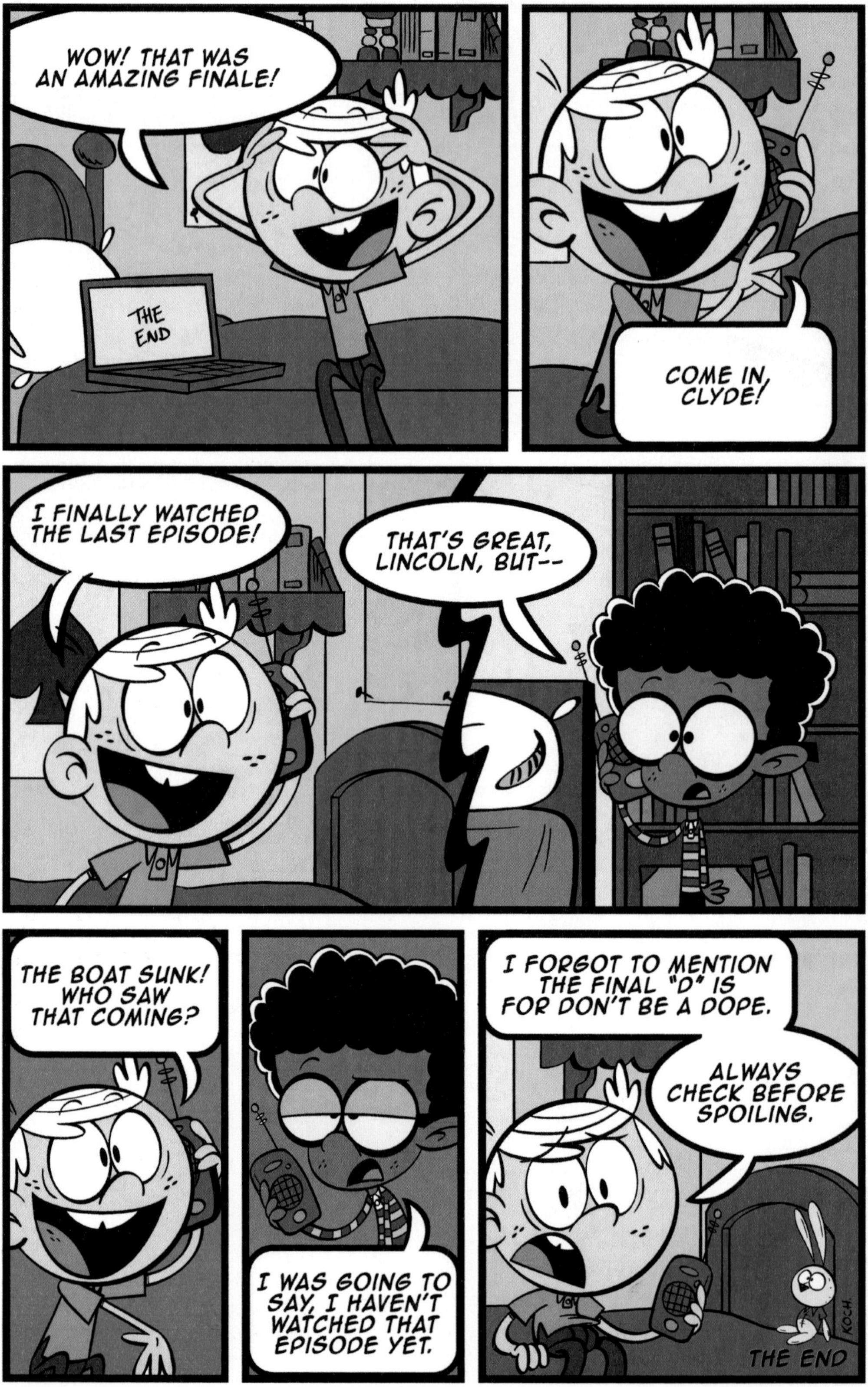
WOW! THAT WAS AN AMAZING FINALE!
THE END
COME IN, CLYDE!
I FINALLY WATCHED THE LAST EPISODE!
THAT'S GREAT, LINCOLN, BUT--
THE BOAT SUNK! WHO SAW THAT COMING?
I WAS GOING TO SAY, I HAVEN'T WATCHED THAT EPISODE YET.
I FORGOT TO MENTION THE FINAL "D" IS FOR DON'T BE A DOPE.
ALWAYS CHECK BEFORE SPOILING.
KOCH.
THE END

"THE CALL"

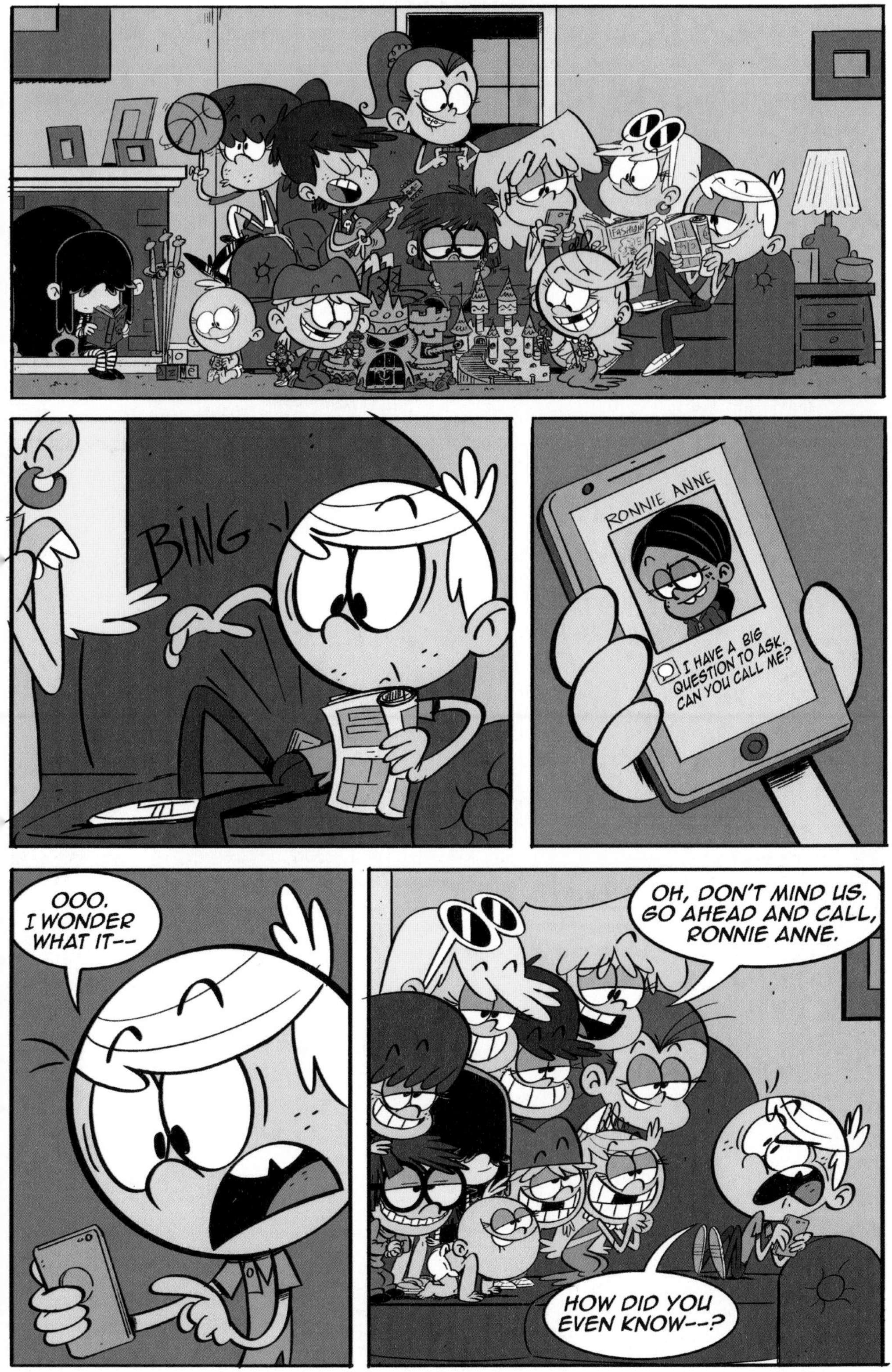
BING
RONNIE ANNE
I HAVE A BIG QUESTION TO ASK. CAN YOU CALL ME?
OOO. I WONDER WHAT IT--
OH, DON'T MIND US. GO AHEAD AND CALL, RONNIE ANNE.
HOW DID YOU EVEN KNOW--?

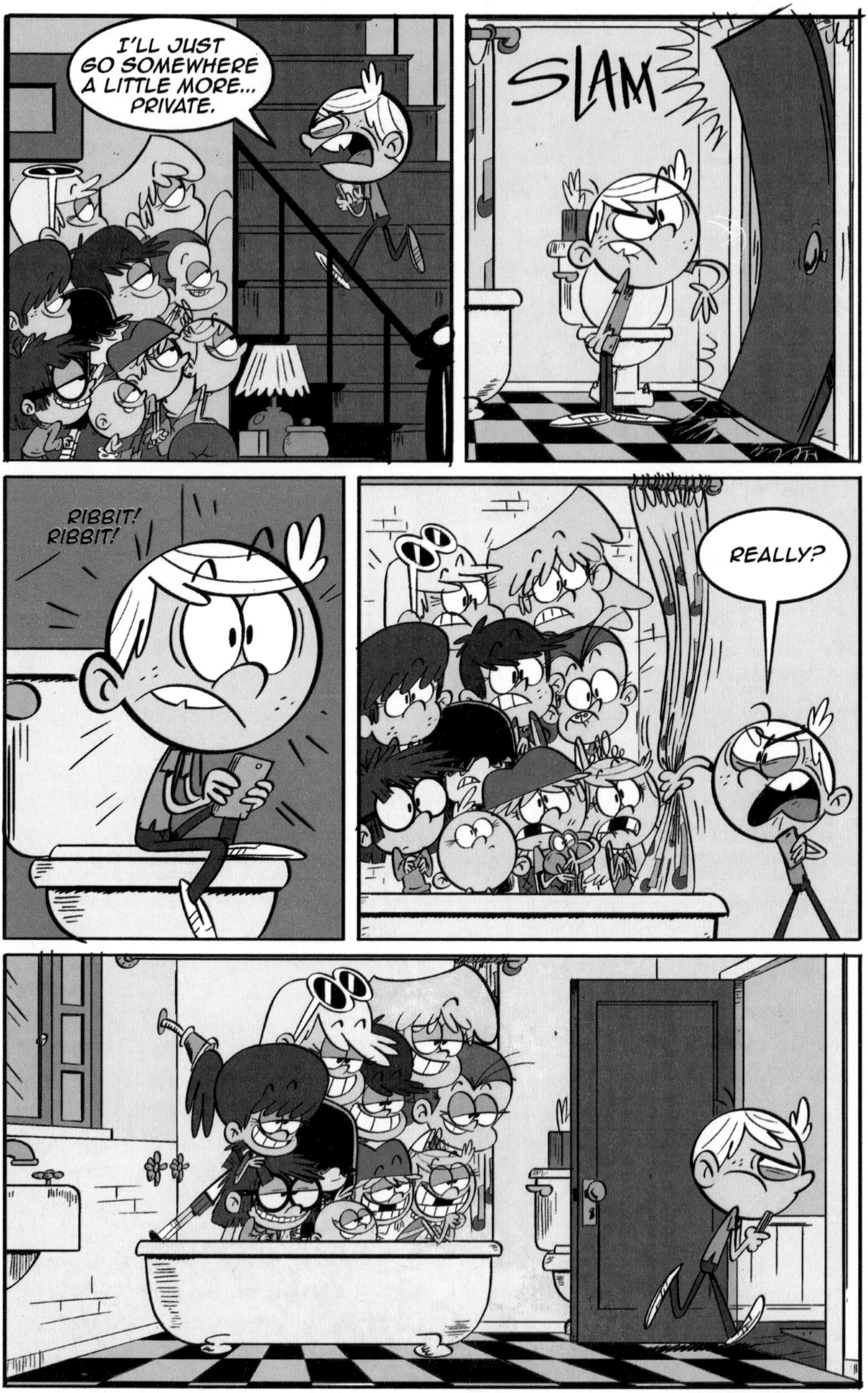
I'LL JUST GO SOMEWHERE A LITTLE MORE... PRIVATE.
SLAM
RIBBIT! RIBBIT!
REALLY?

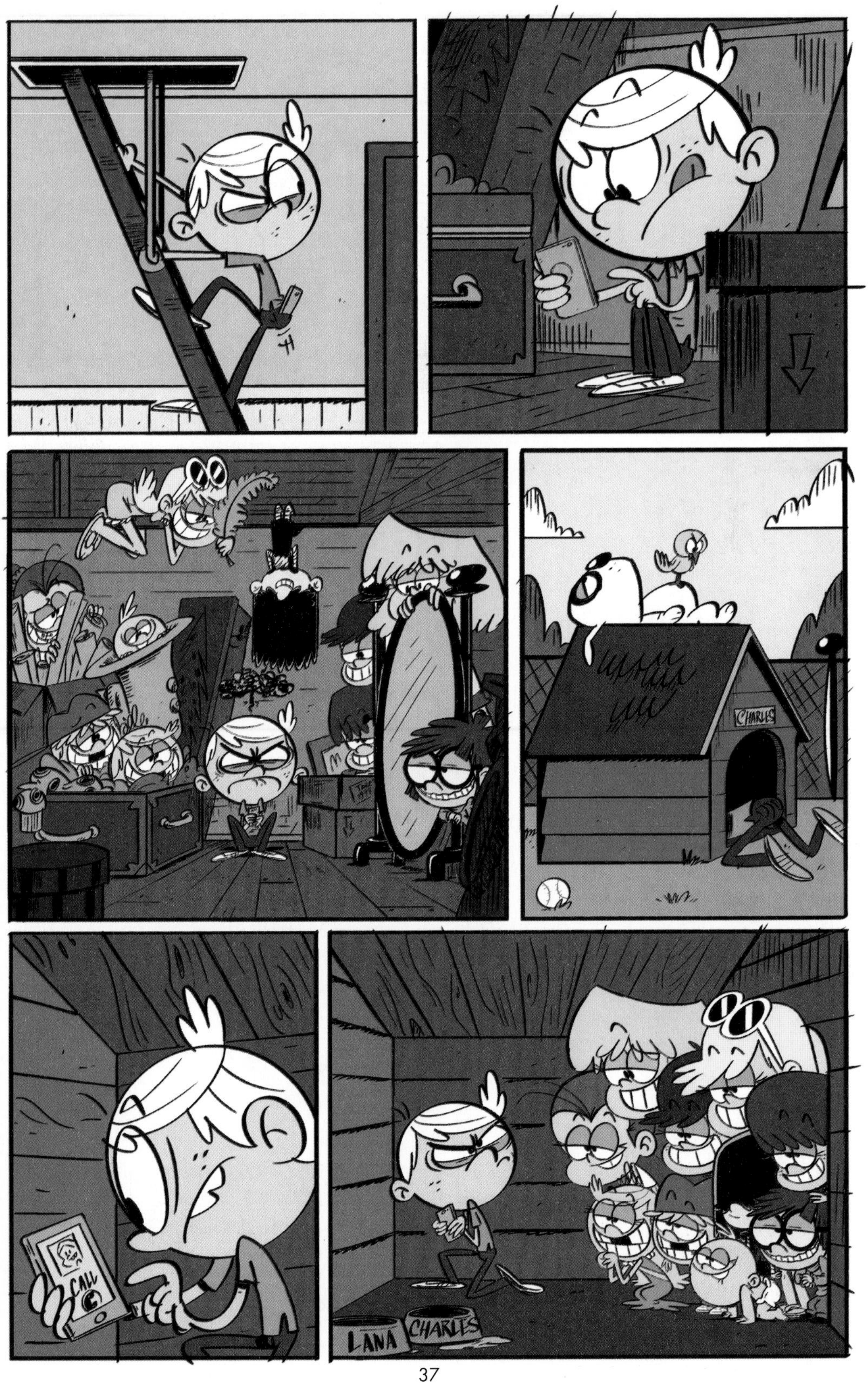
CHARLES
CALL
LANA
CHARLES

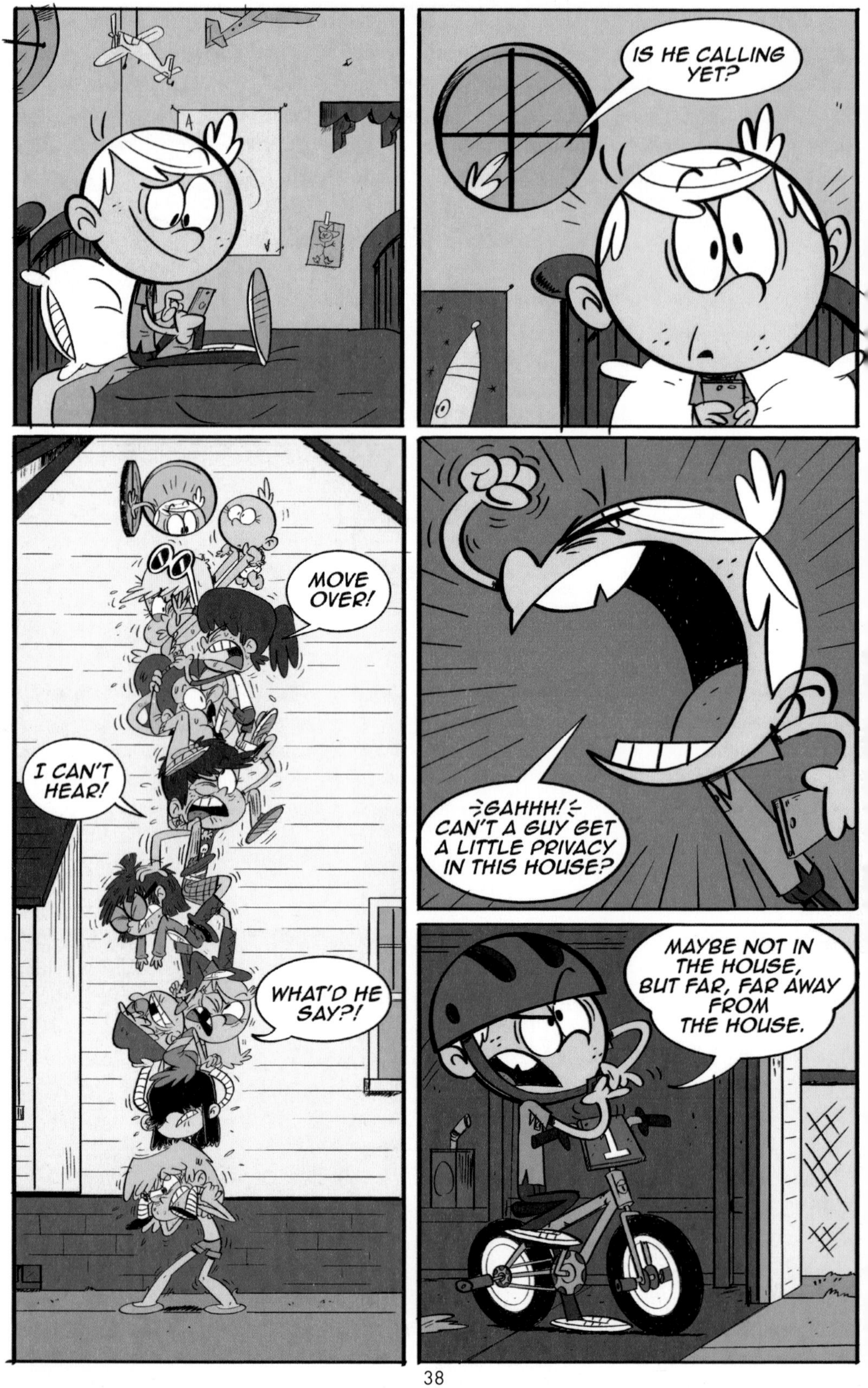
IS HE CALLING YET?
MOVE OVER!
I CAN'T HEAR!
WHAT'D HE SAY?!
GAHHH! CAN'T A GUY GET A LITTLE PRIVACY IN THIS HOUSE?
MAYBE NOT IN THE HOUSE, BUT FAR, FAR AWAY FROM THE HOUSE.

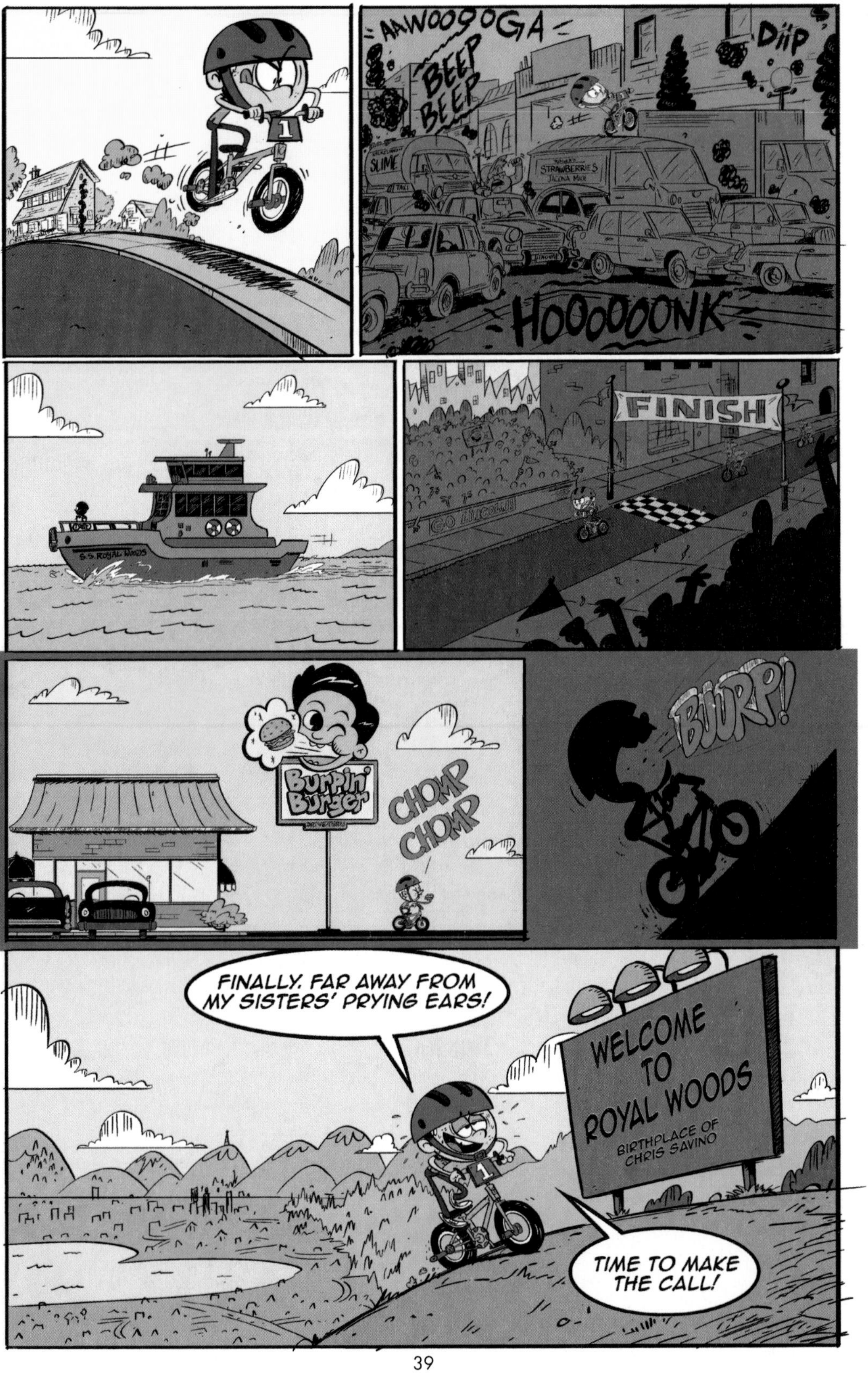
AAWOOOGA
BEEP BEEP
DIIP
SLIME
STRAWBERRIES
TAXI
HOOOOOONK
S.S. ROYAL WOODS
FINISH
Burpin' Burger
CHOMP CHOMP
BURP!
FINALLY. FAR AWAY FROM MY SISTERS' PRYING EARS!
WELCOME TO ROYAL WOODS
BIRTHPLACE OF CHRIS SAVINO
TIME TO MAKE THE CALL!

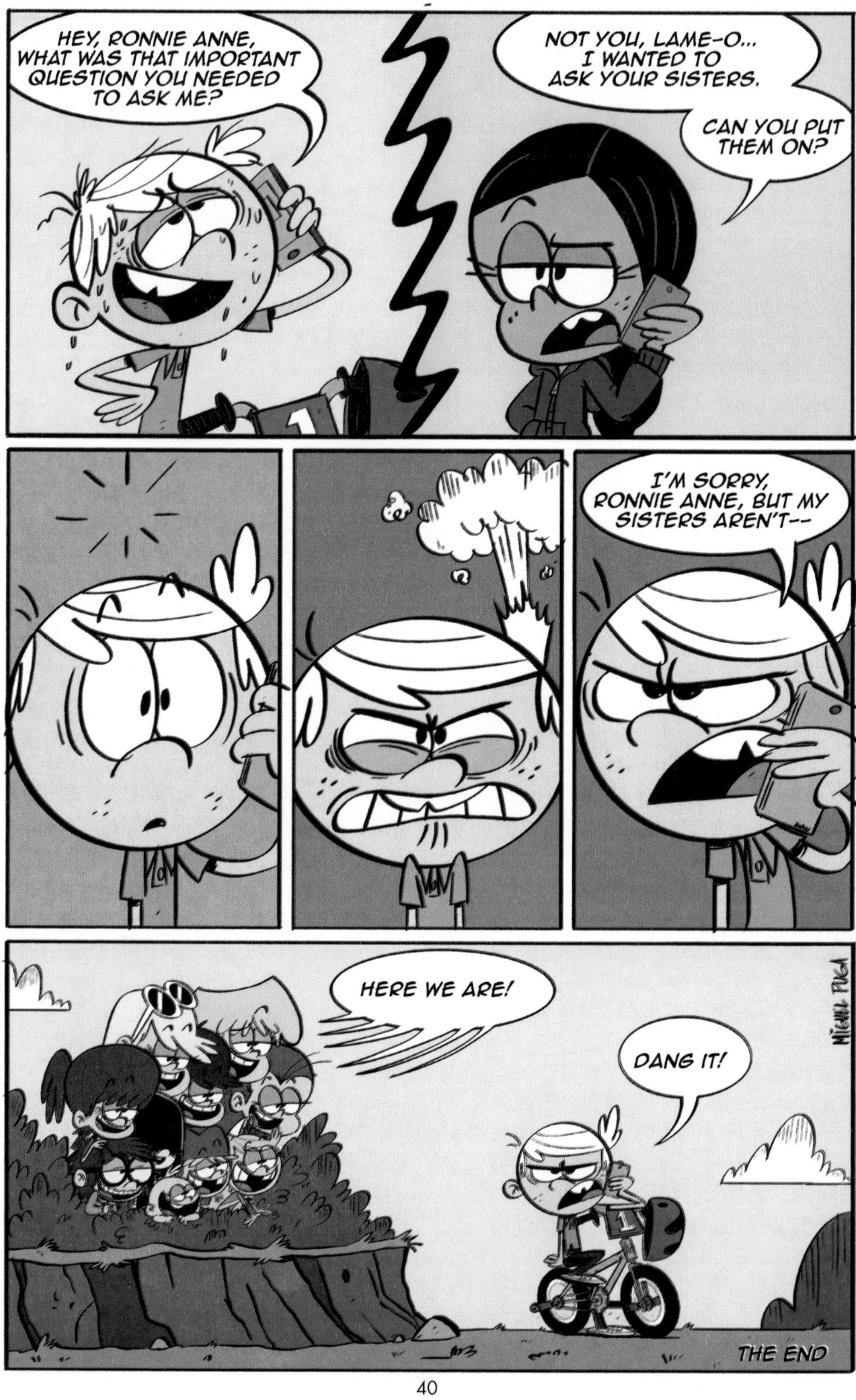
HEY, RONNIE ANNE, WHAT WAS THAT IMPORTANT QUESTION YOU NEEDED TO ASK ME?
NOT YOU, LAME-O... I WANTED TO ASK YOUR SISTERS.
CAN YOU PUT THEM ON?
I'M SORRY, RONNIE ANNE, BUT MY SISTERS AREN'T--
HERE WE ARE!
DANG IT!
MIGUEL PUGA
THE END

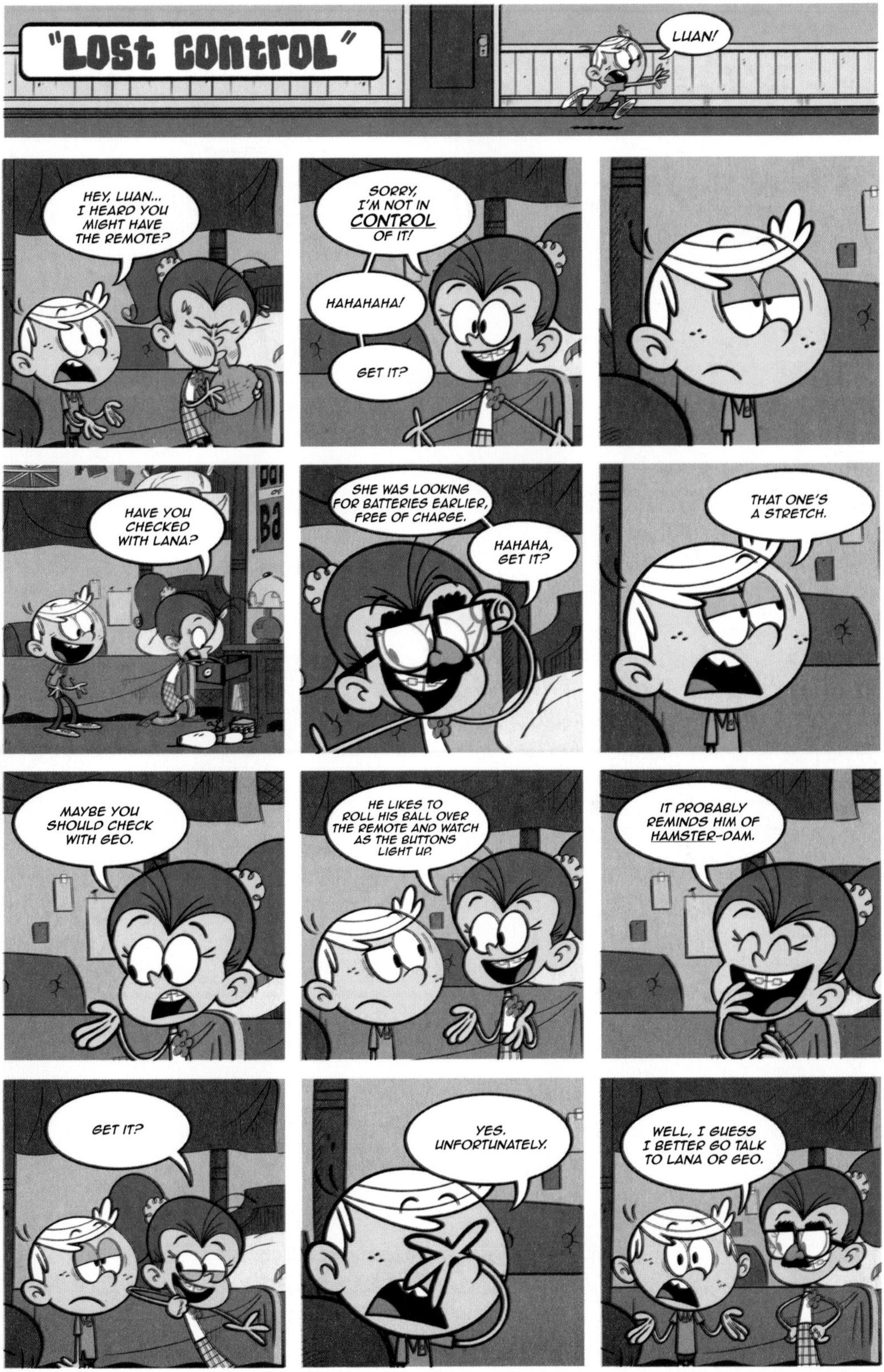
"LOST CONTROL"
LUAN!
HEY, LUAN... I HEARD YOU MIGHT HAVE THE REMOTE?
SORRY, I'M NOT IN CONTROL OF IT!
HAHAHAHA!
GET IT?
HAVE YOU CHECKED WITH LANA?
SHE WAS LOOKING FOR BATTERIES EARLIER, FREE OF CHARGE.
HAHAHA, GET IT?
THAT ONE'S A STRETCH.
MAYBE YOU SHOULD CHECK WITH GEO.
HE LIKES TO ROLL HIS BALL OVER THE REMOTE AND WATCH AS THE BUTTONS LIGHT UP.
IT PROBABLY REMINDS HIM OF HAMSTER-DAM.
GET IT?
YES. UNFORTUNATELY.
WELL, I GUESS I BETTER GO TALK TO LANA OR GEO.

TO TALK TO LANA, GO TO PAGE 104. TO TALK TO GEO, GO TO PAGE 137.

"VERY SUPERSTITIOUS"

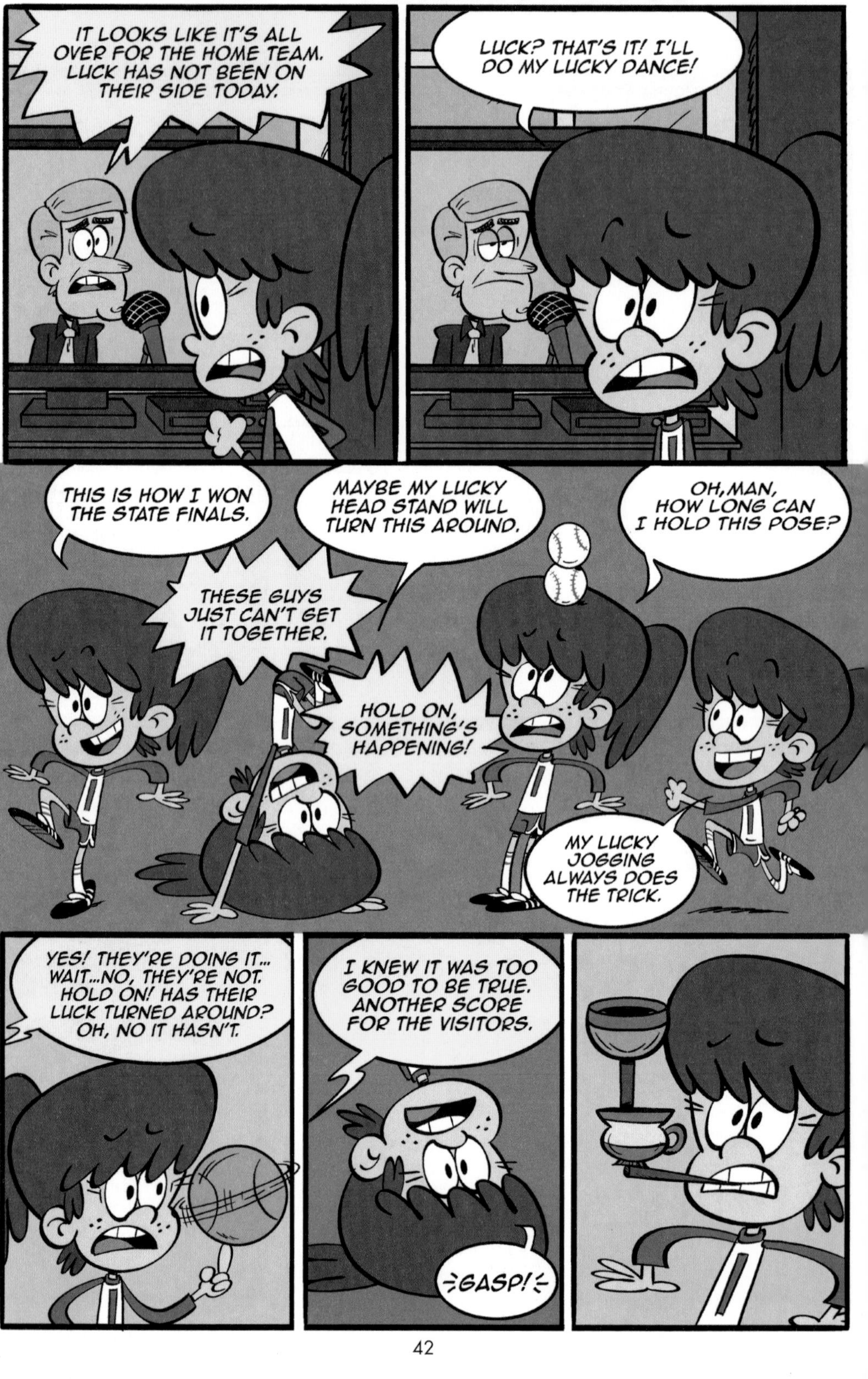

IT LOOKS LIKE IT'S ALL OVER FOR THE HOME TEAM. LUCK HAS NOT BEEN ON THEIR SIDE TODAY.
LUCK? THAT'S IT! I'LL DO MY LUCKY DANCE!
THIS IS HOW I WON THE STATE FINALS.
THESE GUYS JUST CAN'T GET IT TOGETHER.
MAYBE MY LUCKY HEAD STAND WILL TURN THIS AROUND.
HOLD ON, SOMETHING'S HAPPENING!
OH, MAN, HOW LONG CAN I HOLD THIS POSE?
MY LUCKY JOGGING ALWAYS DOES THE TRICK.
YES! THEY'RE DOING IT... WAIT...NO, THEY'RE NOT. HOLD ON! HAS THEIR LUCK TURNED AROUND? OH, NO IT HASN'T.
I KNEW IT WAS TOO GOOD TO BE TRUE. ANOTHER SCORE FOR THE VISITORS.
GASP!

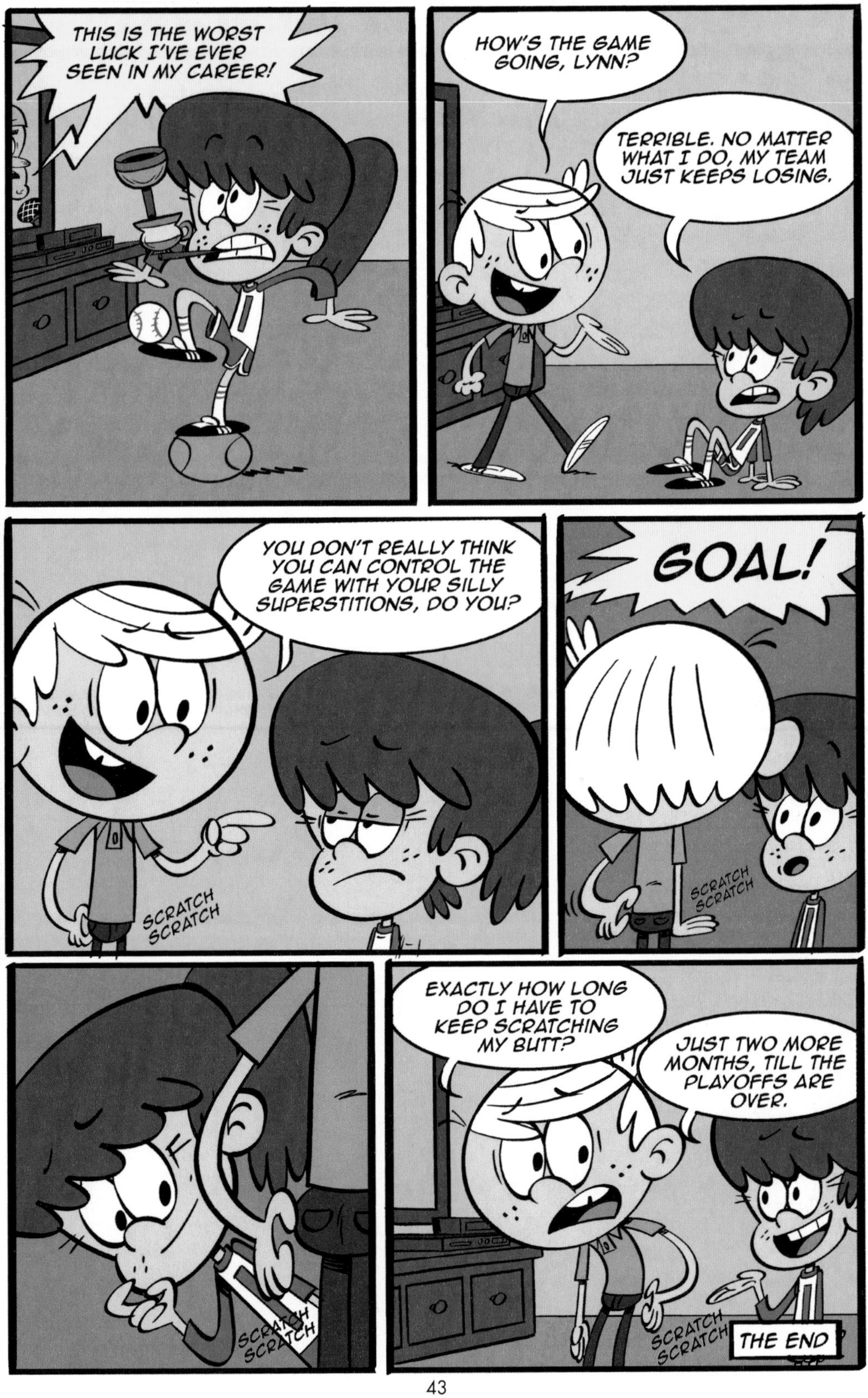
THIS IS THE WORST LUCK I'VE EVER SEEN IN MY CAREER!
HOW'S THE GAME GOING, LYNN?
TERRIBLE. NO MATTER WHAT I DO, MY TEAM JUST KEEPS LOSING.
YOU DON'T REALLY THINK YOU CAN CONTROL THE GAME WITH YOUR SILLY SUPERSTITIONS, DO YOU?
SCRATCH SCRATCH
GOAL!
SCRATCH SCRATCH
SCRATCH SCRATCH
EXACTLY HOW LONG DO I HAVE TO KEEP SCRATCHING MY BUTT?
JUST TWO MORE MONTHS, TILL THE PLAYOFFS ARE OVER.
SCRATCH SCRATCH
THE END

"HERE COMES THE AIRPLANE"

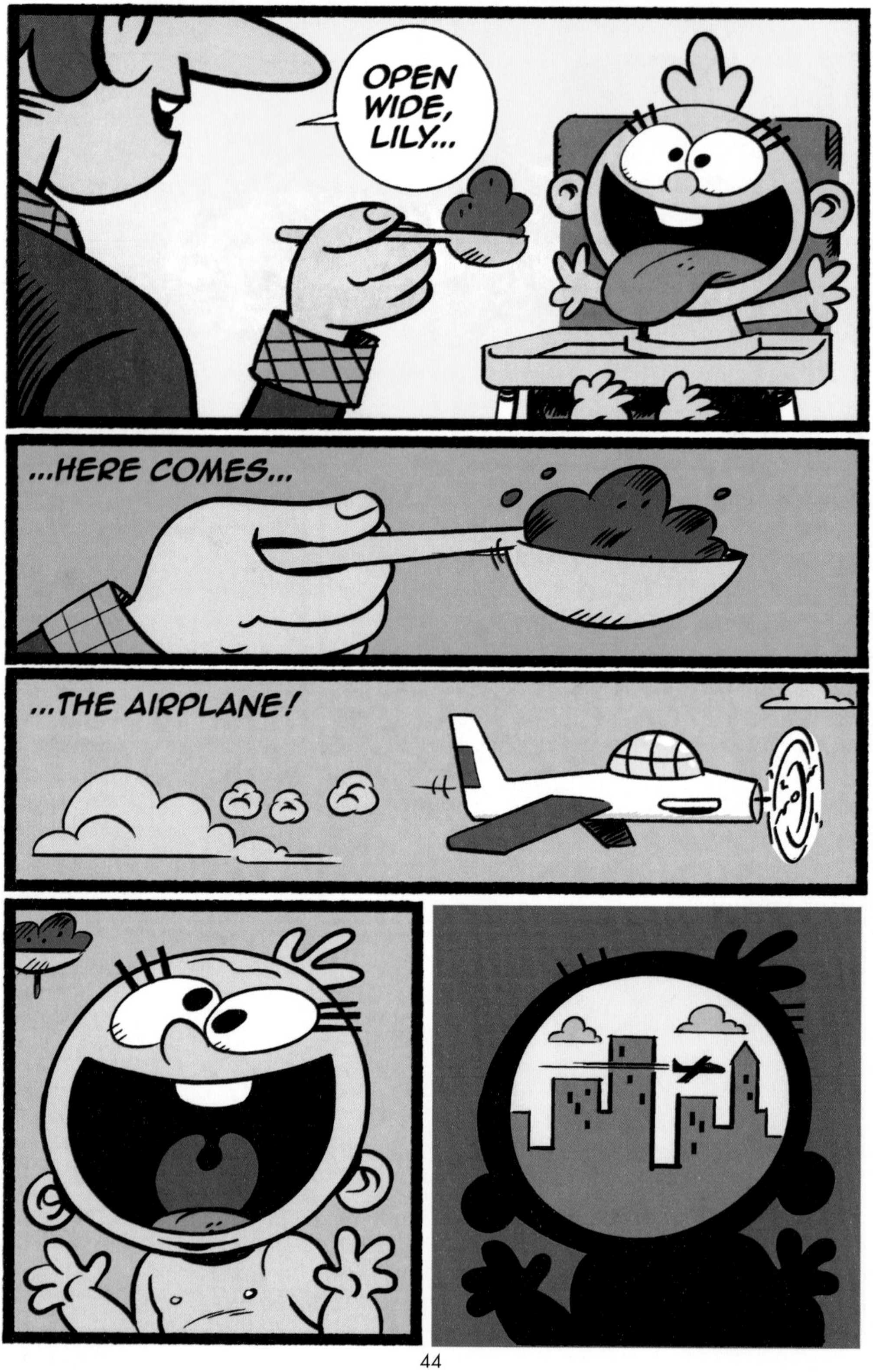

OPEN WIDE, LILY...
...HERE COMES...
...THE AIRPLANE!

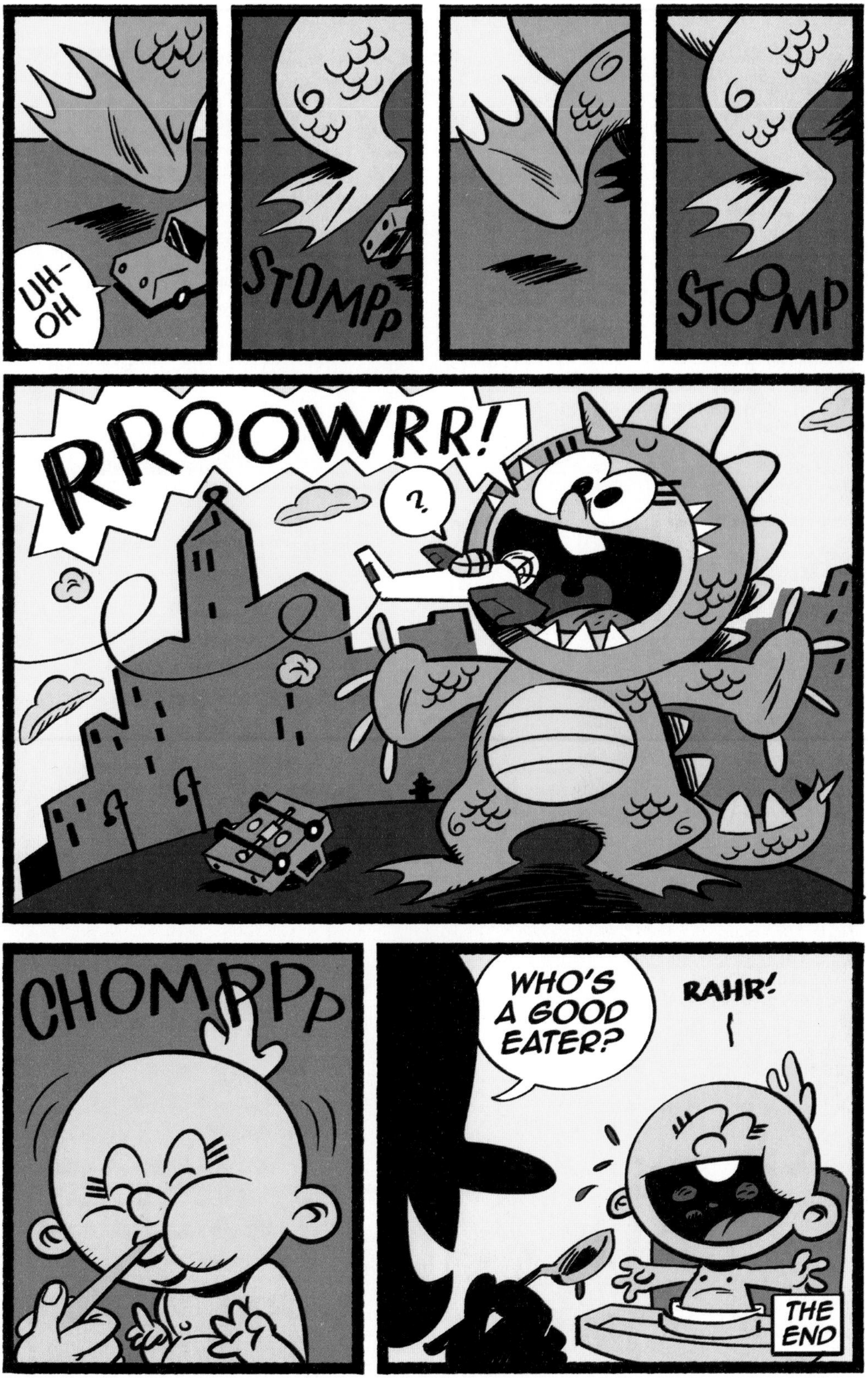
UH-OH
STOMPP
STOOMP
RROOWRR!
?
CHOMPPP
WHO'S A GOOD EATER?
RAHR!
THE END

"WALL WALKER"

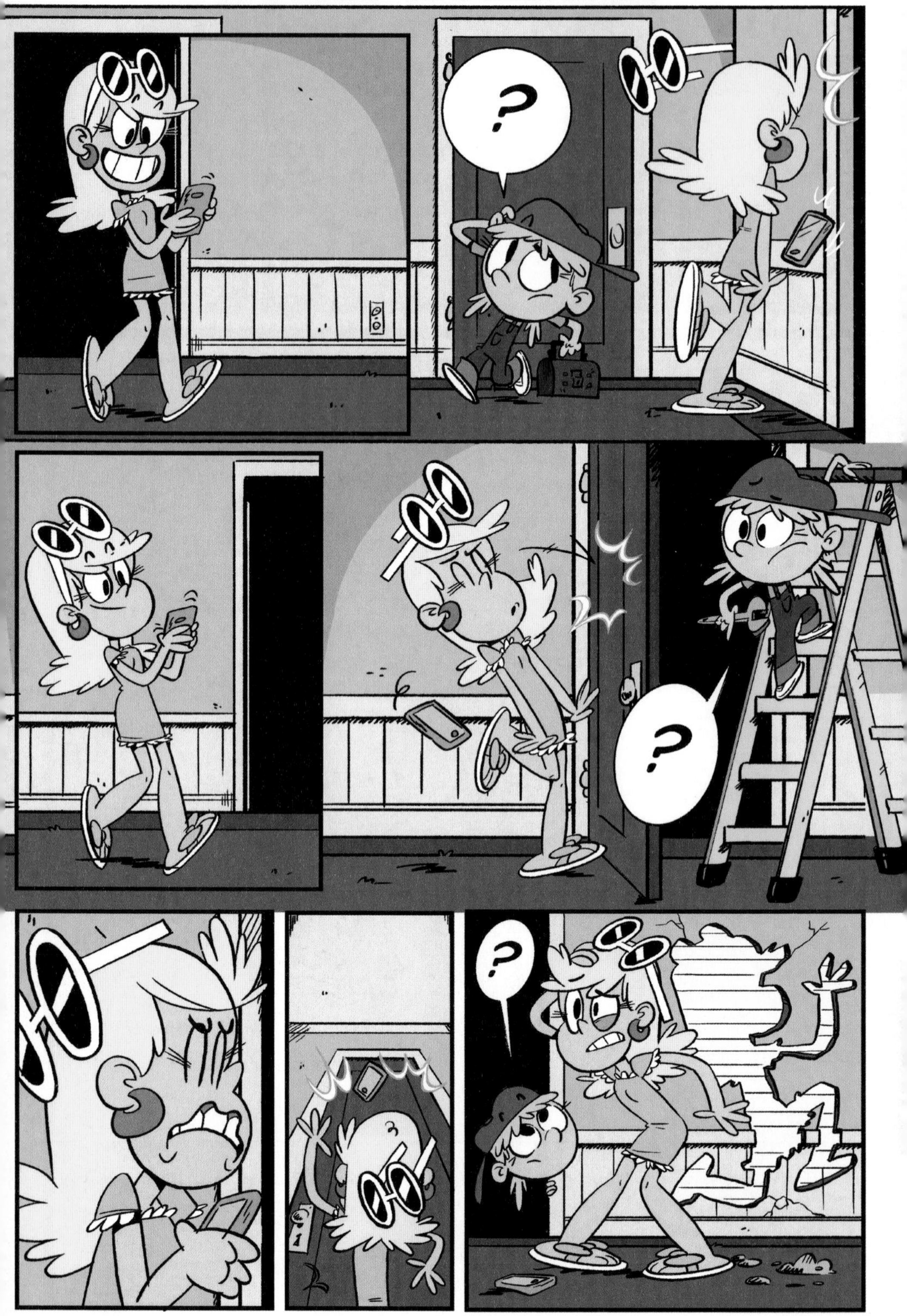
?
?
?

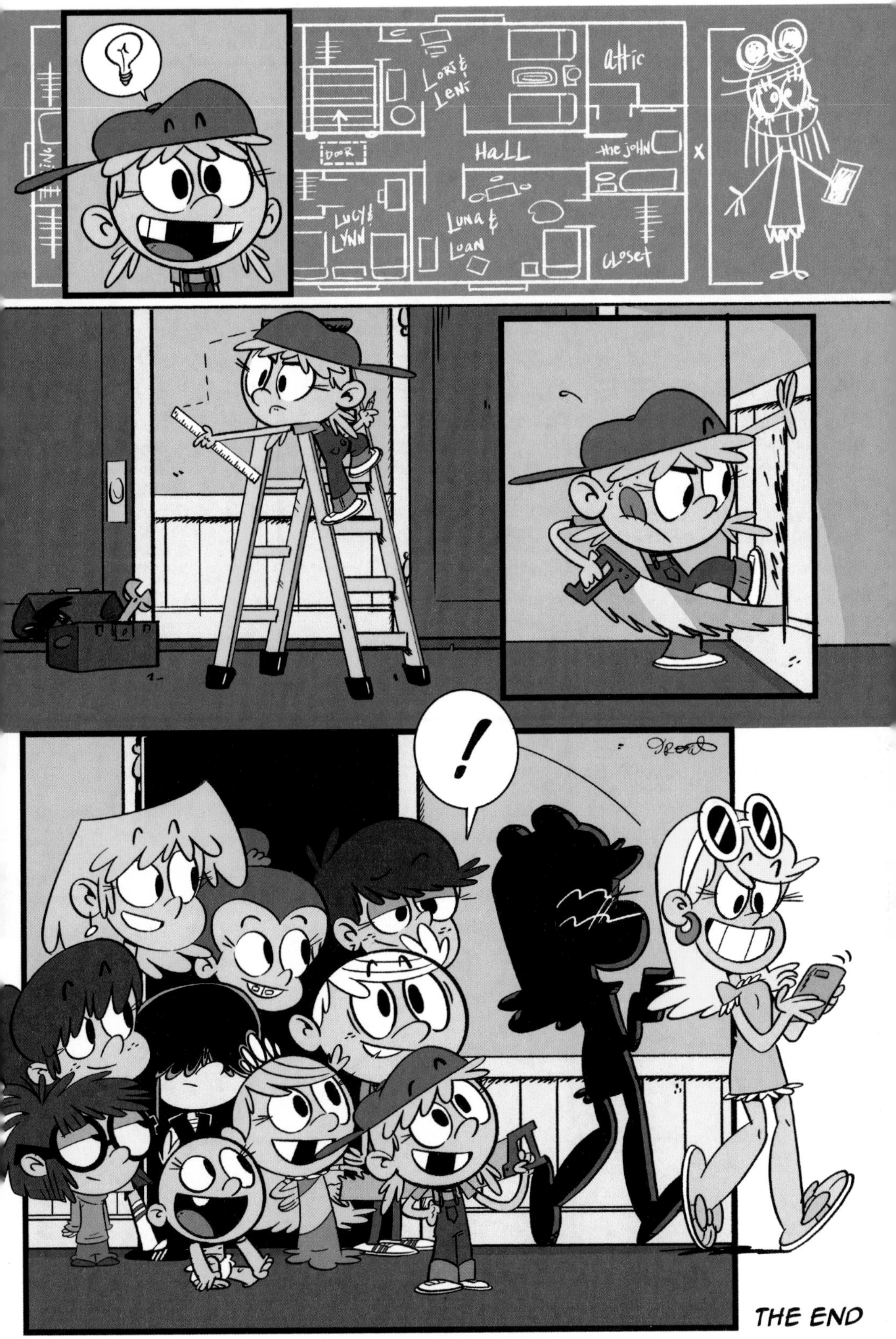

Lori & Leni
attic
DOOR
HALL
the john
Lucy & Lynn
Luna & Loan
closet
!
THE END

"SIBLING SPEAK"

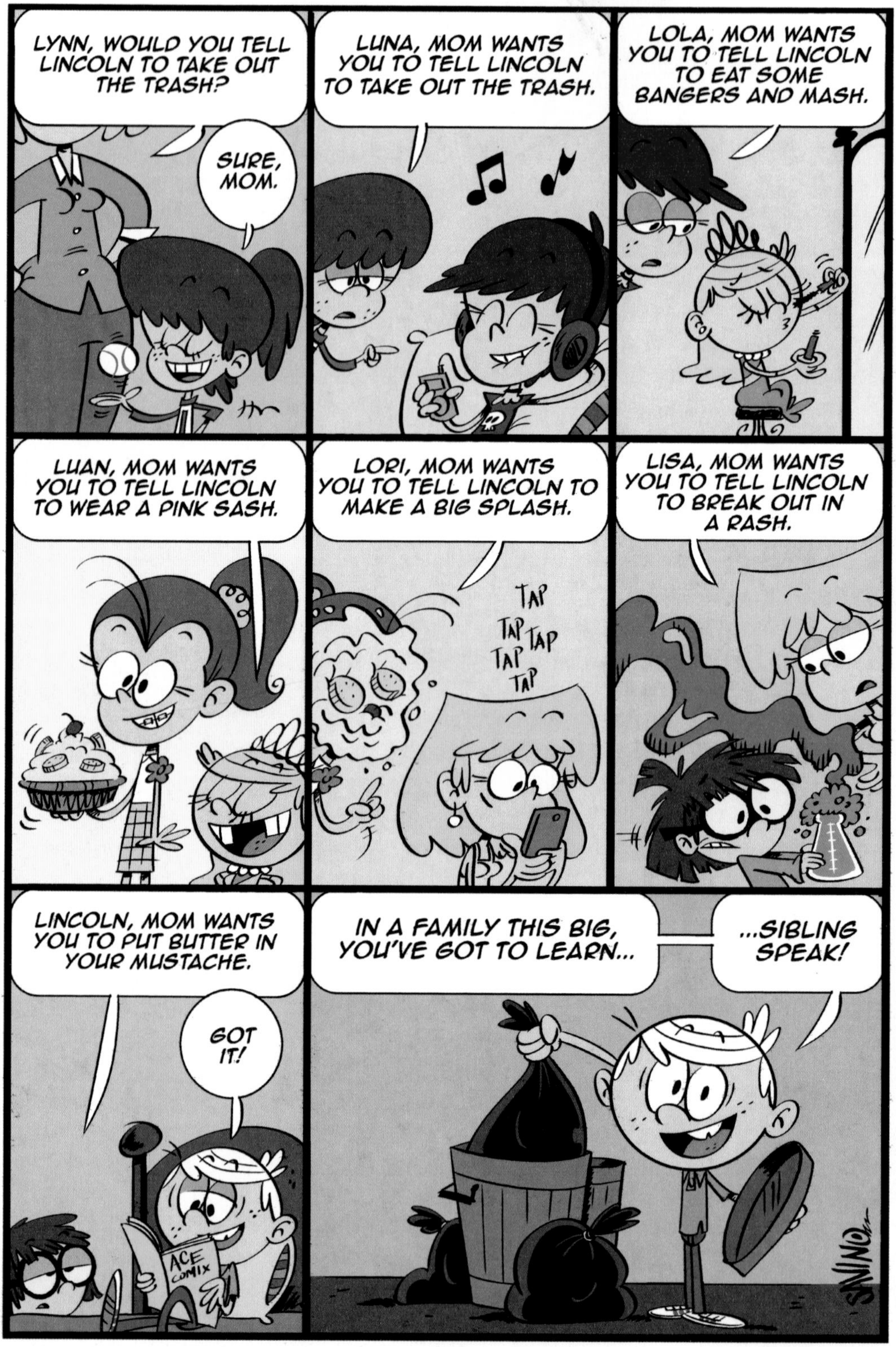

LYNN, WOULD YOU TELL LINCOLN TO TAKE OUT THE TRASH?
SURE, MOM.
LUNA, MOM WANTS YOU TO TELL LINCOLN TO TAKE OUT THE TRASH.
LOLA, MOM WANTS YOU TO TELL LINCOLN TO EAT SOME BANGERS AND MASH.
LUAN, MOM WANTS YOU TO TELL LINCOLN TO WEAR A PINK SASH.
LORI, MOM WANTS YOU TO TELL LINCOLN TO MAKE A BIG SPLASH.
TAP TAP TAP TAP TAP
LISA, MOM WANTS YOU TO TELL LINCOLN TO BREAK OUT IN A RASH.
LINCOLN, MOM WANTS YOU TO PUT BUTTER IN YOUR MUSTACHE.
GOT IT!
ACE COMIX
IN A FAMILY THIS BIG, YOU'VE GOT TO LEARN...
...SIBLING SPEAK!

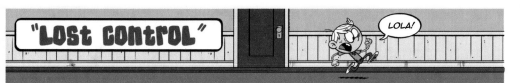

LOLA!

LOLA, DO YOU KNOW WHERE THE REMOTE IS?

MAYBE...MAYBE NOT...DEPENDS ON WHAT YOU HAVE TO OFFER.

FINE. WHAT DO YOU WANT?

IT'S MAKEOVER TIME!

SO WHERE IS THE REMOTE?!

OH. I UM, ACTUALLY DON'T KNOW.

BUT...I DID OVERHEAR LUCY AND LYNN ARGUING ABOUT WHAT TO WATCH AFTER "DREAM BOAT" WAS OVER.

I GUESS I'LL ASK ONE OF THEM...

TO TALK TO LUCY, GO TO PAGE 23. TO TALK TO LYNN, GO TO PAGE 56.

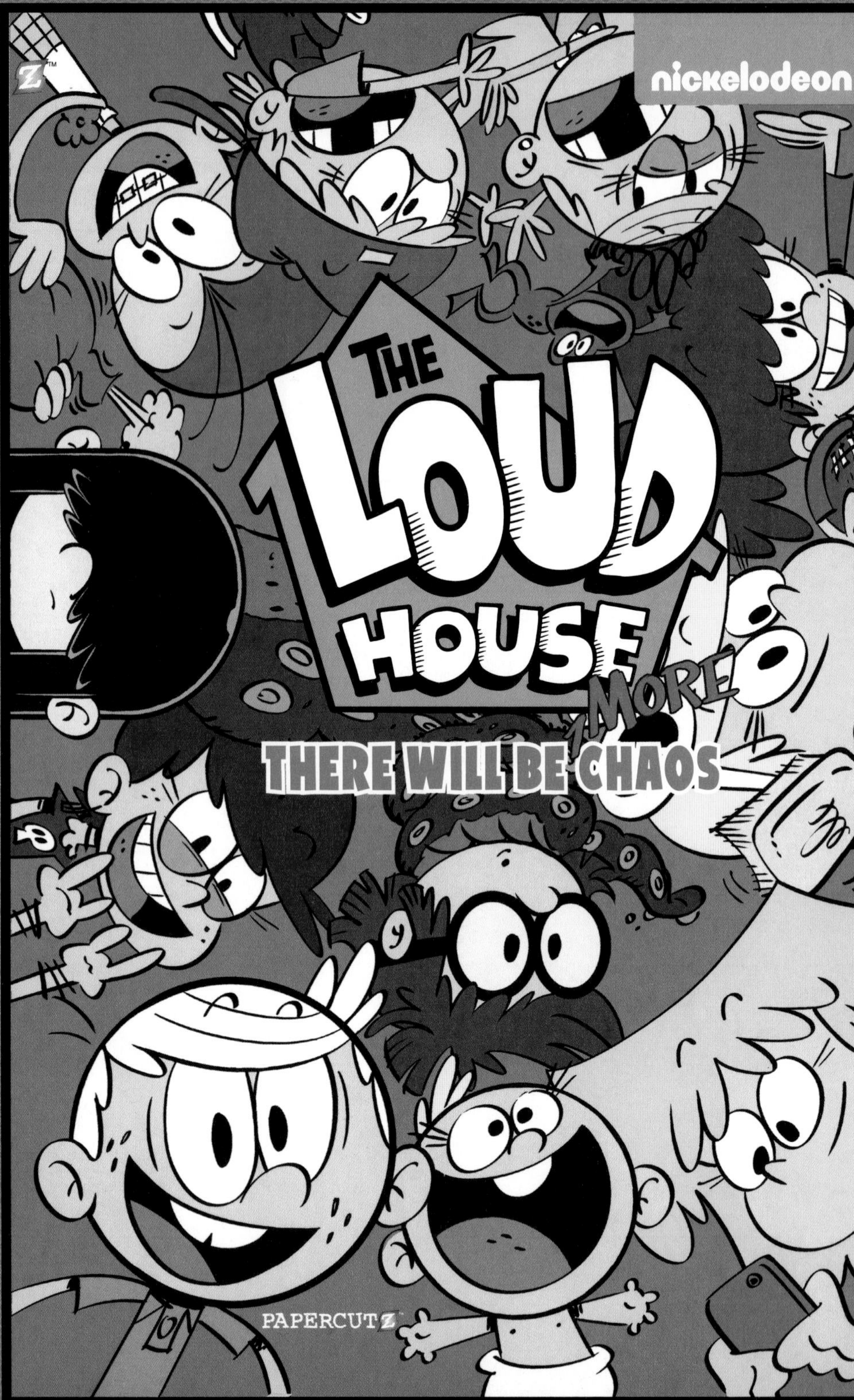
nickelodeon
THE LOUD HOUSE
MORE
THERE WILL BE CHAOS
PAPERCUTZ
THE LOUD HOUSE #2 Cover by Chris Savino

"BACK TO SCHOOL SHOPPING"

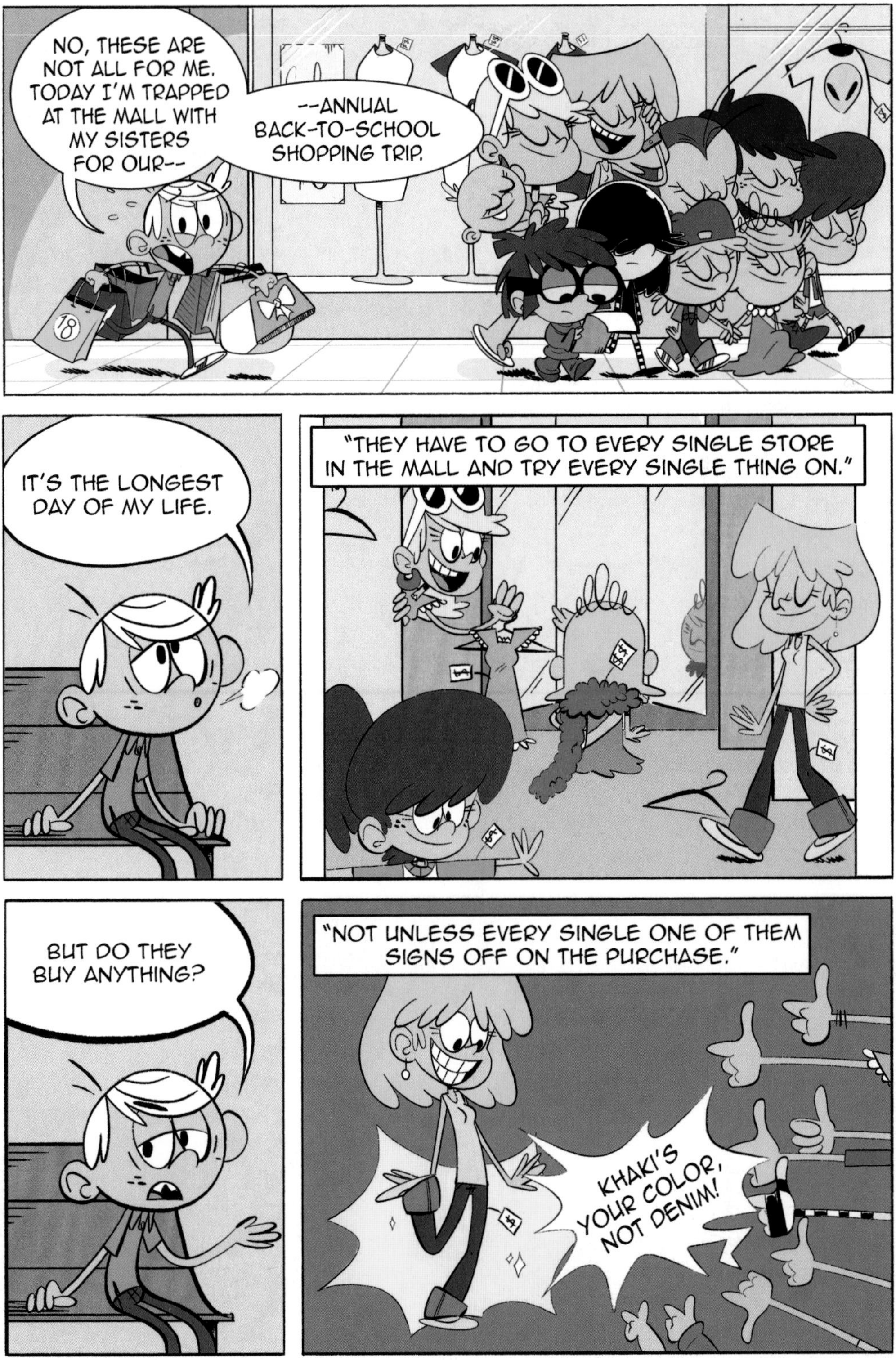
NO, THESE ARE NOT ALL FOR ME. TODAY I'M TRAPPED AT THE MALL WITH MY SISTERS FOR OUR--
--ANNUAL BACK-TO-SCHOOL SHOPPING TRIP.
18
IT'S THE LONGEST DAY OF MY LIFE.
"THEY HAVE TO GO TO EVERY SINGLE STORE IN THE MALL AND TRY EVERY SINGLE THING ON."
BUT DO THEY BUY ANYTHING?
"NOT UNLESS EVERY SINGLE ONE OF THEM SIGNS OFF ON THE PURCHASE."
KHAKI'S YOUR COLOR, NOT DENIM!

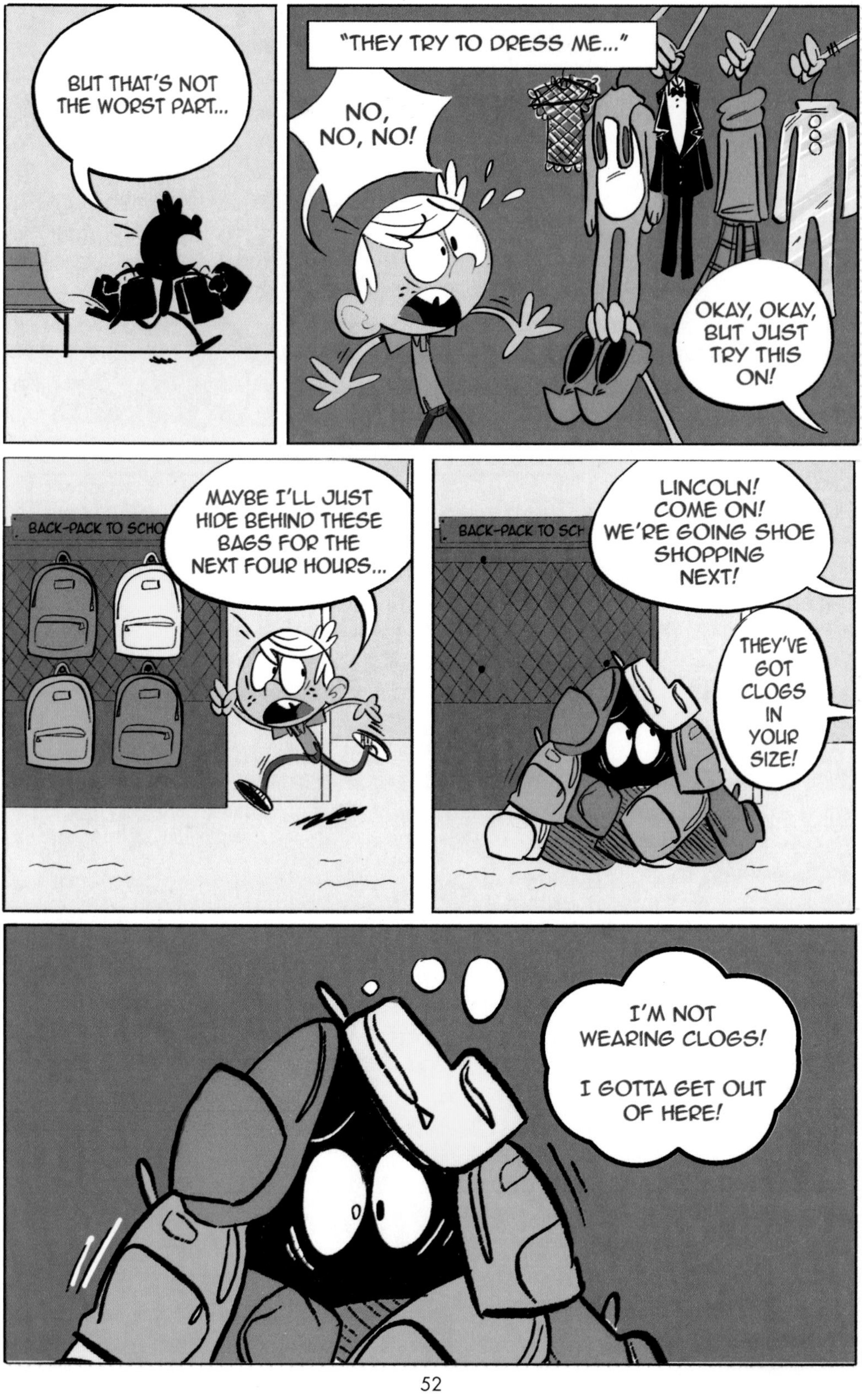
BUT THAT'S NOT THE WORST PART...
"THEY TRY TO DRESS ME..."
NO, NO, NO!
OKAY, OKAY, BUT JUST TRY THIS ON!
BACK-PACK TO SCHO
MAYBE I'LL JUST HIDE BEHIND THESE BAGS FOR THE NEXT FOUR HOURS...
BACK-PACK TO SCH
LINCOLN! COME ON! WE'RE GOING SHOE SHOPPING NEXT!
THEY'VE GOT CLOGS IN YOUR SIZE!
I'M NOT WEARING CLOGS!
I GOTTA GET OUT OF HERE!

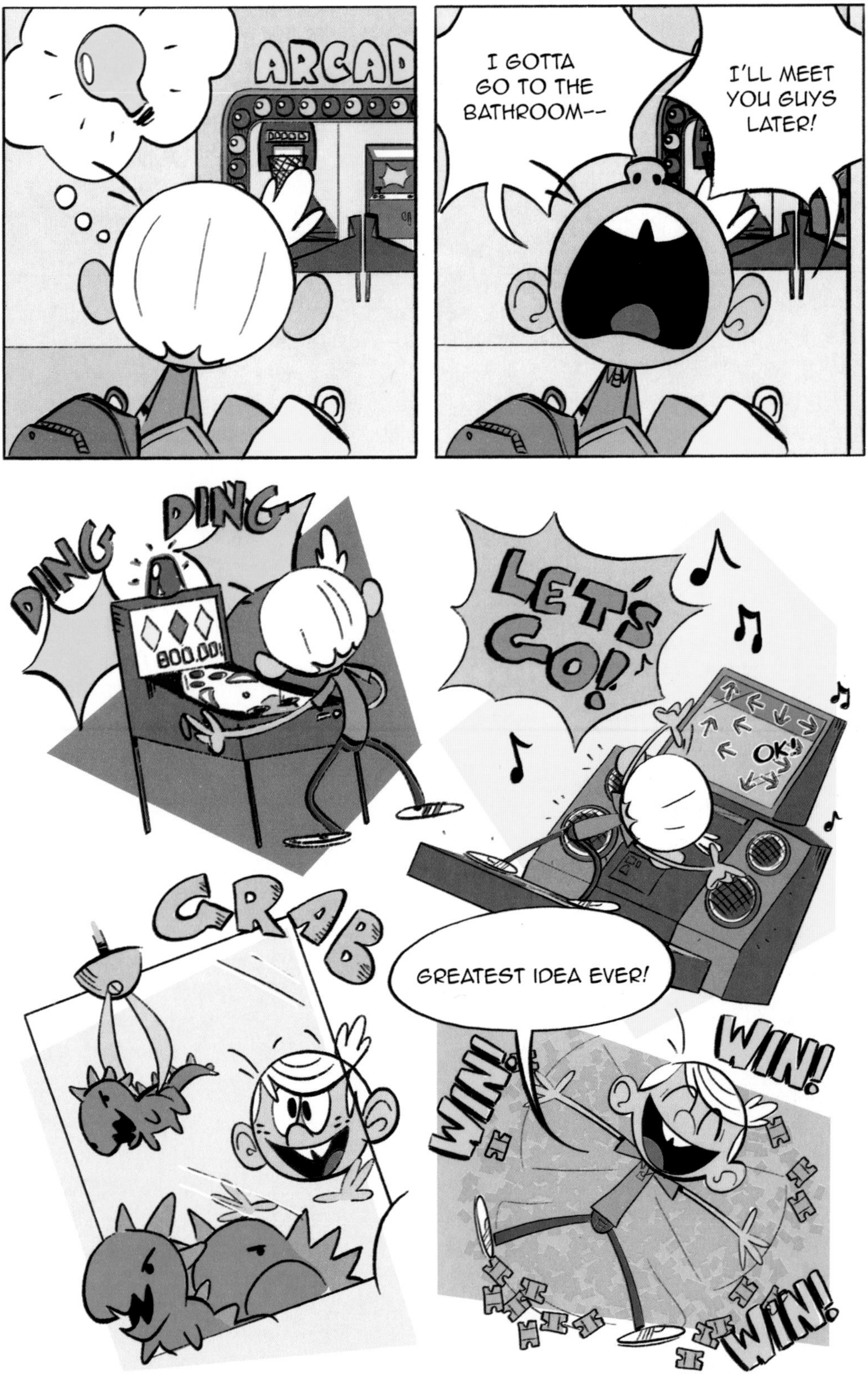
ARCAD
I GOTTA GO TO THE BATHROOM--
I'LL MEET YOU GUYS LATER!
DING DING
800.00!
LET'S GO!
OK!
GRAB
GREATEST IDEA EVER!
WIN!
WIN!
WIN!

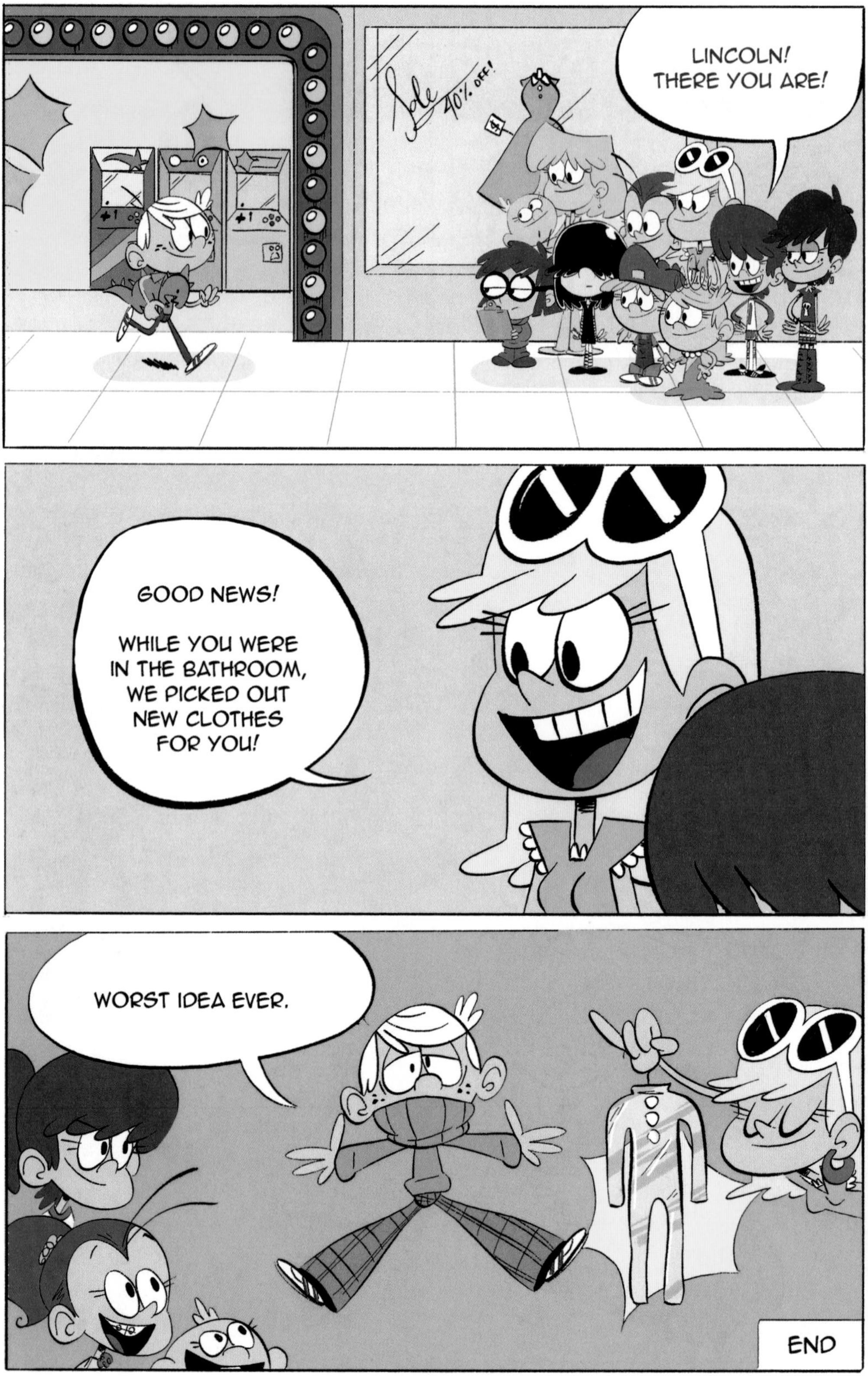

LINCOLN! THERE YOU ARE!
Sale 40% OFF!
GOOD NEWS!
WHILE YOU WERE IN THE BATHROOM, WE PICKED OUT NEW CLOTHES FOR YOU!
WORST IDEA EVER.
END

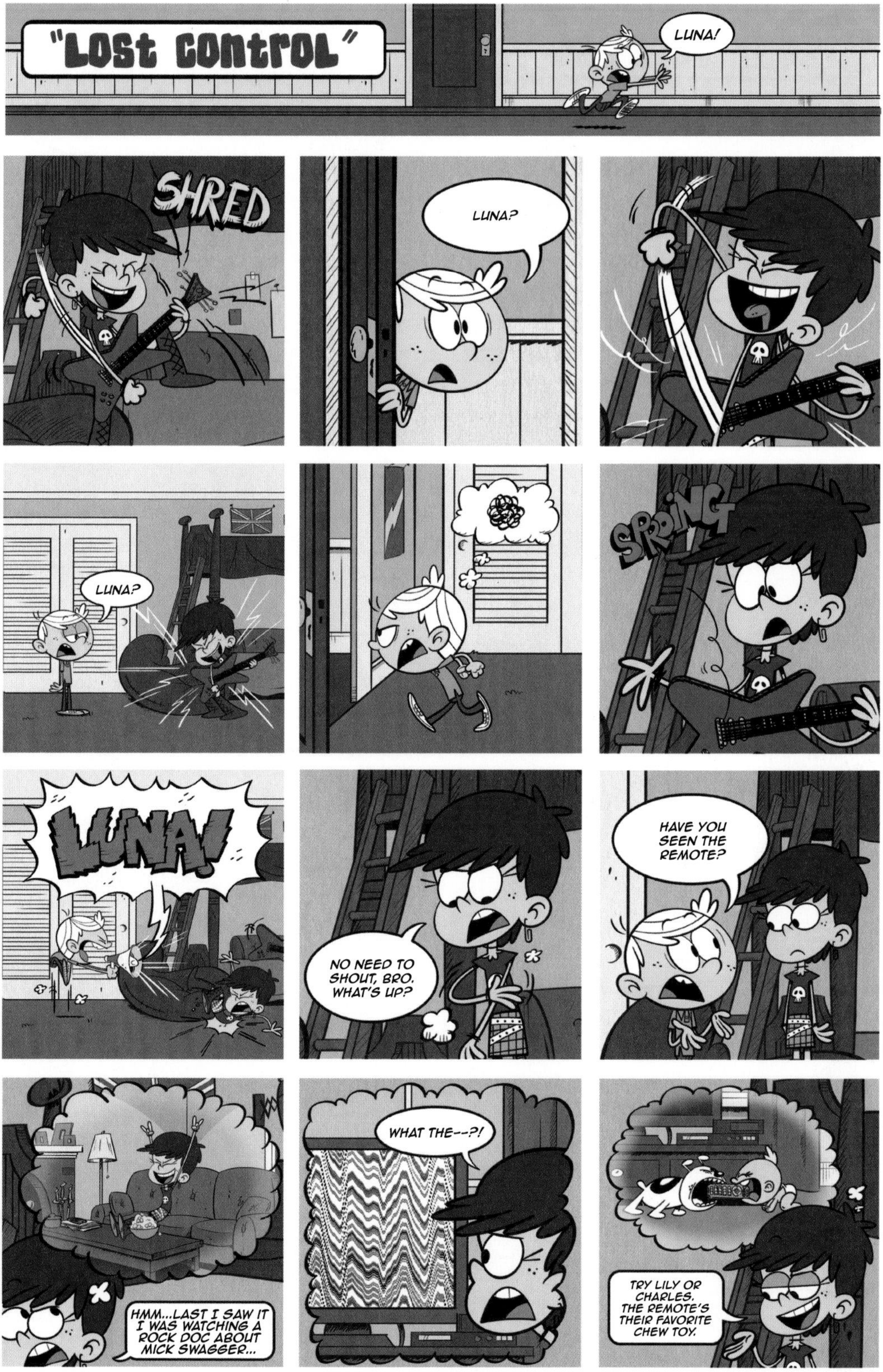
"LOST CONTROL"
LUNA!
SHRED
LUNA?
LUNA?
SPROING
LUNA!
NO NEED TO SHOUT, BRO. WHAT'S UP?
HAVE YOU SEEN THE REMOTE?
HMM...LAST I SAW IT I WAS WATCHING A ROCK DOC ABOUT MICK SWAGGER...
WHAT THE--?!
TRY LILY OR CHARLES. THE REMOTE'S THEIR FAVORITE CHEW TOY.

TO TALK TO LILY, GO TO PAGE 30. TO TALK TO CHARLES, GO TO PAGE 75.

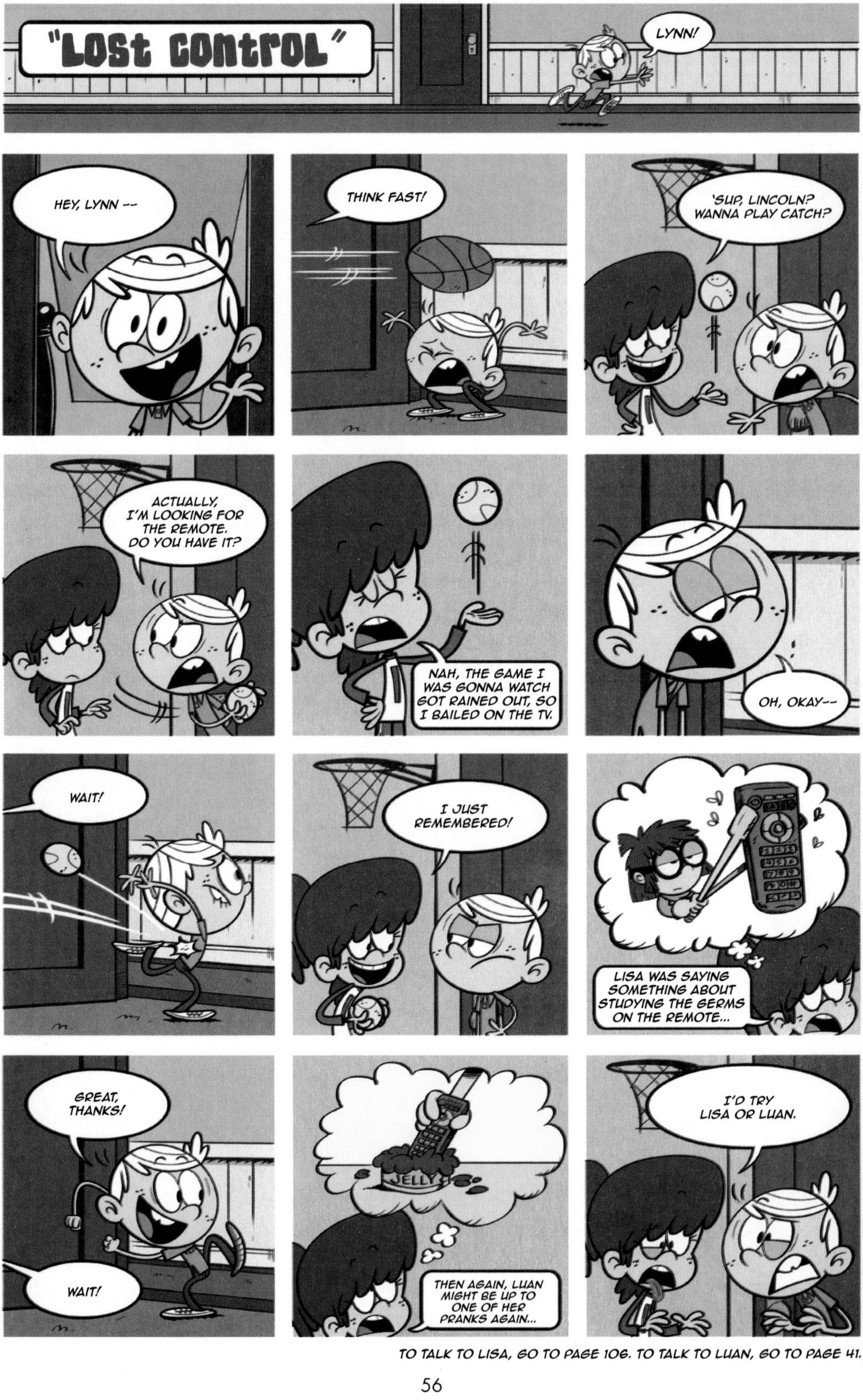
"LOST CONTROL"
LYNN!
HEY, LYNN --
THINK FAST!
'SUP, LINCOLN? WANNA PLAY CATCH?
ACTUALLY, I'M LOOKING FOR THE REMOTE. DO YOU HAVE IT?
NAH, THE GAME I WAS GONNA WATCH GOT RAINED OUT, SO I BAILED ON THE TV.
OH, OKAY--
WAIT!
I JUST REMEMBERED!
LISA WAS SAYING SOMETHING ABOUT STUDYING THE GERMS ON THE REMOTE...
GREAT, THANKS!
WAIT!
JELLY
THEN AGAIN, LUAN MIGHT BE UP TO ONE OF HER PRANKS AGAIN...
I'D TRY LISA OR LUAN.

TO TALK TO LISA, GO TO PAGE 106. TO TALK TO LUAN, GO TO PAGE 41.

"POPSICLE PROBLEMS"

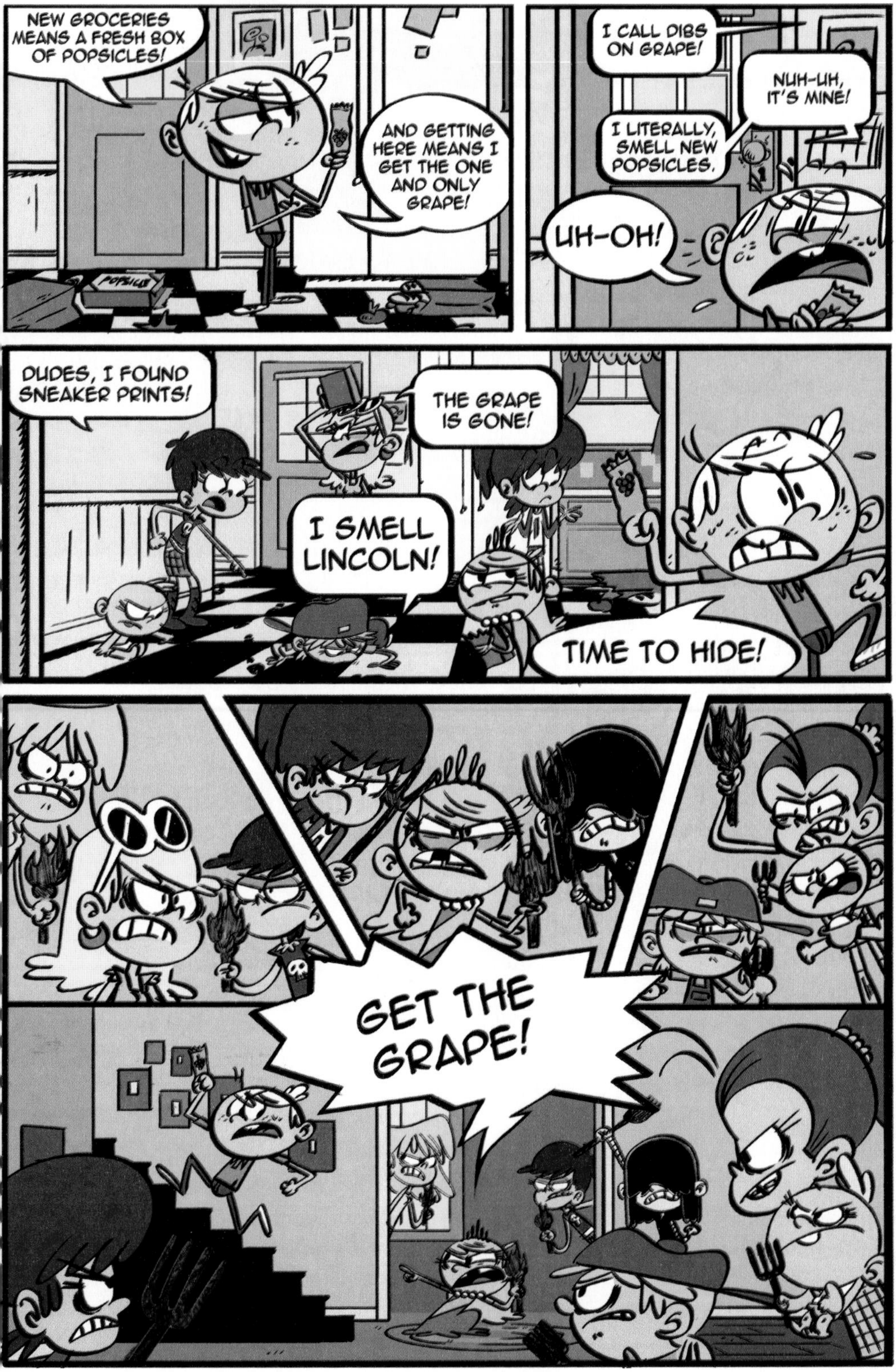

NEW GROCERIES MEANS A FRESH BOX OF POPSICLES!
AND GETTING HERE MEANS I GET THE ONE AND ONLY GRAPE!
POPSICLE
I CALL DIBS ON GRAPE!
NUH-UH, IT'S MINE!
I LITERALLY, SMELL NEW POPSICLES.
UH-OH!
DUDES, I FOUND SNEAKER PRINTS!
THE GRAPE IS GONE!
I SMELL LINCOLN!
TIME TO HIDE!
GET THE GRAPE!

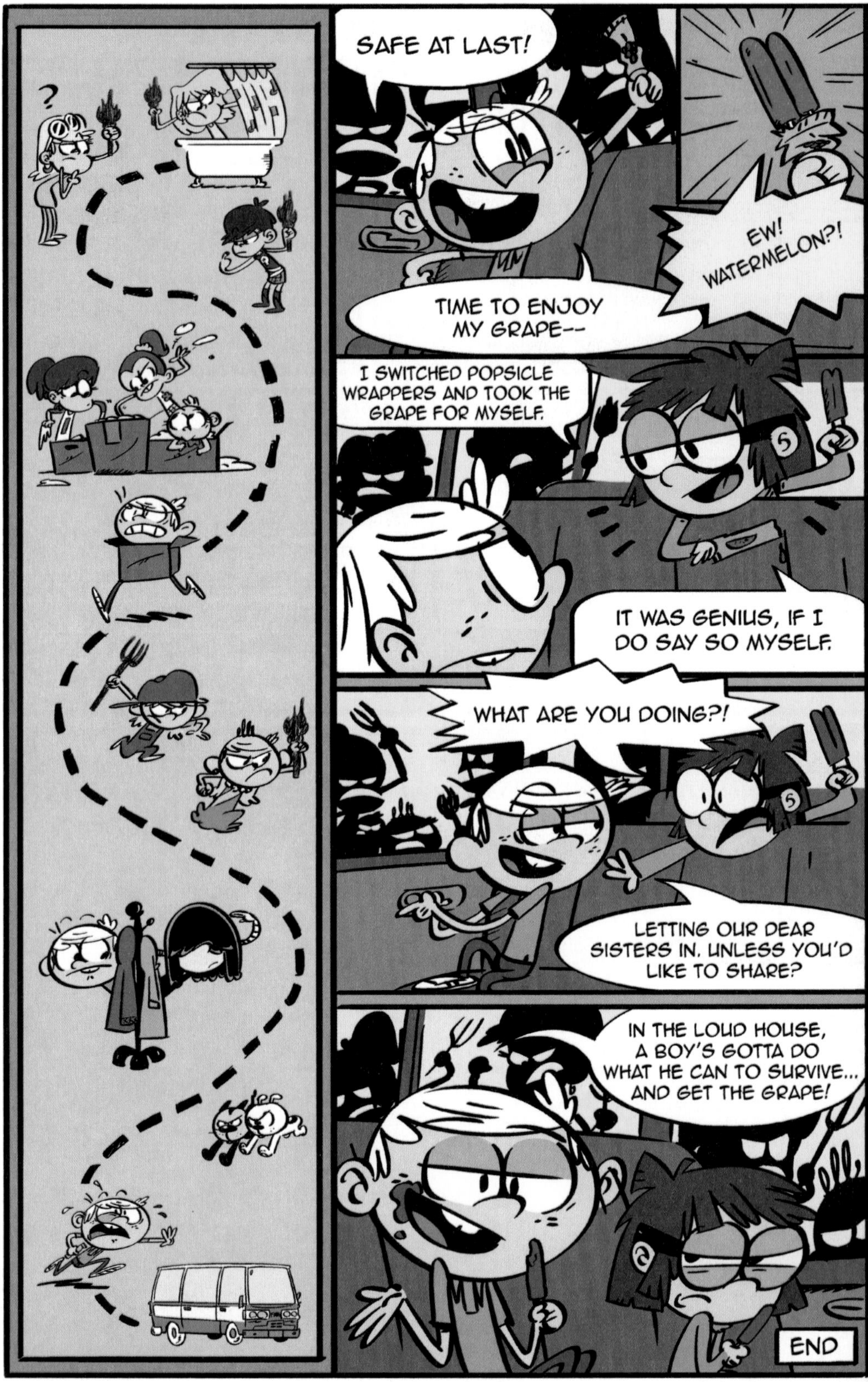
?
SAFE AT LAST!
TIME TO ENJOY MY GRAPE--
EW! WATERMELON?!
I SWITCHED POPSICLE WRAPPERS AND TOOK THE GRAPE FOR MYSELF.
IT WAS GENIUS, IF I DO SAY SO MYSELF.
WHAT ARE YOU DOING?!
LETTING OUR DEAR SISTERS IN. UNLESS YOU'D LIKE TO SHARE?
IN THE LOUD HOUSE, A BOY'S GOTTA DO WHAT HE CAN TO SURVIVE... AND GET THE GRAPE!
END

"HOPPILY EVER AFTER"

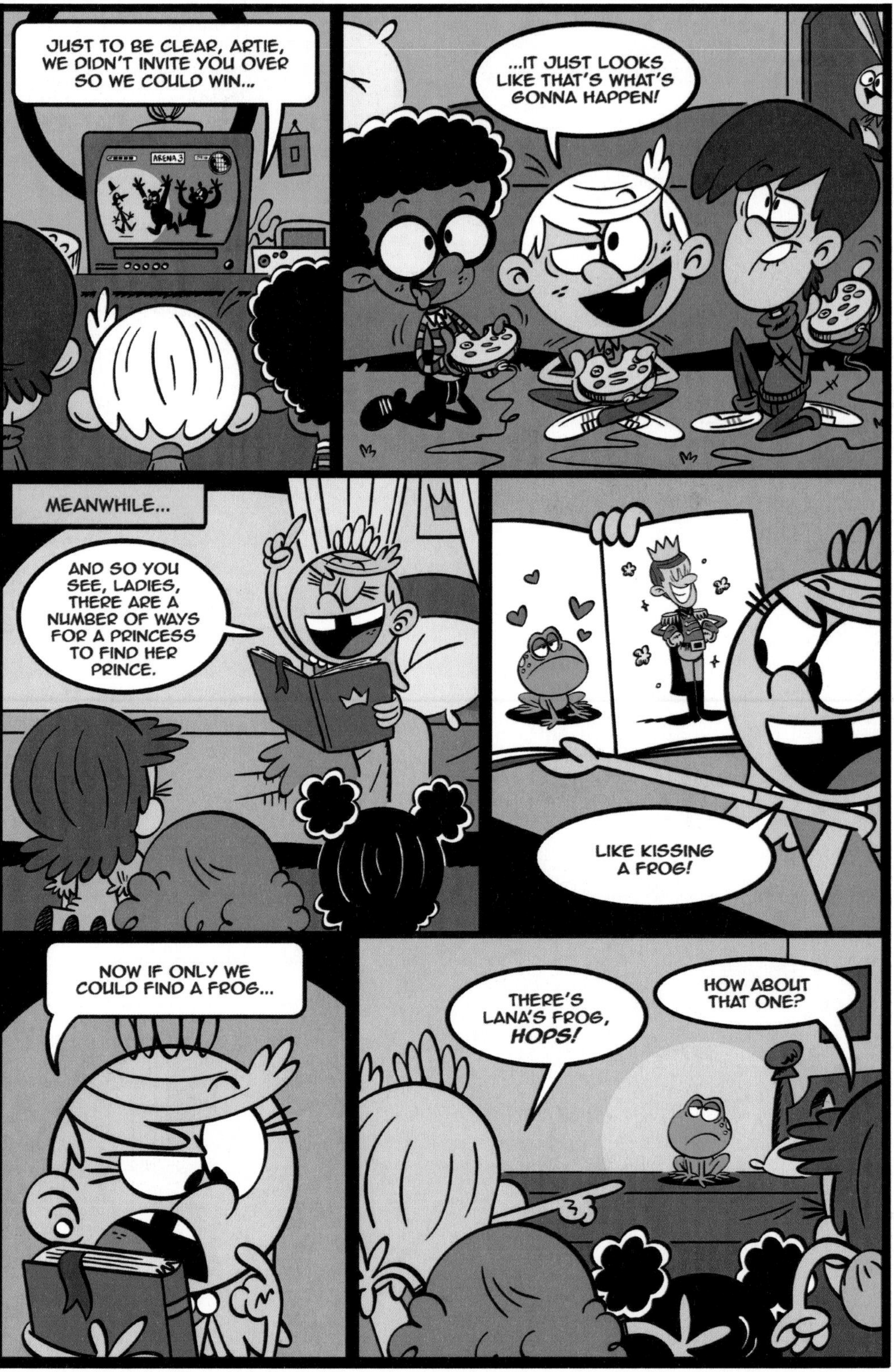

JUST TO BE CLEAR, ARTIE, WE DIDN'T INVITE YOU OVER SO WE COULD WIN...
ARENA 3
...IT JUST LOOKS LIKE THAT'S WHAT'S GONNA HAPPEN!
MEANWHILE...
AND SO YOU SEE, LADIES, THERE ARE A NUMBER OF WAYS FOR A PRINCESS TO FIND HER PRINCE.
LIKE KISSING A FROG!
NOW IF ONLY WE COULD FIND A FROG...
THERE'S LANA'S FROG, *HOPS!*
HOW ABOUT THAT ONE?

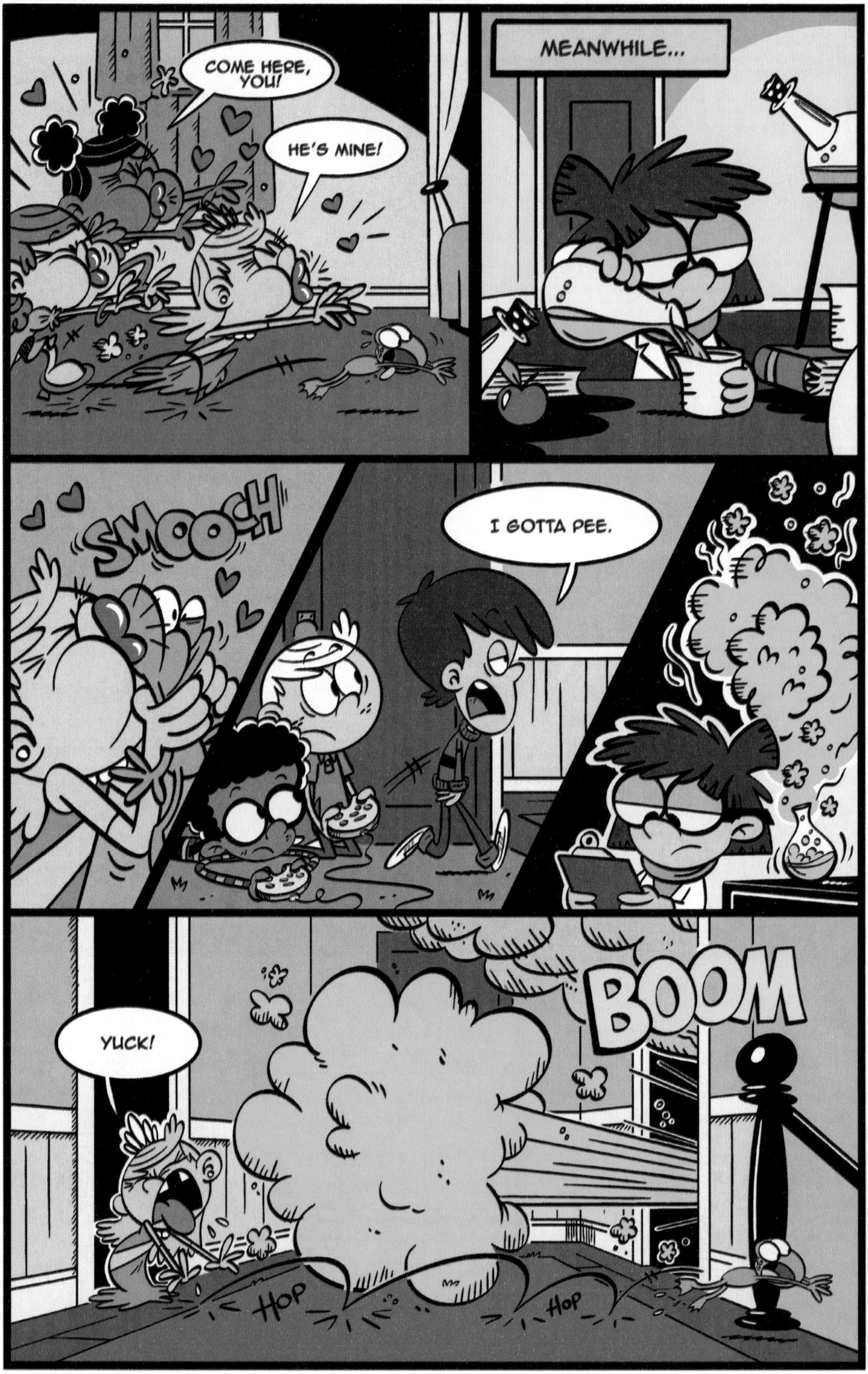

COME HERE, YOU!
HE'S MINE!
MEANWHILE...
SMOOCH
I GOTTA PEE.
BOOM
YUCK!
HOP
HOP

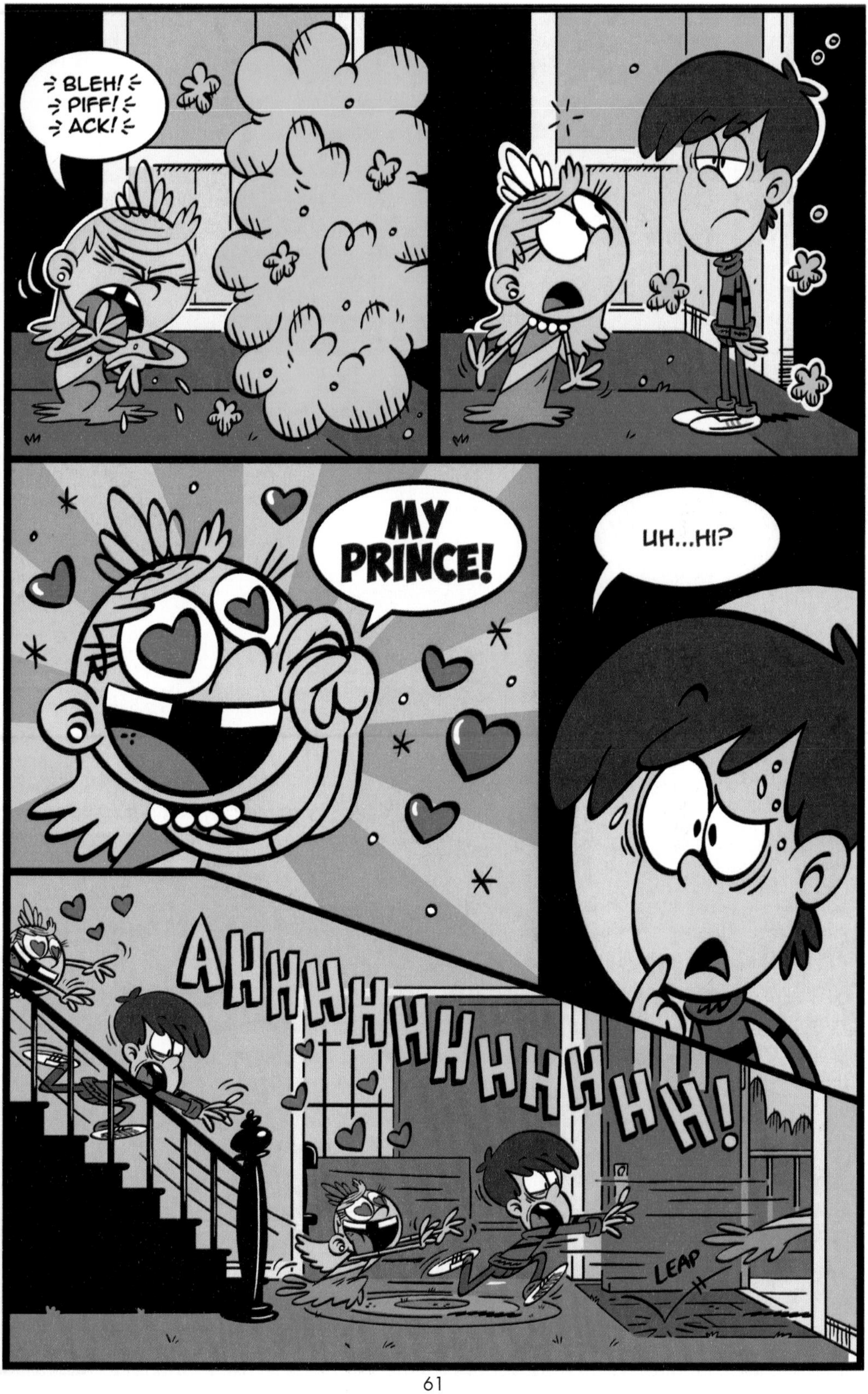
BLEH! PIFF! ACK!
MY PRINCE!
UH...HI?
AHHHHHHHHHHHHH!
LEAP

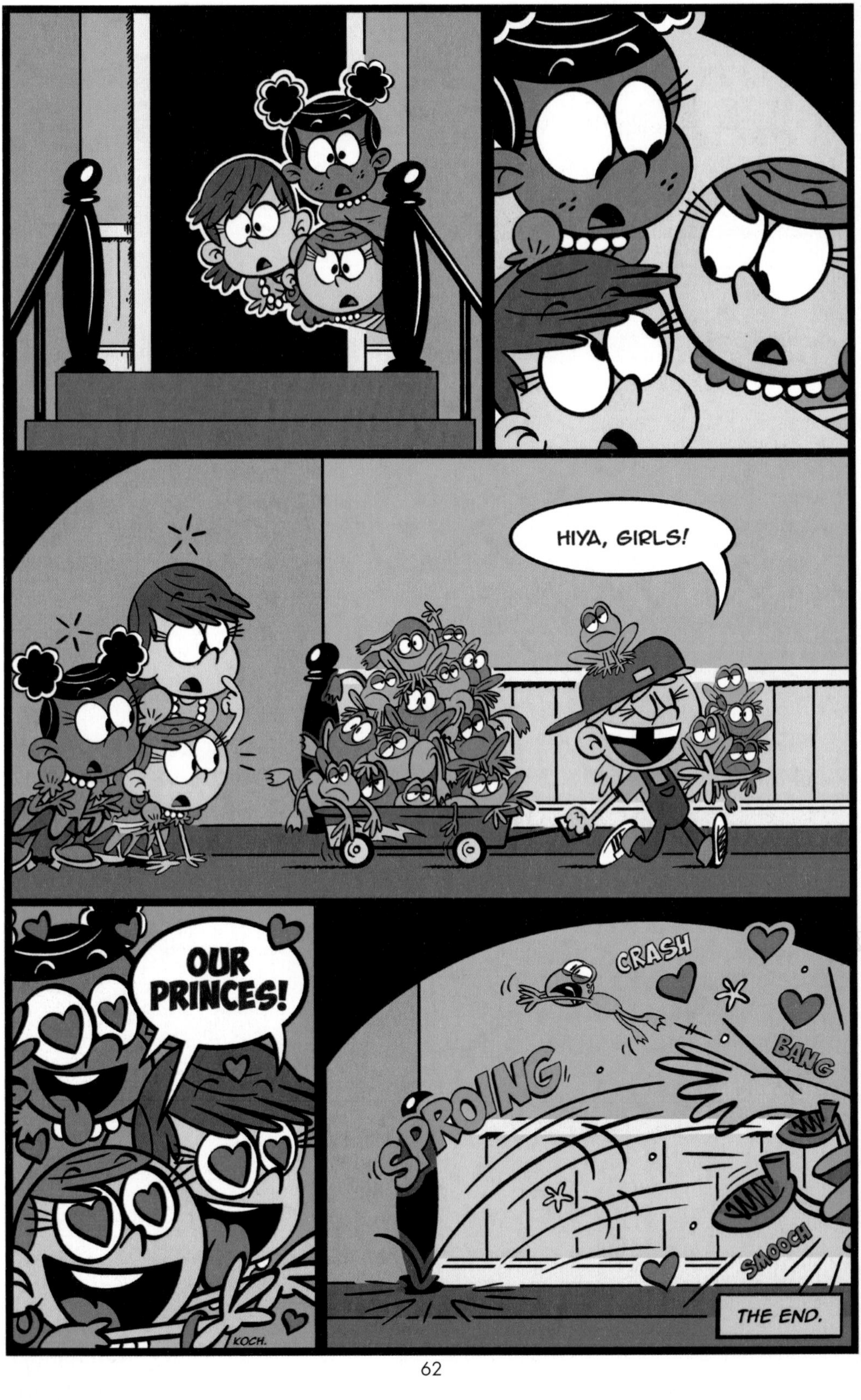
HIYA, GIRLS!
OUR PRINCES!
KOCH.
SPROING
CRASH
BANG
SMOOCH
THE END.

"DATE NIGHT"

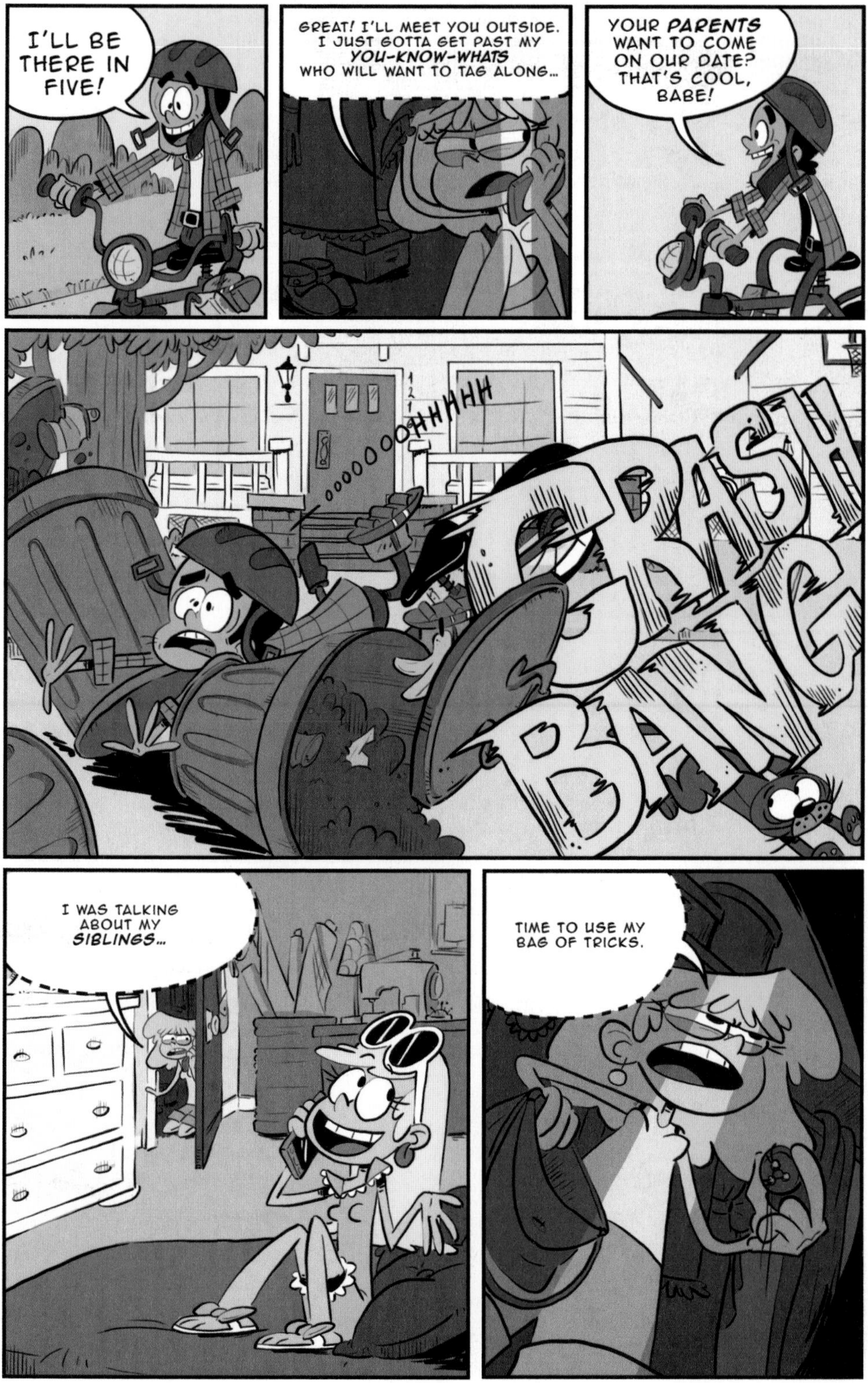
I'LL BE THERE IN FIVE!
GREAT! I'LL MEET YOU OUTSIDE. I JUST GOTTA GET PAST MY YOU-KNOW-WHATS WHO WILL WANT TO TAG ALONG...
YOUR PARENTS WANT TO COME ON OUR DATE? THAT'S COOL, BABE!
OOOOOOOHHHHH
CRASH
BANG
I WAS TALKING ABOUT MY SIBLINGS...
TIME TO USE MY BAG OF TRICKS.

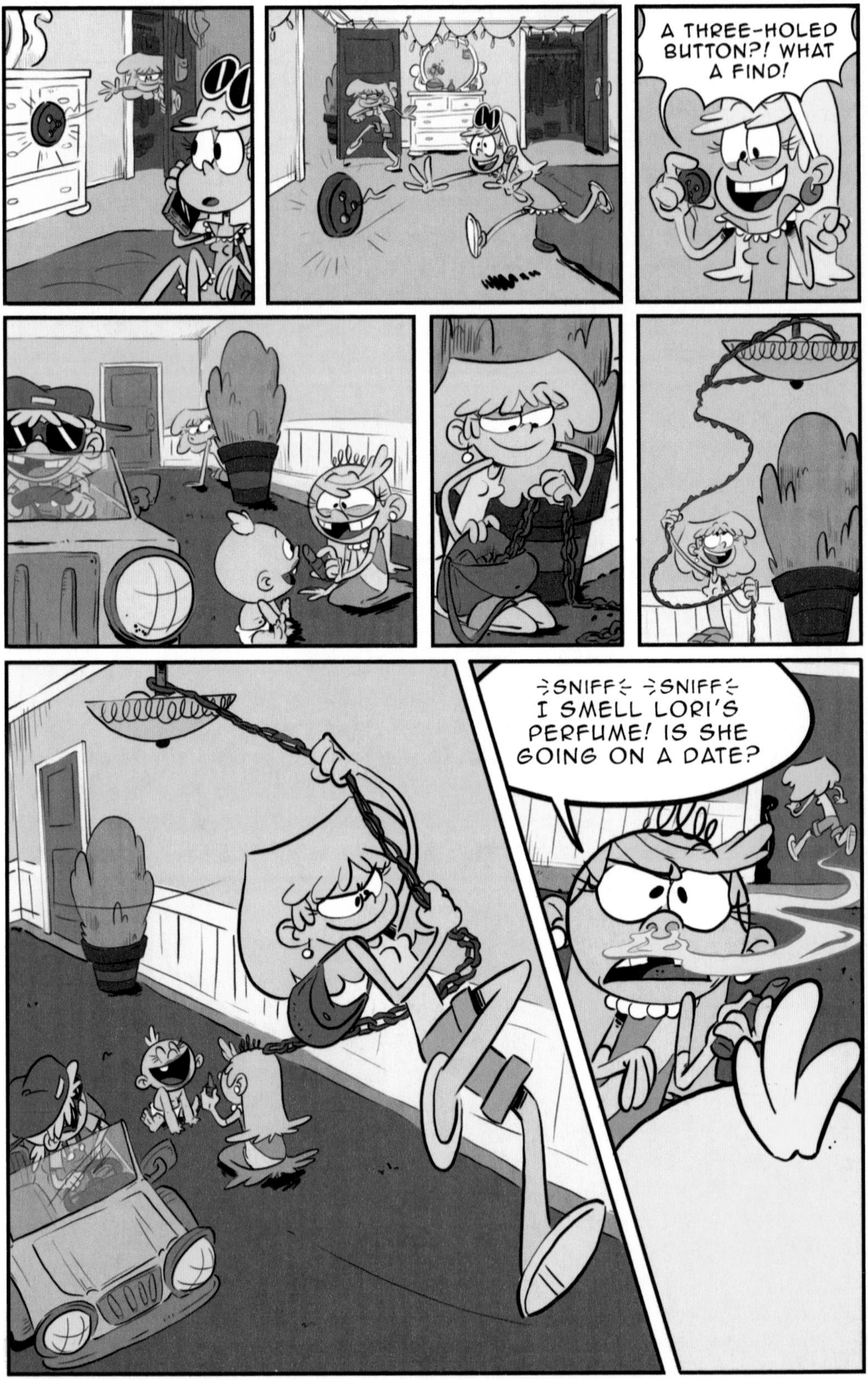
A THREE-HOLED BUTTON?! WHAT A FIND!
SNIFF SNIFF I SMELL LORI'S PERFUME! IS SHE GOING ON A DATE?

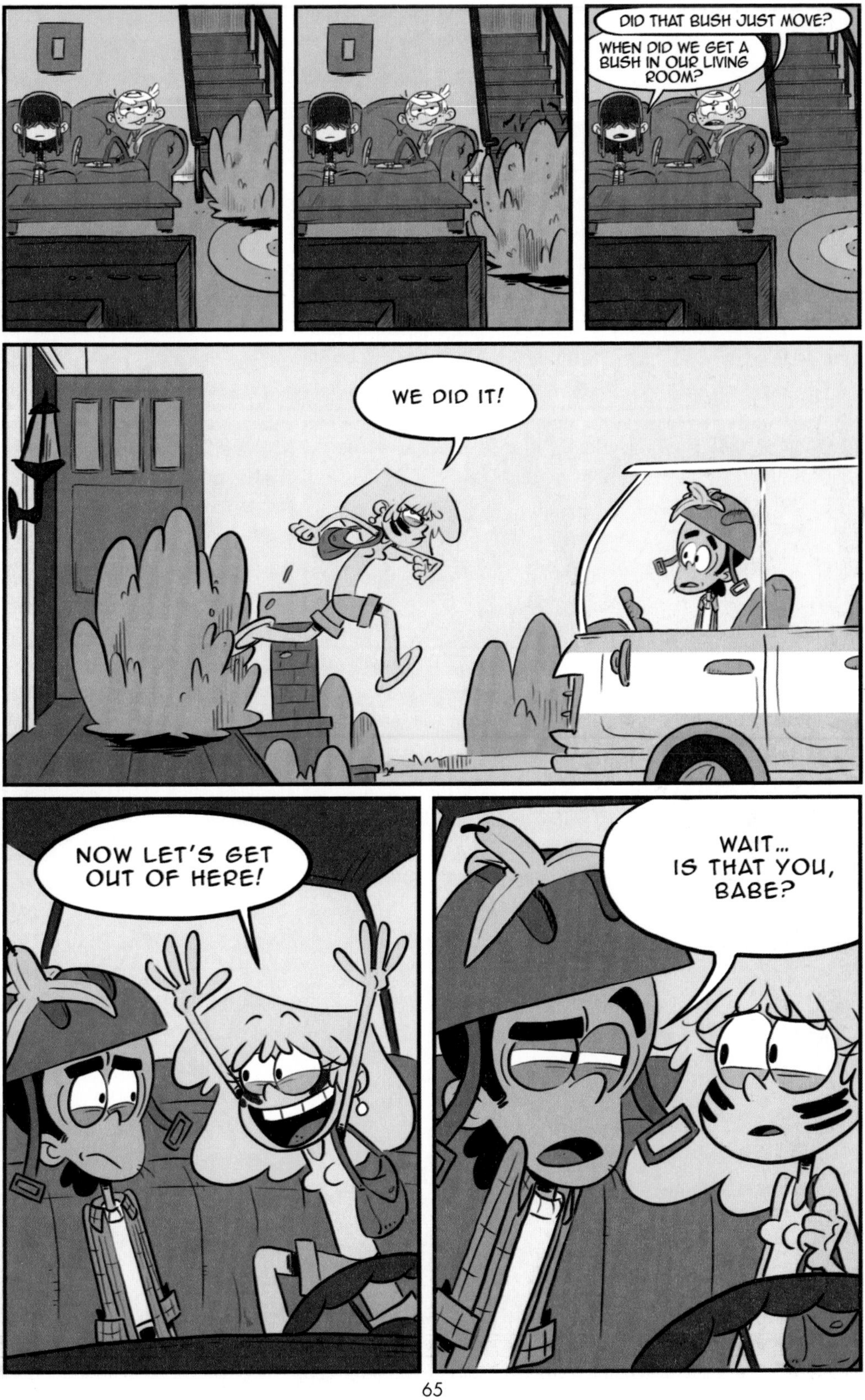
DID THAT BUSH JUST MOVE?
WHEN DID WE GET A BUSH IN OUR LIVING ROOM?
WE DID IT!
NOW LET'S GET OUT OF HERE!
WAIT... IS THAT YOU, BABE?

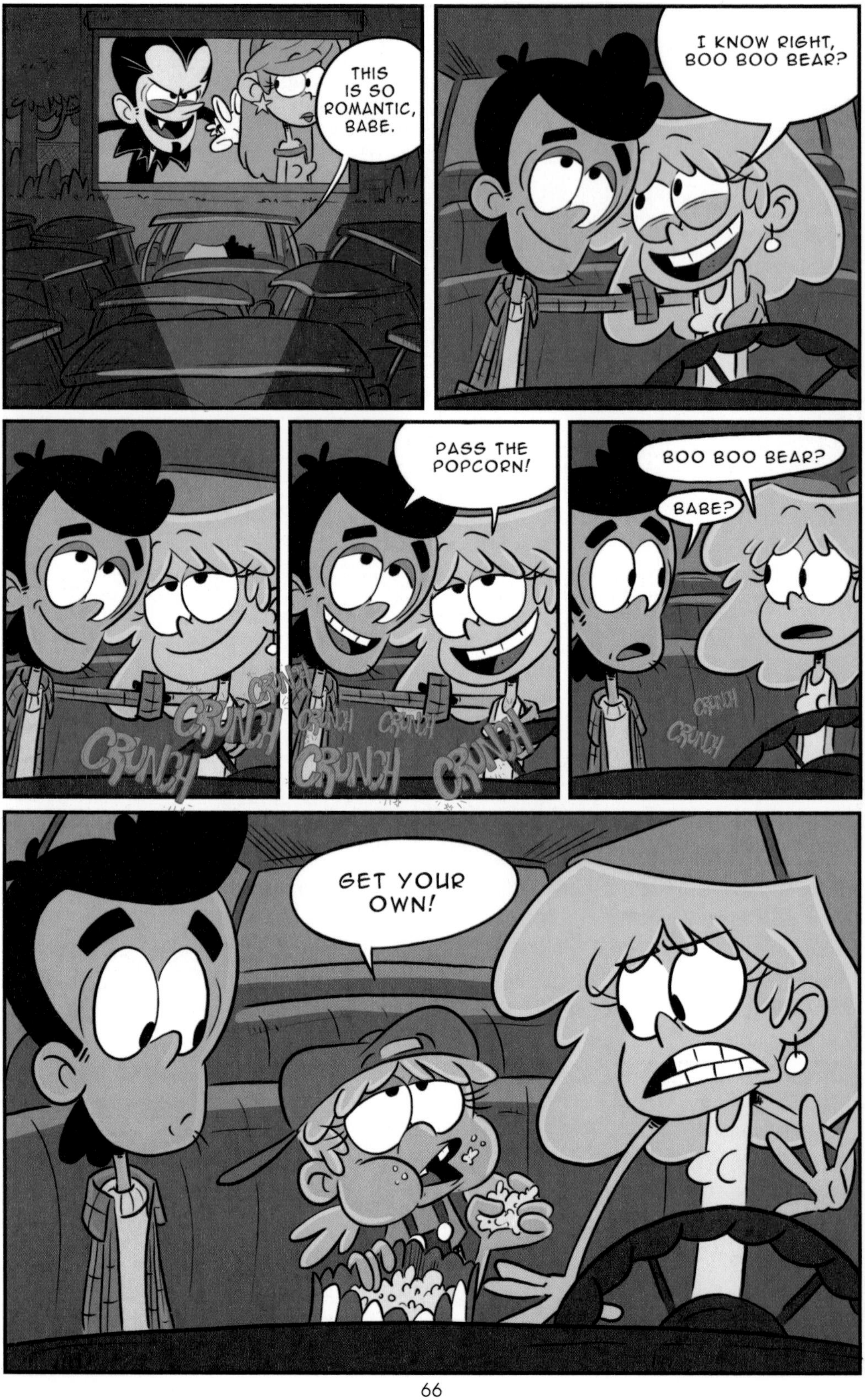
THIS IS SO ROMANTIC, BABE.
I KNOW RIGHT, BOO BOO BEAR?
CRUNCH
CRUNCH
CRUNCH
PASS THE POPCORN!
CRUNCH
CRUNCH
CRUNCH
CRUNCH
BOO BOO BEAR?
BABE?
CRUNCH
CRUNCH
GET YOUR OWN!

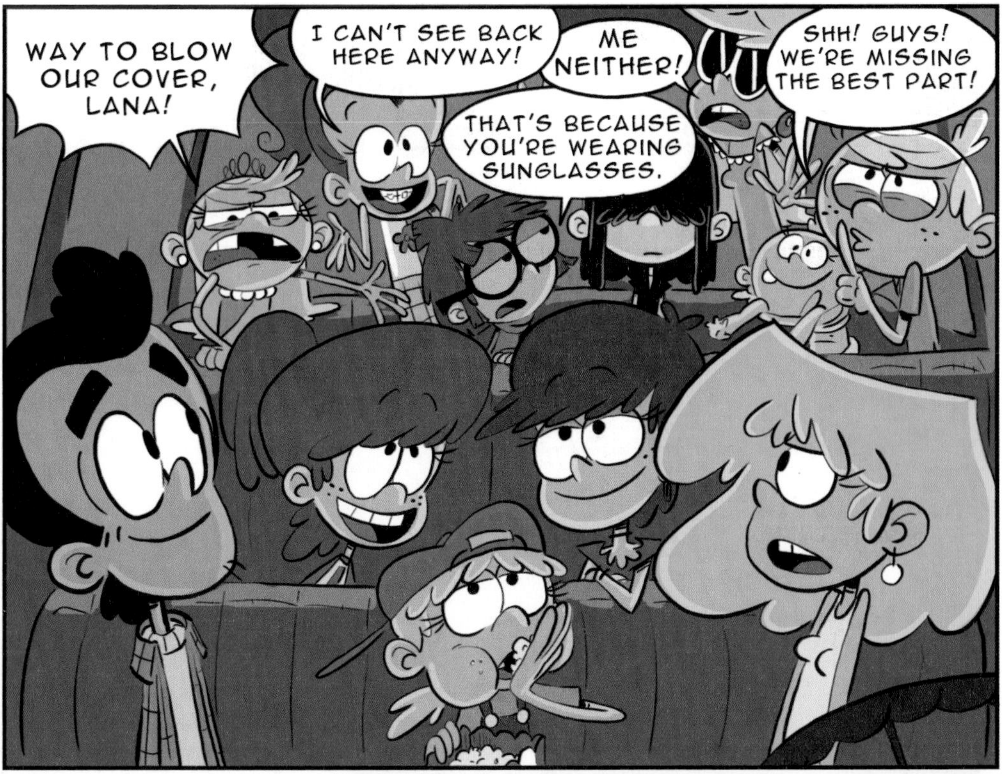
WAY TO BLOW OUR COVER, LANA!
I CAN'T SEE BACK HERE ANYWAY!
ME NEITHER!
THAT'S BECAUSE YOU'RE WEARING SUNGLASSES.
SHH! GUYS! WE'RE MISSING THE BEST PART!

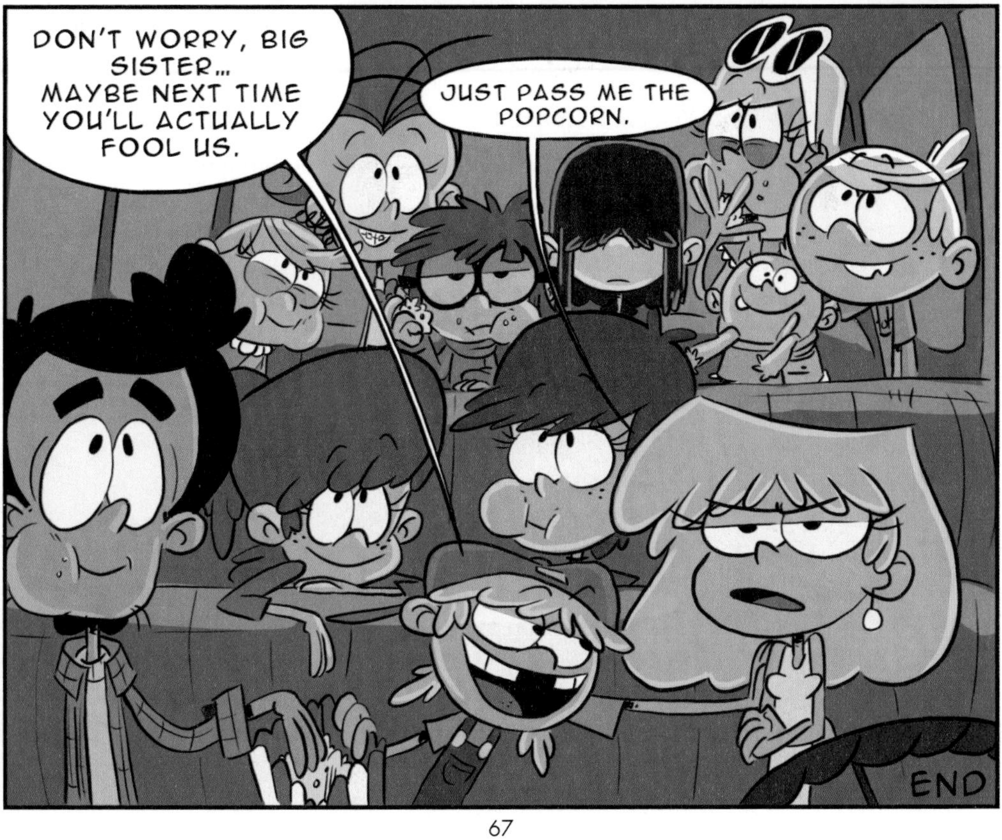
DON'T WORRY, BIG SISTER... MAYBE NEXT TIME YOU'LL ACTUALLY FOOL US.
JUST PASS ME THE POPCORN.
END

"THE SNEEZE!"

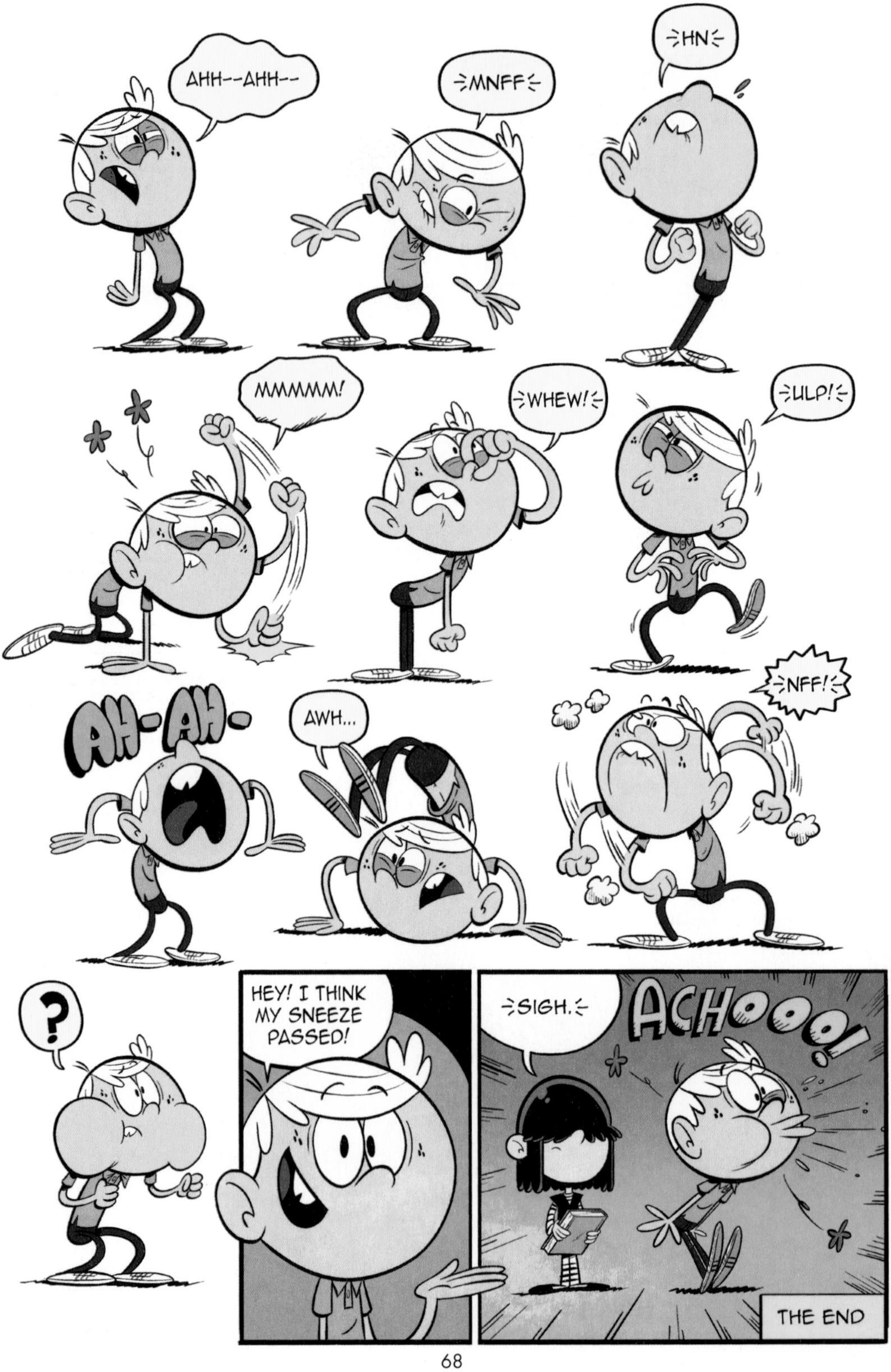
AHH--AHH--
MNFF
HN
MMMMM!
WHEW!
ULP!
AH-AH-
AWH...
NFF!
?
HEY! I THINK MY SNEEZE PASSED!
SIGH.
ACHOOO!
THE END

"CLYDE'S CAT-ASTROPHE"

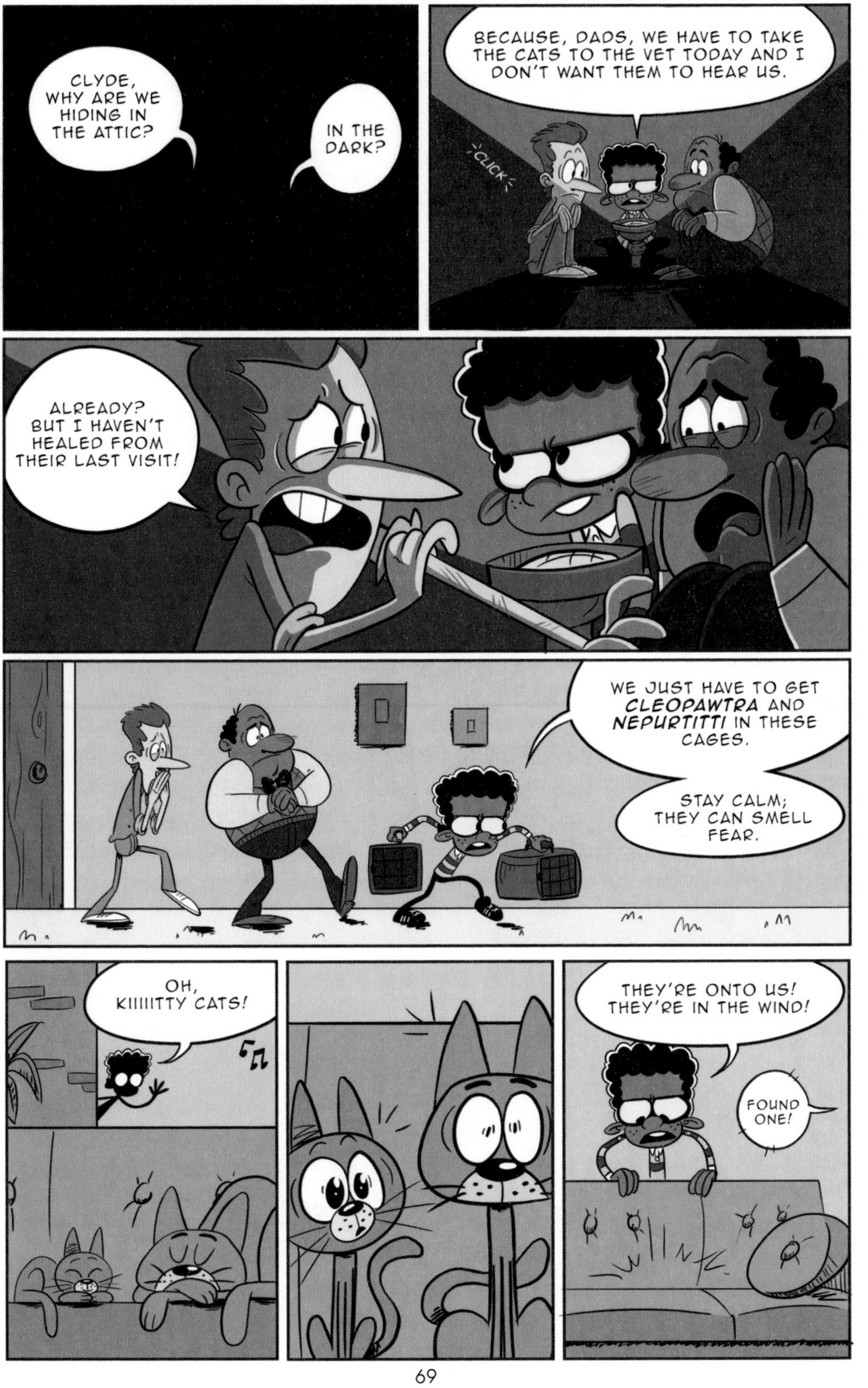
CLYDE, WHY ARE WE HIDING IN THE ATTIC?
IN THE DARK?
BECAUSE, DADS, WE HAVE TO TAKE THE CATS TO THE VET TODAY AND I DON'T WANT THEM TO HEAR US.
CLICK
ALREADY? BUT I HAVEN'T HEALED FROM THEIR LAST VISIT!
WE JUST HAVE TO GET *CLEOPAWTRA* AND *NEPURTITTI* IN THESE CAGES.
STAY CALM; THEY CAN SMELL FEAR.
OH, KIIIIITTY CATS!
THEY'RE ONTO US! THEY'RE IN THE WIND!
FOUND ONE!

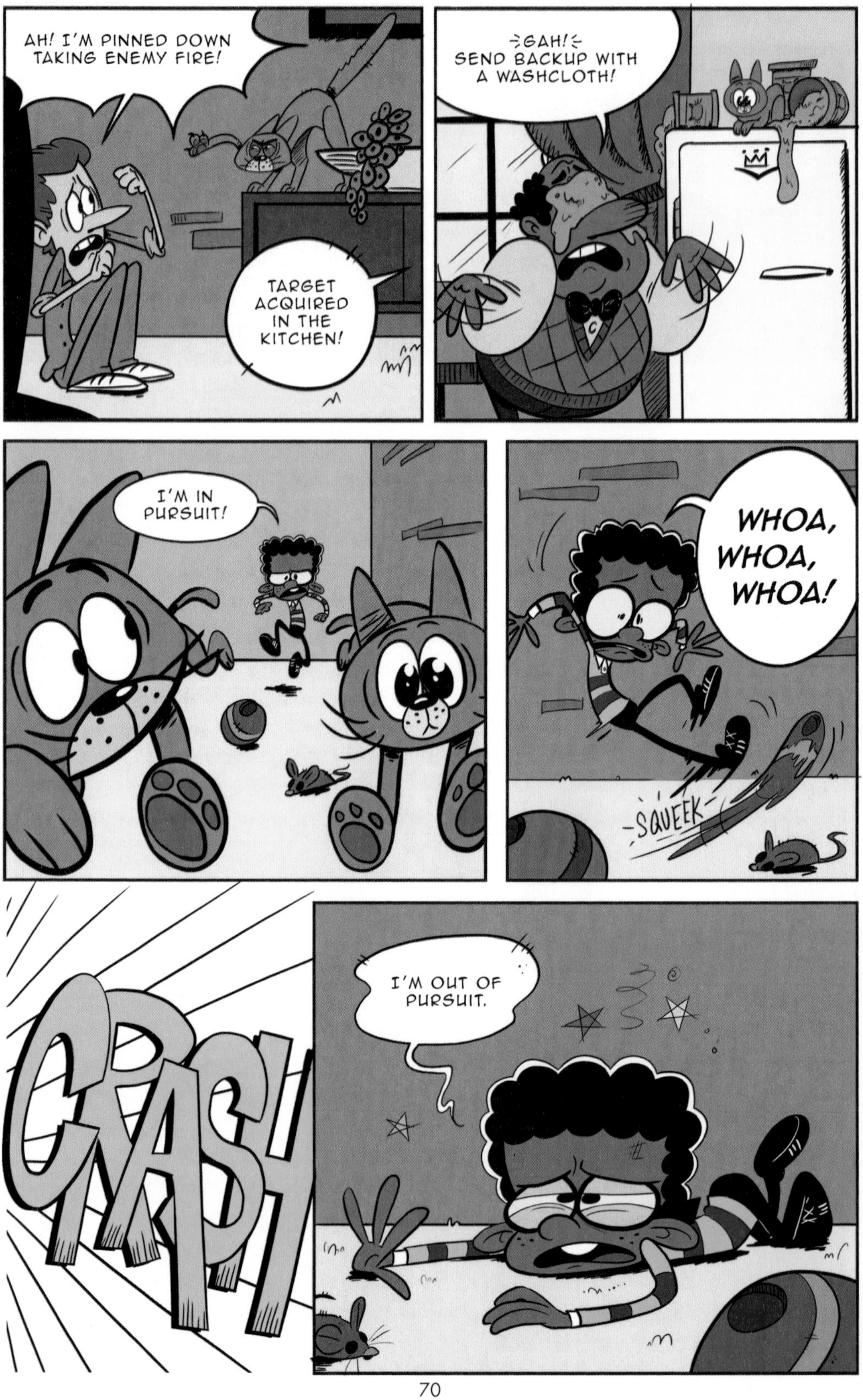
AH! I'M PINNED DOWN TAKING ENEMY FIRE!
TARGET ACQUIRED IN THE KITCHEN!
GAH! SEND BACKUP WITH A WASHCLOTH!
I'M IN PURSUIT!
WHOA, WHOA, WHOA!
SQUEEK
CRASH
I'M OUT OF PURSUIT.

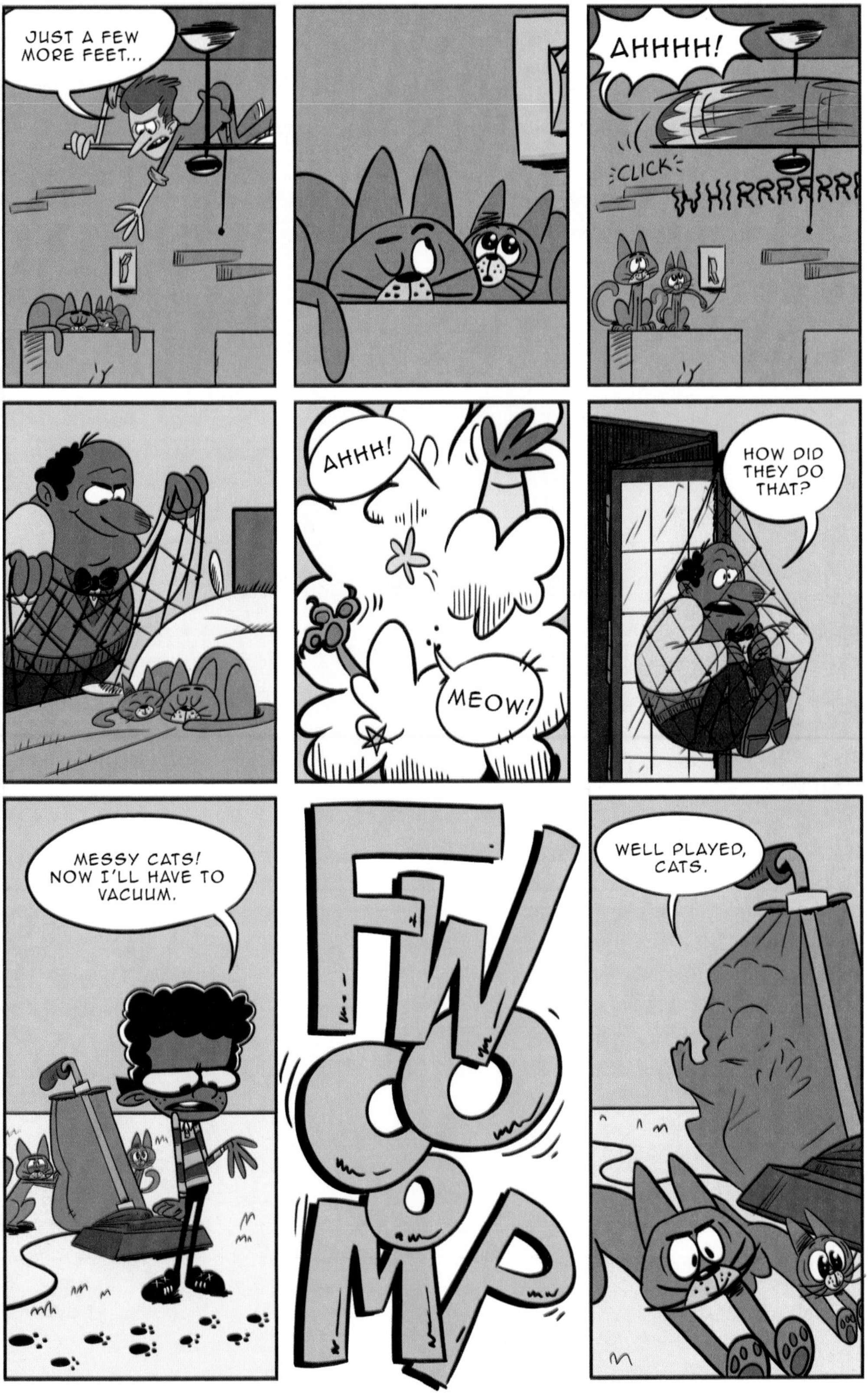
JUST A FEW MORE FEET...
AHHHH!
CLICK
WHIRRRRRRR
AHHH!
MEOW!
HOW DID THEY DO THAT?
MESSY CATS! NOW I'LL HAVE TO VACUUM.
FWOOMP
WELL PLAYED, CATS.

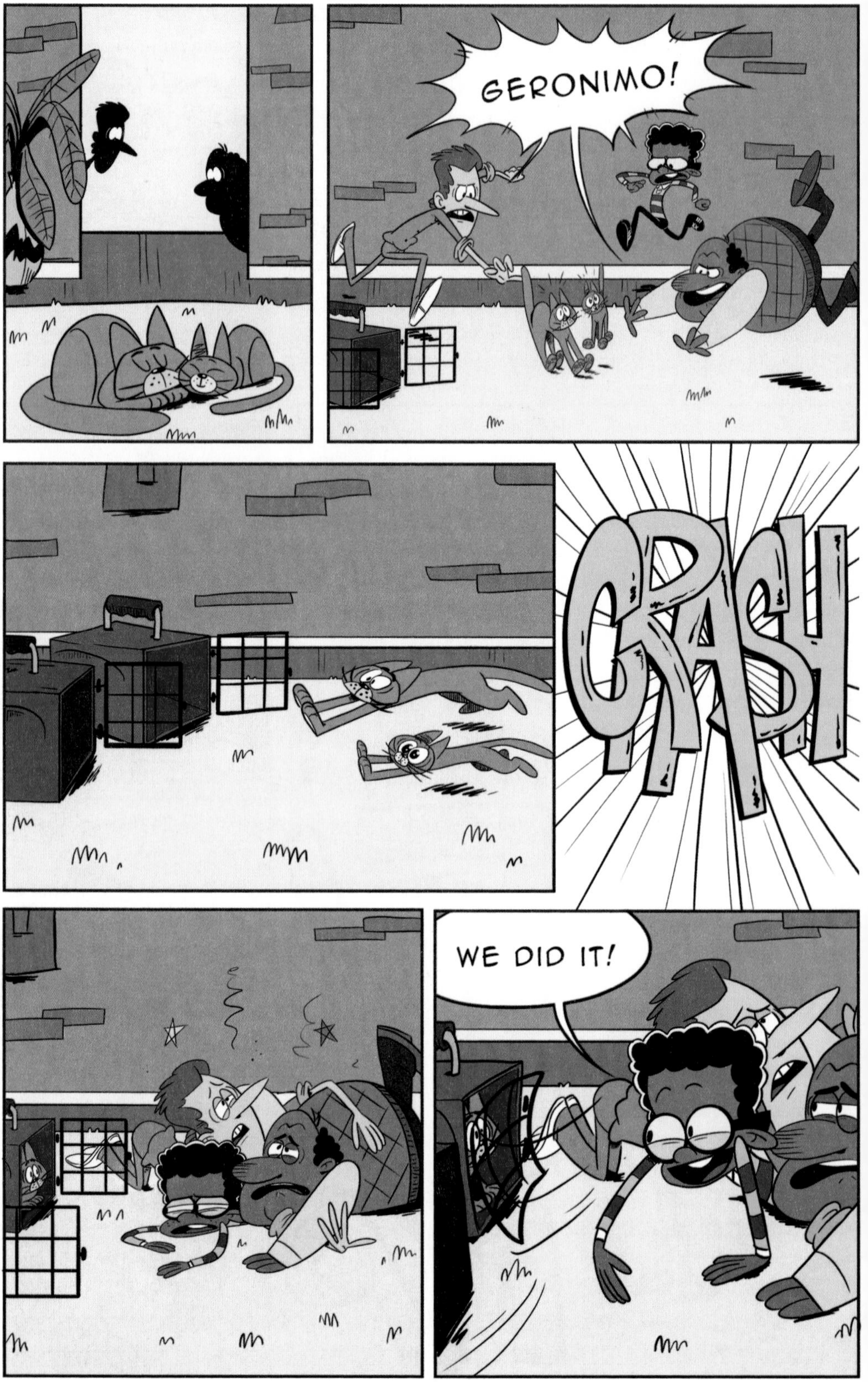
GERONIMO!
CRASH
WE DID IT!

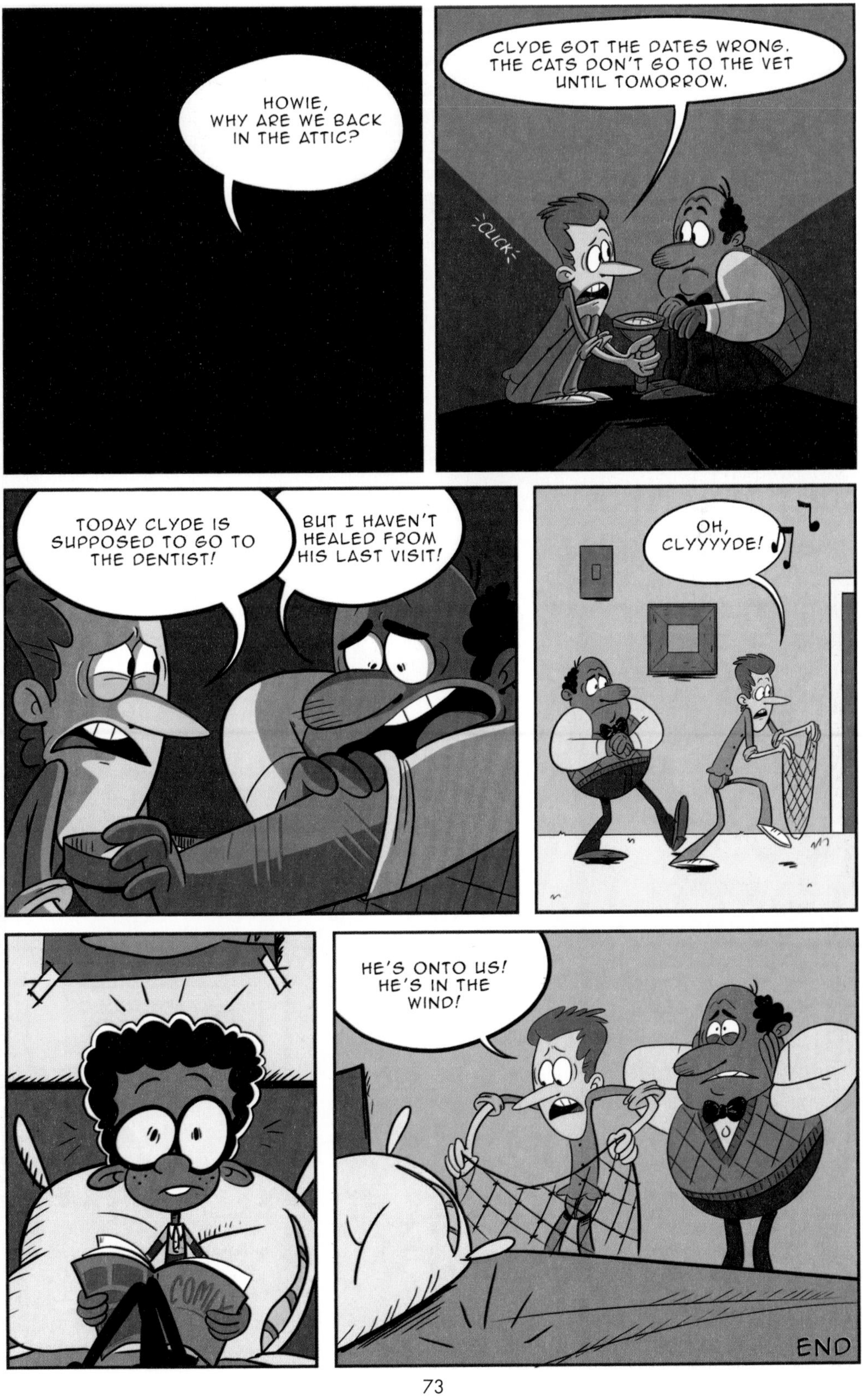
HOWIE,
WHY ARE WE BACK
IN THE ATTIC?
CLYDE GOT THE DATES WRONG.
THE CATS DON'T GO TO THE VET
UNTIL TOMORROW.
CLICK
TODAY CLYDE IS
SUPPOSED TO GO TO
THE DENTIST!
BUT I HAVEN'T
HEALED FROM
HIS LAST VISIT!
OH,
CLYYYYDE!
HE'S ONTO US!
HE'S IN THE
WIND!
END

"LAND ESCAPE"

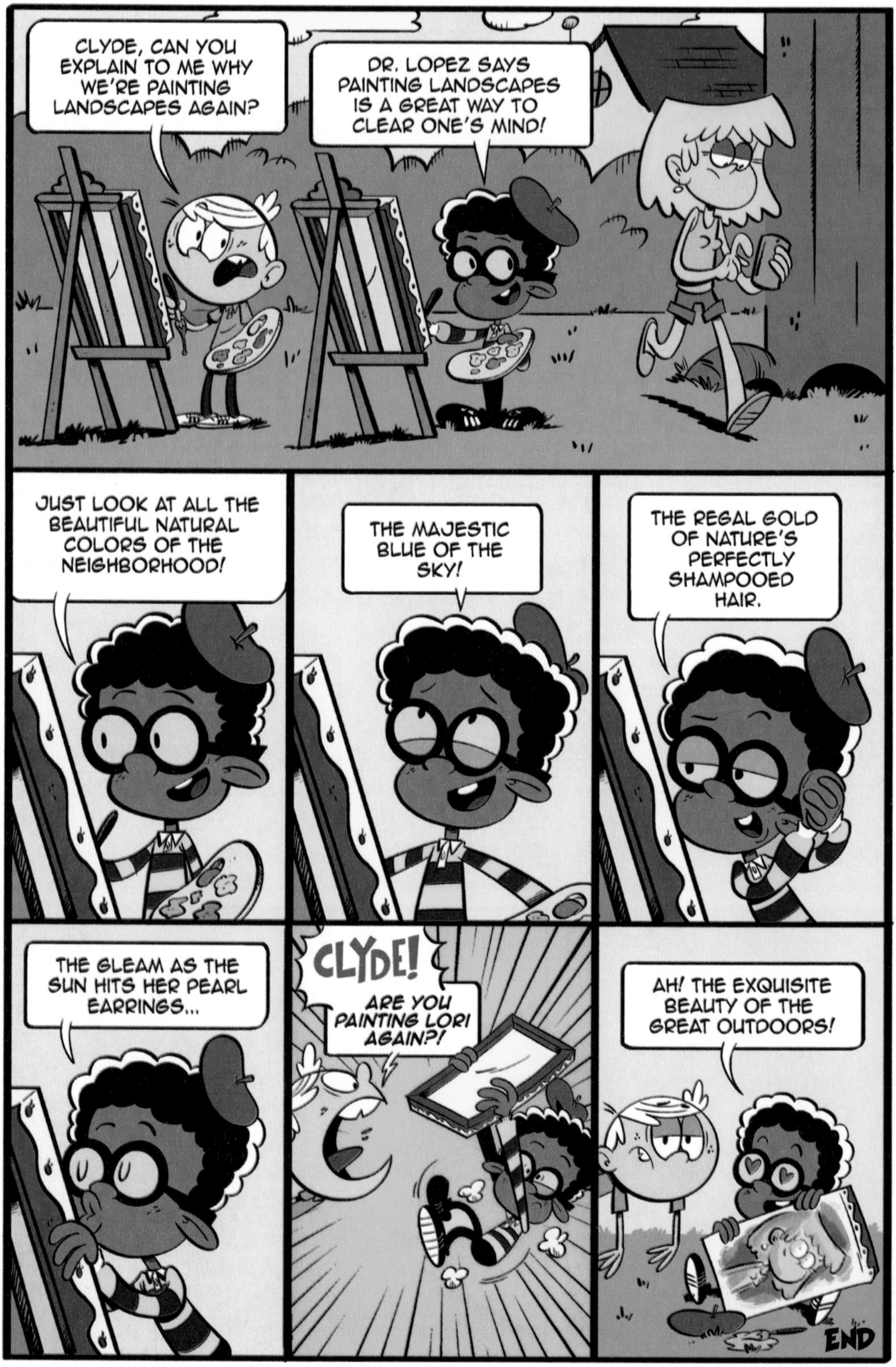

CLYDE, CAN YOU EXPLAIN TO ME WHY WE'RE PAINTING LANDSCAPES AGAIN?
DR. LOPEZ SAYS PAINTING LANDSCAPES IS A GREAT WAY TO CLEAR ONE'S MIND!
JUST LOOK AT ALL THE BEAUTIFUL NATURAL COLORS OF THE NEIGHBORHOOD!
THE MAJESTIC BLUE OF THE SKY!
THE REGAL GOLD OF NATURE'S PERFECTLY SHAMPOOED HAIR.
THE GLEAM AS THE SUN HITS HER PEARL EARRINGS...
CLYDE!
ARE YOU PAINTING LORI AGAIN?!
AH! THE EXQUISITE BEAUTY OF THE GREAT OUTDOORS!
END

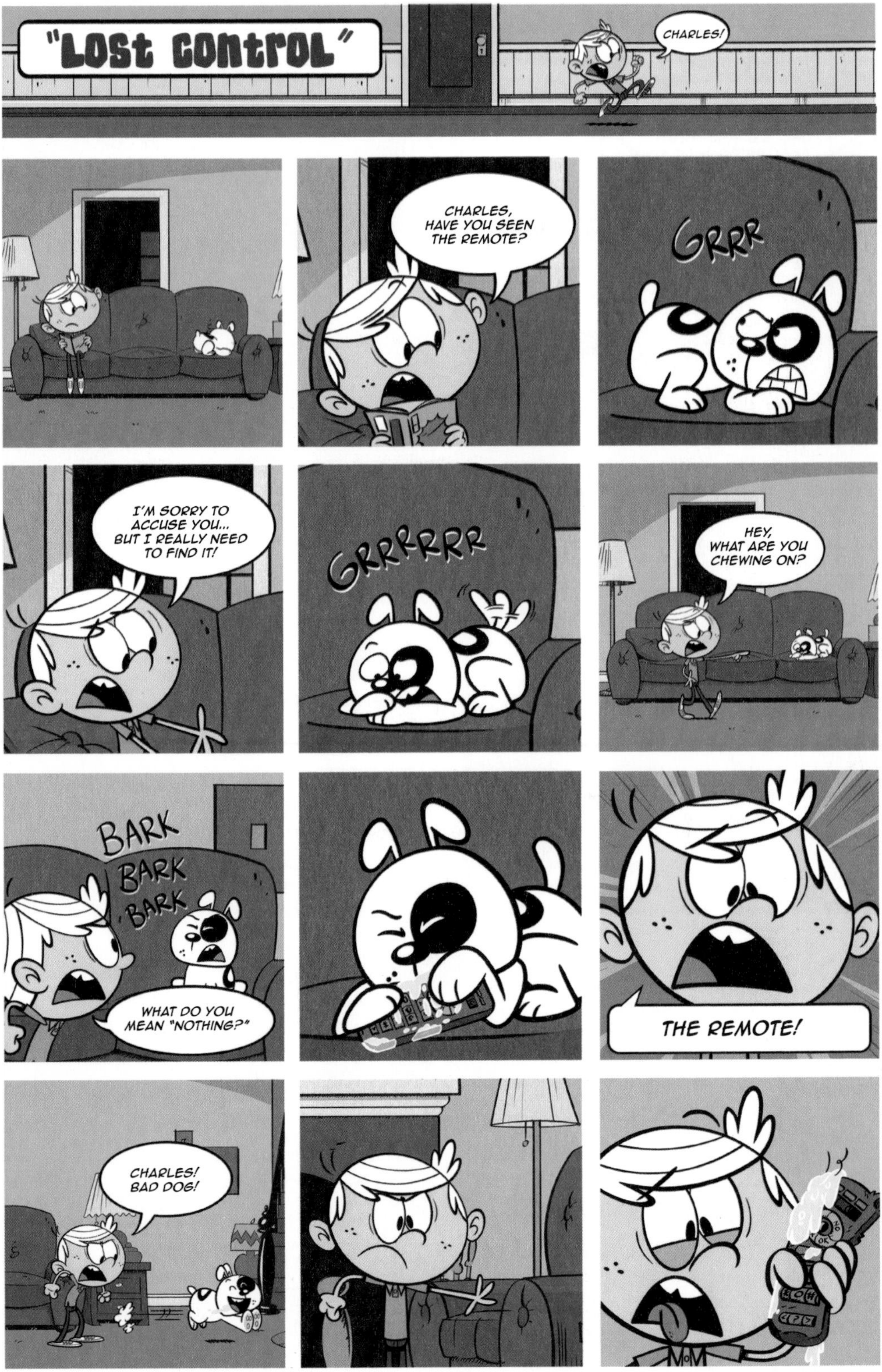
"LOST CONTROL"
CHARLES!
CHARLES, HAVE YOU SEEN THE REMOTE?
GRRR
I'M SORRY TO ACCUSE YOU... BUT I REALLY NEED TO FIND IT!
GRRRRRR
HEY, WHAT ARE YOU CHEWING ON?
BARK
BARK
BARK
WHAT DO YOU MEAN "NOTHING?"
THE REMOTE!
CHARLES! BAD DOG!

OH, NO! YOU'VE HIT A DEAD END. TO TRY AGAIN, GO TALK TO LORI ON PAGE 7.

"TROPICAL PARADISE"

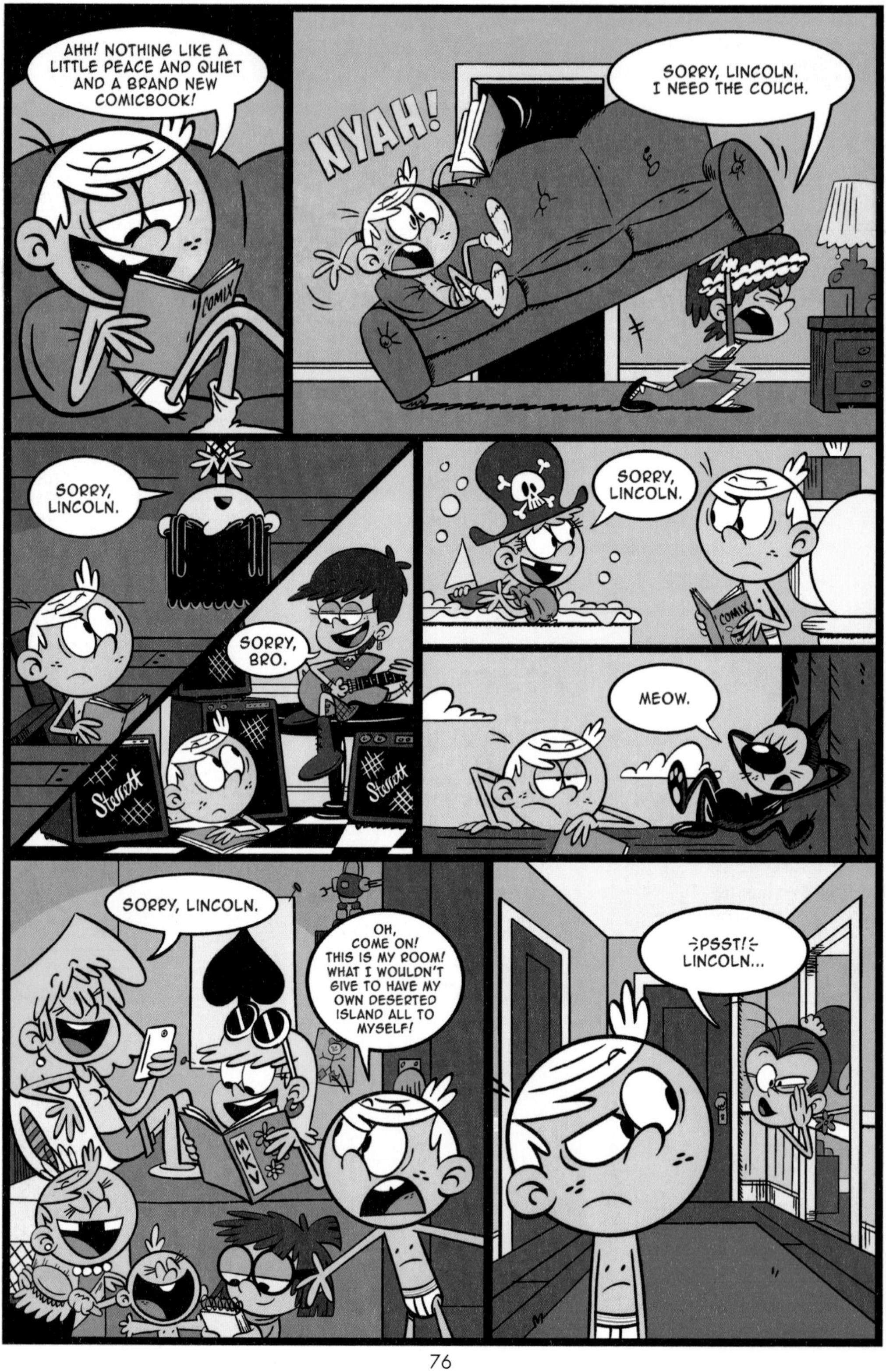
AHH! NOTHING LIKE A LITTLE PEACE AND QUIET AND A BRAND NEW COMICBOOK!
COMIX
NYAH!
SORRY, LINCOLN. I NEED THE COUCH.
SORRY, LINCOLN.
SORRY, BRO.
Sterrett
Sterrett
SORRY, LINCOLN.
COMIX
MEOW.
SORRY, LINCOLN.
MKV
OH, COME ON! THIS IS MY ROOM! WHAT I WOULDN'T GIVE TO HAVE MY OWN DESERTED ISLAND ALL TO MYSELF!
PSST! LINCOLN...

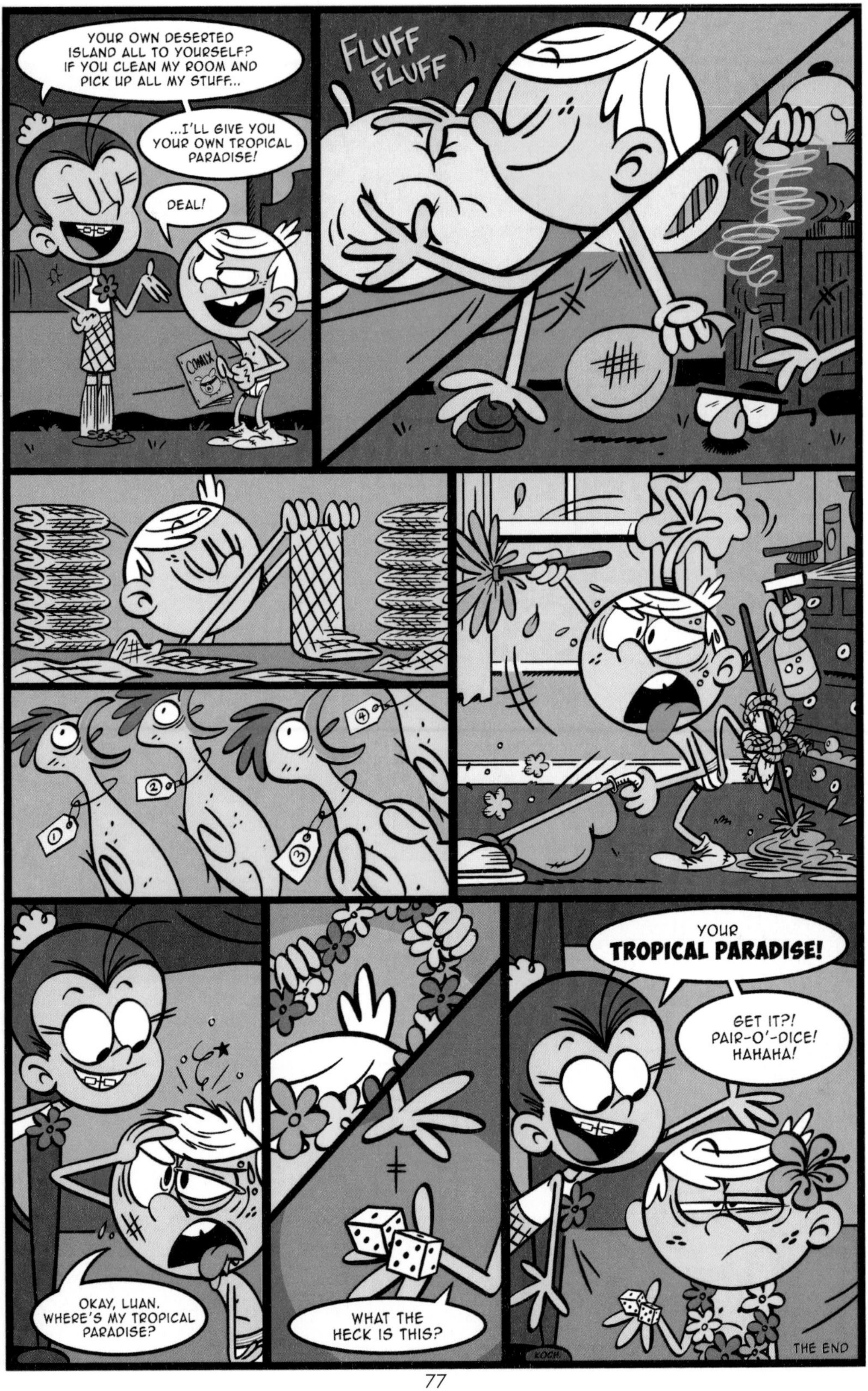
YOUR OWN DESERTED ISLAND ALL TO YOURSELF? IF YOU CLEAN MY ROOM AND PICK UP ALL MY STUFF...
...I'LL GIVE YOU YOUR OWN TROPICAL PARADISE!
DEAL!
COMIX
FLUFF FLUFF
1
2
3
4
OKAY, LUAN. WHERE'S MY TROPICAL PARADISE?
WHAT THE HECK IS THIS?
YOUR TROPICAL PARADISE!
GET IT?! PAIR-O'-DICE! HAHAHA!
THE END

"HOUSE TRAINING"

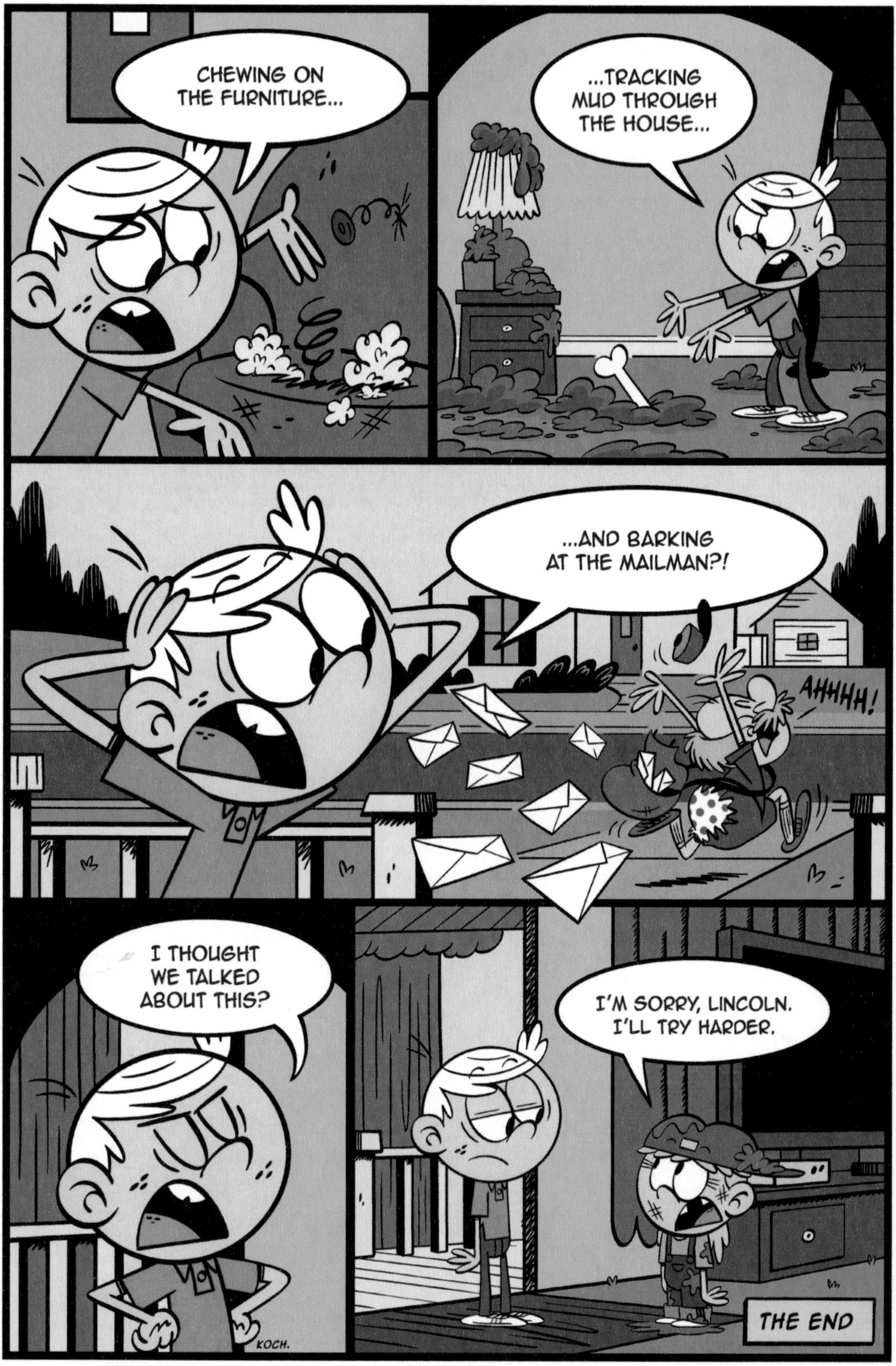
CHEWING ON THE FURNITURE...
...TRACKING MUD THROUGH THE HOUSE...
...AND BARKING AT THE MAILMAN?!
AHHHH!
I THOUGHT WE TALKED ABOUT THIS?
I'M SORRY, LINCOLN. I'LL TRY HARDER.
THE END
KOCH.

"TIRED OUT"

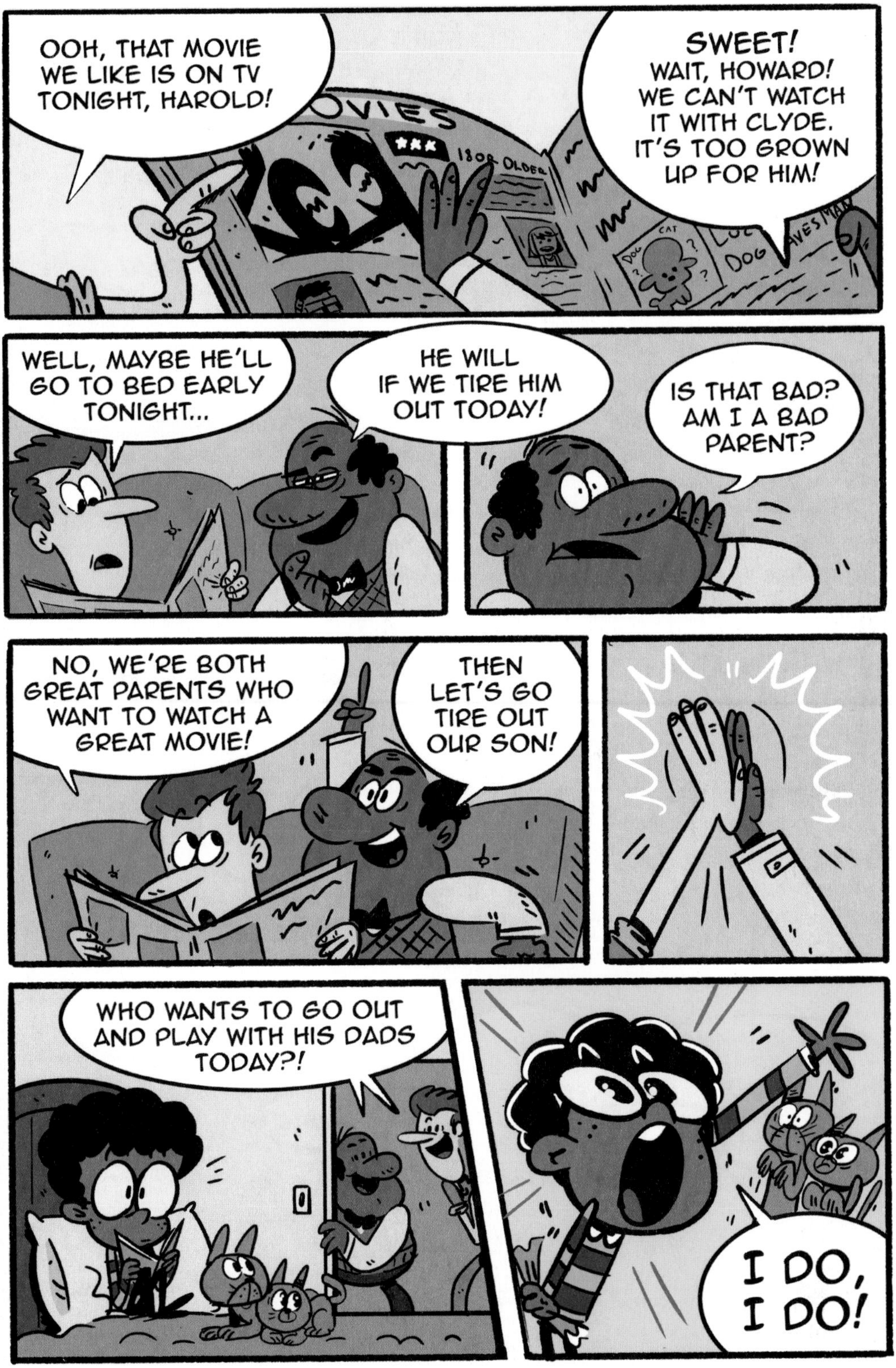
OOH, THAT MOVIE WE LIKE IS ON TV TONIGHT, HAROLD!
MOVIES
18 OR OLDER
SWEET! WAIT, HOWARD! WE CAN'T WATCH IT WITH CLYDE. IT'S TOO GROWN UP FOR HIM!
WELL, MAYBE HE'LL GO TO BED EARLY TONIGHT...
HE WILL IF WE TIRE HIM OUT TODAY!
IS THAT BAD? AM I A BAD PARENT?
NO, WE'RE BOTH GREAT PARENTS WHO WANT TO WATCH A GREAT MOVIE!
THEN LET'S GO TIRE OUT OUR SON!
WHO WANTS TO GO OUT AND PLAY WITH HIS DADS TODAY?!
I DO, I DO!

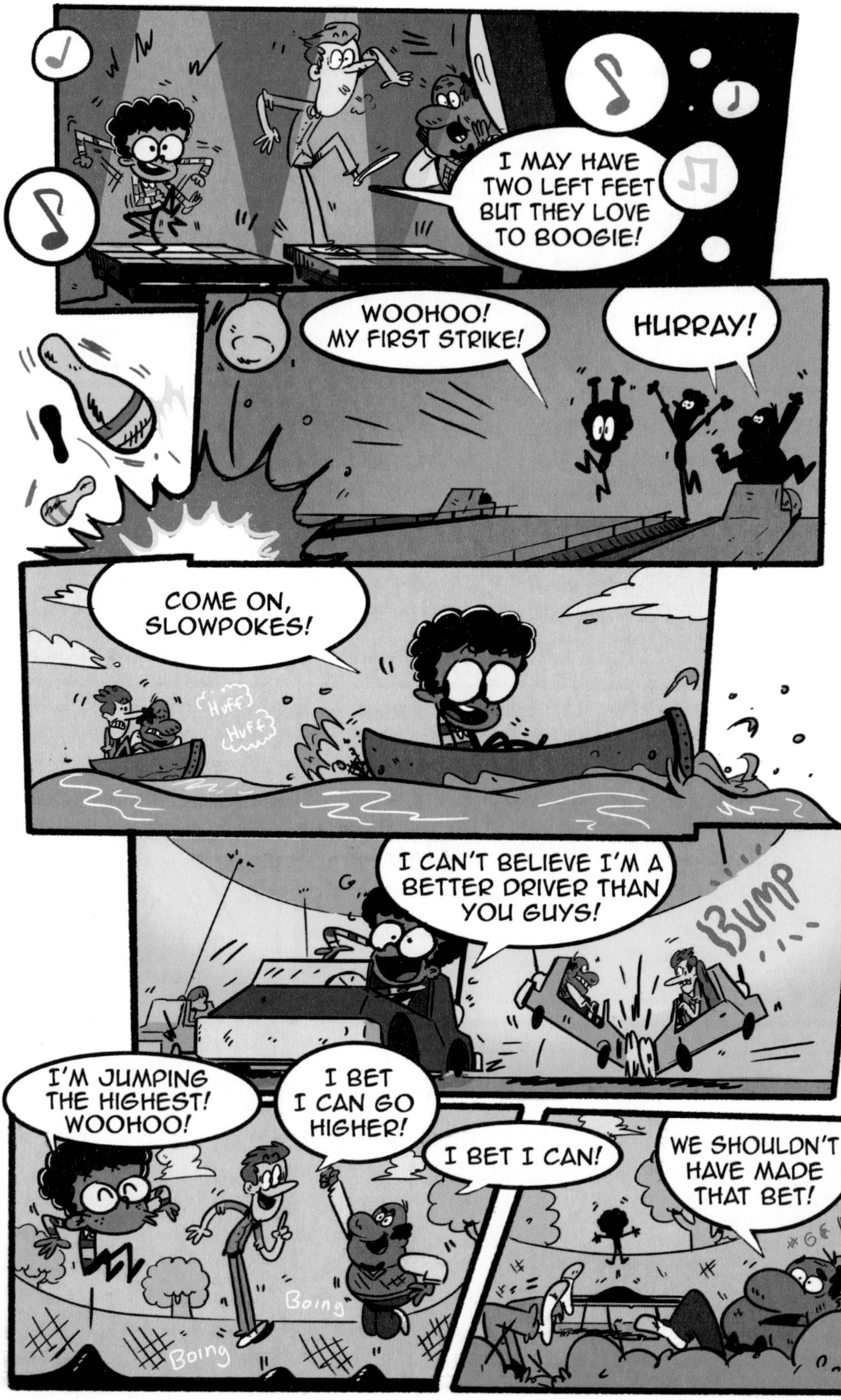
I MAY HAVE TWO LEFT FEET BUT THEY LOVE TO BOOGIE!
WOOHOO! MY FIRST STRIKE!
HURRAY!
COME ON, SLOWPOKES!
Huff
Huff
I CAN'T BELIEVE I'M A BETTER DRIVER THAN YOU GUYS!
BUMP
I'M JUMPING THE HIGHEST! WOOHOO!
I BET I CAN GO HIGHER!
Boing
Boing
I BET I CAN!
WE SHOULDN'T HAVE MADE THAT BET!

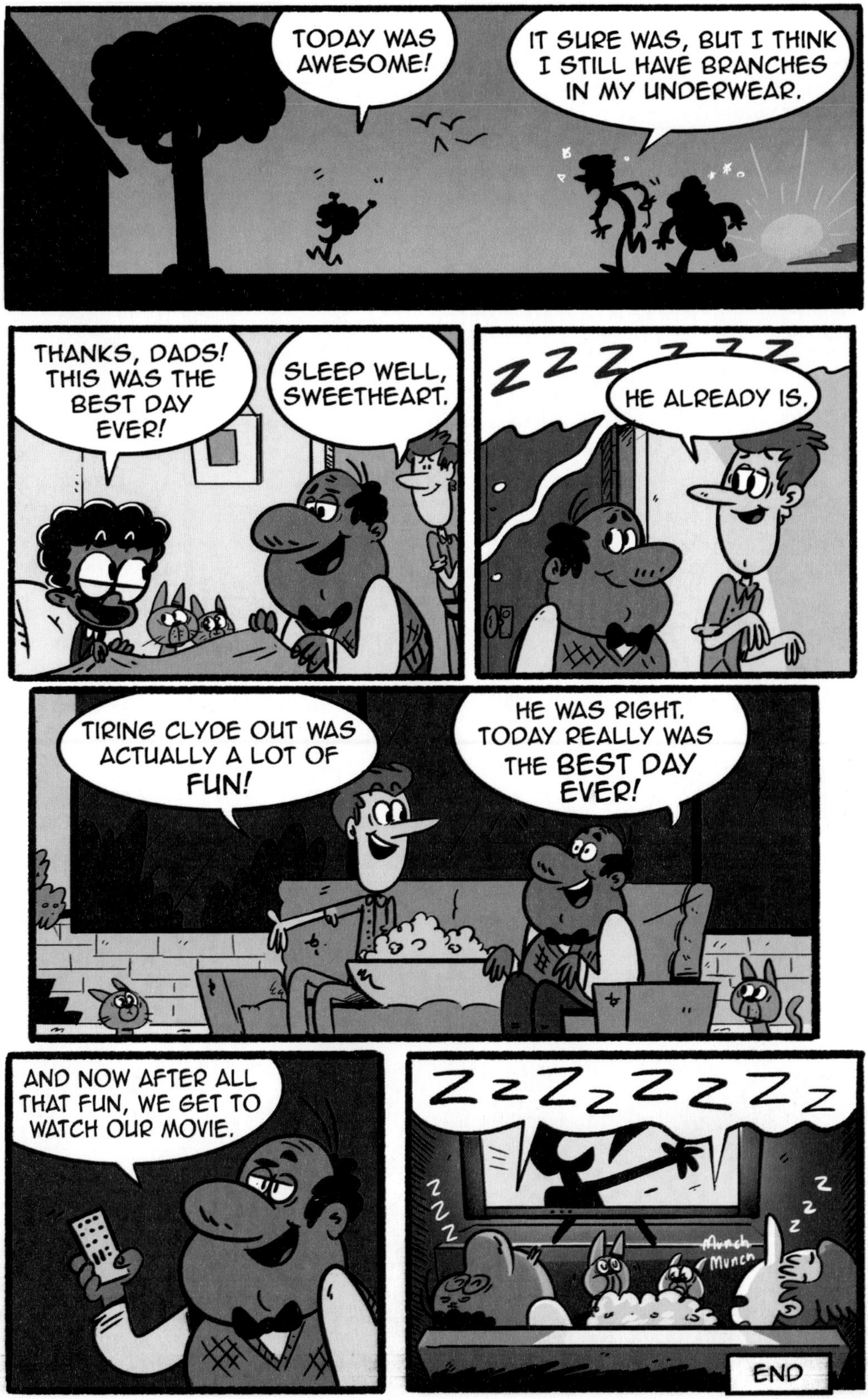
TODAY WAS AWESOME!
IT SURE WAS, BUT I THINK I STILL HAVE BRANCHES IN MY UNDERWEAR.
THANKS, DADS! THIS WAS THE BEST DAY EVER!
SLEEP WELL, SWEETHEART.
ZZZZZZZ
HE ALREADY IS.
TIRING CLYDE OUT WAS ACTUALLY A LOT OF FUN!
HE WAS RIGHT. TODAY REALLY WAS THE BEST DAY EVER!
AND NOW AFTER ALL THAT FUN, WE GET TO WATCH OUR MOVIE.
ZzZzZZZZz
Munch Munch
END

"LIGHTS OUT"

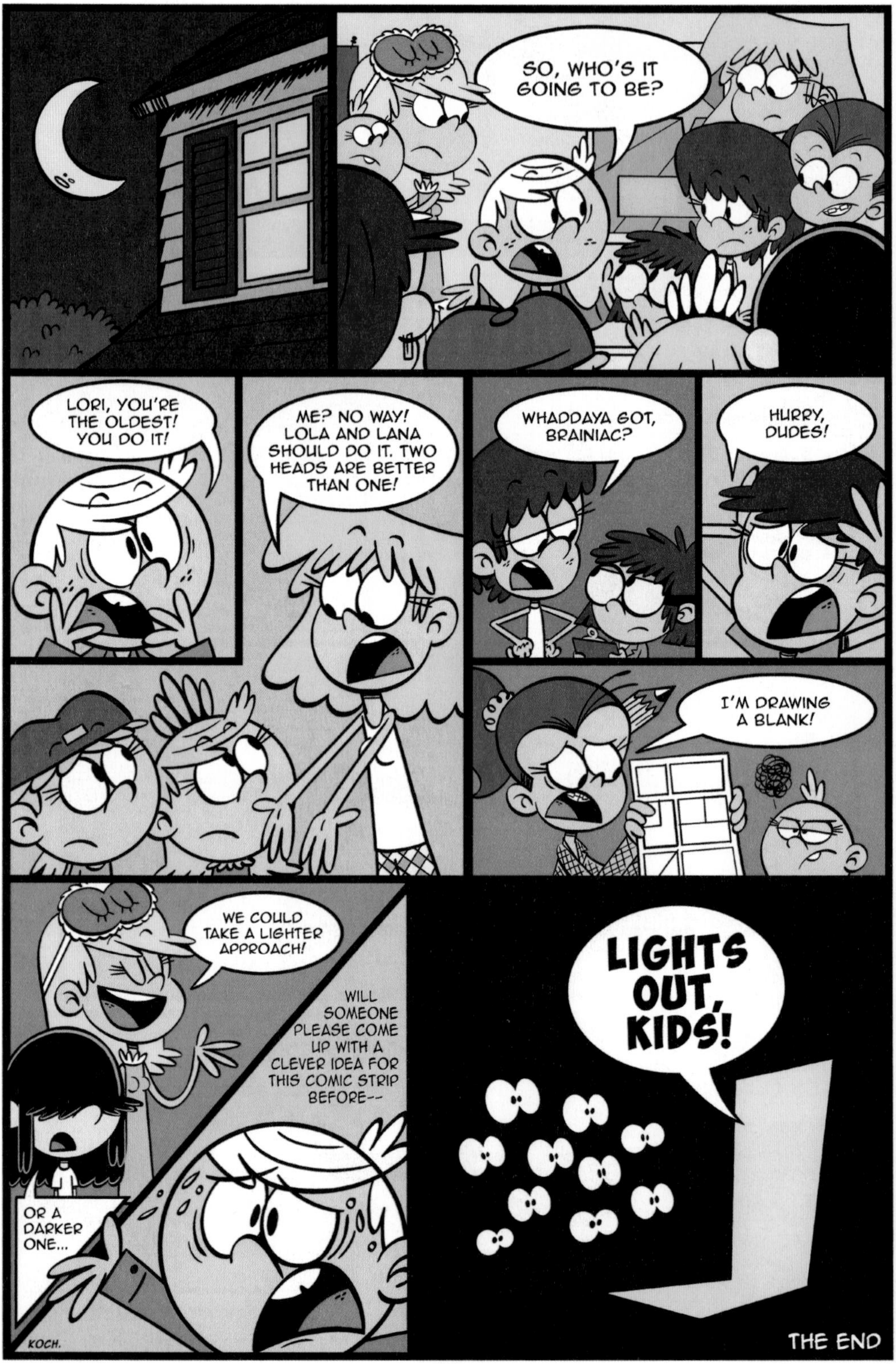
SO, WHO'S IT GOING TO BE?
LORI, YOU'RE THE OLDEST! YOU DO IT!
ME? NO WAY! LOLA AND LANA SHOULD DO IT. TWO HEADS ARE BETTER THAN ONE!
WHADDAYA GOT, BRAINIAC?
HURRY, DUDES!
I'M DRAWING A BLANK!
WE COULD TAKE A LIGHTER APPROACH!
OR A DARKER ONE...
WILL SOMEONE PLEASE COME UP WITH A CLEVER IDEA FOR THIS COMIC STRIP BEFORE--
LIGHTS OUT, KIDS!
THE END
KOCH.

"THE 10-HEADED BEAST"

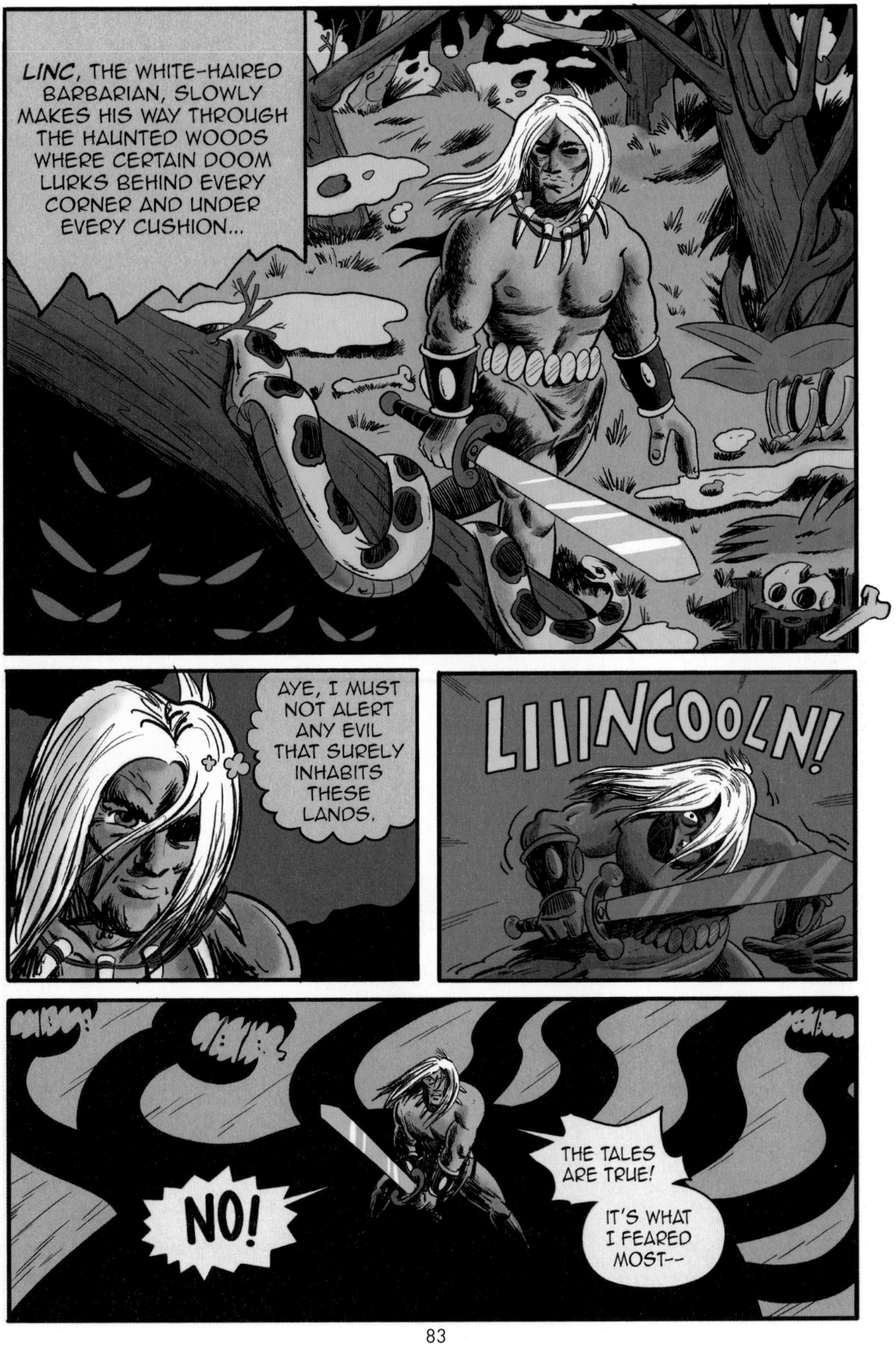

LINC, THE WHITE-HAIRED BARBARIAN, SLOWLY MAKES HIS WAY THROUGH THE HAUNTED WOODS WHERE CERTAIN DOOM LURKS BEHIND EVERY CORNER AND UNDER EVERY CUSHION...
AYE, I MUST NOT ALERT ANY EVIL THAT SURELY INHABITS THESE LANDS.
LIIINCOOLN!
NO!
THE TALES ARE TRUE!
IT'S WHAT I FEARED MOST--

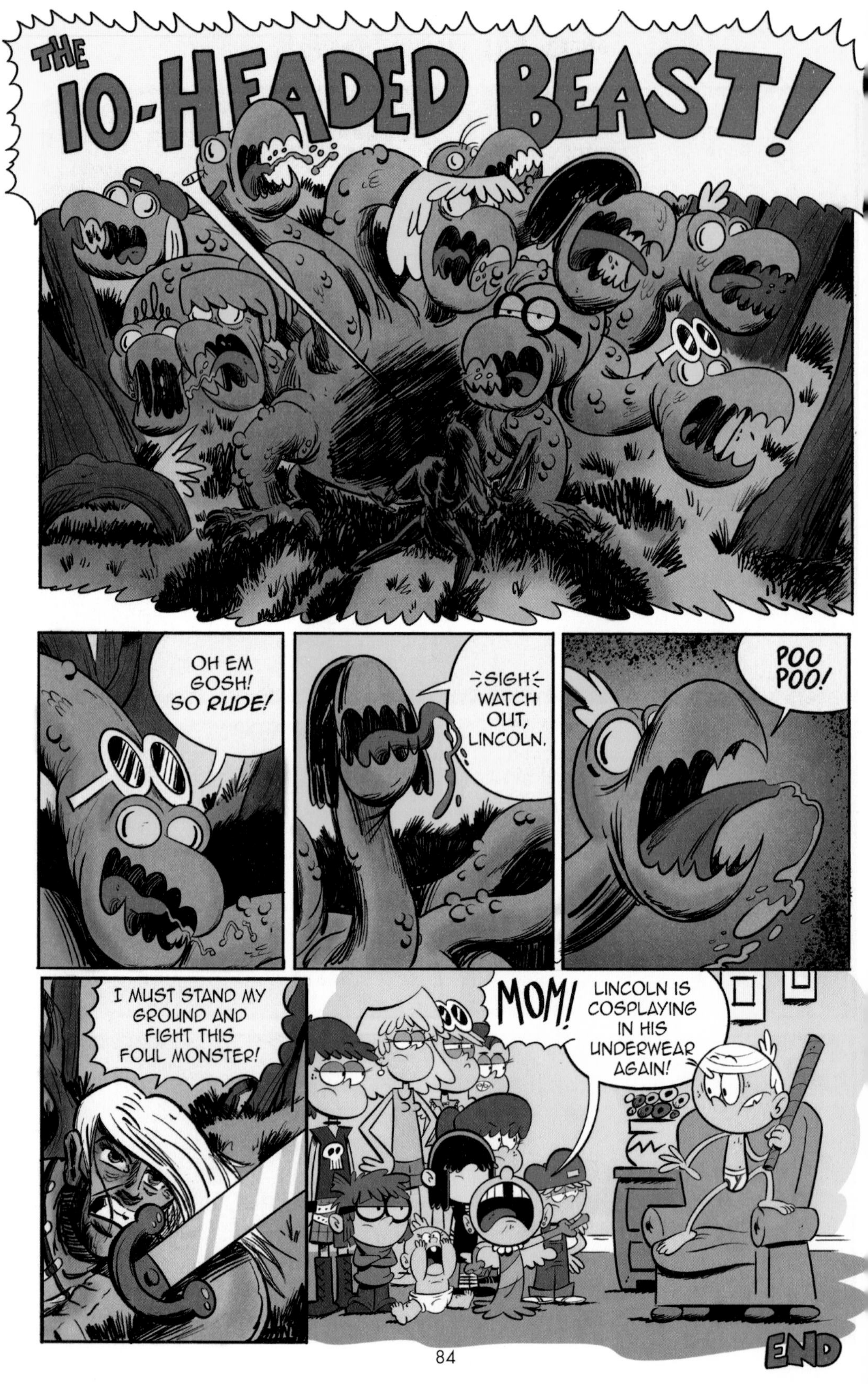
THE 10-HEADED BEAST!
OH EM GOSH! SO RUDE!
SIGH WATCH OUT, LINCOLN.
POO POO!
I MUST STAND MY GROUND AND FIGHT THIS FOUL MONSTER!
MOM!
LINCOLN IS COSPLAYING IN HIS UNDERWEAR AGAIN!
END

"TRAFFIC JAM"

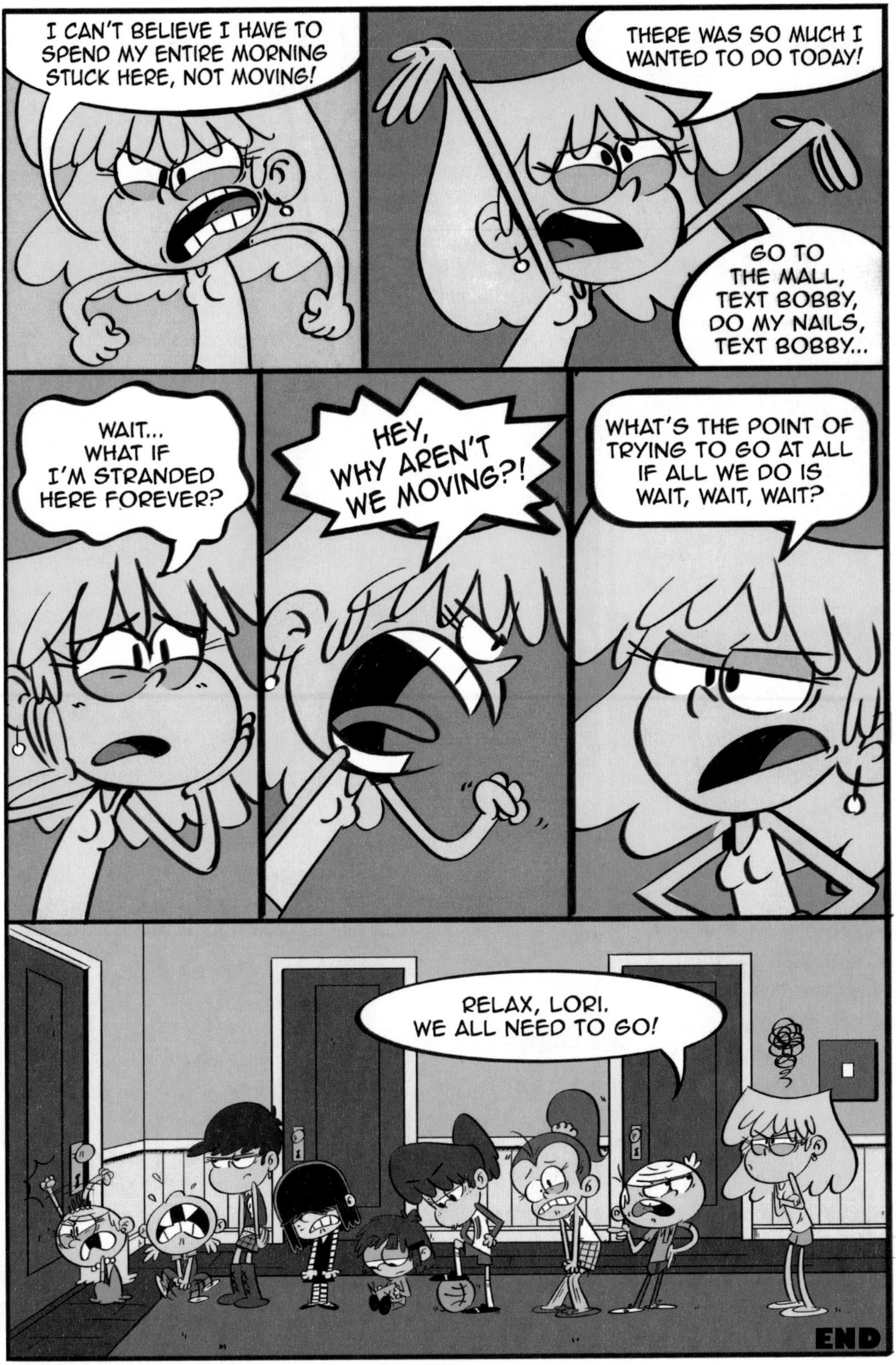
I CAN'T BELIEVE I HAVE TO SPEND MY ENTIRE MORNING STUCK HERE, NOT MOVING!
THERE WAS SO MUCH I WANTED TO DO TODAY!
GO TO THE MALL, TEXT BOBBY, DO MY NAILS, TEXT BOBBY...
WAIT... WHAT IF I'M STRANDED HERE FOREVER?
HEY, WHY AREN'T WE MOVING?!
WHAT'S THE POINT OF TRYING TO GO AT ALL IF ALL WE DO IS WAIT, WAIT, WAIT?
RELAX, LORI. WE ALL NEED TO GO!
END

"BAGGED AND BOARDED"

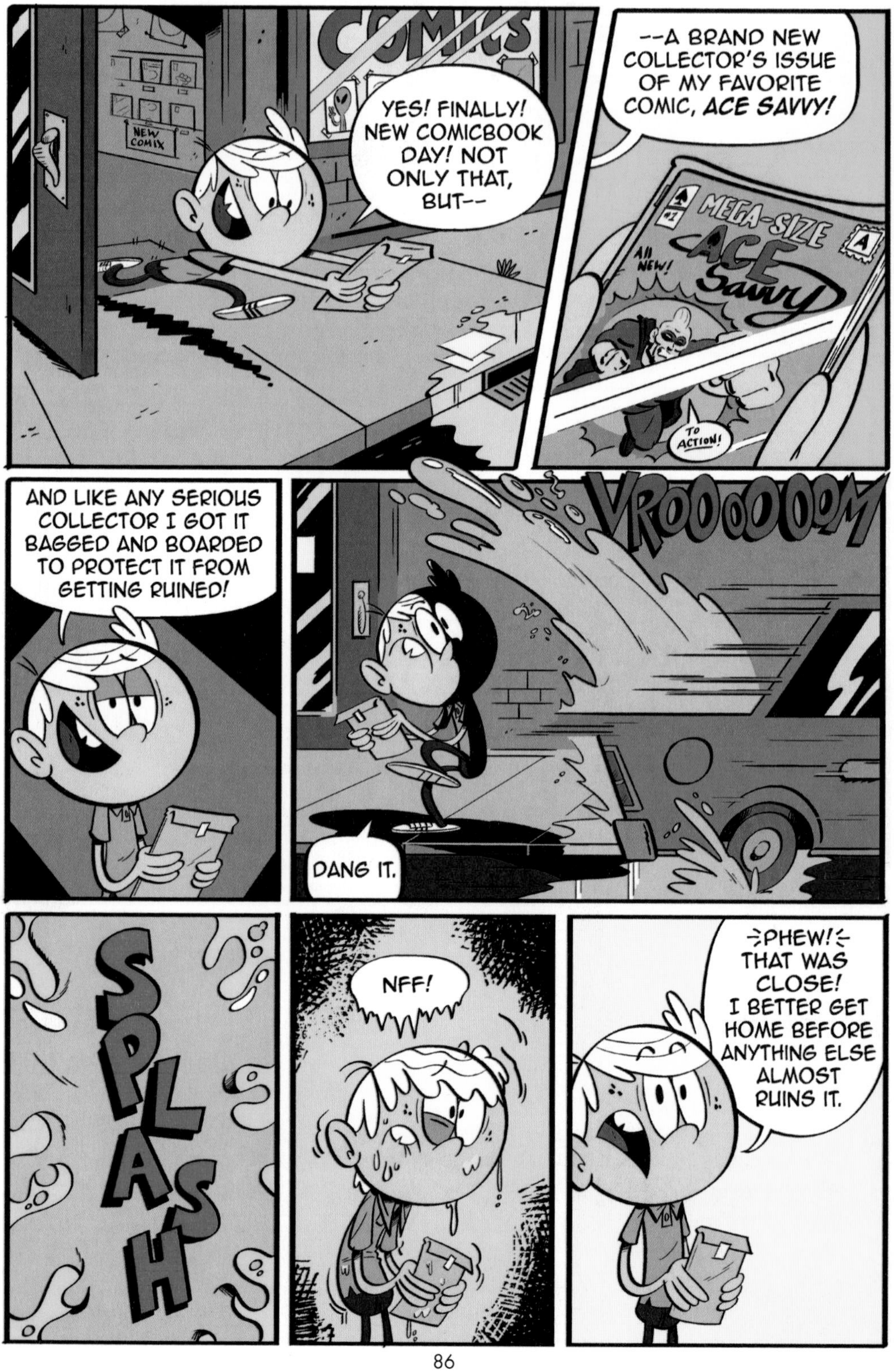
NEW COMIX
COMICS
YES! FINALLY! NEW COMICBOOK DAY! NOT ONLY THAT, BUT--
--A BRAND NEW COLLECTOR'S ISSUE OF MY FAVORITE COMIC, ACE SAVVY!
MEGA-SIZE ACE Savvy
ALL NEW!
A
TO ACTION!
AND LIKE ANY SERIOUS COLLECTOR I GOT IT BAGGED AND BOARDED TO PROTECT IT FROM GETTING RUINED!
VROOOOOOOM
DANG IT.
SPLASH
NFF!
PHEW! THAT WAS CLOSE! I BETTER GET HOME BEFORE ANYTHING ELSE ALMOST RUINS IT.

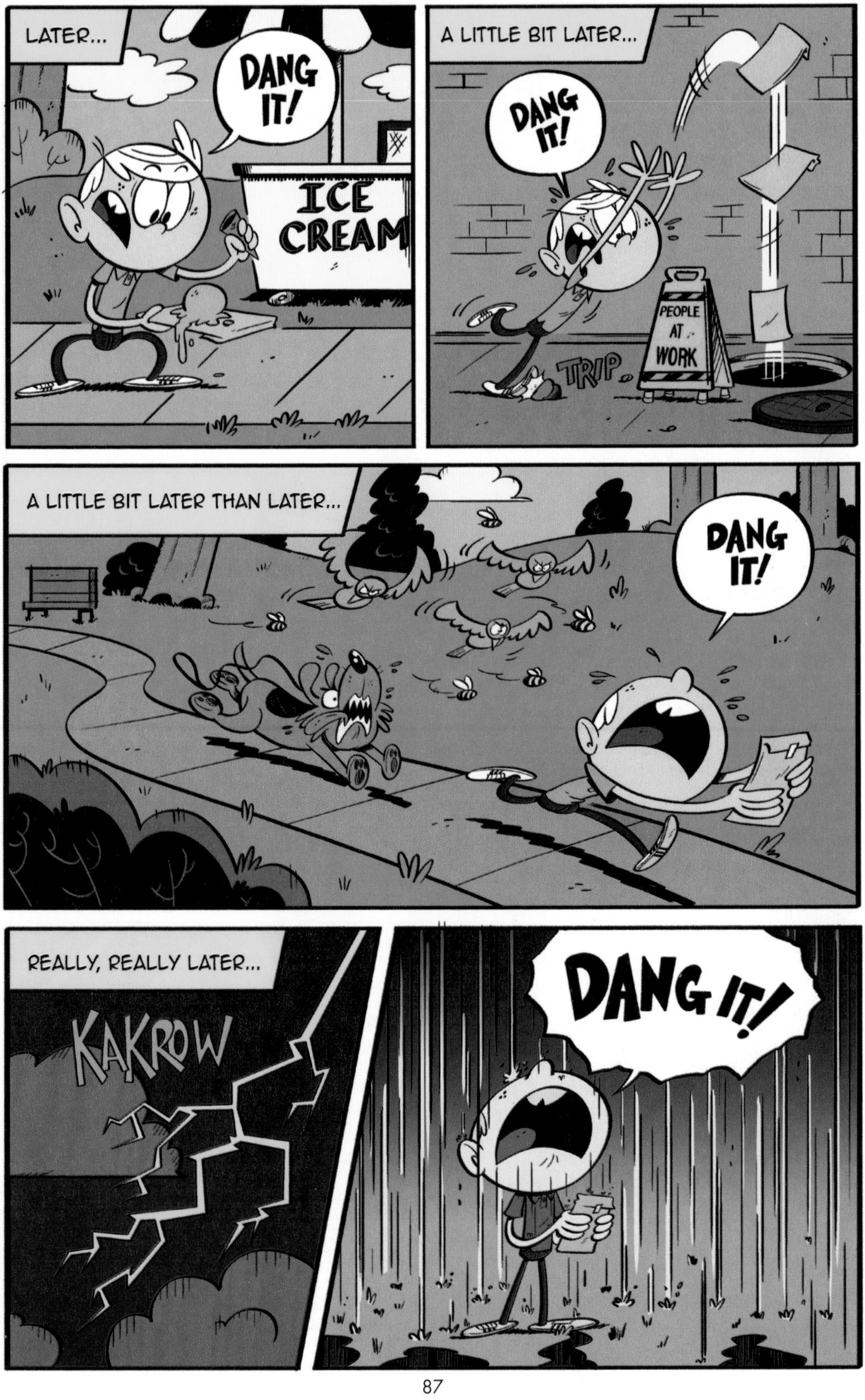
LATER...
DANG IT!
ICE CREAM
A LITTLE BIT LATER...
DANG IT!
PEOPLE AT WORK
TRIP
A LITTLE BIT LATER THAN LATER...
DANG IT!
REALLY, REALLY LATER...
KAKROW
DANG IT!

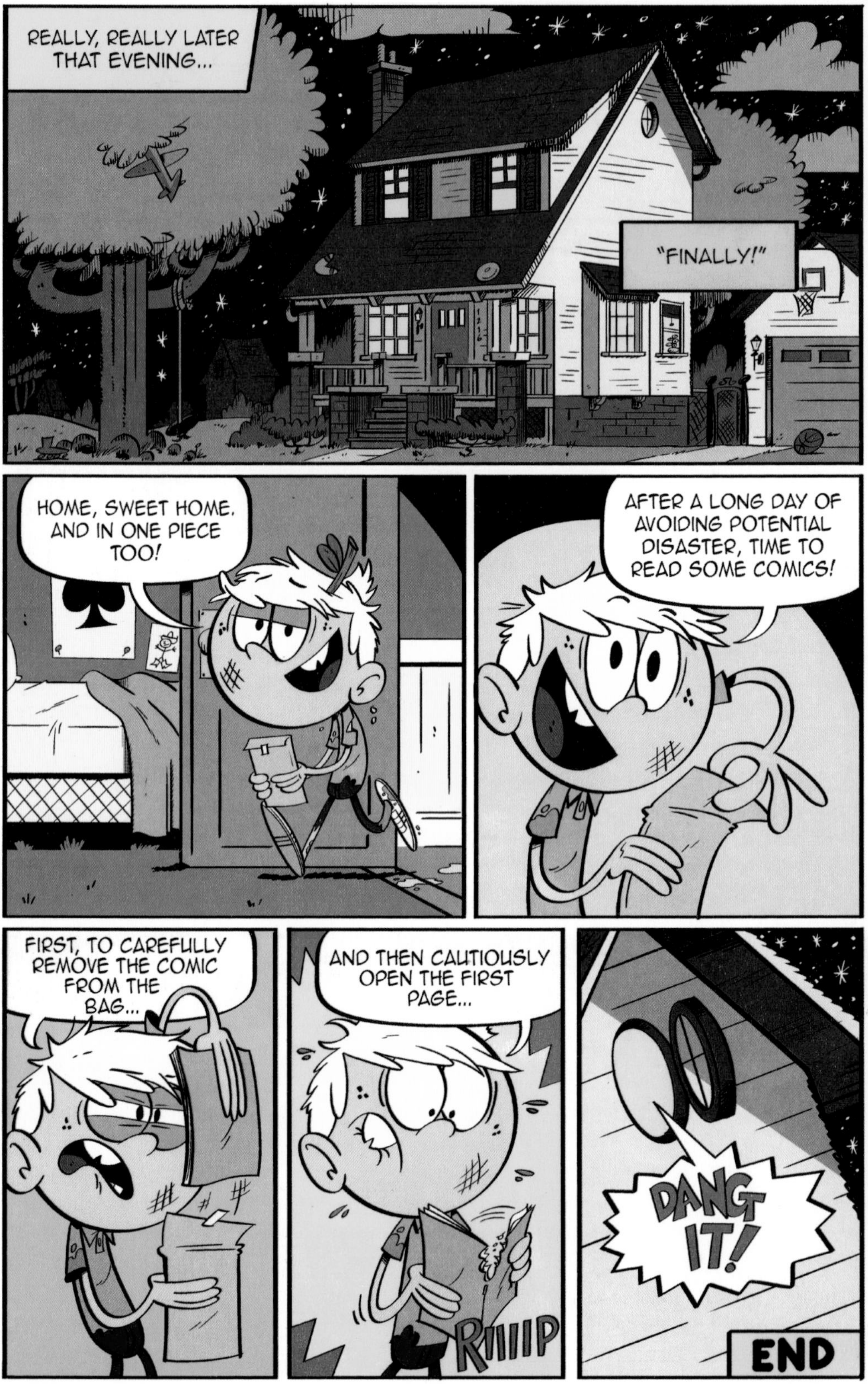
REALLY, REALLY LATER THAT EVENING...
"FINALLY!"
HOME, SWEET HOME. AND IN ONE PIECE TOO!
AFTER A LONG DAY OF AVOIDING POTENTIAL DISASTER, TIME TO READ SOME COMICS!
FIRST, TO CAREFULLY REMOVE THE COMIC FROM THE BAG...
AND THEN CAUTIOUSLY OPEN THE FIRST PAGE...
RIIIIP
DANG IT!
END

"SHOE STYLIN'"

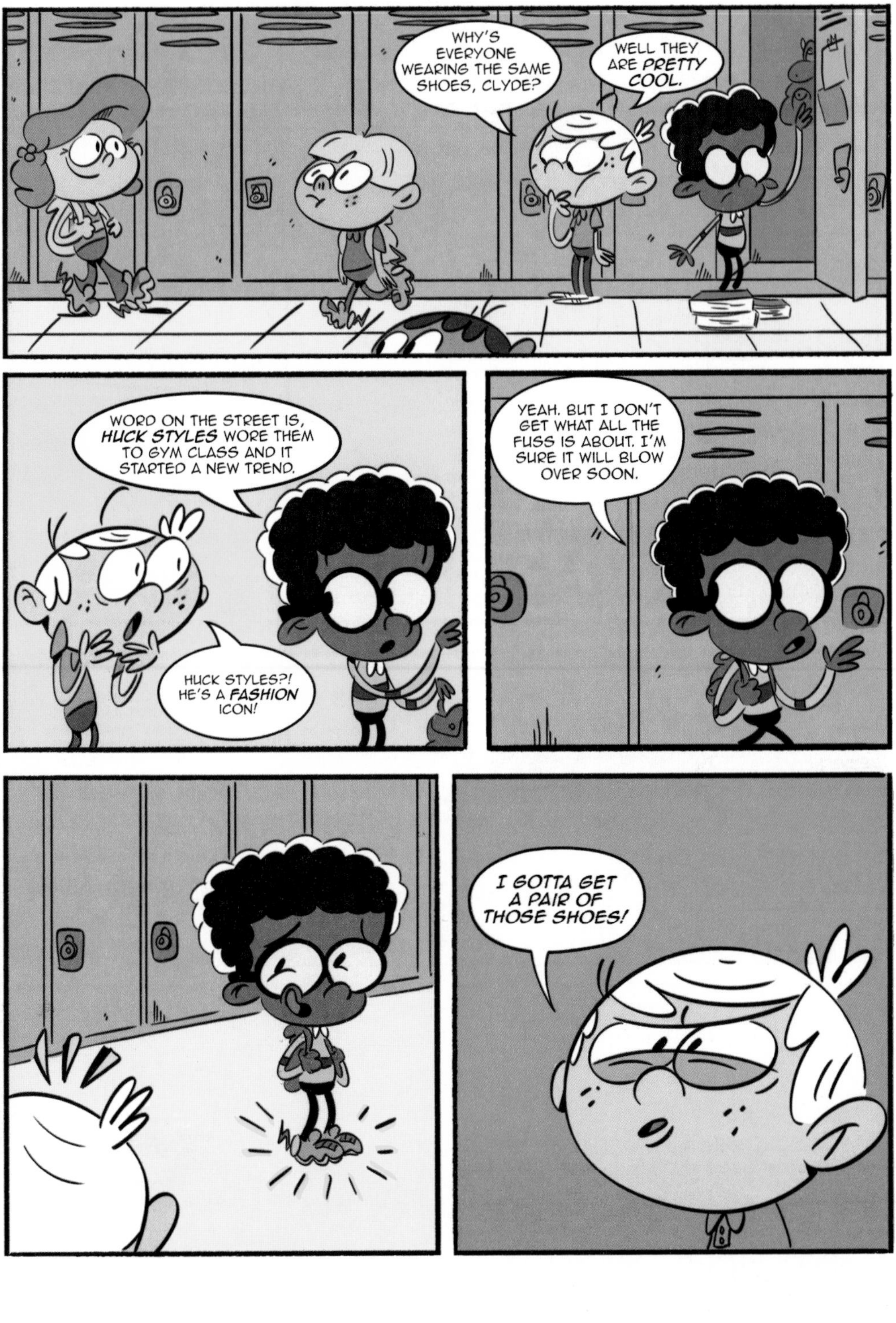
WHY'S EVERYONE WEARING THE SAME SHOES, CLYDE?
WELL THEY ARE PRETTY COOL.
WORD ON THE STREET IS, HUCK STYLES WORE THEM TO GYM CLASS AND IT STARTED A NEW TREND.
HUCK STYLES?! HE'S A FASHION ICON!
YEAH. BUT I DON'T GET WHAT ALL THE FUSS IS ABOUT. I'M SURE IT WILL BLOW OVER SOON.
I GOTTA GET A PAIR OF THOSE SHOES!

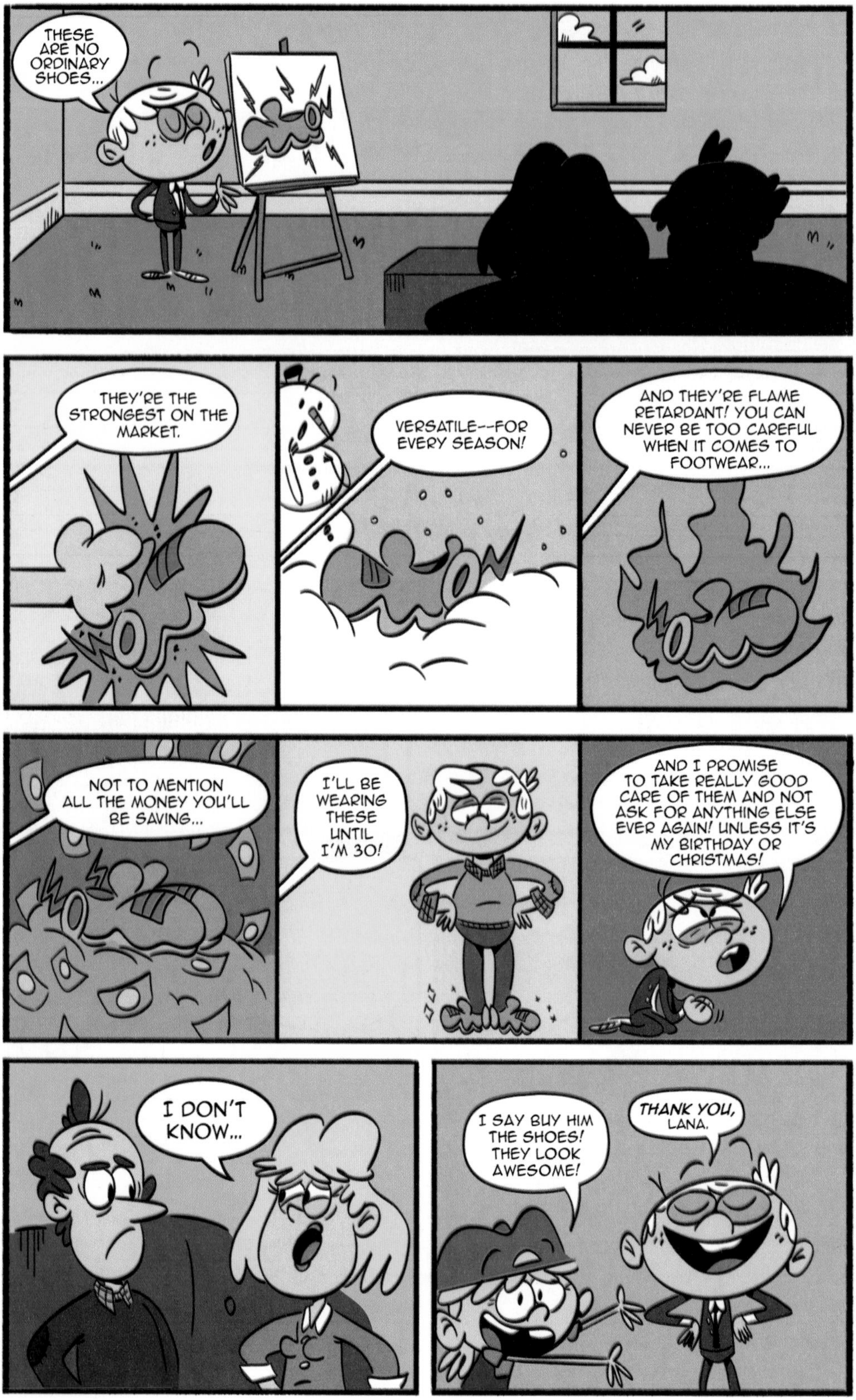
THESE ARE NO ORDINARY SHOES...
THEY'RE THE STRONGEST ON THE MARKET.
VERSATILE--FOR EVERY SEASON!
AND THEY'RE FLAME RETARDANT! YOU CAN NEVER BE TOO CAREFUL WHEN IT COMES TO FOOTWEAR...
NOT TO MENTION ALL THE MONEY YOU'LL BE SAVING...
I'LL BE WEARING THESE UNTIL I'M 30!
AND I PROMISE TO TAKE REALLY GOOD CARE OF THEM AND NOT ASK FOR ANYTHING ELSE EVER AGAIN! UNLESS IT'S MY BIRTHDAY OR CHRISTMAS!
I DON'T KNOW...
I SAY BUY HIM THE SHOES! THEY LOOK AWESOME!
THANK YOU, LANA.

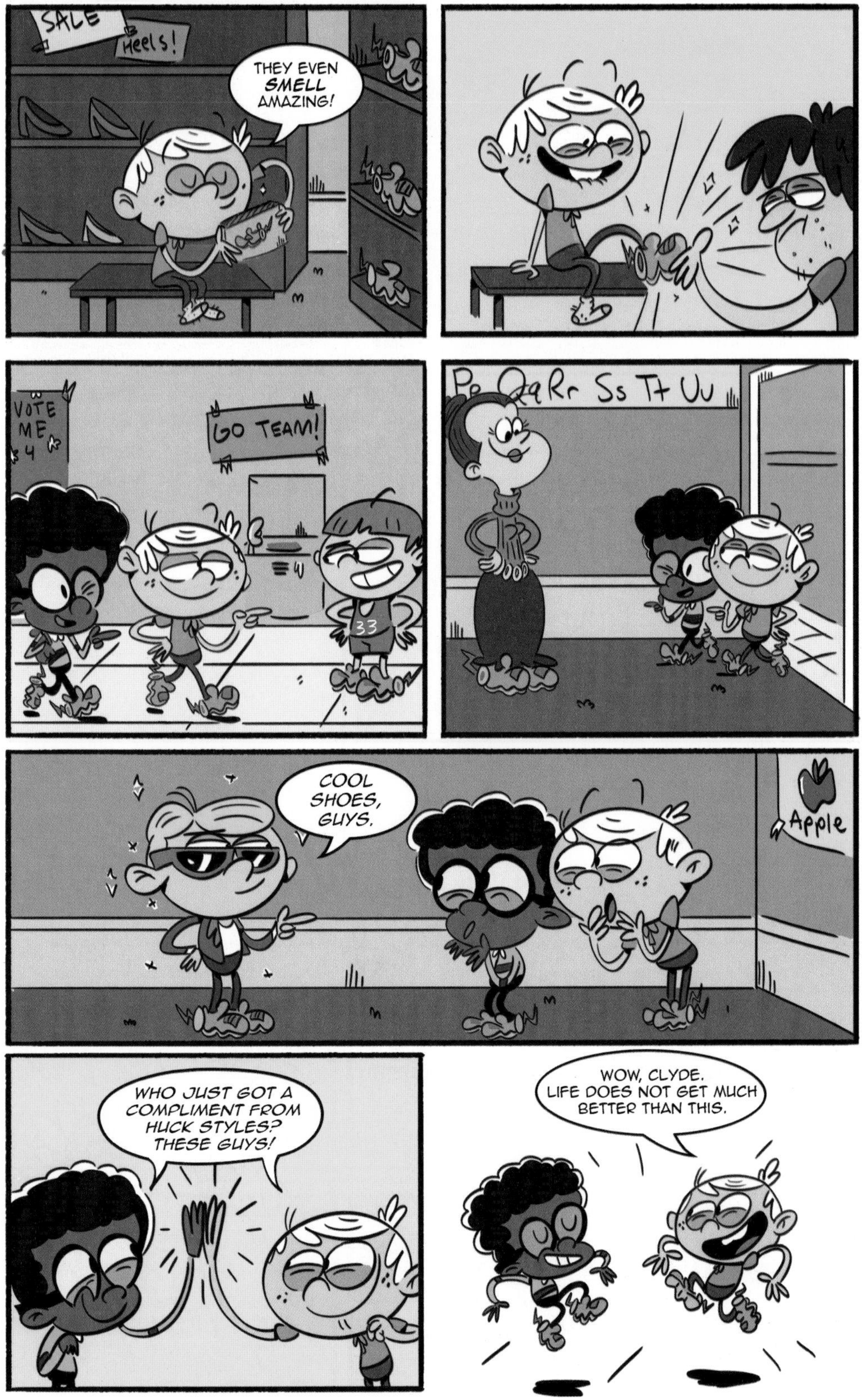
SALE
Heels!
THEY EVEN SMELL AMAZING!
VOTE ME 4
GO TEAM!
33
Pp Qq Rr Ss Tt Uu
COOL SHOES, GUYS.
Apple
WHO JUST GOT A COMPLIMENT FROM HUCK STYLES? THESE GUYS!
WOW, CLYDE. LIFE DOES NOT GET MUCH BETTER THAN THIS.

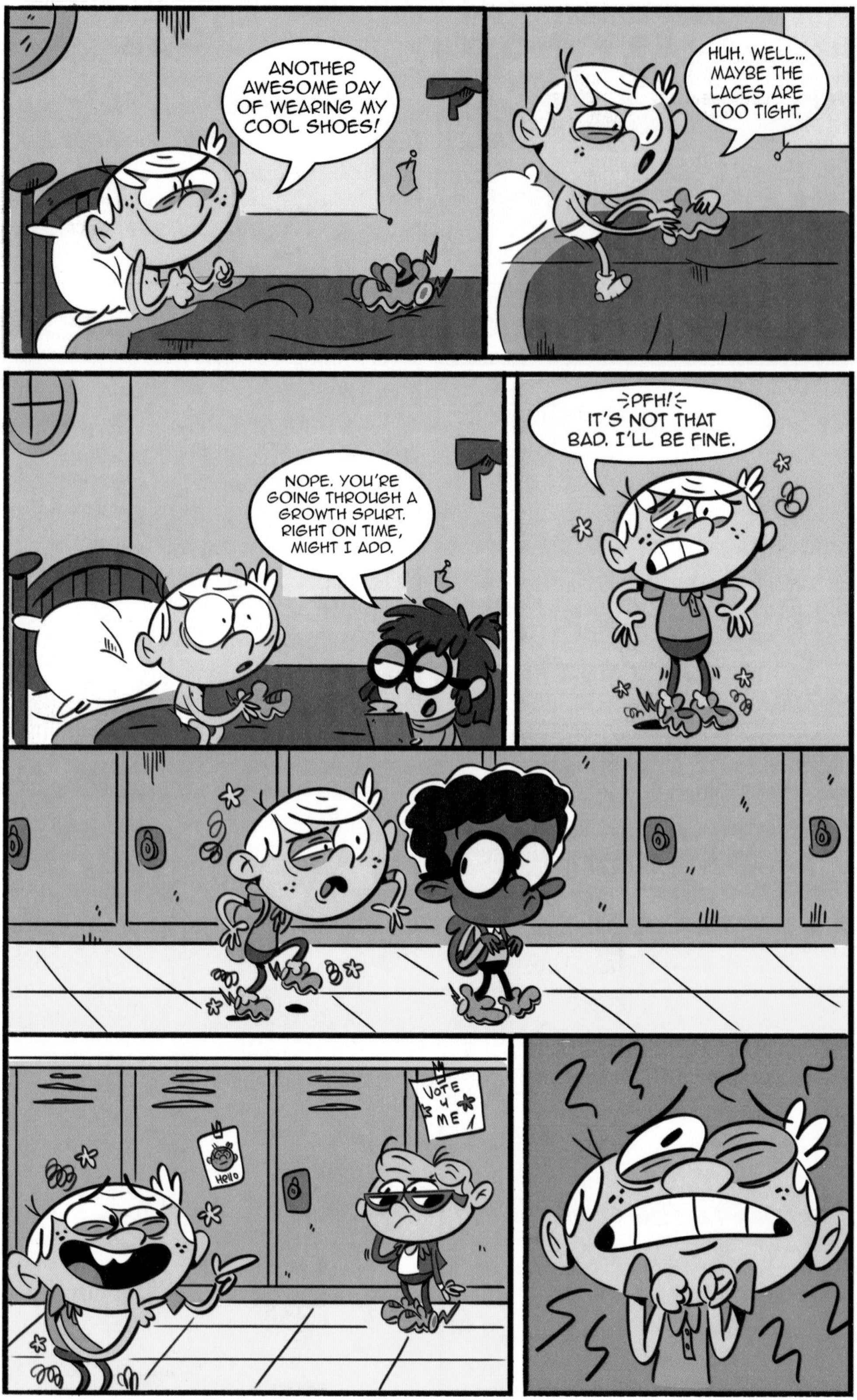
ANOTHER AWESOME DAY OF WEARING MY COOL SHOES!
HUH. WELL... MAYBE THE LACES ARE TOO TIGHT.
NOPE. YOU'RE GOING THROUGH A GROWTH SPURT. RIGHT ON TIME, MIGHT I ADD.
PFH! IT'S NOT THAT BAD. I'LL BE FINE.
VOTE 4 ME
Hello

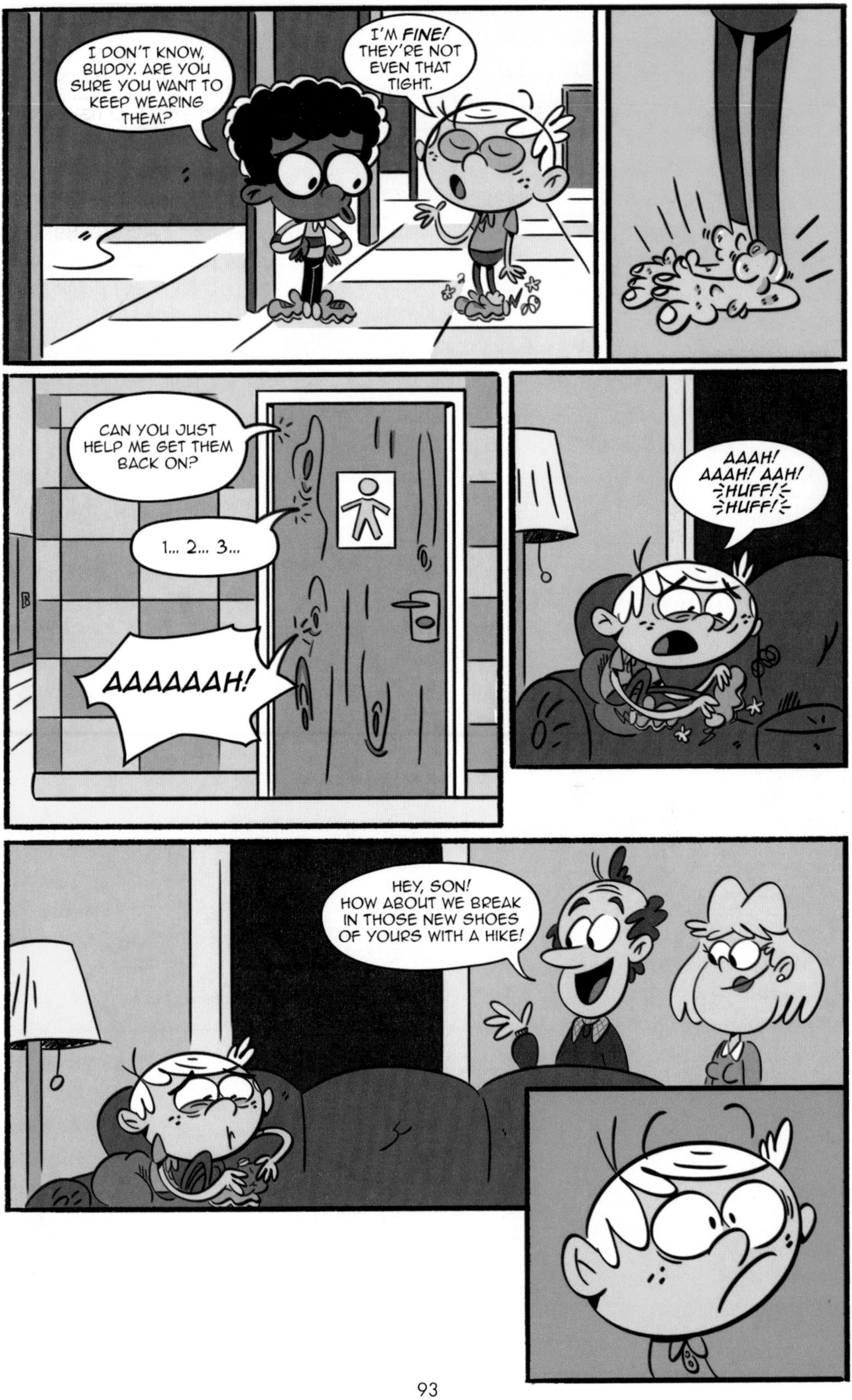
I DON'T KNOW, BUDDY. ARE YOU SURE YOU WANT TO KEEP WEARING THEM?
I'M FINE! THEY'RE NOT EVEN THAT TIGHT.
CAN YOU JUST HELP ME GET THEM BACK ON?
1... 2... 3...
AAAAAAH!
AAAH! AAAH! AAH! HUFF! HUFF!
HEY, SON! HOW ABOUT WE BREAK IN THOSE NEW SHOES OF YOURS WITH A HIKE!

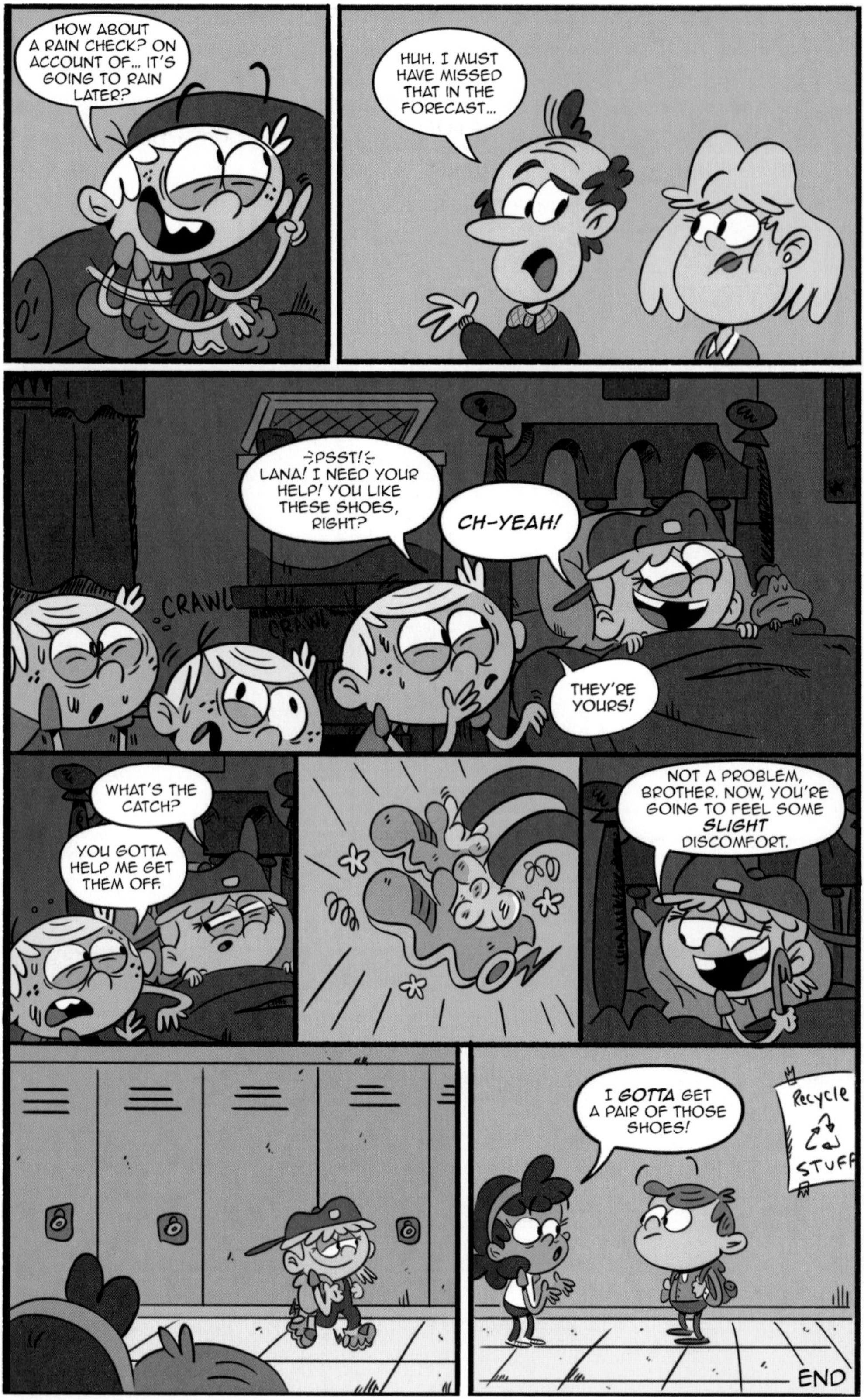
HOW ABOUT A RAIN CHECK? ON ACCOUNT OF... IT'S GOING TO RAIN LATER?
HUH. I MUST HAVE MISSED THAT IN THE FORECAST...
PSST! LANA! I NEED YOUR HELP! YOU LIKE THESE SHOES, RIGHT?
CH-YEAH!
CRAWL
CRAWL
THEY'RE YOURS!
WHAT'S THE CATCH?
YOU GOTTA HELP ME GET THEM OFF.
NOT A PROBLEM, BROTHER. NOW, YOU'RE GOING TO FEEL SOME SLIGHT DISCOMFORT.
I GOTTA GET A PAIR OF THOSE SHOES!
Recycle
STUFF
END

"THE ART OF COOKING"

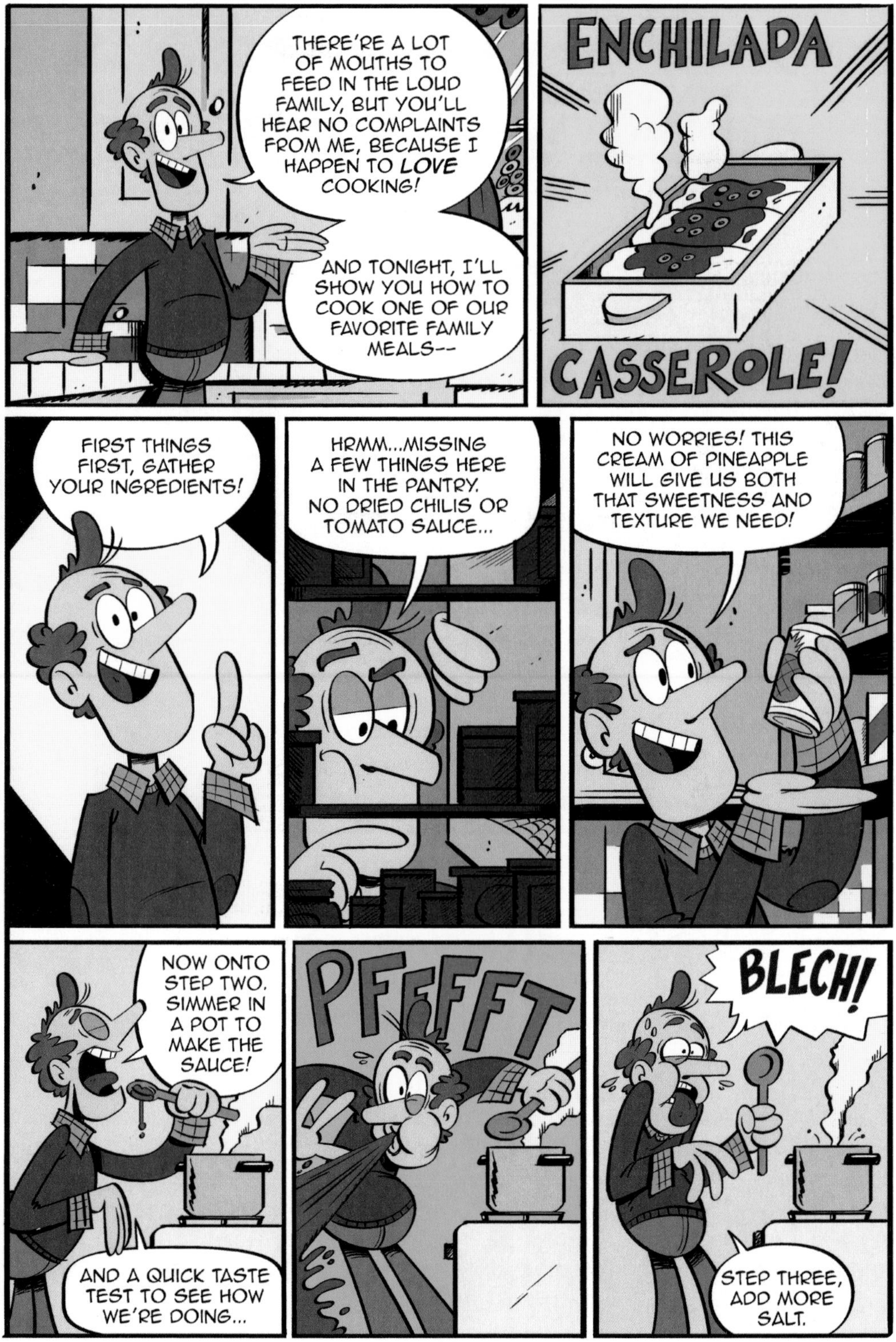
THERE'RE A LOT OF MOUTHS TO FEED IN THE LOUD FAMILY, BUT YOU'LL HEAR NO COMPLAINTS FROM ME, BECAUSE I HAPPEN TO *LOVE* COOKING!
AND TONIGHT, I'LL SHOW YOU HOW TO COOK ONE OF OUR FAVORITE FAMILY MEALS--
ENCHILADA
CASSEROLE!
FIRST THINGS FIRST, GATHER YOUR INGREDIENTS!
HRMM...MISSING A FEW THINGS HERE IN THE PANTRY. NO DRIED CHILIS OR TOMATO SAUCE...
NO WORRIES! THIS CREAM OF PINEAPPLE WILL GIVE US BOTH THAT SWEETNESS AND TEXTURE WE NEED!
NOW ONTO STEP TWO. SIMMER IN A POT TO MAKE THE SAUCE!
AND A QUICK TASTE TEST TO SEE HOW WE'RE DOING...
PFFFFT
BLECH!
STEP THREE, ADD MORE SALT.

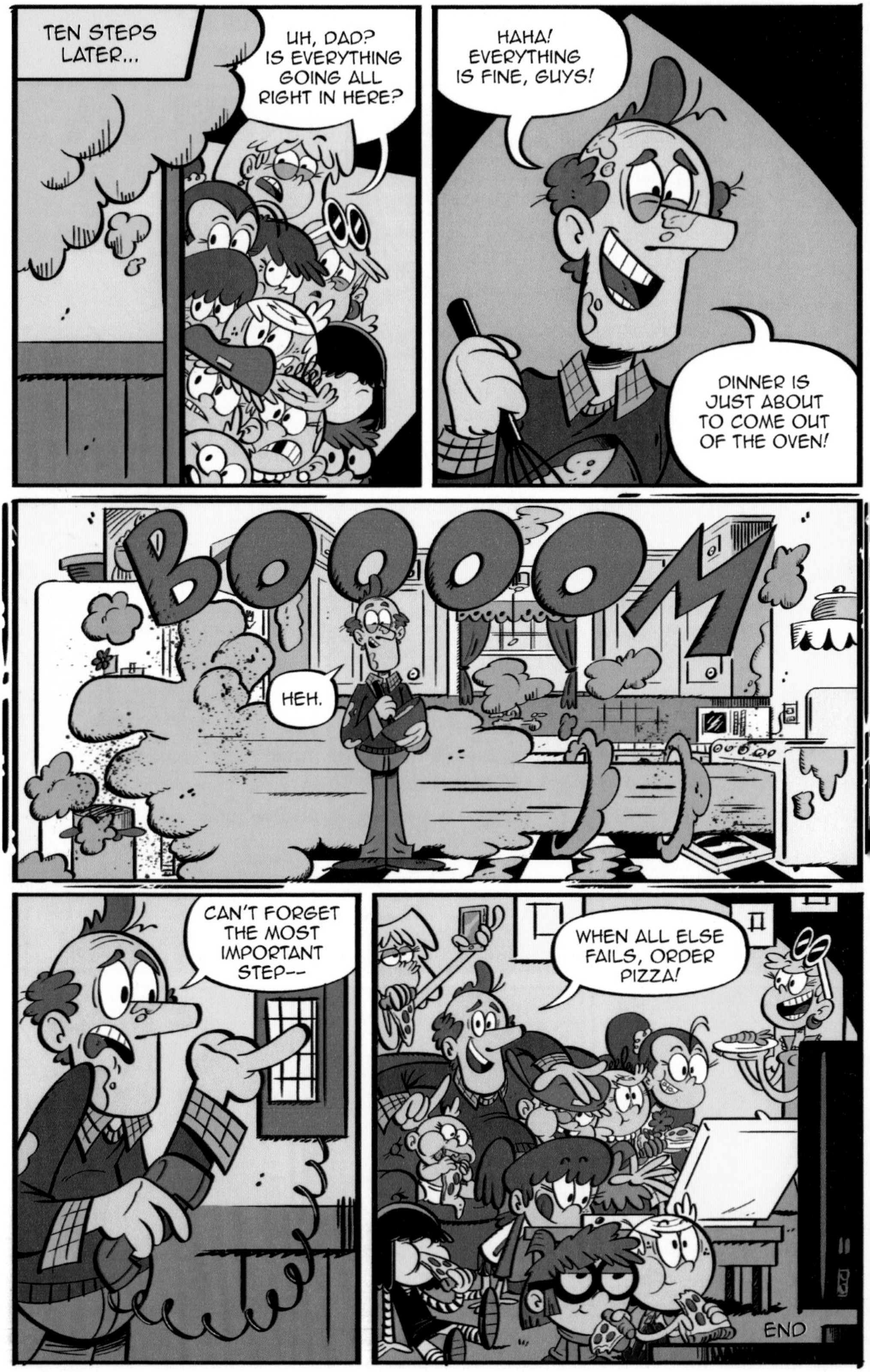
TEN STEPS LATER...
UH, DAD? IS EVERYTHING GOING ALL RIGHT IN HERE?
HAHA! EVERYTHING IS FINE, GUYS!
DINNER IS JUST ABOUT TO COME OUT OF THE OVEN!
BOOOOM
HEH.
CAN'T FORGET THE MOST IMPORTANT STEP--
WHEN ALL ELSE FAILS, ORDER PIZZA!
END

"THE BORROWERS"

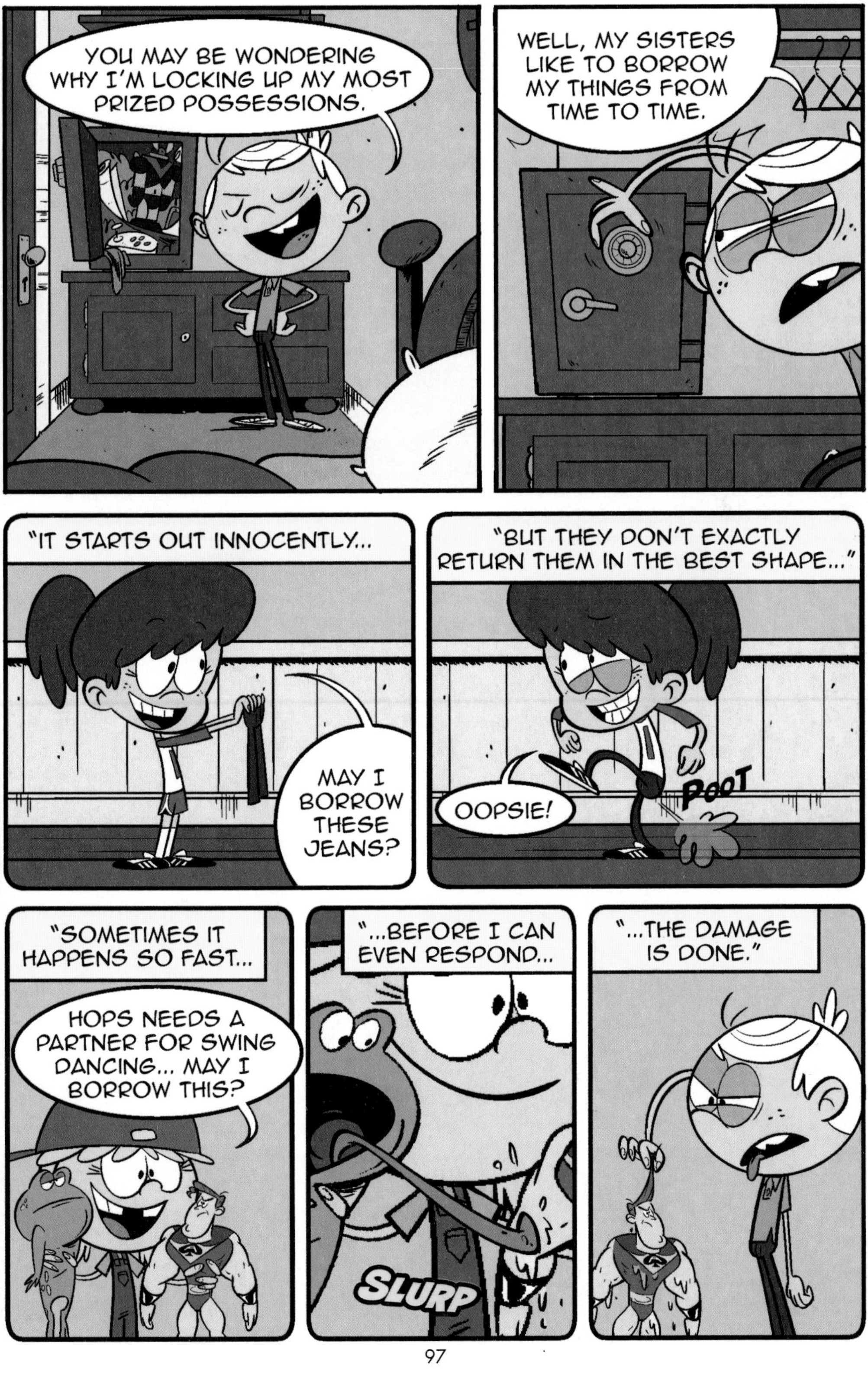

YOU MAY BE WONDERING WHY I'M LOCKING UP MY MOST PRIZED POSSESSIONS.
WELL, MY SISTERS LIKE TO BORROW MY THINGS FROM TIME TO TIME.
"IT STARTS OUT INNOCENTLY...
MAY I BORROW THESE JEANS?
"BUT THEY DON'T EXACTLY RETURN THEM IN THE BEST SHAPE..."
OOPSIE!
POOT
"SOMETIMES IT HAPPENS SO FAST...
HOPS NEEDS A PARTNER FOR SWING DANCING... MAY I BORROW THIS?
"...BEFORE I CAN EVEN RESPOND...
SLURP
"...THE DAMAGE IS DONE."

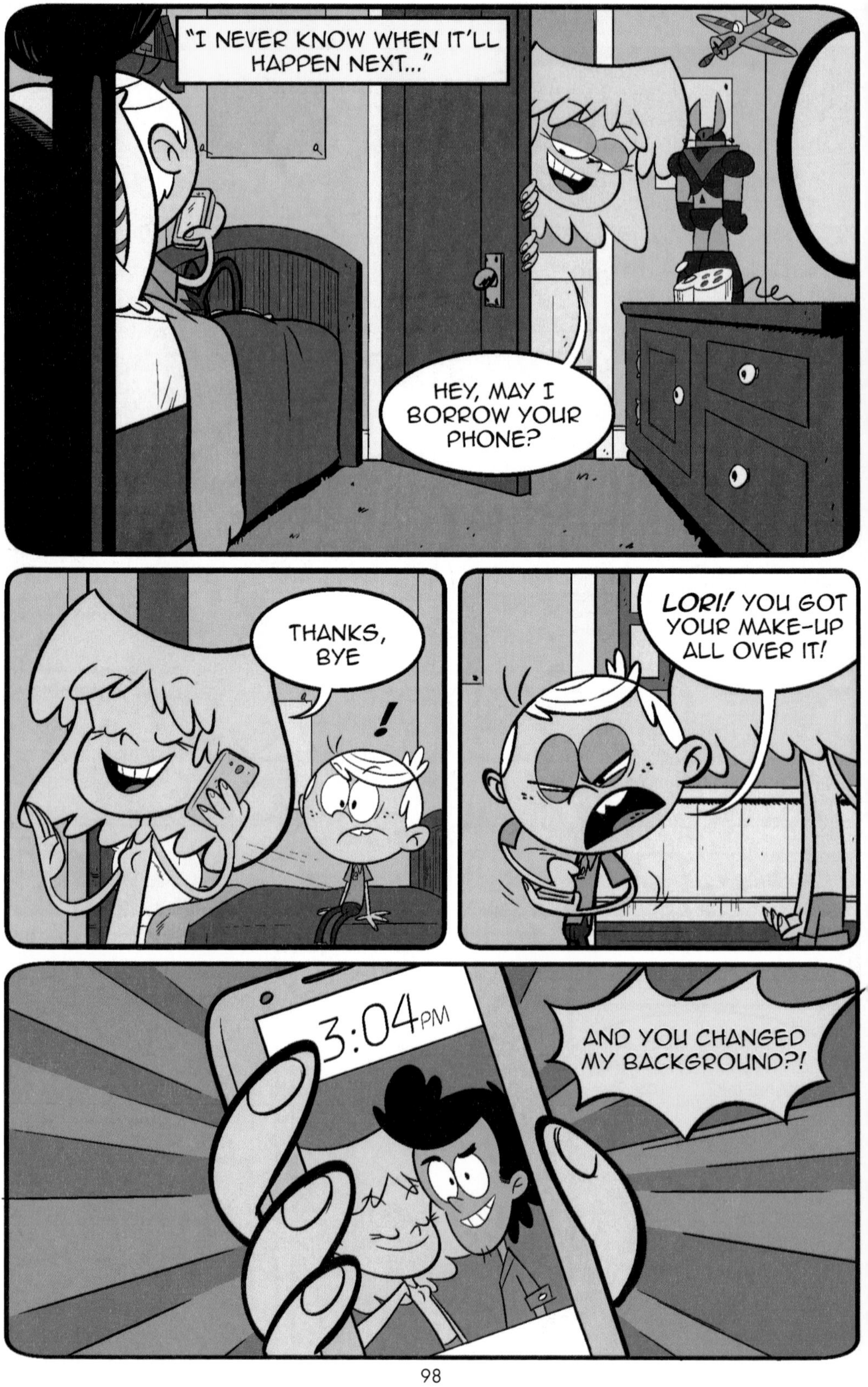
"I NEVER KNOW WHEN IT'LL HAPPEN NEXT..."
HEY, MAY I BORROW YOUR PHONE?
THANKS, BYE
!
LORI! YOU GOT YOUR MAKE-UP ALL OVER IT!
3:04PM
AND YOU CHANGED MY BACKGROUND?!

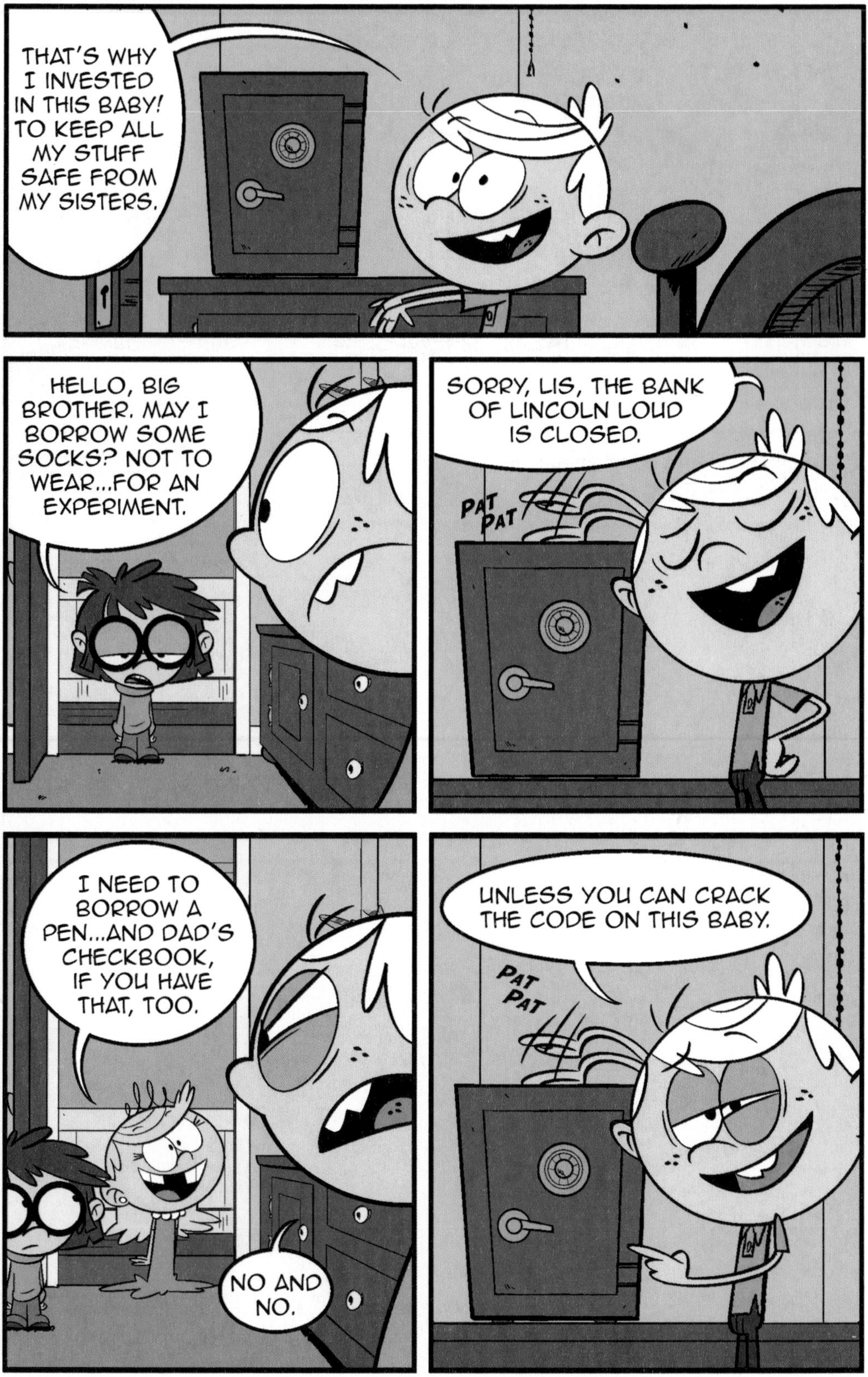
THAT'S WHY I INVESTED IN THIS BABY! TO KEEP ALL MY STUFF SAFE FROM MY SISTERS.
HELLO, BIG BROTHER. MAY I BORROW SOME SOCKS? NOT TO WEAR...FOR AN EXPERIMENT.
SORRY, LIS, THE BANK OF LINCOLN LOUD IS CLOSED.
PAT PAT
I NEED TO BORROW A PEN...AND DAD'S CHECKBOOK, IF YOU HAVE THAT, TOO.
NO AND NO.
UNLESS YOU CAN CRACK THE CODE ON THIS BABY.
PAT PAT

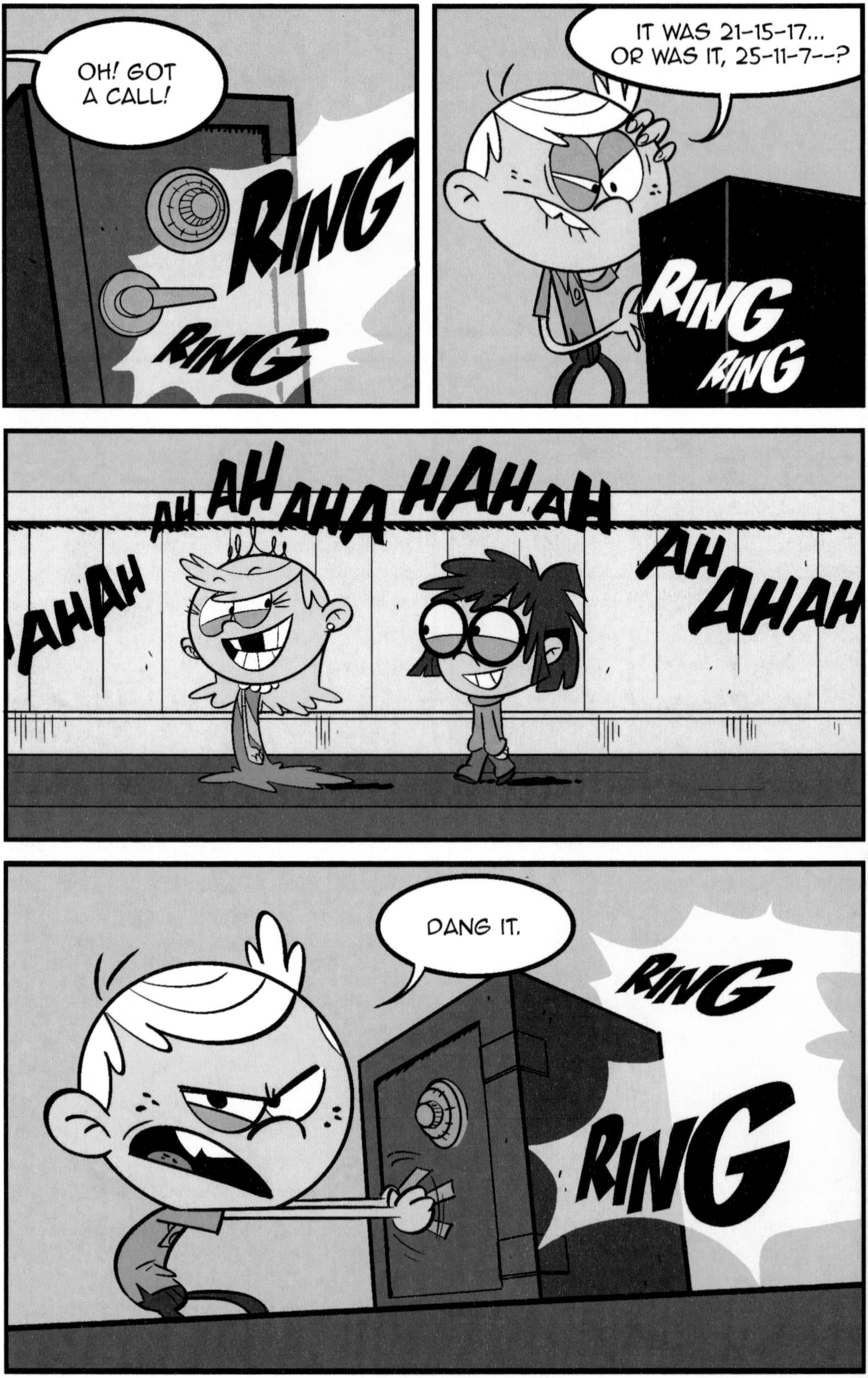
OH! GOT A CALL!
RING
RING
IT WAS 21-15-17... OR WAS IT, 25-11-7--?
RING
RING
AHAH
AH AH AHA HAH AH
AH
AHAH
DANG IT.
RING
RING

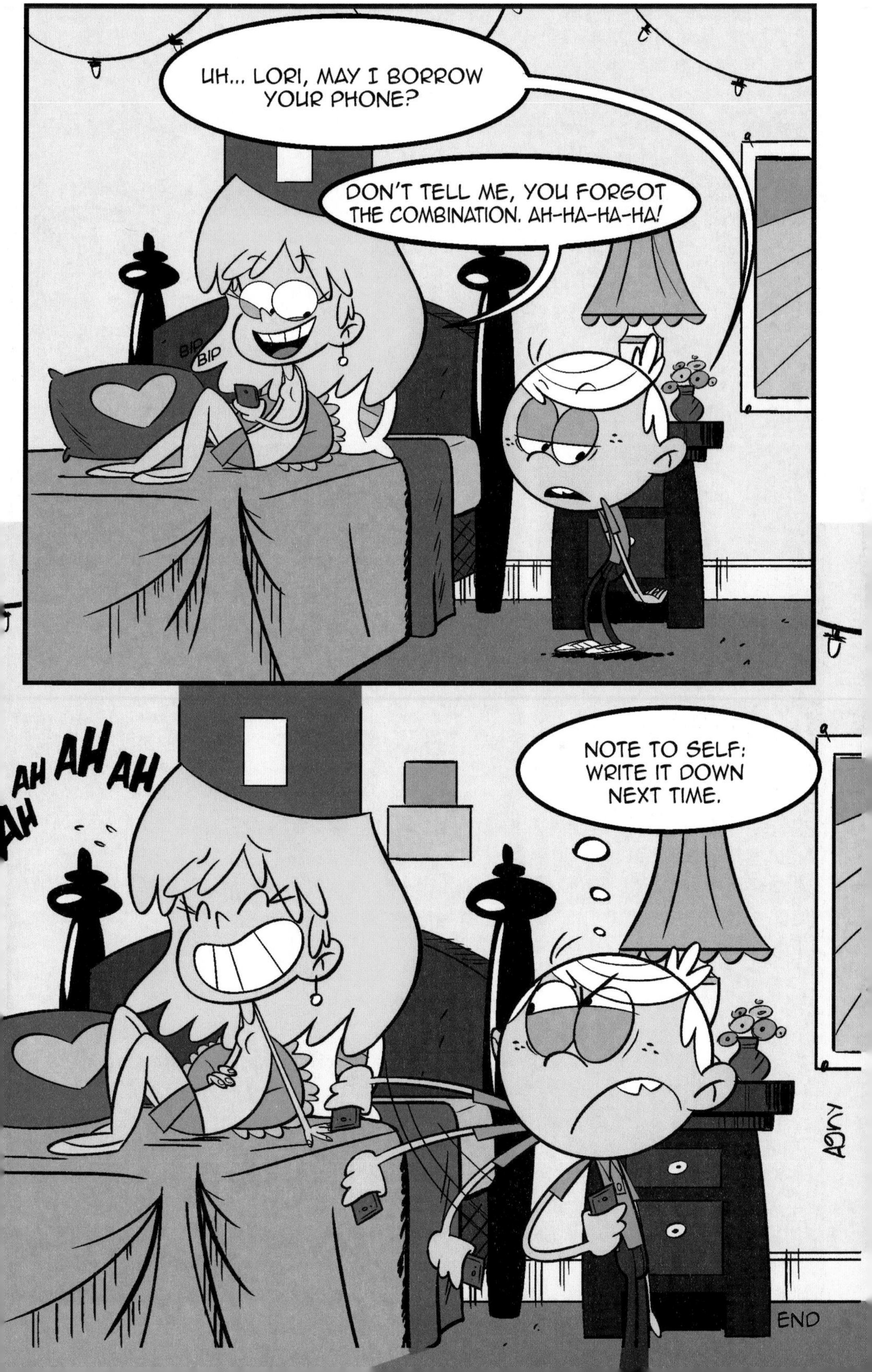
UH... LORI, MAY I BORROW YOUR PHONE?
DON'T TELL ME, YOU FORGOT THE COMBINATION. AH-HA-HA-HA!
BIP BIP
AH AH AH AH AH
NOTE TO SELF: WRITE IT DOWN NEXT TIME.
END

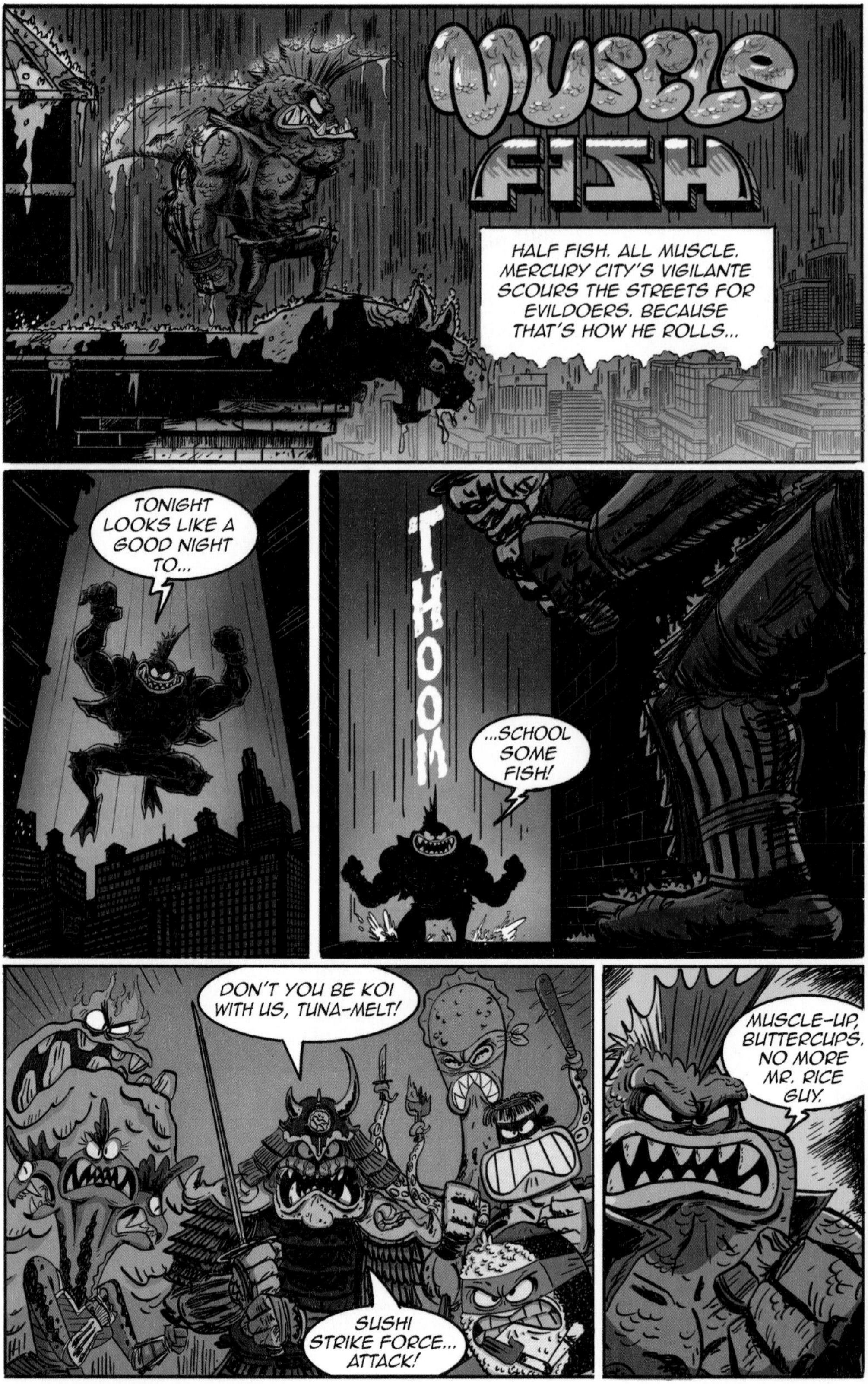
MUSCLE FISH
HALF FISH. ALL MUSCLE. MERCURY CITY'S VIGILANTE SCOURS THE STREETS FOR EVILDOERS. BECAUSE THAT'S HOW HE ROLLS...
TONIGHT LOOKS LIKE A GOOD NIGHT TO...
THOOM
...SCHOOL SOME FISH!
DON'T YOU BE KOI WITH US, TUNA-MELT!
SUSHI STRIKE FORCE... ATTACK!
MUSCLE-UP, BUTTERCUPS. NO MORE MR. RICE GUY.

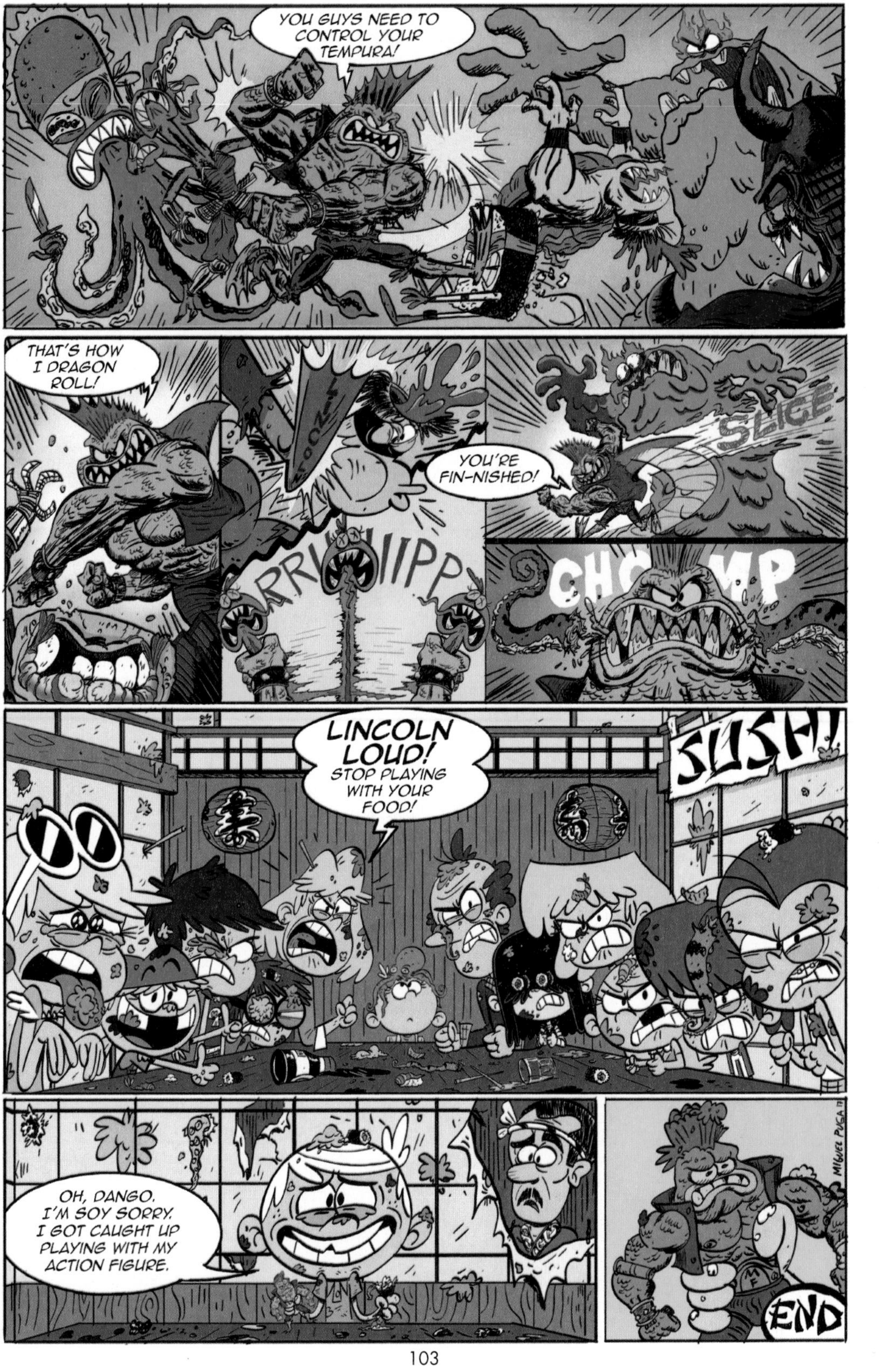

YOU GUYS NEED TO CONTROL YOUR TEMPURA!
THAT'S HOW I DRAGON ROLL!
YOU'RE FIN-NISHED!
SLICE
RRIIIIPP
CHOMP
LINCOLN LOUD! STOP PLAYING WITH YOUR FOOD!
SUSHI
OH, DANGO. I'M SOY SORRY. I GOT CAUGHT UP PLAYING WITH MY ACTION FIGURE.
MIGUEL PUGA
END

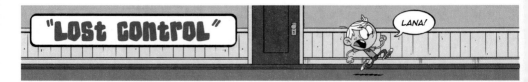

"LOST CONTROL"

LANA!

SCRATCH SCRATCH

LANA, DO YOU KNOW WHERE THE REMOTE IS?

ITCH ITCH ITCH

UHH...NOPE!

I CAN TELL YOU'RE LYING!

POW

SOK

POKE

SORRY, LINCOLN, I NEED IT!

IT'S MY BACK-SCRATCHER!

BUT, LANA, "ARGGH!" IS COMING ON!

WELL, I ROLLED IN POISON IVY SO MY BACK'S REALLY ITCHY.

SCRATCH SCRATCH

HMMM, THAT GIVES ME AN IDEA!

SCRATCH SCRATCH

ARGGH!

AHHH. NOW THIS IS MORE LIKE IT.

I'LL SAY! HEY, A LITTLE TO THE LEFT. YEAH THAT'S THE SPOT!

CONGRATULATIONS! YOU FOUND THE REMOTE!

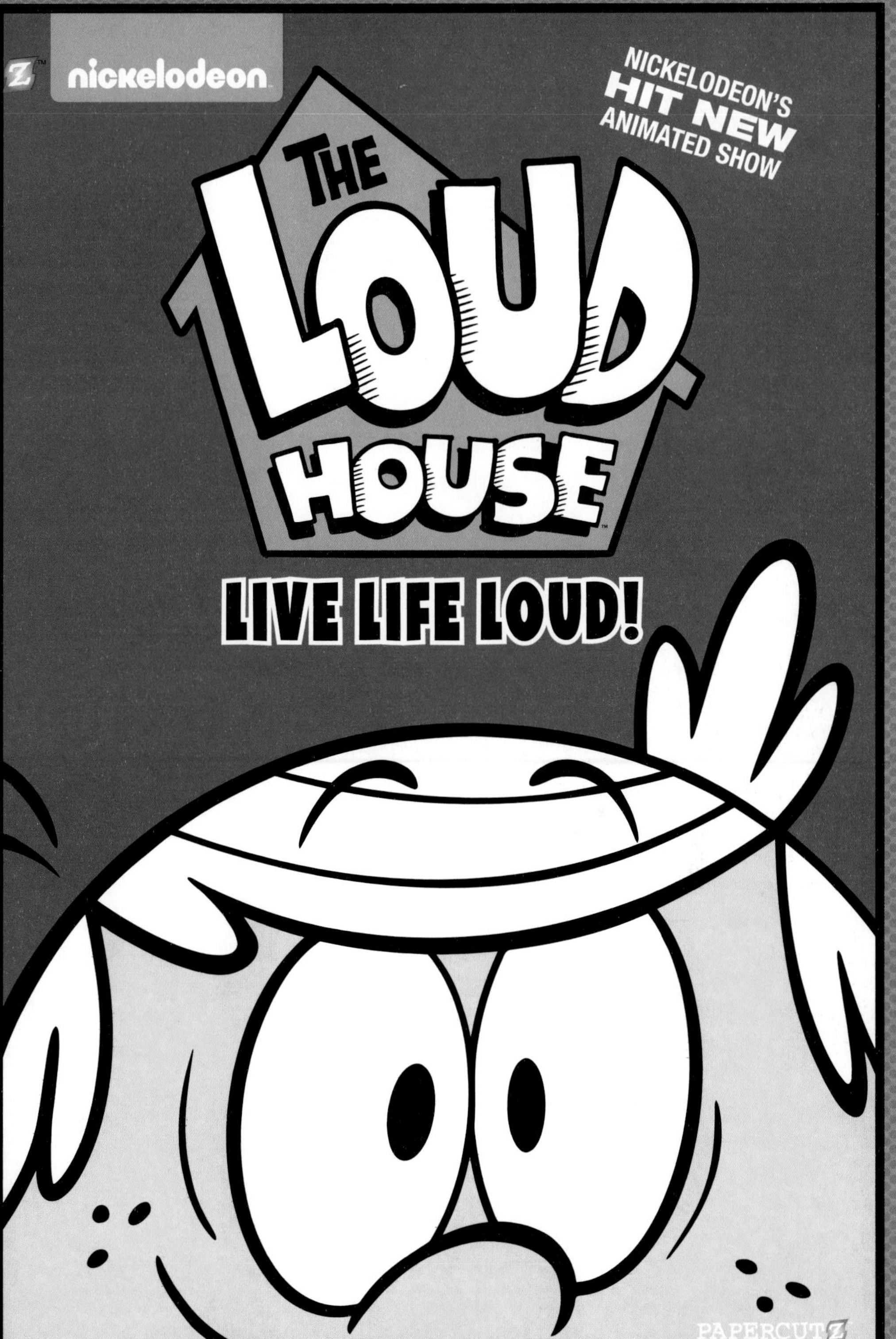
nickelodeon
NICKELODEON'S HIT NEW ANIMATED SHOW
THE LOUD HOUSE
LIVE LIFE LOUD!
PAPERCUTZ

THE LOUD HOUSE #3 Cover by Chris Savino

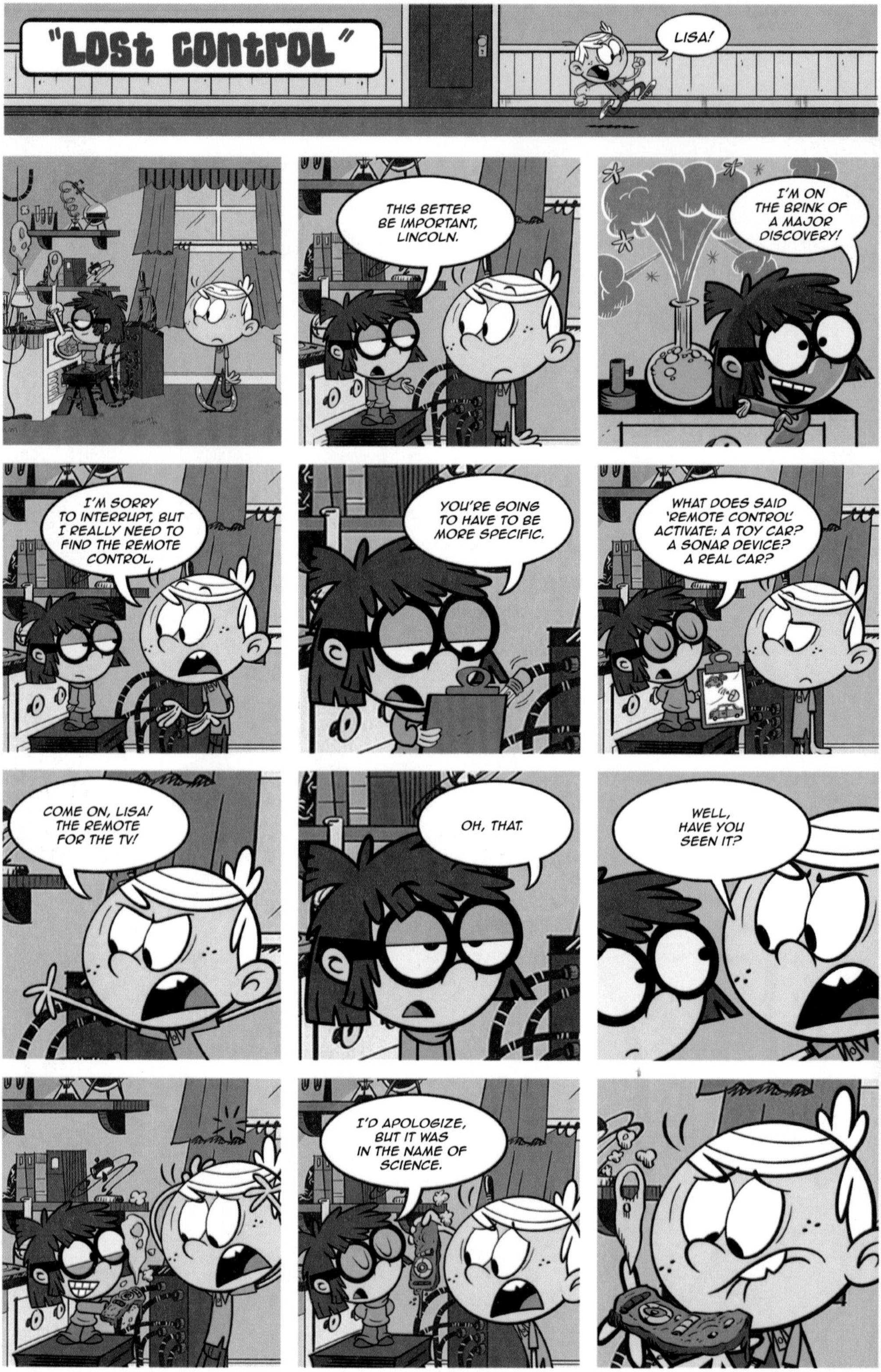
"LOST CONTROL"
LISA!
THIS BETTER BE IMPORTANT, LINCOLN.
I'M ON THE BRINK OF A MAJOR DISCOVERY!
I'M SORRY TO INTERRUPT, BUT I REALLY NEED TO FIND THE REMOTE CONTROL.
YOU'RE GOING TO HAVE TO BE MORE SPECIFIC.
WHAT DOES SAID 'REMOTE CONTROL' ACTIVATE: A TOY CAR? A SONAR DEVICE? A REAL CAR?
COME ON, LISA! THE REMOTE FOR THE TV!
OH, THAT.
WELL, HAVE YOU SEEN IT?
I'D APOLOGIZE, BUT IT WAS IN THE NAME OF SCIENCE.

OH, NO! YOU'VE HIT A DEAD END. TO TRY AGAIN, GO TALK TO LORI ON PAGE 7.

"PRIVATE EYES"

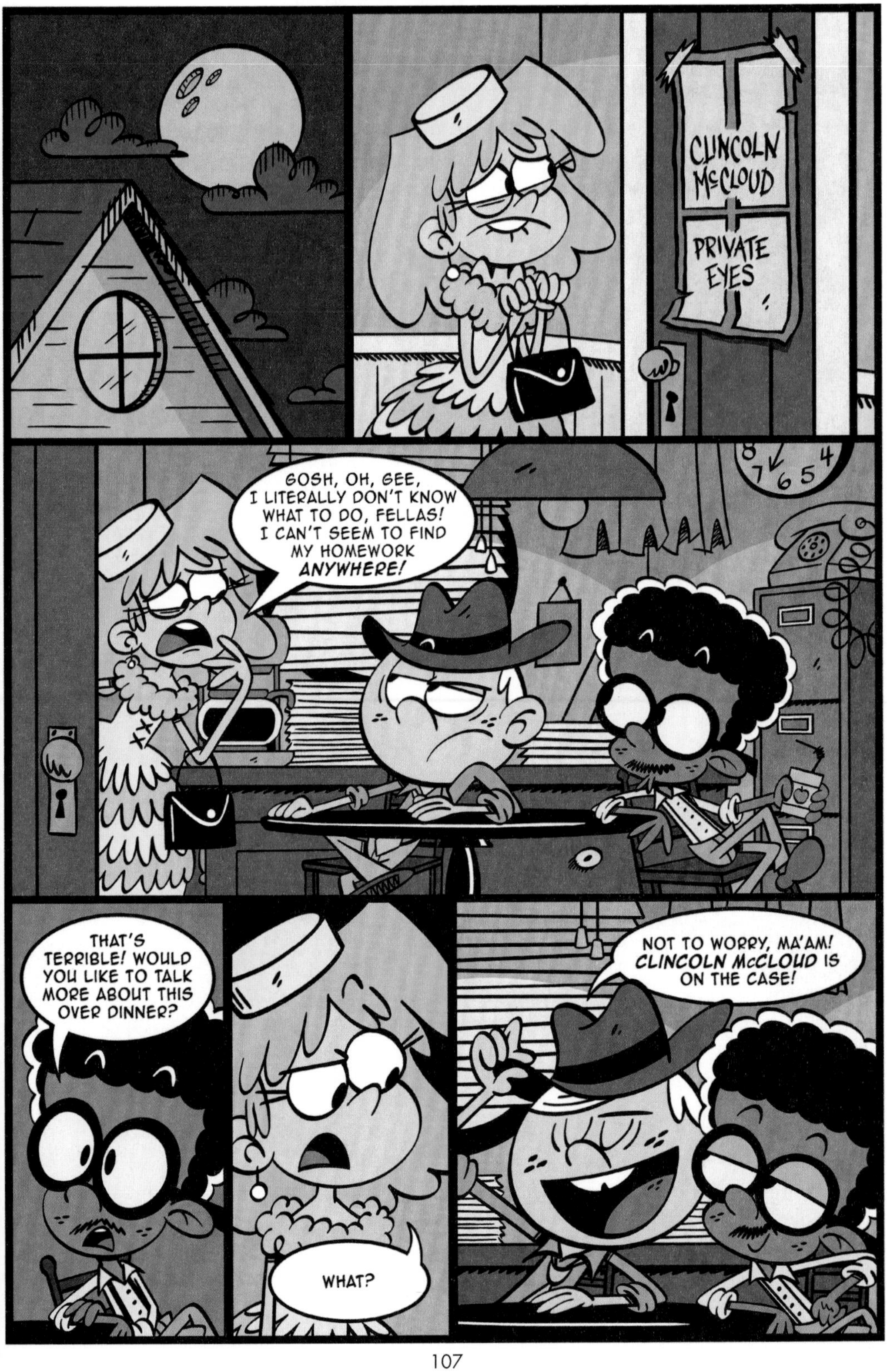
CLINCOLN McCLOUD
PRIVATE EYES
GOSH, OH, GEE, I LITERALLY DON'T KNOW WHAT TO DO, FELLAS! I CAN'T SEEM TO FIND MY HOMEWORK *ANYWHERE!*
THAT'S TERRIBLE! WOULD YOU LIKE TO TALK MORE ABOUT THIS OVER DINNER?
WHAT?
NOT TO WORRY, MA'AM! *CLINCOLN McCLOUD* IS ON THE CASE!

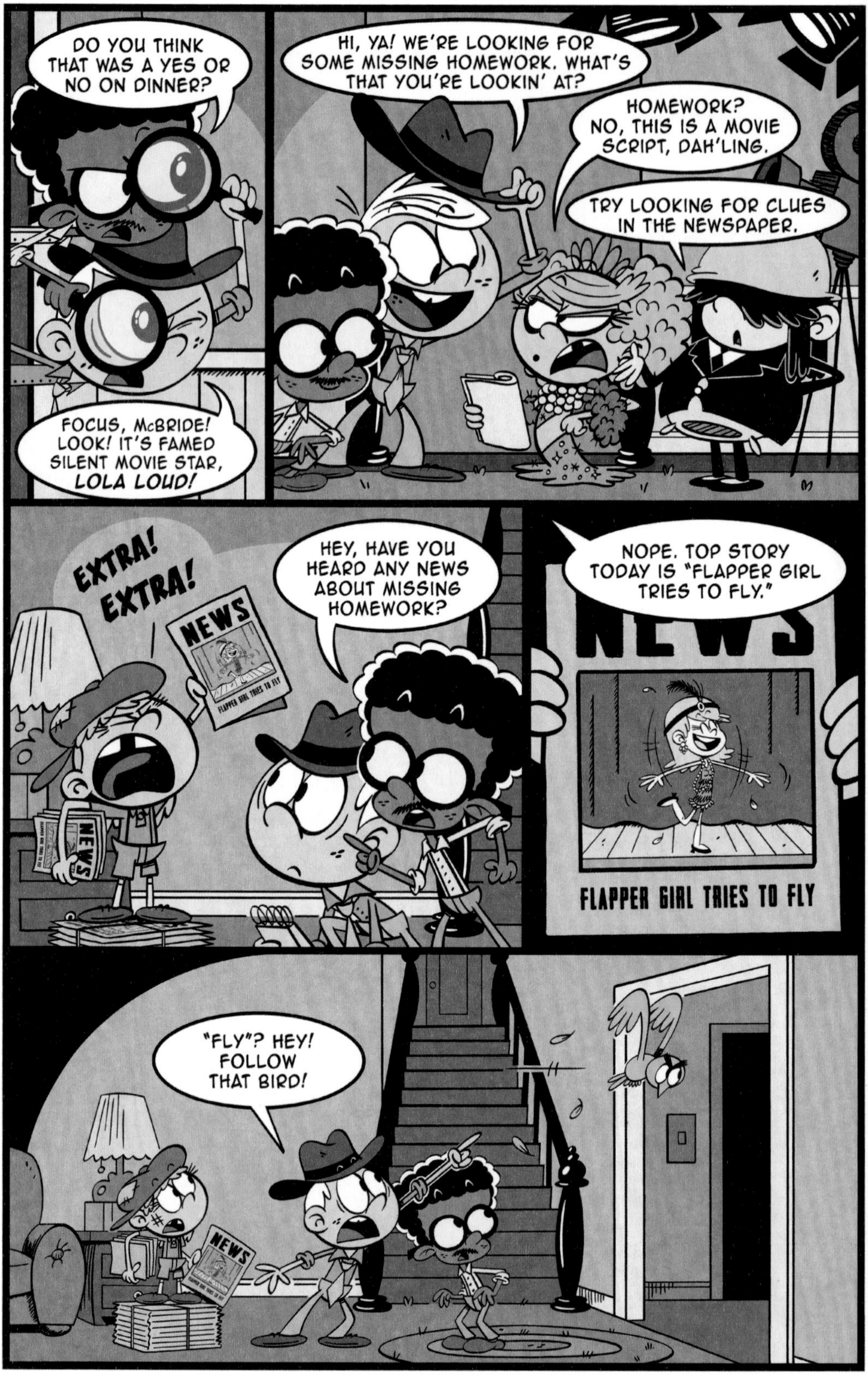
DO YOU THINK THAT WAS A YES OR NO ON DINNER?
FOCUS, McBRIDE! LOOK! IT'S FAMED SILENT MOVIE STAR, LOLA LOUD!
HI, YA! WE'RE LOOKING FOR SOME MISSING HOMEWORK. WHAT'S THAT YOU'RE LOOKIN' AT?
HOMEWORK? NO, THIS IS A MOVIE SCRIPT, DAH'LING.
TRY LOOKING FOR CLUES IN THE NEWSPAPER.
EXTRA! EXTRA!
NEWS
FLAPPER GIRL TRIES TO FLY
HEY, HAVE YOU HEARD ANY NEWS ABOUT MISSING HOMEWORK?
NOPE. TOP STORY TODAY IS "FLAPPER GIRL TRIES TO FLY."
NEWS
FLAPPER GIRL TRIES TO FLY
"FLY"? HEY! FOLLOW THAT BIRD!
NEWS

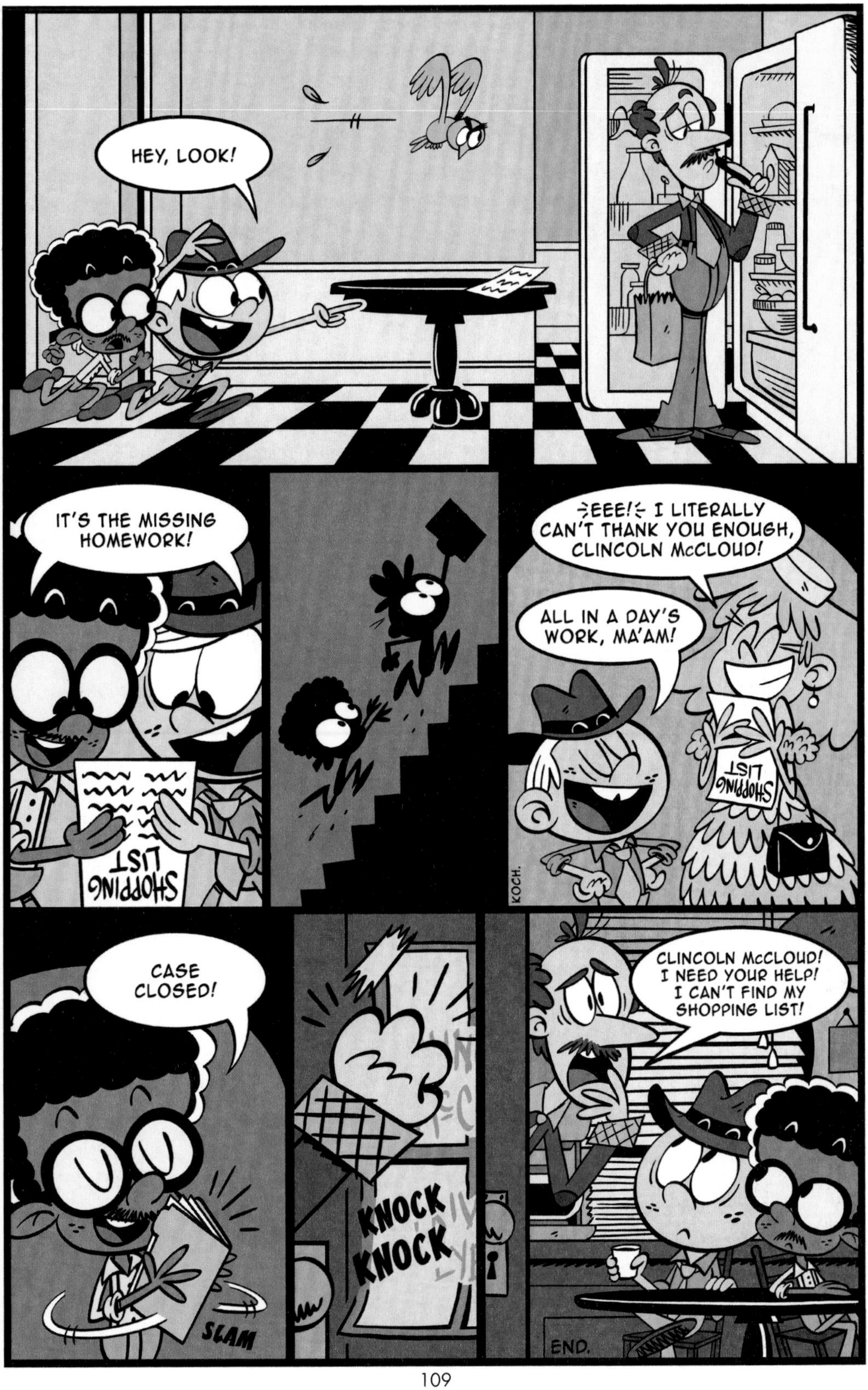
HEY, LOOK!
IT'S THE MISSING HOMEWORK!
SHOPPING LIST
EEEE! I LITERALLY CAN'T THANK YOU ENOUGH, CLINCOLN McCLOUD!
ALL IN A DAY'S WORK, MA'AM!
SHOPPING LIST
KOCH.
CASE CLOSED!
SLAM
KNOCK KNOCK
CLINCOLN McCLOUD! I NEED YOUR HELP! I CAN'T FIND MY SHOPPING LIST!
END.

"MY YARD, MY PROPERTY"

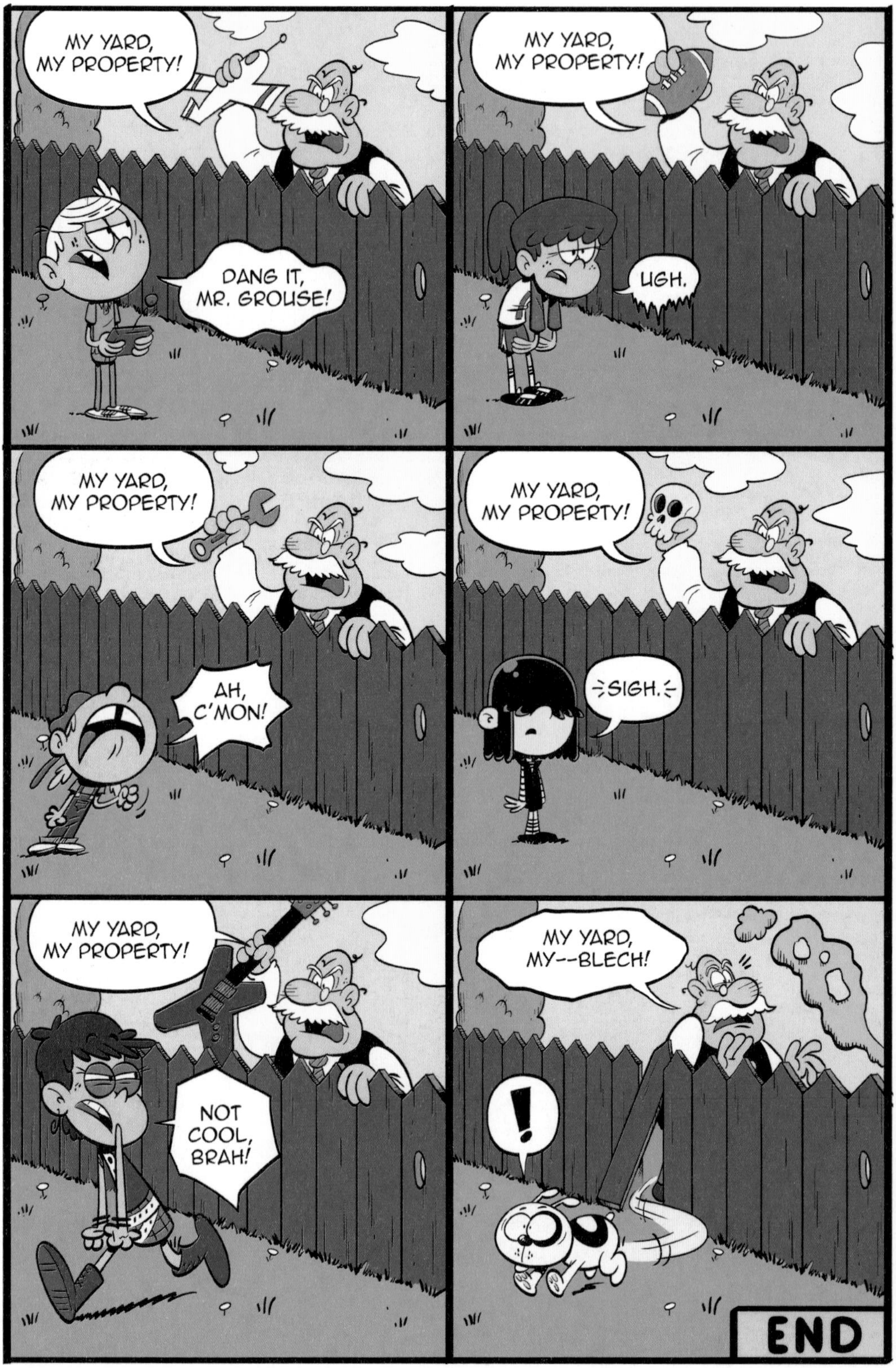
MY YARD, MY PROPERTY!
DANG IT, MR. GROUSE!
MY YARD, MY PROPERTY!
UGH.
MY YARD, MY PROPERTY!
AH, C'MON!
MY YARD, MY PROPERTY!
SIGH.
MY YARD, MY PROPERTY!
NOT COOL, BRAH!
MY YARD, MY--BLECH!
!
END

"A PIRATE'S LIFE FOR CJ"

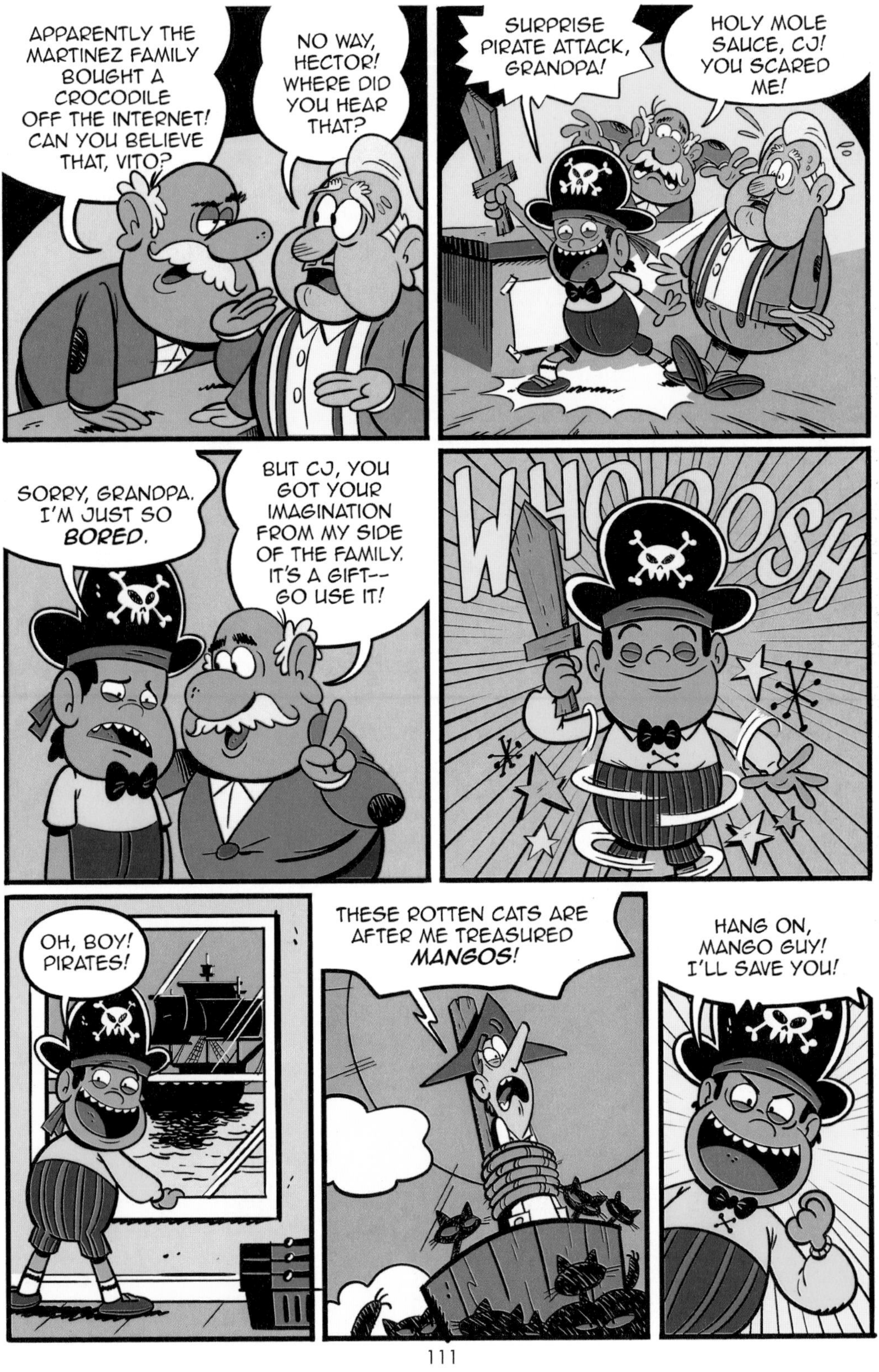
APPARENTLY THE MARTINEZ FAMILY BOUGHT A CROCODILE OFF THE INTERNET! CAN YOU BELIEVE THAT, VITO?
NO WAY, HECTOR! WHERE DID YOU HEAR THAT?
SURPRISE PIRATE ATTACK, GRANDPA!
HOLY MOLE SAUCE, CJ! YOU SCARED ME!
SORRY, GRANDPA. I'M JUST SO BORED.
BUT CJ, YOU GOT YOUR IMAGINATION FROM MY SIDE OF THE FAMILY. IT'S A GIFT-- GO USE IT!
WHOOOOSH
OH, BOY! PIRATES!
THESE ROTTEN CATS ARE AFTER ME TREASURED MANGOS!
HANG ON, MANGO GUY! I'LL SAVE YOU!

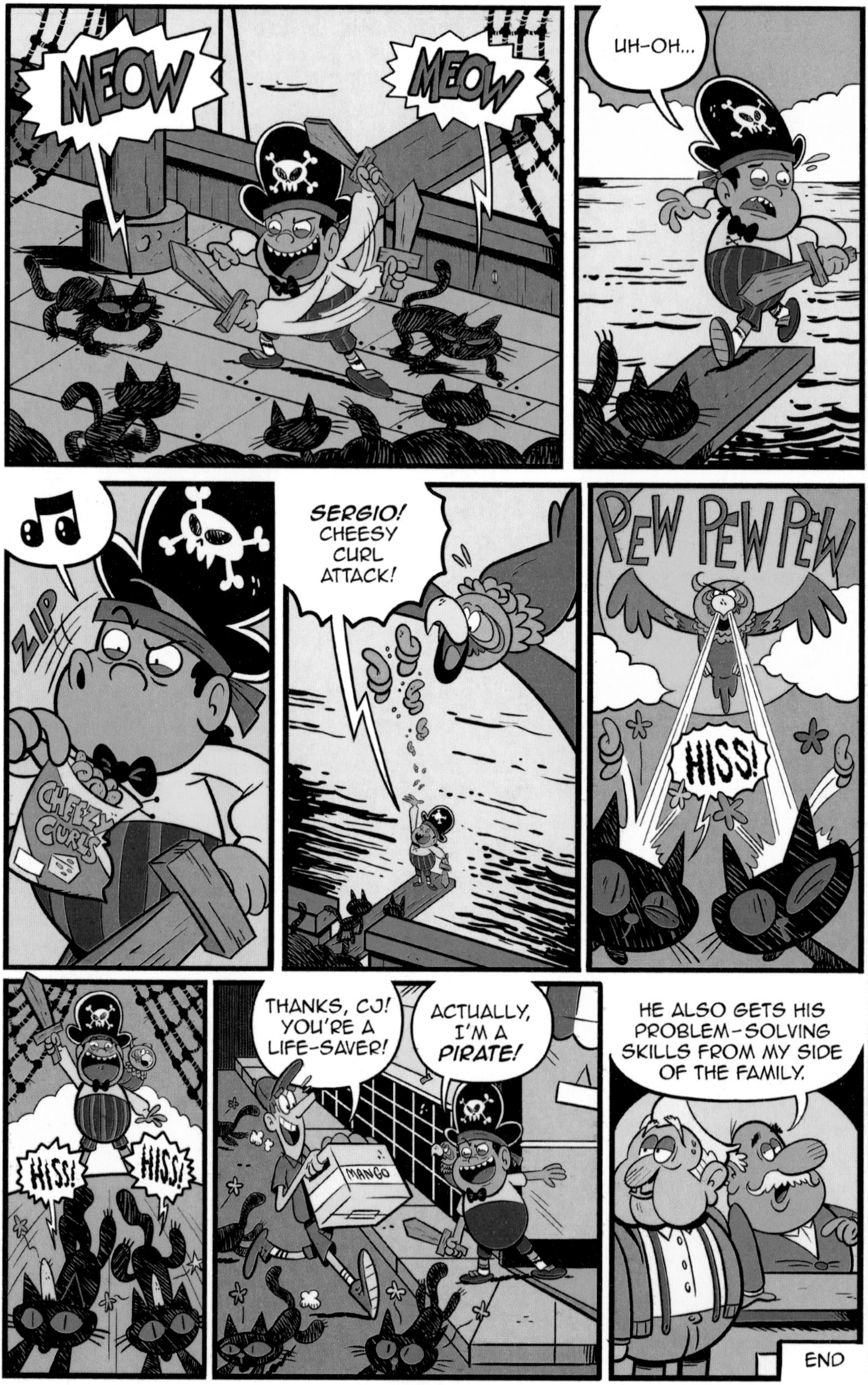
MEOW
MEOW
UH-OH...
ZIP
CHEEZY CURLS
SERGIO! CHEESY CURL ATTACK!
PEW PEW PEW
HISS!
HISS!
HISS!
THANKS, CJ! YOU'RE A LIFE-SAVER!
ACTUALLY, I'M A PIRATE!
MANGO
HE ALSO GETS HIS PROBLEM-SOLVING SKILLS FROM MY SIDE OF THE FAMILY.
END

"HICCUP HIJINKS"

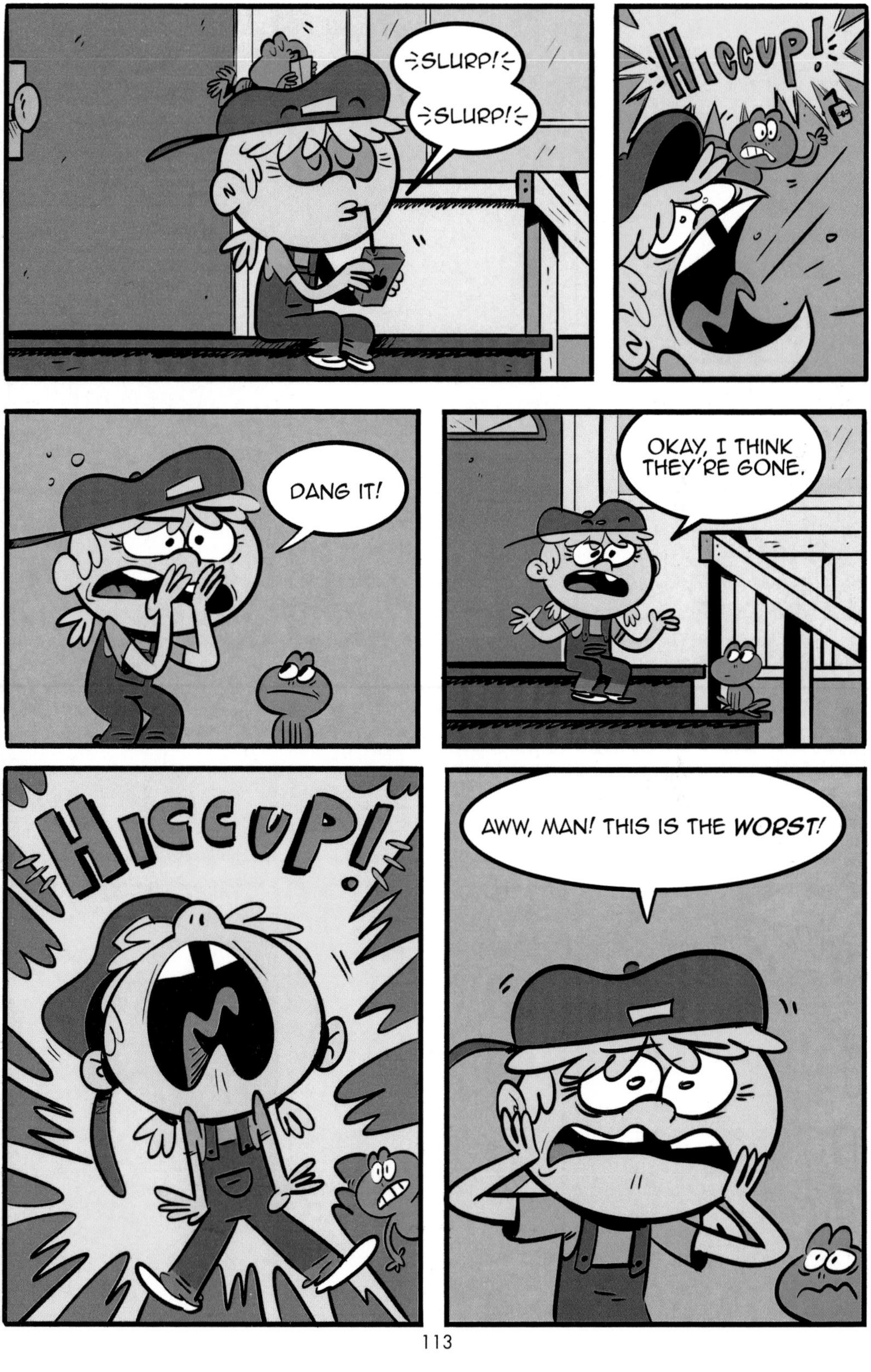
SLURP!
SLURP!
HICCUP!
DANG IT!
OKAY, I THINK THEY'RE GONE.
HICCUP!
AWW, MAN! THIS IS THE WORST!

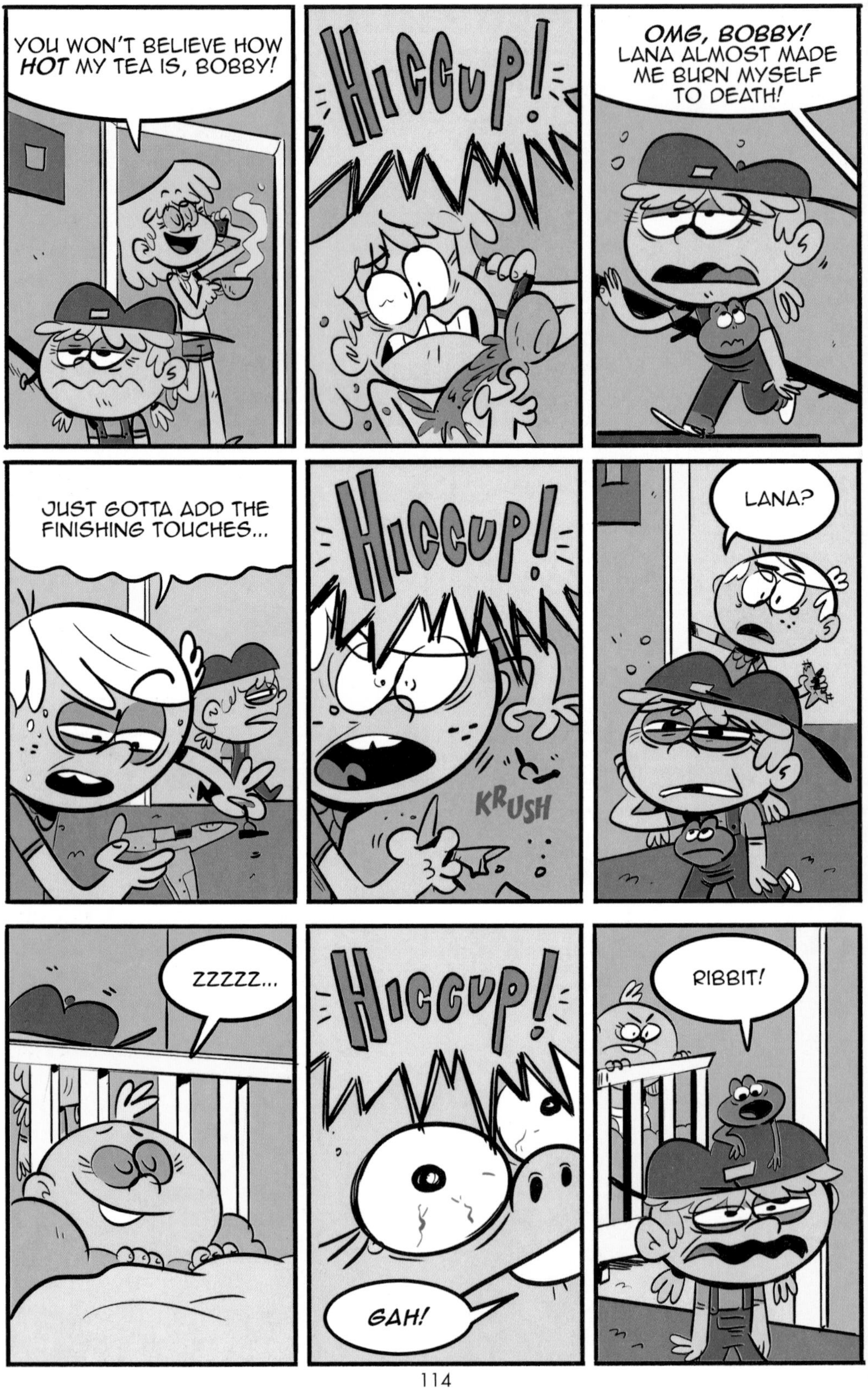
YOU WON'T BELIEVE HOW HOT MY TEA IS, BOBBY!
HICCUP!
OMG, BOBBY! LANA ALMOST MADE ME BURN MYSELF TO DEATH!
JUST GOTTA ADD THE FINISHING TOUCHES...
HICCUP!
KRUSH
LANA?
ZZZZZ...
HICCUP!
GAH!
RIBBIT!

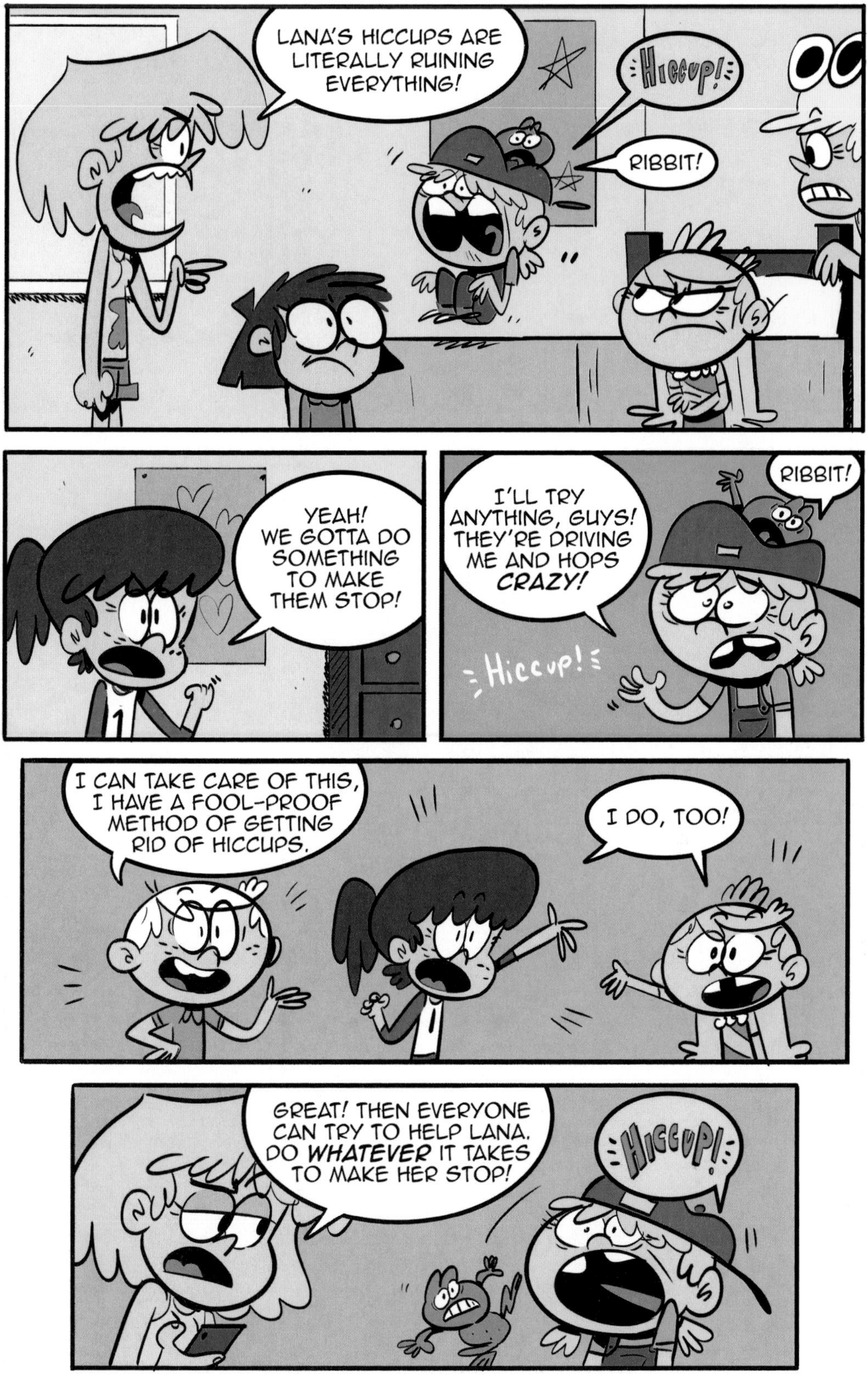
LANA'S HICCUPS ARE LITERALLY RUINING EVERYTHING!
HICCUP!
RIBBIT!
YEAH! WE GOTTA DO SOMETHING TO MAKE THEM STOP!
I'LL TRY ANYTHING, GUYS! THEY'RE DRIVING ME AND HOPS CRAZY!
RIBBIT!
Hiccup!
I CAN TAKE CARE OF THIS, I HAVE A FOOL-PROOF METHOD OF GETTING RID OF HICCUPS.
I DO, TOO!
GREAT! THEN EVERYONE CAN TRY TO HELP LANA. DO WHATEVER IT TAKES TO MAKE HER STOP!
HICCUP!

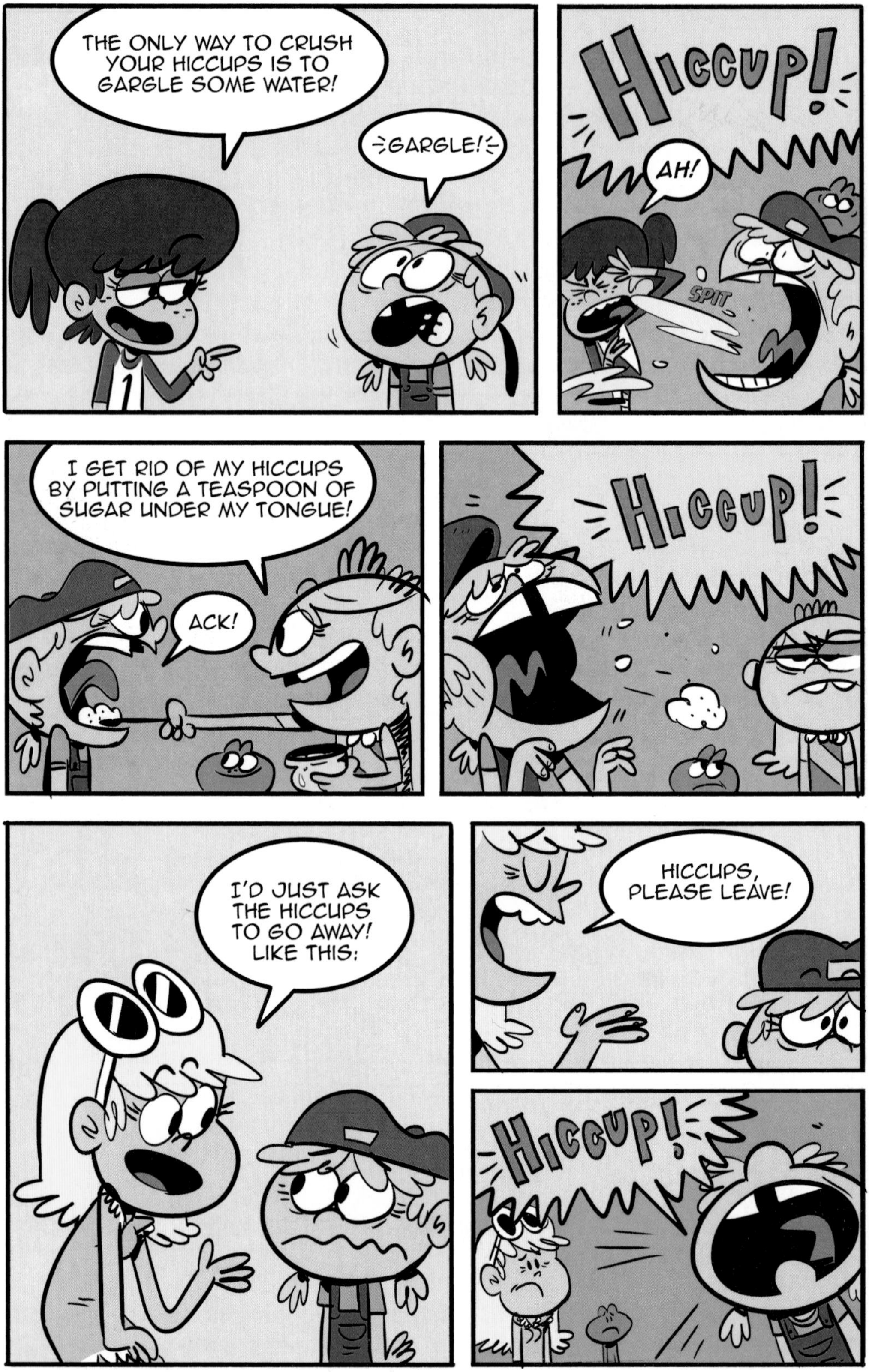
THE ONLY WAY TO CRUSH YOUR HICCUPS IS TO GARGLE SOME WATER!
GARGLE!
HICCUP!
AH!
SPIT
I GET RID OF MY HICCUPS BY PUTTING A TEASPOON OF SUGAR UNDER MY TONGUE!
ACK!
HICCUP!
I'D JUST ASK THE HICCUPS TO GO AWAY! LIKE THIS:
HICCUPS, PLEASE LEAVE!
HICCUP!

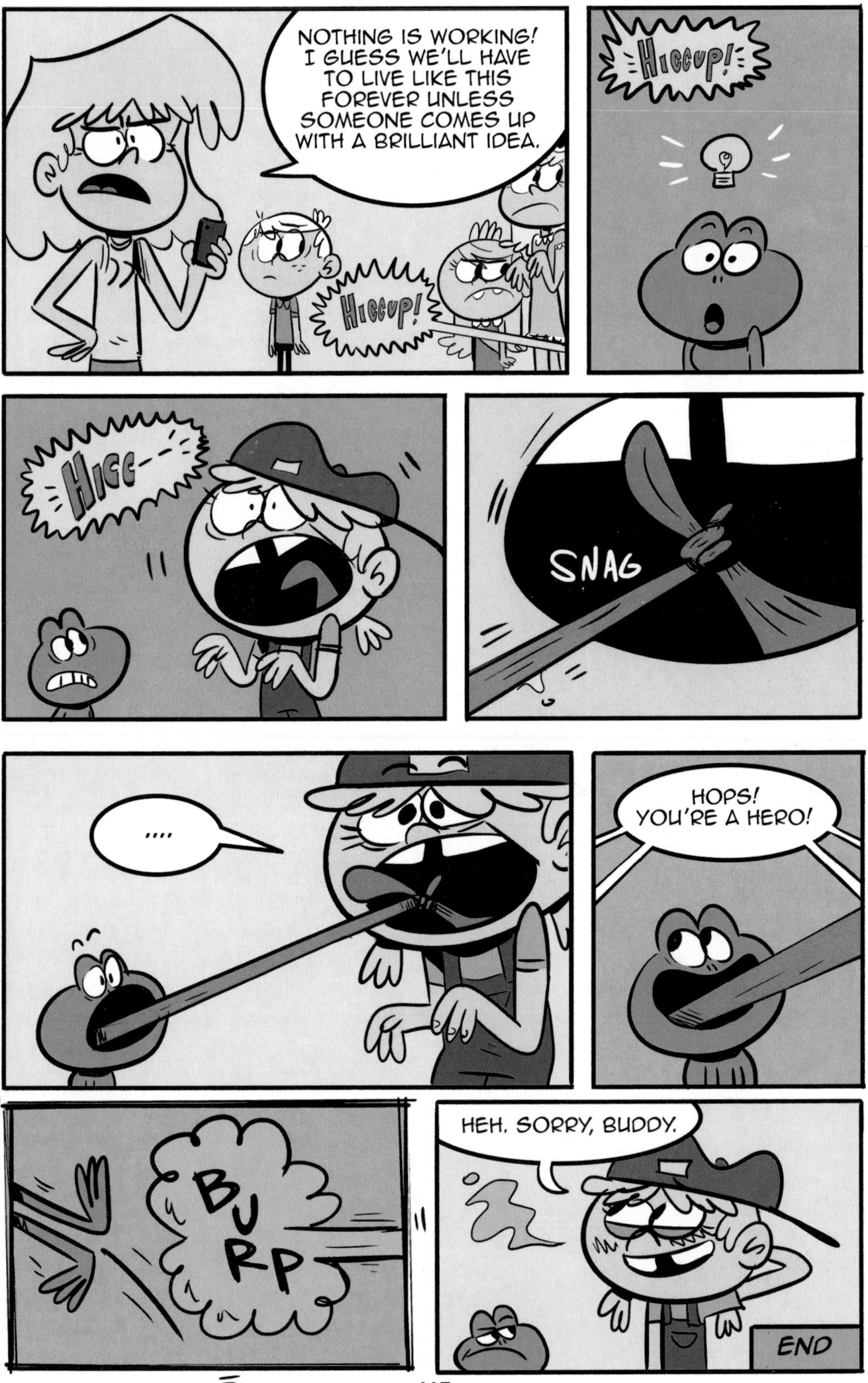
NOTHING IS WORKING! I GUESS WE'LL HAVE TO LIVE LIKE THIS FOREVER UNLESS SOMEONE COMES UP WITH A BRILLIANT IDEA.
HICCUP!
HICCUP!
HICC---
SNAG
....
HOPS! YOU'RE A HERO!
BURP
HEH. SORRY, BUDDY.
END

"MOM'S NIGHT IN"

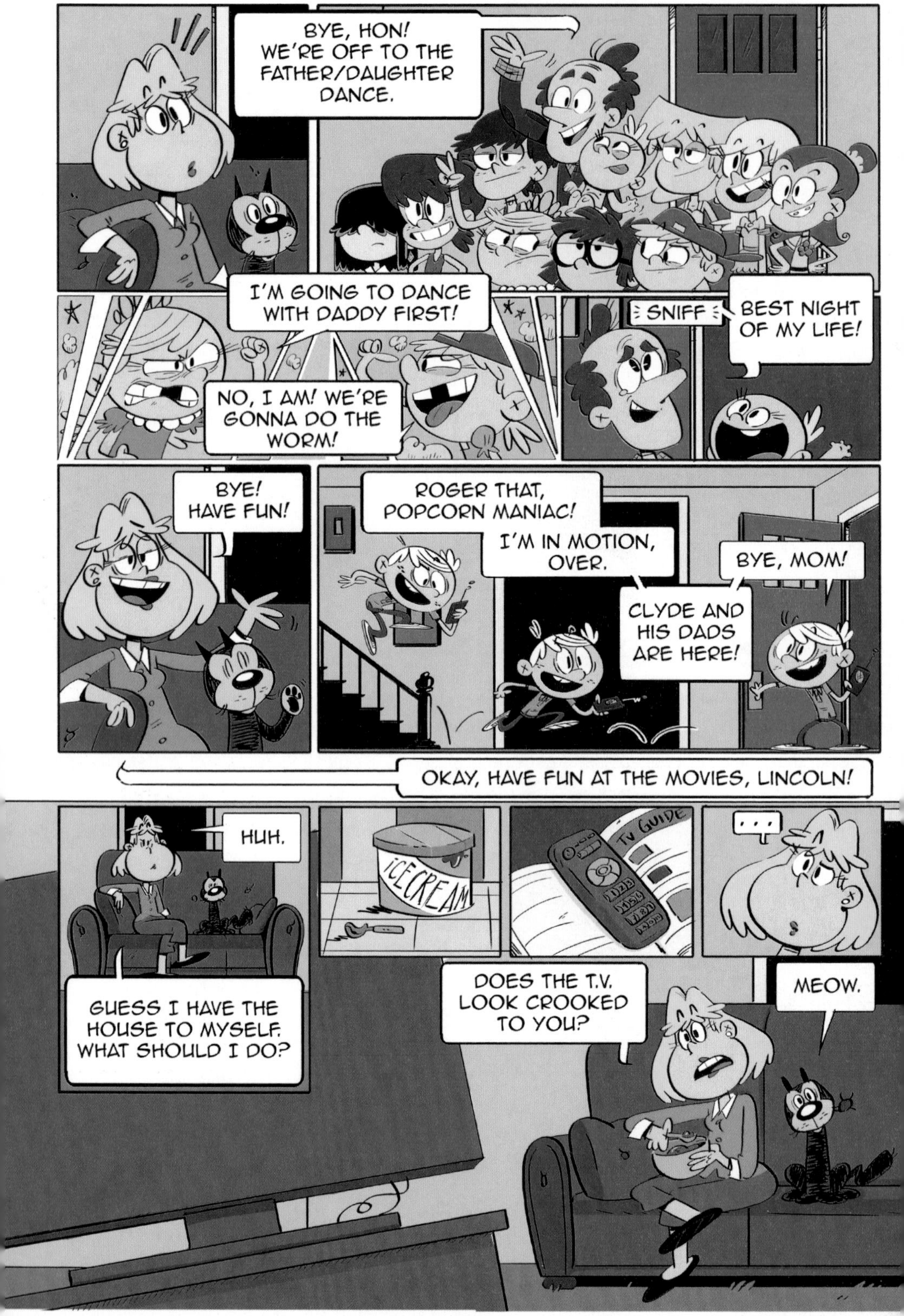
BYE, HON! WE'RE OFF TO THE FATHER/DAUGHTER DANCE.
I'M GOING TO DANCE WITH DADDY FIRST!
NO, I AM! WE'RE GONNA DO THE WORM!
SNIFF
BEST NIGHT OF MY LIFE!
BYE! HAVE FUN!
ROGER THAT, POPCORN MANIAC!
I'M IN MOTION, OVER.
CLYDE AND HIS DADS ARE HERE!
BYE, MOM!
OKAY, HAVE FUN AT THE MOVIES, LINCOLN!
HUH.
GUESS I HAVE THE HOUSE TO MYSELF. WHAT SHOULD I DO?
ICE CREAM
TV GUIDE
...
DOES THE T.V. LOOK CROOKED TO YOU?
MEOW.

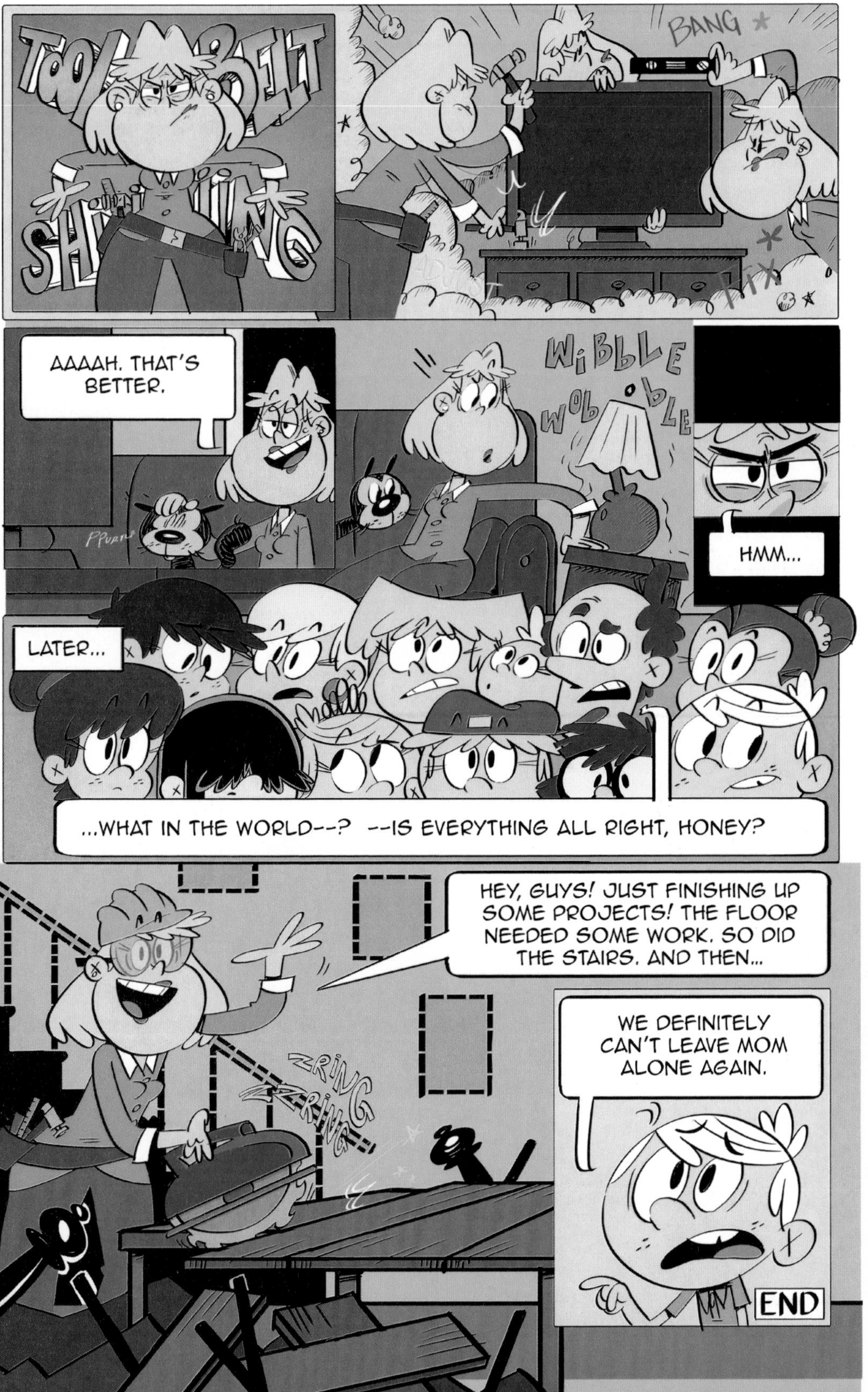
BANG
AAAAH. THAT'S BETTER.
WIBBLE
WOBBLE
HMM...
LATER...
...WHAT IN THE WORLD--? --IS EVERYTHING ALL RIGHT, HONEY?
HEY, GUYS! JUST FINISHING UP SOME PROJECTS! THE FLOOR NEEDED SOME WORK. SO DID THE STAIRS. AND THEN...
ZRING
ZRING
WE DEFINITELY CAN'T LEAVE MOM ALONE AGAIN.
END

"GOTH PERKS"

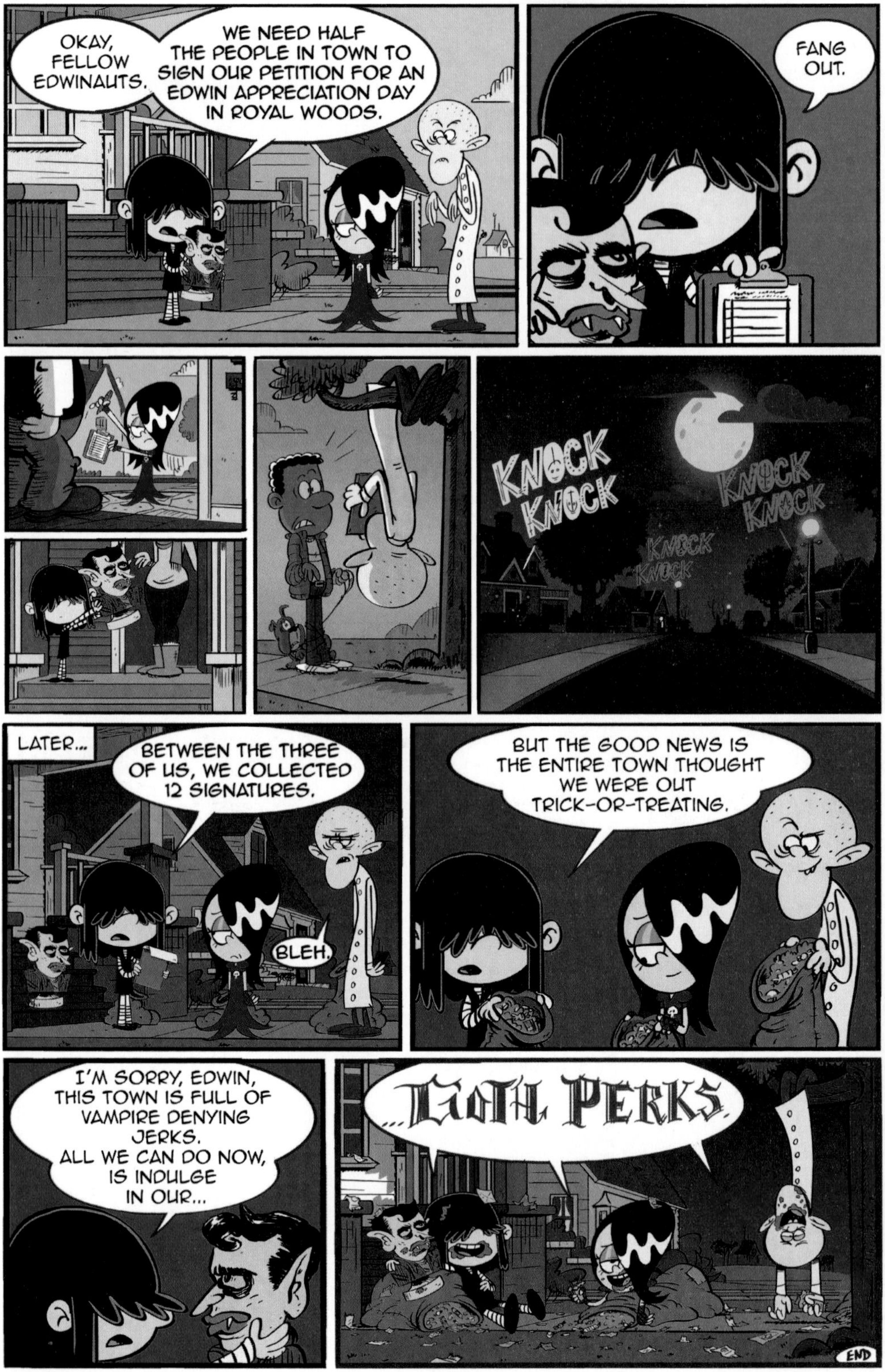

OKAY, FELLOW EDWINAUTS.
WE NEED HALF THE PEOPLE IN TOWN TO SIGN OUR PETITION FOR AN EDWIN APPRECIATION DAY IN ROYAL WOODS.
FANG OUT.
KNOCK KNOCK
KNOCK KNOCK
KNOCK KNOCK
LATER...
BETWEEN THE THREE OF US, WE COLLECTED 12 SIGNATURES.
BLEH.
BUT THE GOOD NEWS IS THE ENTIRE TOWN THOUGHT WE WERE OUT TRICK-OR-TREATING.
I'M SORRY, EDWIN, THIS TOWN IS FULL OF VAMPIRE DENYING JERKS. ALL WE CAN DO NOW, IS INDULGE IN OUR...
...GOTH PERKS
END

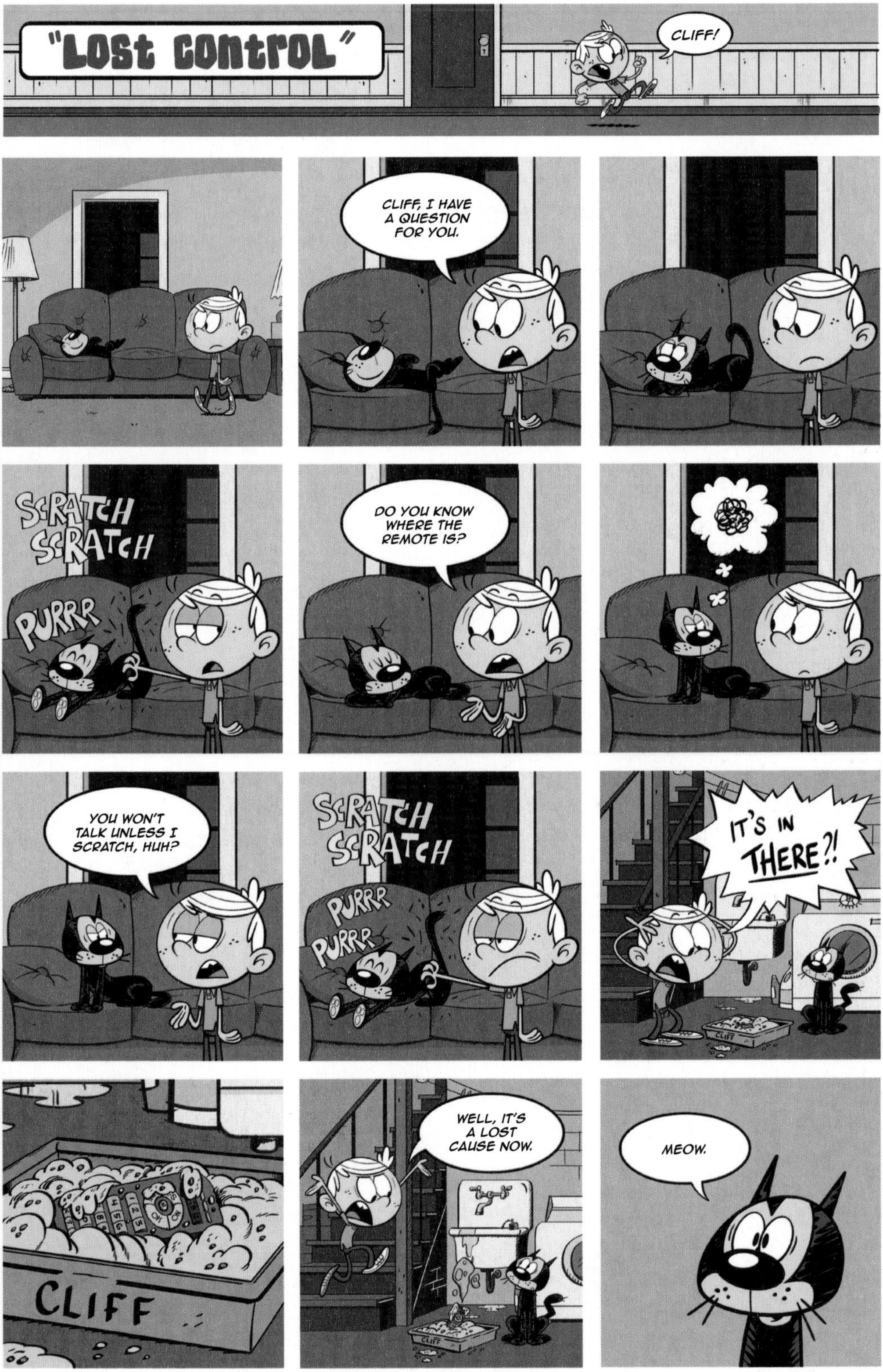
"LOST CONTROL"
CLIFF!
CLIFF, I HAVE A QUESTION FOR YOU.
SCRATCH SCRATCH
PURRR
DO YOU KNOW WHERE THE REMOTE IS?
YOU WON'T TALK UNLESS I SCRATCH, HUH?
SCRATCH SCRATCH
PURRR PURRR
IT'S IN THERE?!
CLIFF
WELL, IT'S A LOST CAUSE NOW.
MEOW.

OH, NO! YOU'VE HIT A DEAD END. TO TRY AGAIN, GO TALK TO LORI ON PAGE 7.

"BABY BROTHER"

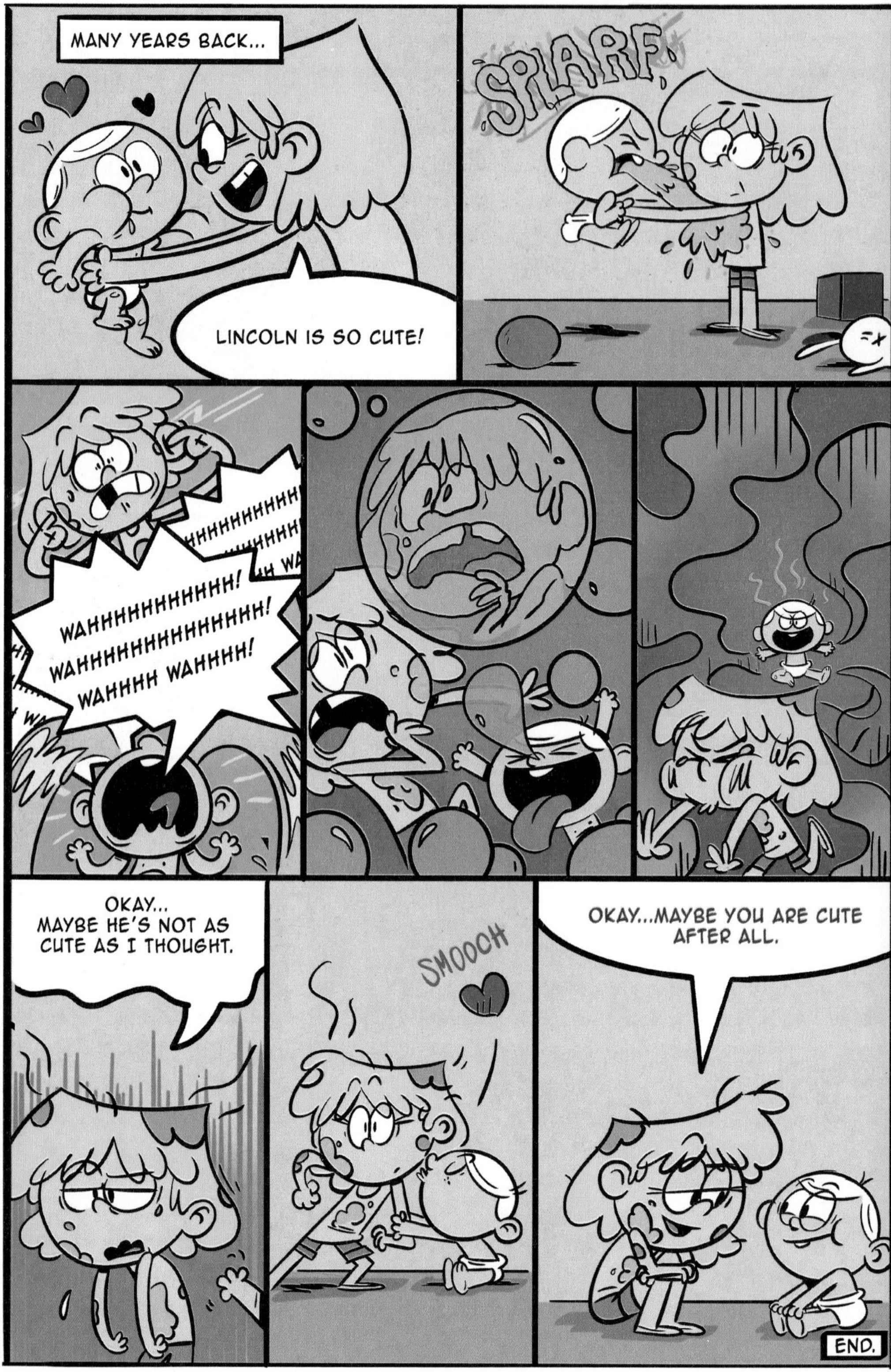
MANY YEARS BACK...
LINCOLN IS SO CUTE!
SPLARF
WAHHHHHHHHHHHH! WAHHHHHHHHHHHHHHH! WAHHHH WAHHHH!
OKAY... MAYBE HE'S NOT AS CUTE AS I THOUGHT.
SMOOCH
OKAY...MAYBE YOU ARE CUTE AFTER ALL.
END.

"BABES IN THE CITY"

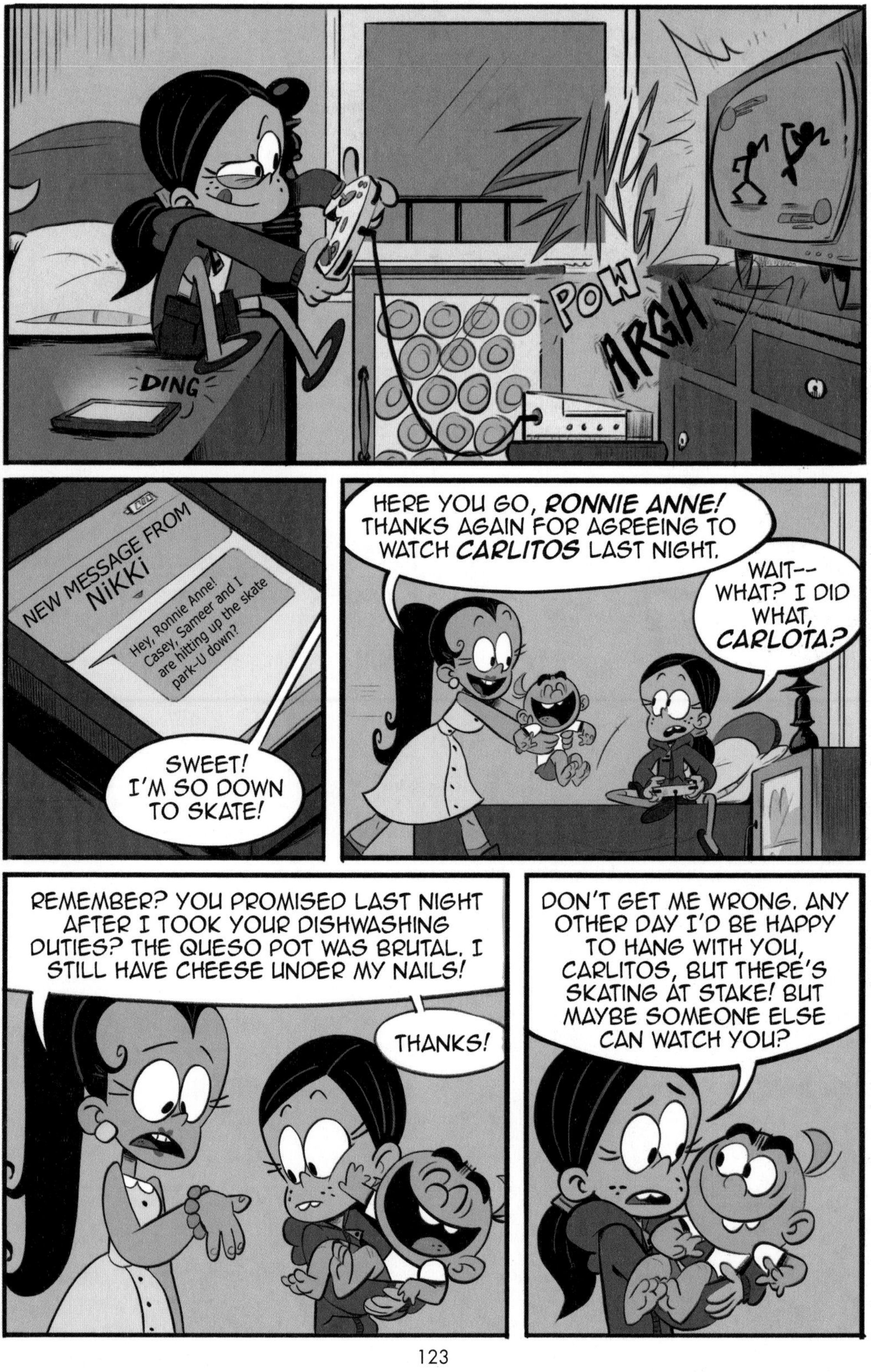

ZING
ZING
POW
ARGH
DING
NEW MESSAGE FROM
NiKKi
Hey, Ronnie Anne! Casey, Sameer and I are hitting up the skate park-U down?
SWEET! I'M SO DOWN TO SKATE!
HERE YOU GO, RONNIE ANNE! THANKS AGAIN FOR AGREEING TO WATCH CARLITOS LAST NIGHT.
WAIT-- WHAT? I DID WHAT, CARLOTA?
REMEMBER? YOU PROMISED LAST NIGHT AFTER I TOOK YOUR DISHWASHING DUTIES? THE QUESO POT WAS BRUTAL. I STILL HAVE CHEESE UNDER MY NAILS!
THANKS!
DON'T GET ME WRONG. ANY OTHER DAY I'D BE HAPPY TO HANG WITH YOU, CARLITOS, BUT THERE'S SKATING AT STAKE! BUT MAYBE SOMEONE ELSE CAN WATCH YOU?

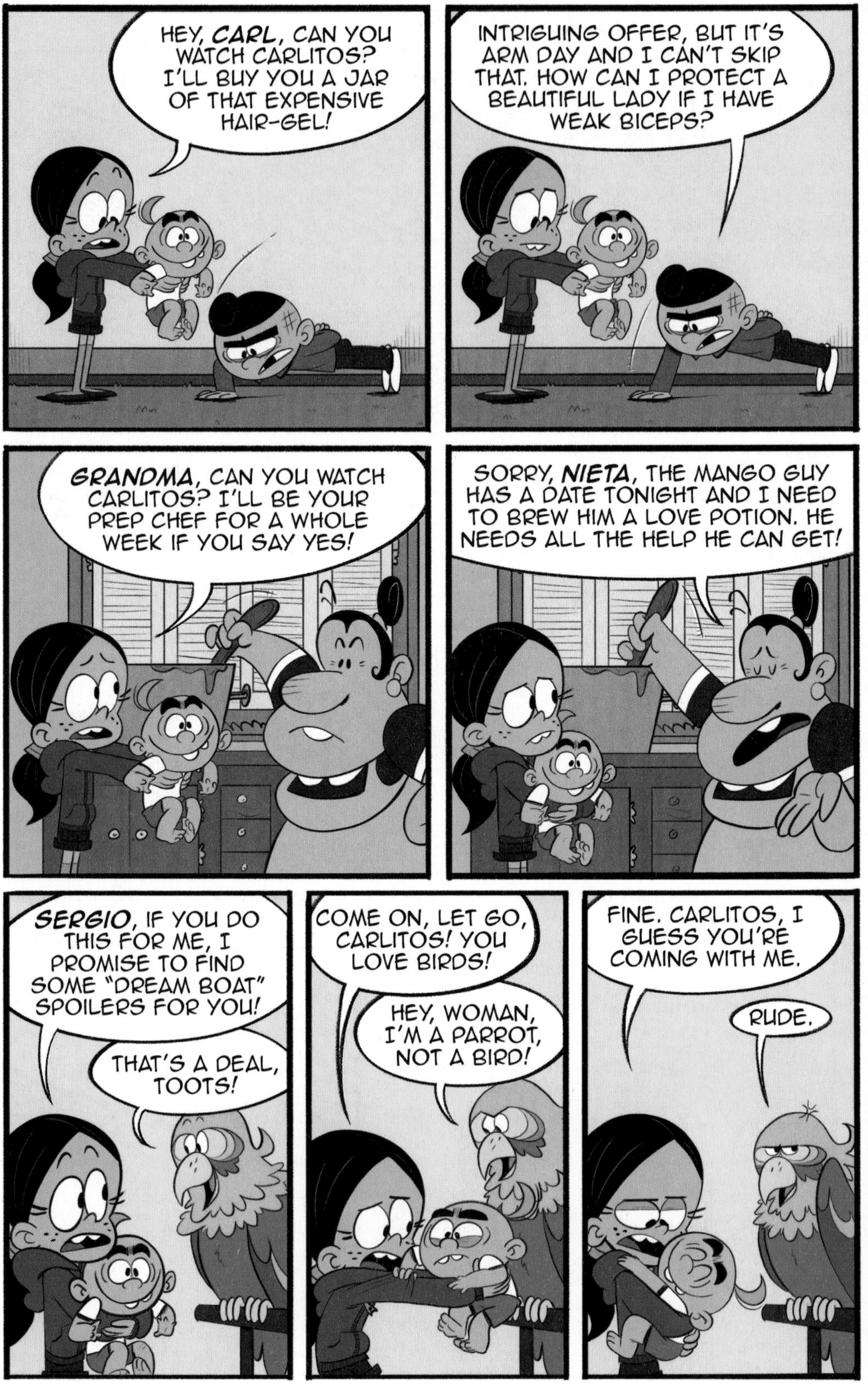
HEY, CARL, CAN YOU WATCH CARLITOS? I'LL BUY YOU A JAR OF THAT EXPENSIVE HAIR-GEL!
INTRIGUING OFFER, BUT IT'S ARM DAY AND I CAN'T SKIP THAT. HOW CAN I PROTECT A BEAUTIFUL LADY IF I HAVE WEAK BICEPS?
GRANDMA, CAN YOU WATCH CARLITOS? I'LL BE YOUR PREP CHEF FOR A WHOLE WEEK IF YOU SAY YES!
SORRY, NIETA, THE MANGO GUY HAS A DATE TONIGHT AND I NEED TO BREW HIM A LOVE POTION. HE NEEDS ALL THE HELP HE CAN GET!
SERGIO, IF YOU DO THIS FOR ME, I PROMISE TO FIND SOME "DREAM BOAT" SPOILERS FOR YOU!
THAT'S A DEAL, TOOTS!
COME ON, LET GO, CARLITOS! YOU LOVE BIRDS!
HEY, WOMAN, I'M A PARROT, NOT A BIRD!
FINE. CARLITOS, I GUESS YOU'RE COMING WITH ME.
RUDE.

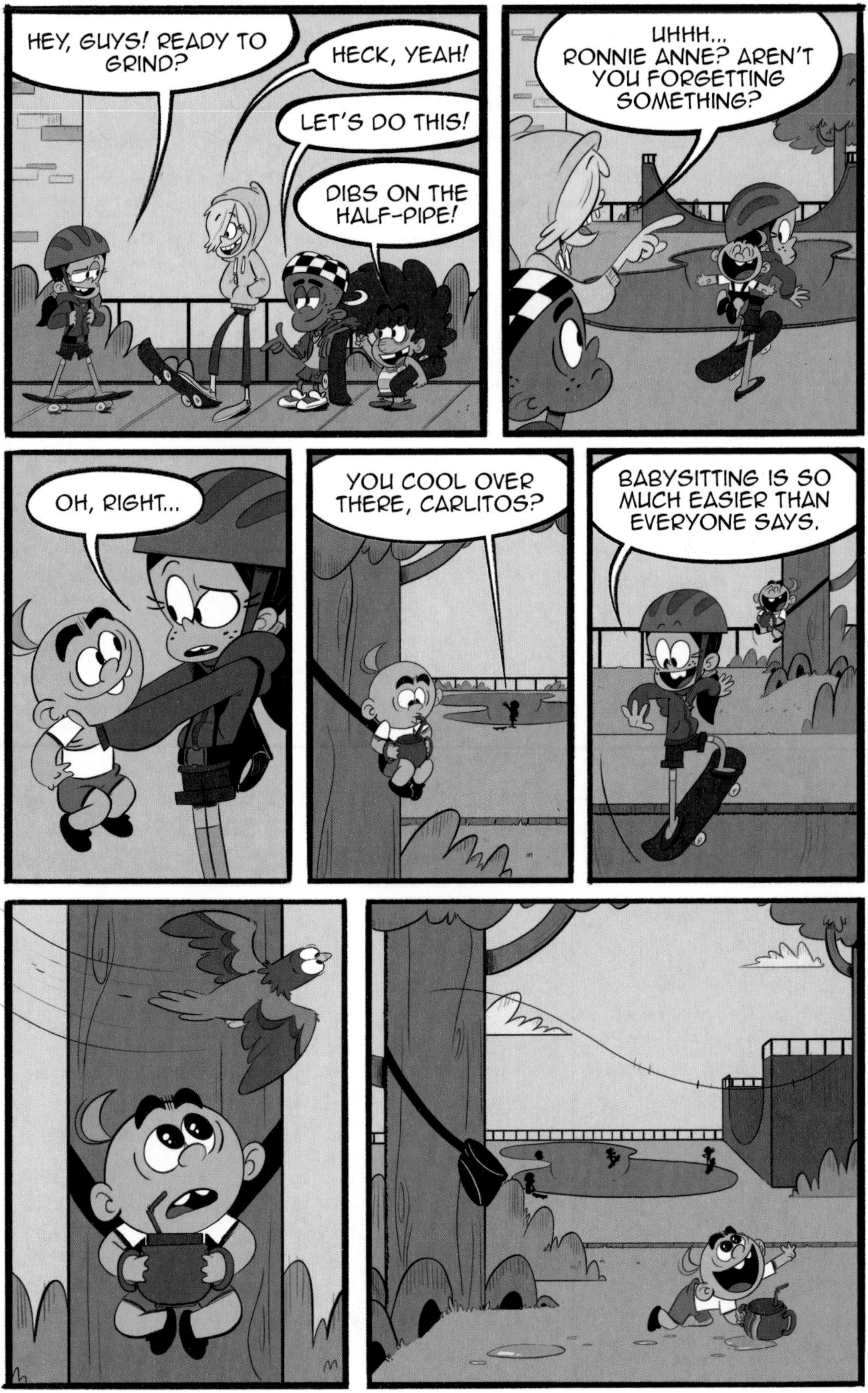
HEY, GUYS! READY TO GRIND?
HECK, YEAH!
LET'S DO THIS!
DIBS ON THE HALF-PIPE!
UHHH... RONNIE ANNE? AREN'T YOU FORGETTING SOMETHING?
OH, RIGHT...
YOU COOL OVER THERE, CARLITOS?
BABYSITTING IS SO MUCH EASIER THAN EVERYONE SAYS.

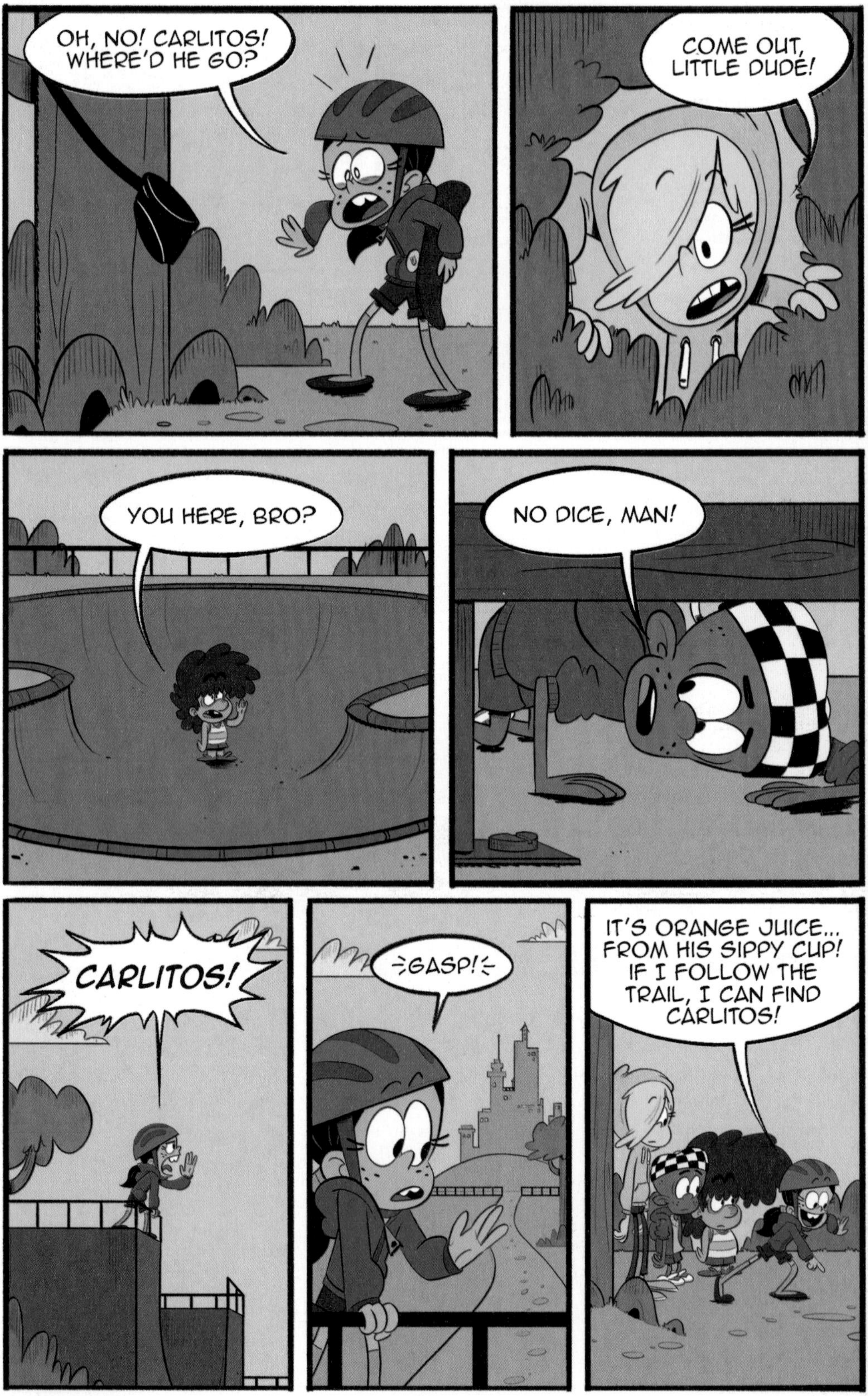
OH, NO! CARLITOS! WHERE'D HE GO?
COME OUT, LITTLE DUDE!
YOU HERE, BRO?
NO DICE, MAN!
CARLITOS!
GASP!
IT'S ORANGE JUICE... FROM HIS SIPPY CUP! IF I FOLLOW THE TRAIL, I CAN FIND CARLITOS!

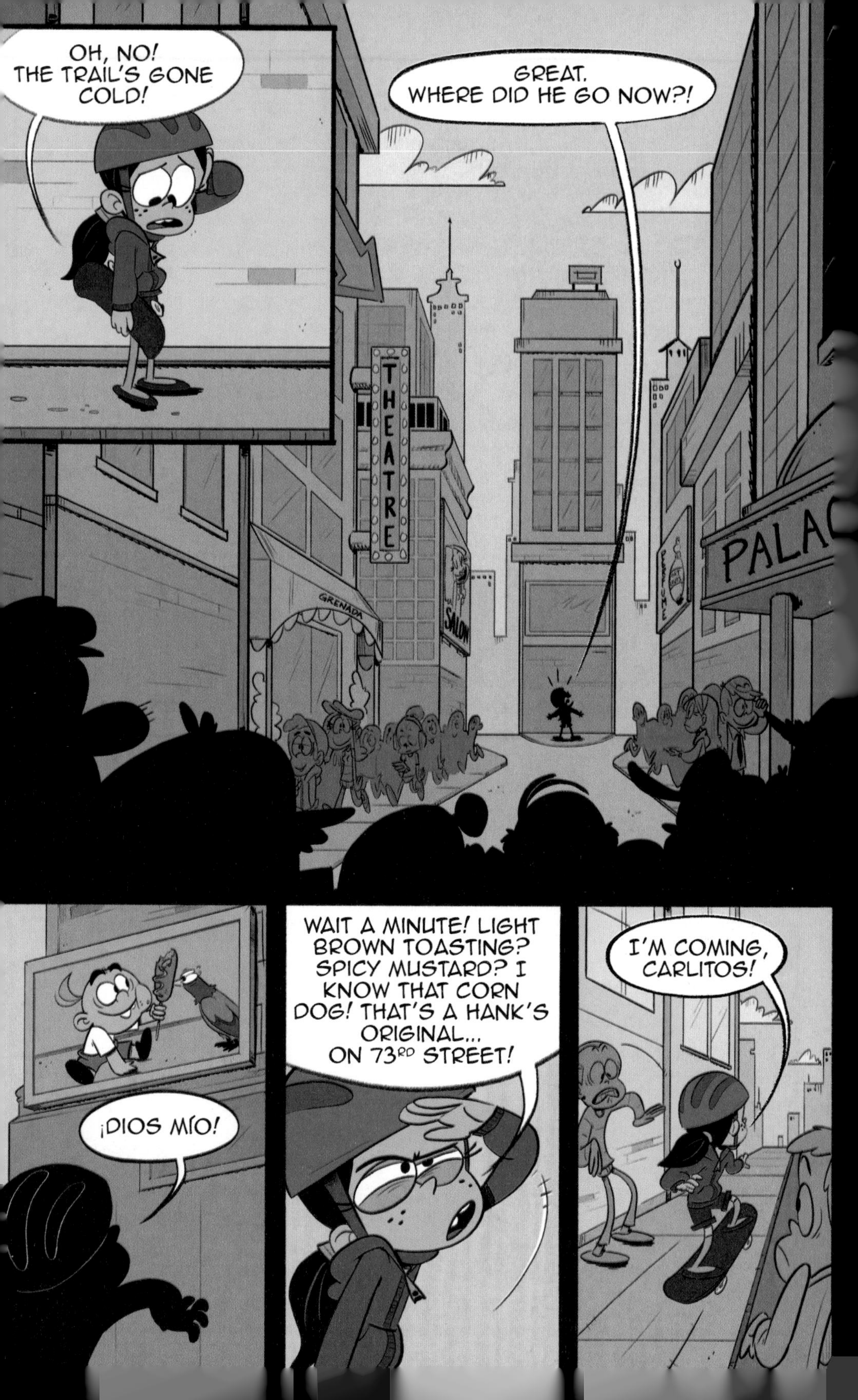
OH, NO! THE TRAIL'S GONE COLD!
GREAT. WHERE DID HE GO NOW?!
THEATRE
GRENADA
SALON
PALAC
¡DIOS MÍO!
WAIT A MINUTE! LIGHT BROWN TOASTING? SPICY MUSTARD? I KNOW THAT CORN DOG! THAT'S A HANK'S ORIGINAL... ON 73RD STREET!
I'M COMING, CARLITOS!

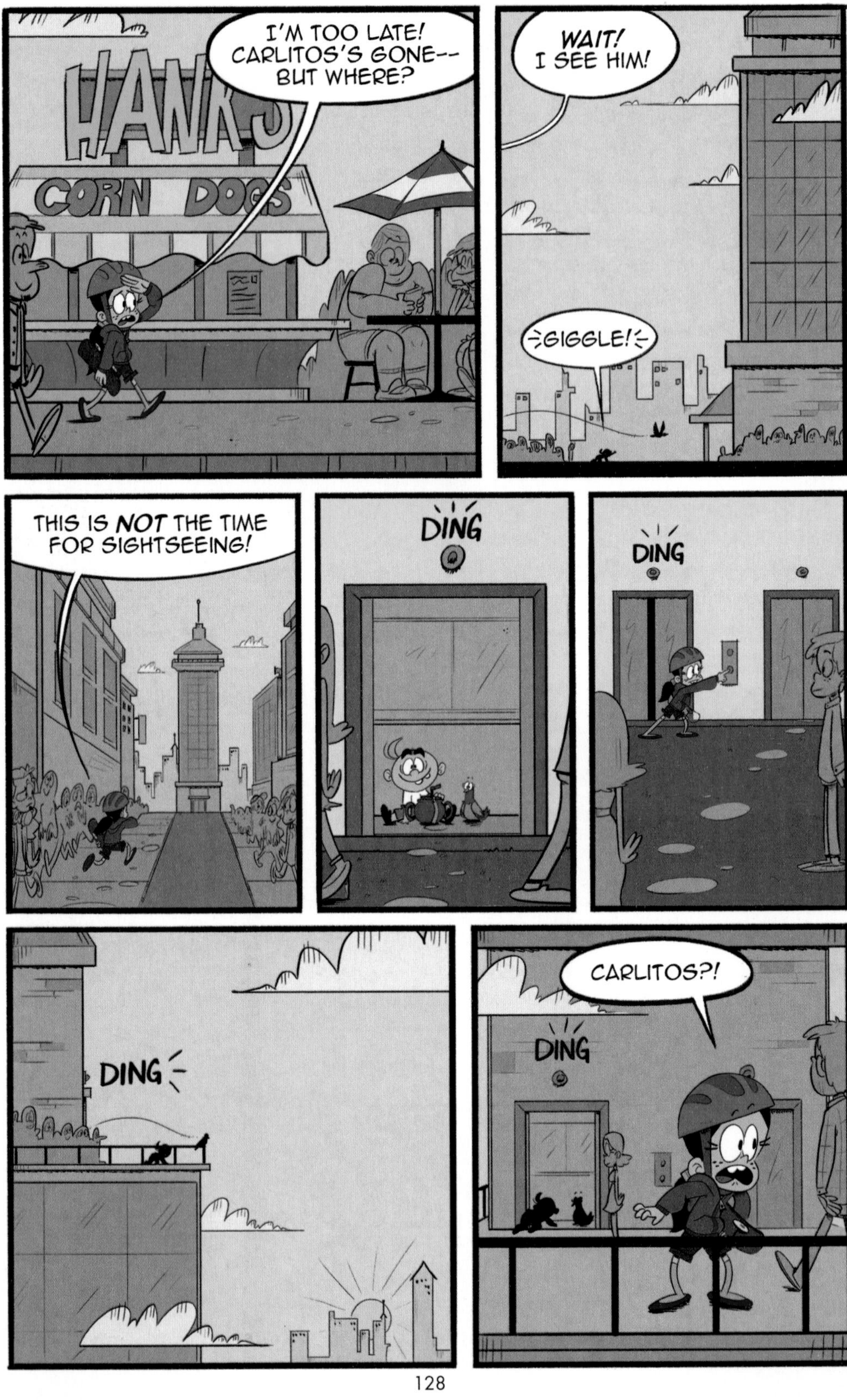
HANK'S
CORN DOGS
I'M TOO LATE! CARLITOS'S GONE-- BUT WHERE?
WAIT! I SEE HIM!
GIGGLE!
THIS IS NOT THE TIME FOR SIGHTSEEING!
DING
DING
DING
DING
CARLITOS?!

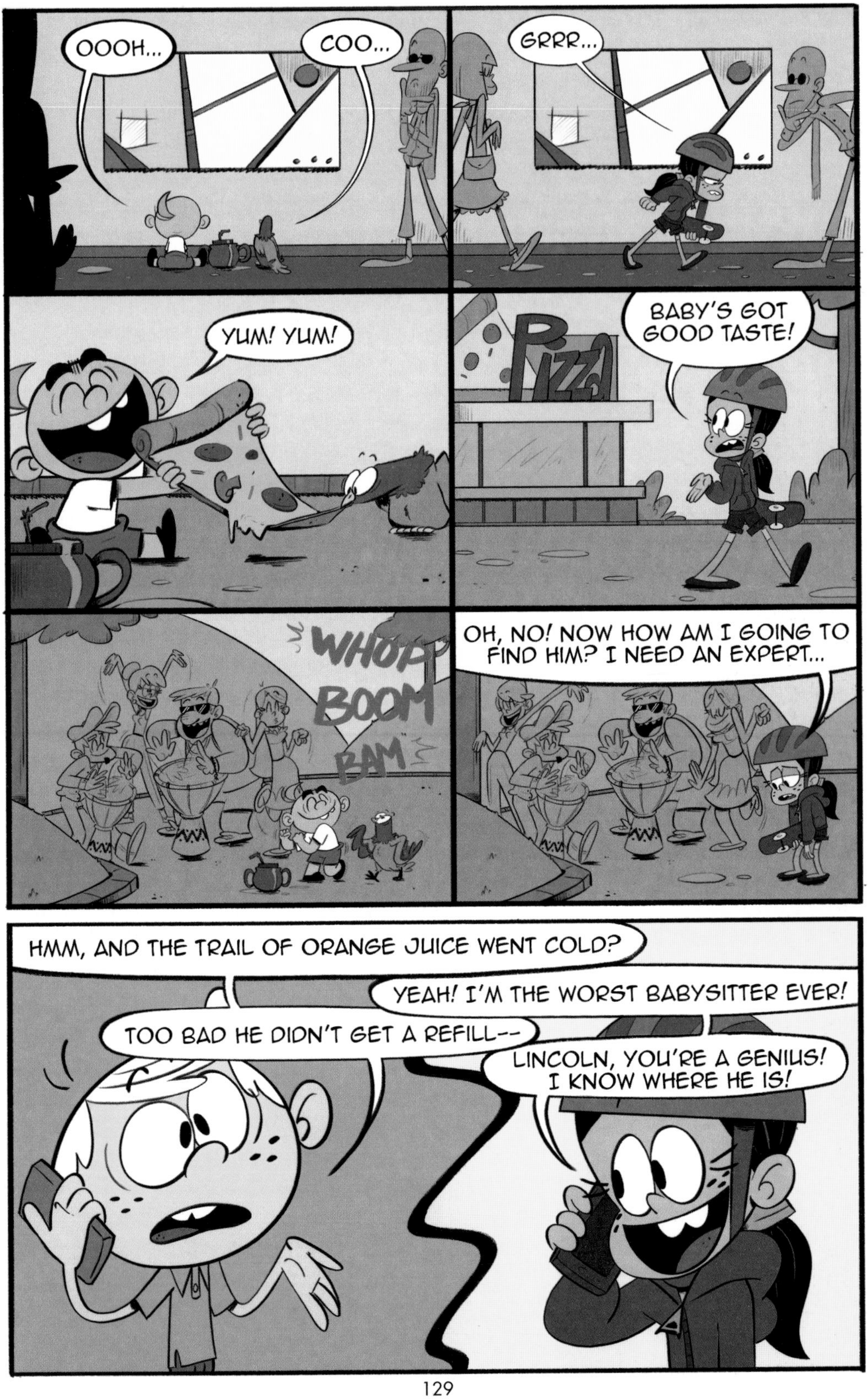
OOOH...
COO...
GRRR...
YUM! YUM!
BABY'S GOT GOOD TASTE!
PIZZA
WHOP
BOOM
BAM
OH, NO! NOW HOW AM I GOING TO FIND HIM? I NEED AN EXPERT...
HMM, AND THE TRAIL OF ORANGE JUICE WENT COLD?
YEAH! I'M THE WORST BABYSITTER EVER!
TOO BAD HE DIDN'T GET A REFILL--
LINCOLN, YOU'RE A GENIUS! I KNOW WHERE HE IS!

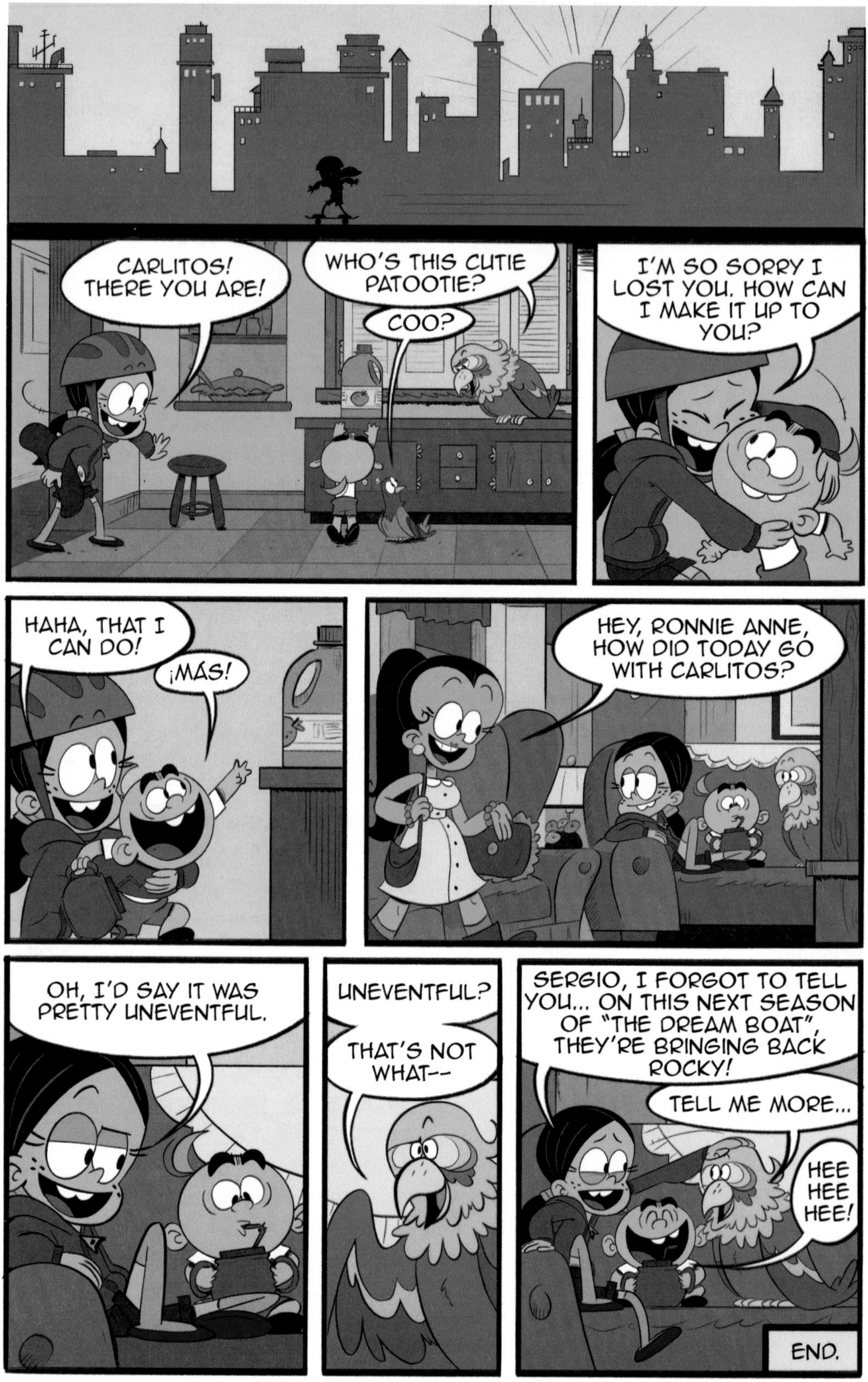
CARLITOS! THERE YOU ARE!
WHO'S THIS CUTIE PATOOTIE?
COO?
I'M SO SORRY I LOST YOU. HOW CAN I MAKE IT UP TO YOU?
HAHA, THAT I CAN DO!
¡MÁS!
HEY, RONNIE ANNE, HOW DID TODAY GO WITH CARLITOS?
OH, I'D SAY IT WAS PRETTY UNEVENTFUL.
UNEVENTFUL?
THAT'S NOT WHAT--
SERGIO, I FORGOT TO TELL YOU... ON THIS NEXT SEASON OF "THE DREAM BOAT", THEY'RE BRINGING BACK ROCKY!
TELL ME MORE...
HEE HEE HEE!
END.

"PACKING PARENTS"

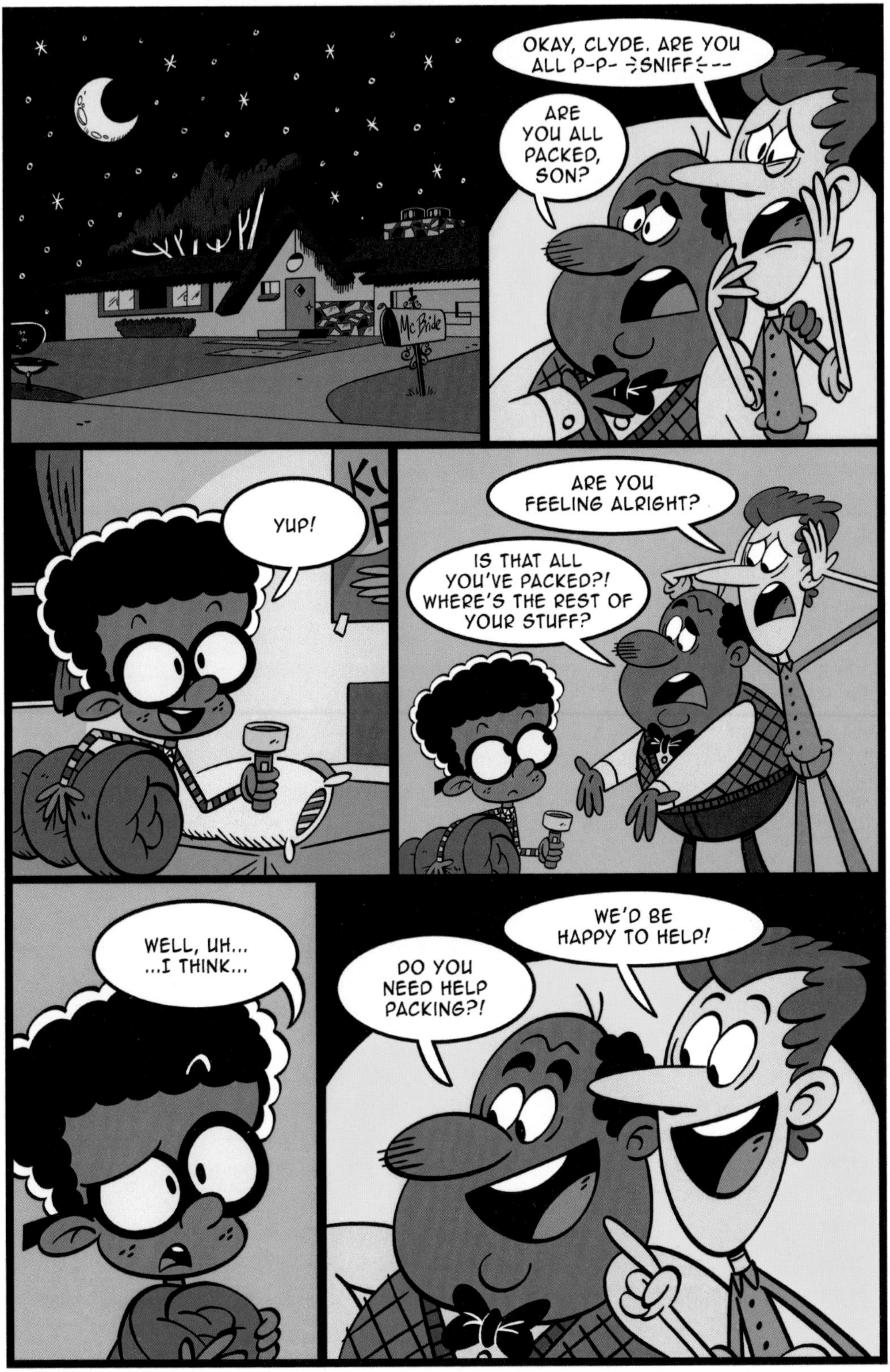

Mc Bride
OKAY, CLYDE. ARE YOU ALL P-P- ⇉SNIFF⇇--
ARE YOU ALL PACKED, SON?
YUP!
ARE YOU FEELING ALRIGHT?
IS THAT ALL YOU'VE PACKED?! WHERE'S THE REST OF YOUR STUFF?
WELL, UH... ...I THINK...
WE'D BE HAPPY TO HELP!
DO YOU NEED HELP PACKING?!

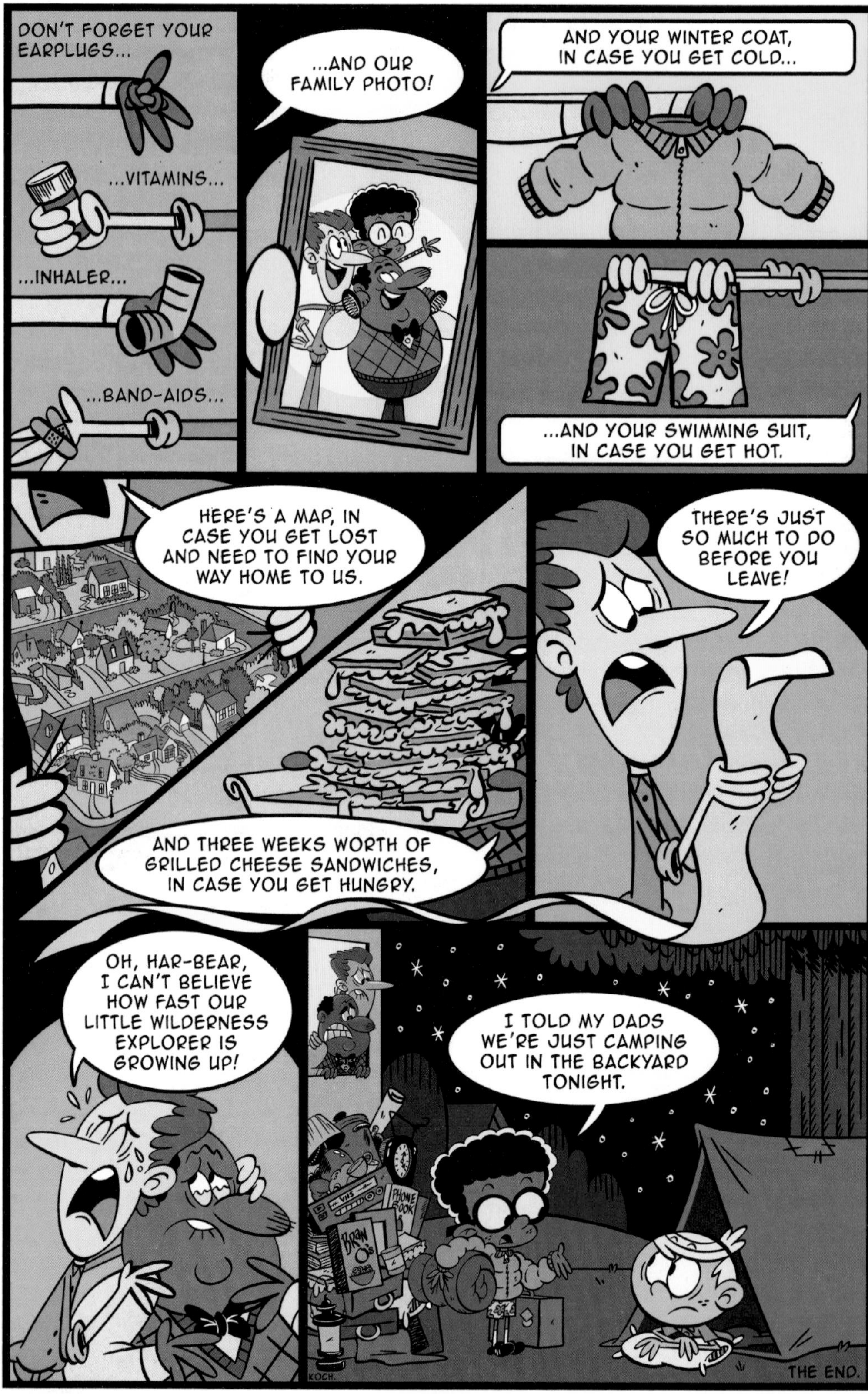
DON'T FORGET YOUR EARPLUGS...
...VITAMINS...
...INHALER...
...BAND-AIDS...
...AND OUR FAMILY PHOTO!
AND YOUR WINTER COAT, IN CASE YOU GET COLD...
...AND YOUR SWIMMING SUIT, IN CASE YOU GET HOT.
HERE'S A MAP, IN CASE YOU GET LOST AND NEED TO FIND YOUR WAY HOME TO US.
THERE'S JUST SO MUCH TO DO BEFORE YOU LEAVE!
AND THREE WEEKS WORTH OF GRILLED CHEESE SANDWICHES, IN CASE YOU GET HUNGRY.
OH, HAR-BEAR, I CAN'T BELIEVE HOW FAST OUR LITTLE WILDERNESS EXPLORER IS GROWING UP!
I TOLD MY DADS WE'RE JUST CAMPING OUT IN THE BACKYARD TONIGHT.
VHS
PHONE BOOK
KOCH.
THE END.

"IT'S JUST A PHASE"

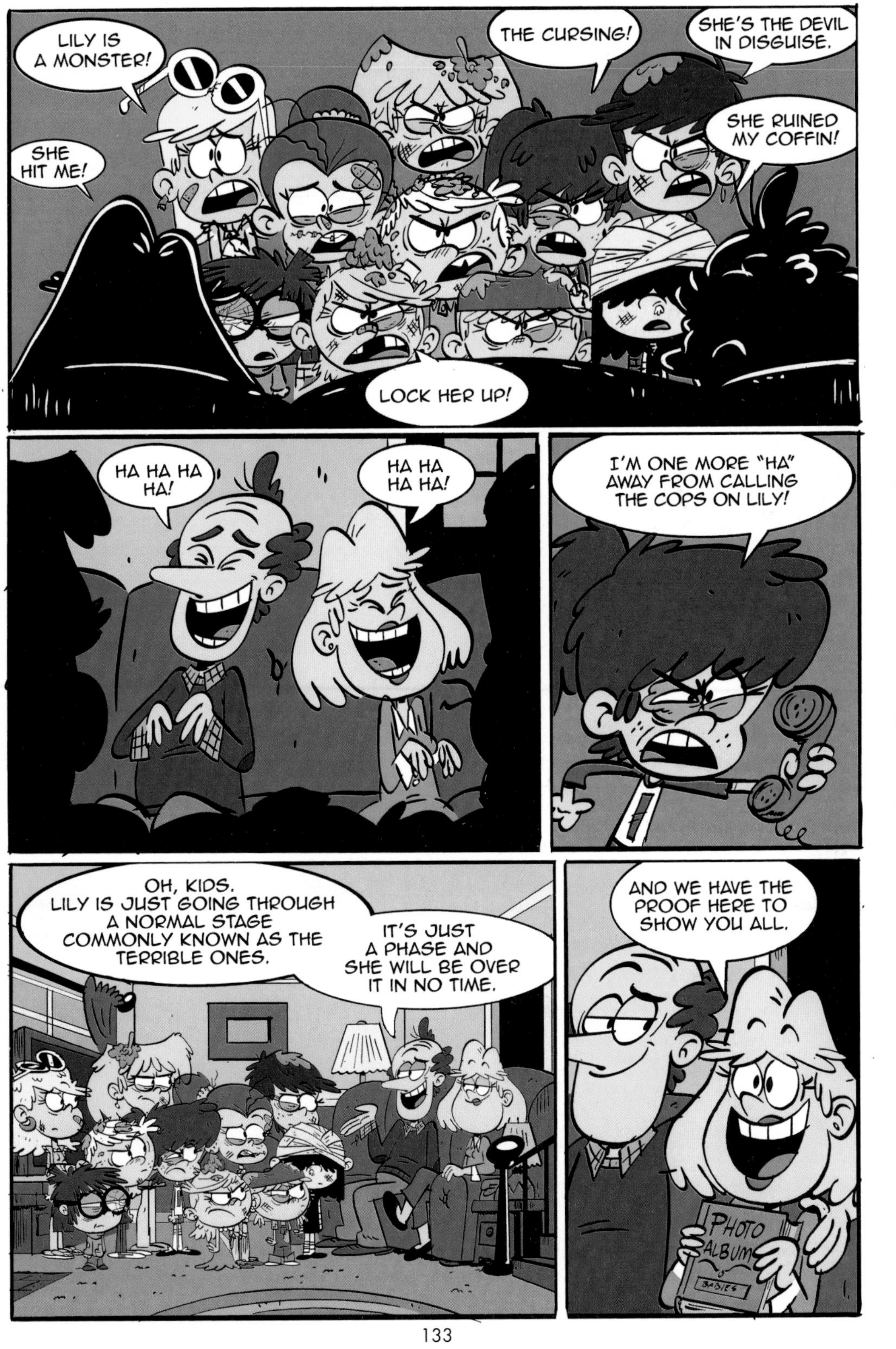
LILY IS A MONSTER!
SHE HIT ME!
THE CURSING!
SHE'S THE DEVIL IN DISGUISE.
SHE RUINED MY COFFIN!
LOCK HER UP!
HA HA HA HA!
HA HA HA HA!
I'M ONE MORE "HA" AWAY FROM CALLING THE COPS ON LILY!
OH, KIDS. LILY IS JUST GOING THROUGH A NORMAL STAGE COMMONLY KNOWN AS THE TERRIBLE ONES.
IT'S JUST A PHASE AND SHE WILL BE OVER IT IN NO TIME.
AND WE HAVE THE PROOF HERE TO SHOW YOU ALL.
PHOTO ALBUM
BABIES

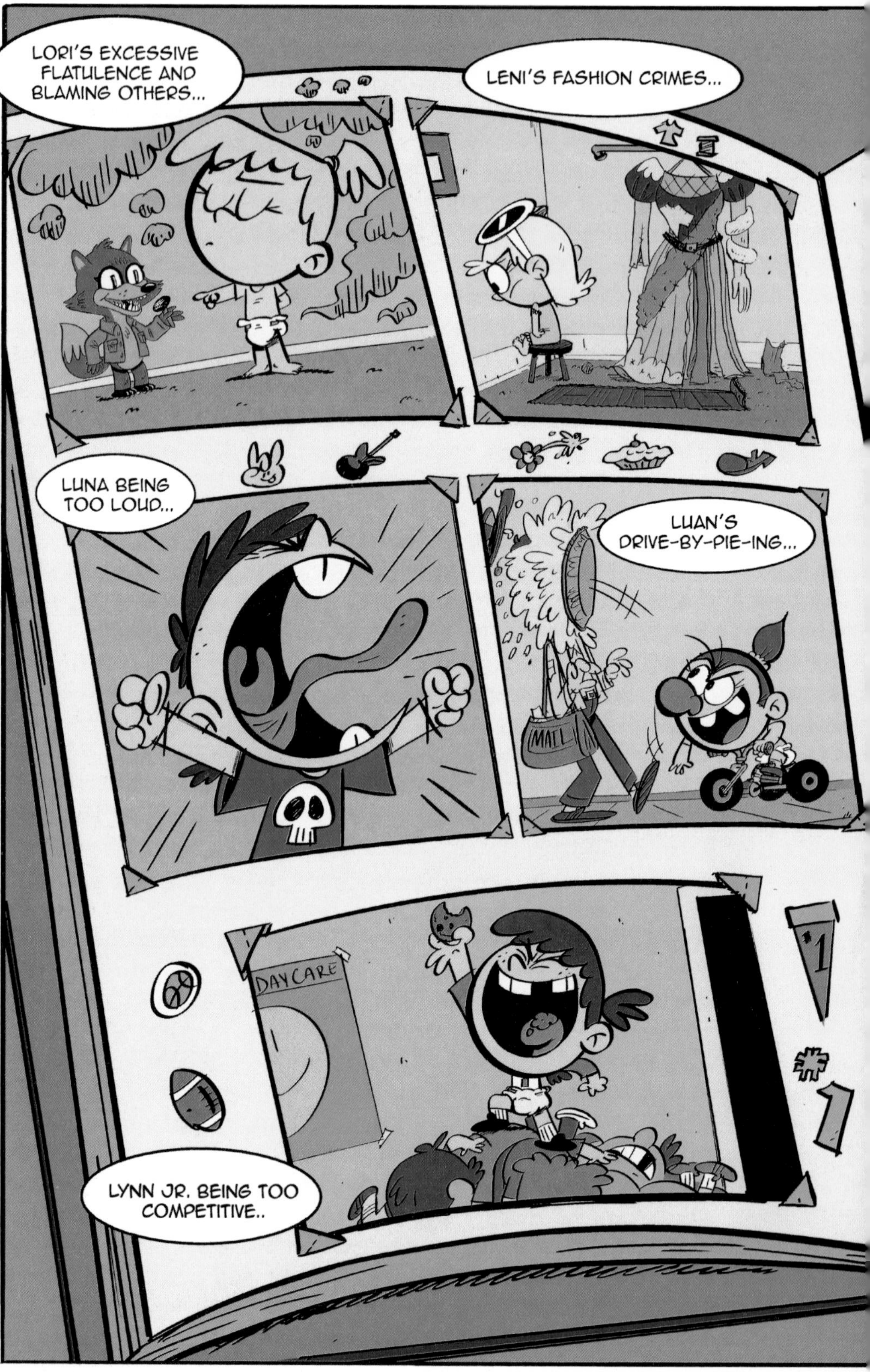

LORI'S EXCESSIVE FLATULENCE AND BLAMING OTHERS...
LENI'S FASHION CRIMES...
LUNA BEING TOO LOUD...
LUAN'S DRIVE-BY-PIE-ING...
MAIL
DAYCARE
#1
#1
LYNN JR. BEING TOO COMPETITIVE..

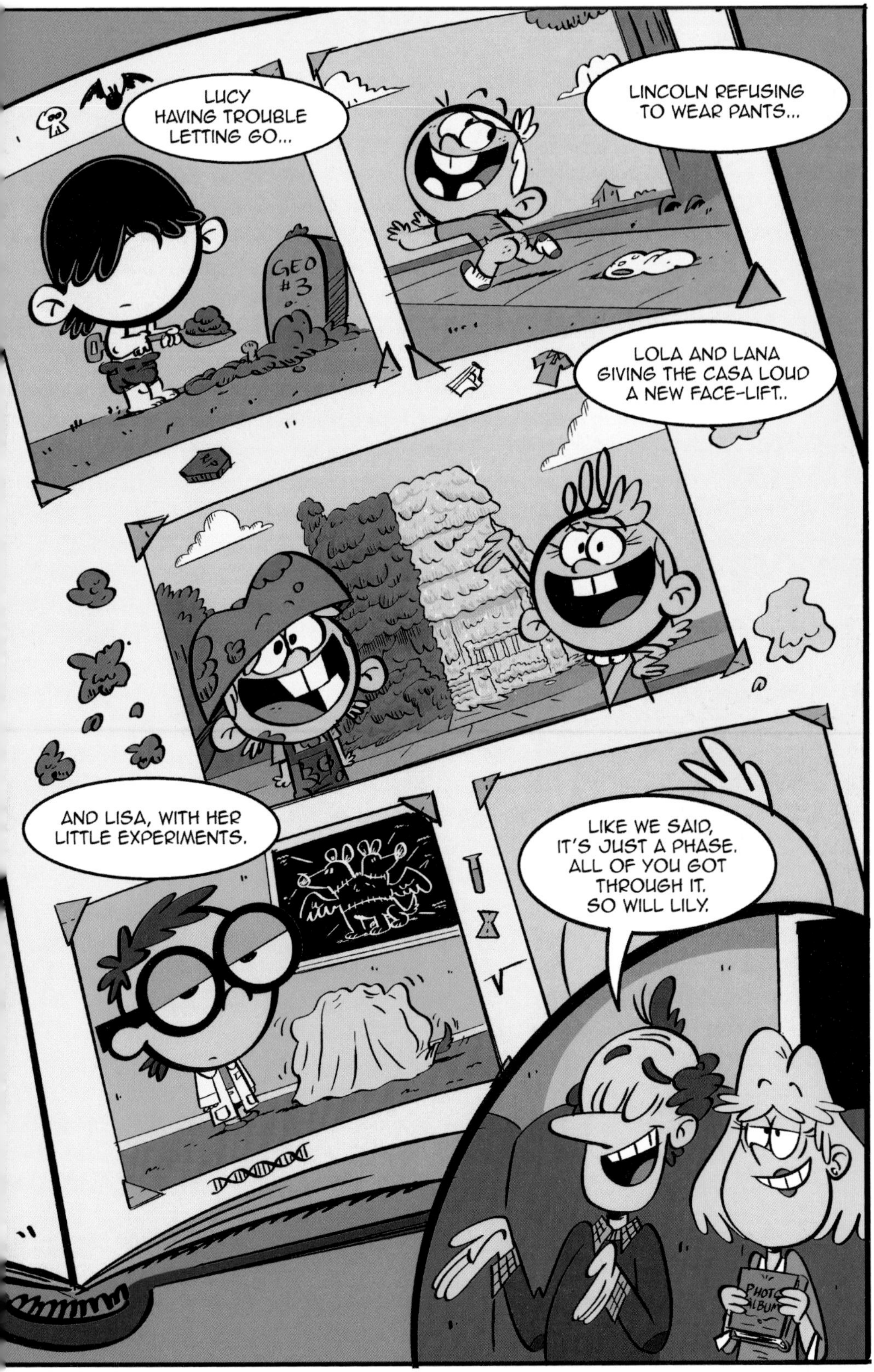
LUCY HAVING TROUBLE LETTING GO...
GEO #3
LINCOLN REFUSING TO WEAR PANTS...
LOLA AND LANA GIVING THE CASA LOUD A NEW FACE-LIFT..
AND LISA, WITH HER LITTLE EXPERIMENTS.
LIKE WE SAID, IT'S JUST A PHASE. ALL OF YOU GOT THROUGH IT. SO WILL LILY.
PHOTO ALBUM

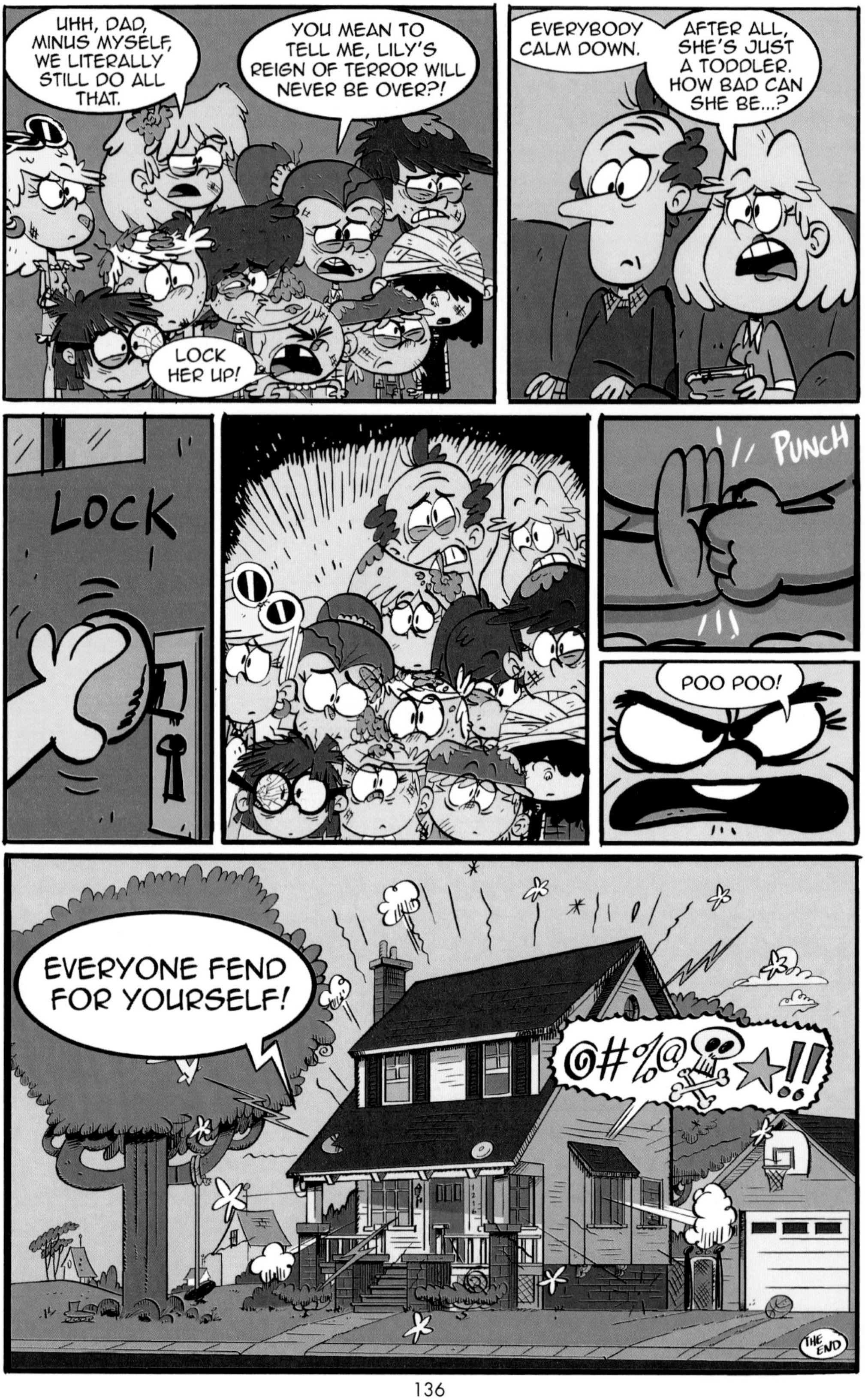
UHH, DAD, MINUS MYSELF, WE LITERALLY STILL DO ALL THAT.
YOU MEAN TO TELL ME, LILY'S REIGN OF TERROR WILL NEVER BE OVER?!
LOCK HER UP!
EVERYBODY CALM DOWN.
AFTER ALL, SHE'S JUST A TODDLER. HOW BAD CAN SHE BE...?
LOCK
PUNCH
POO POO!
EVERYONE FEND FOR YOURSELF!
@#%@!!
THE END

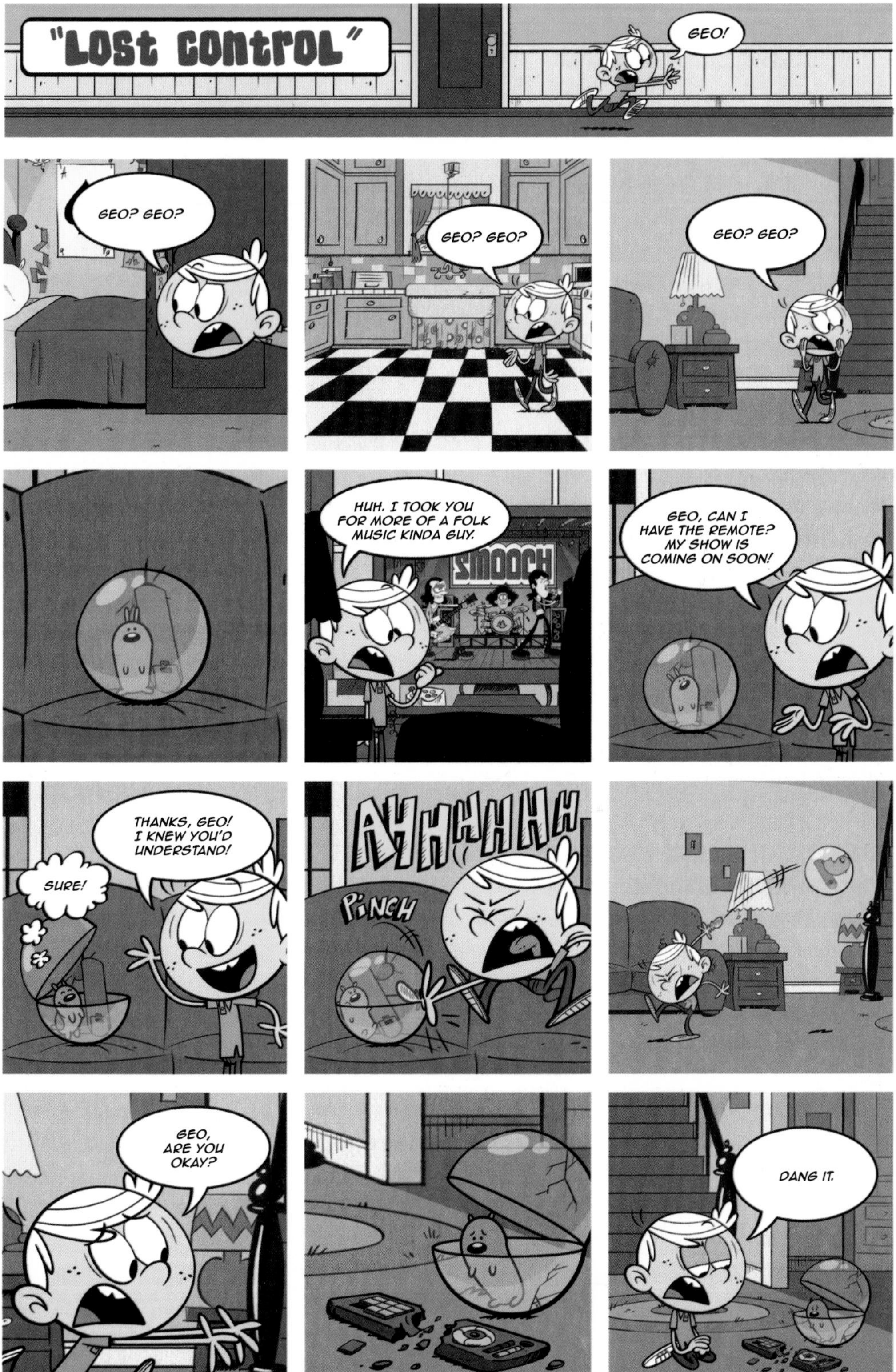
"Lost Control"
GEO!
GEO? GEO?
GEO? GEO?
GEO? GEO?
HUH. I TOOK YOU FOR MORE OF A FOLK MUSIC KINDA GUY.
SMOOCH
GEO, CAN I HAVE THE REMOTE? MY SHOW IS COMING ON SOON!
SURE!
THANKS, GEO! I KNEW YOU'D UNDERSTAND!
AYHHHHHH
PINCH
GEO, ARE YOU OKAY?
DANG IT.

OH, NO! YOU'VE HIT A DEAD END. TO TRY AGAIN, GO TALK TO LORI ON PAGE 7.

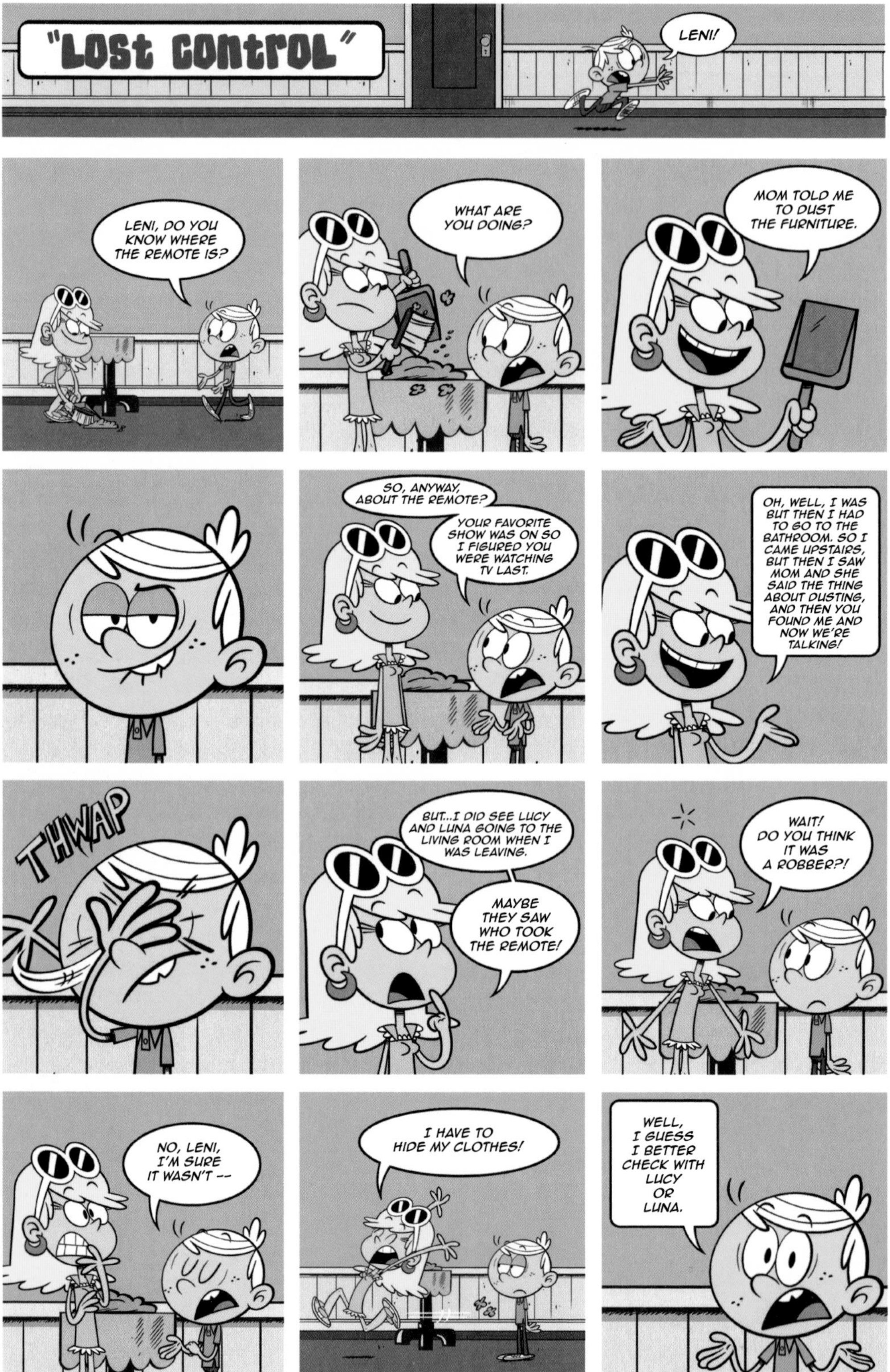
"LOST CONTROL"
LENI!
LENI, DO YOU KNOW WHERE THE REMOTE IS?
WHAT ARE YOU DOING?
MOM TOLD ME TO DUST THE FURNITURE.
SO, ANYWAY, ABOUT THE REMOTE?
YOUR FAVORITE SHOW WAS ON SO I FIGURED YOU WERE WATCHING TV LAST.
OH, WELL, I WAS BUT THEN I HAD TO GO TO THE BATHROOM. SO I CAME UPSTAIRS, BUT THEN I SAW MOM AND SHE SAID THE THING ABOUT DUSTING, AND THEN YOU FOUND ME AND NOW WE'RE TALKING!
THWAP
BUT...I DID SEE LUCY AND LUNA GOING TO THE LIVING ROOM WHEN I WAS LEAVING.
MAYBE THEY SAW WHO TOOK THE REMOTE!
WAIT! DO YOU THINK IT WAS A ROBBER?!
NO, LENI, I'M SURE IT WASN'T --
I HAVE TO HIDE MY CLOTHES!
WELL, I GUESS I BETTER CHECK WITH LUCY OR LUNA.

TO TALK TO LUCY, GO TO PAGE 23. TO TALK TO LUNA, GO TO PAGE 55.

"CLOWNING AROUND"

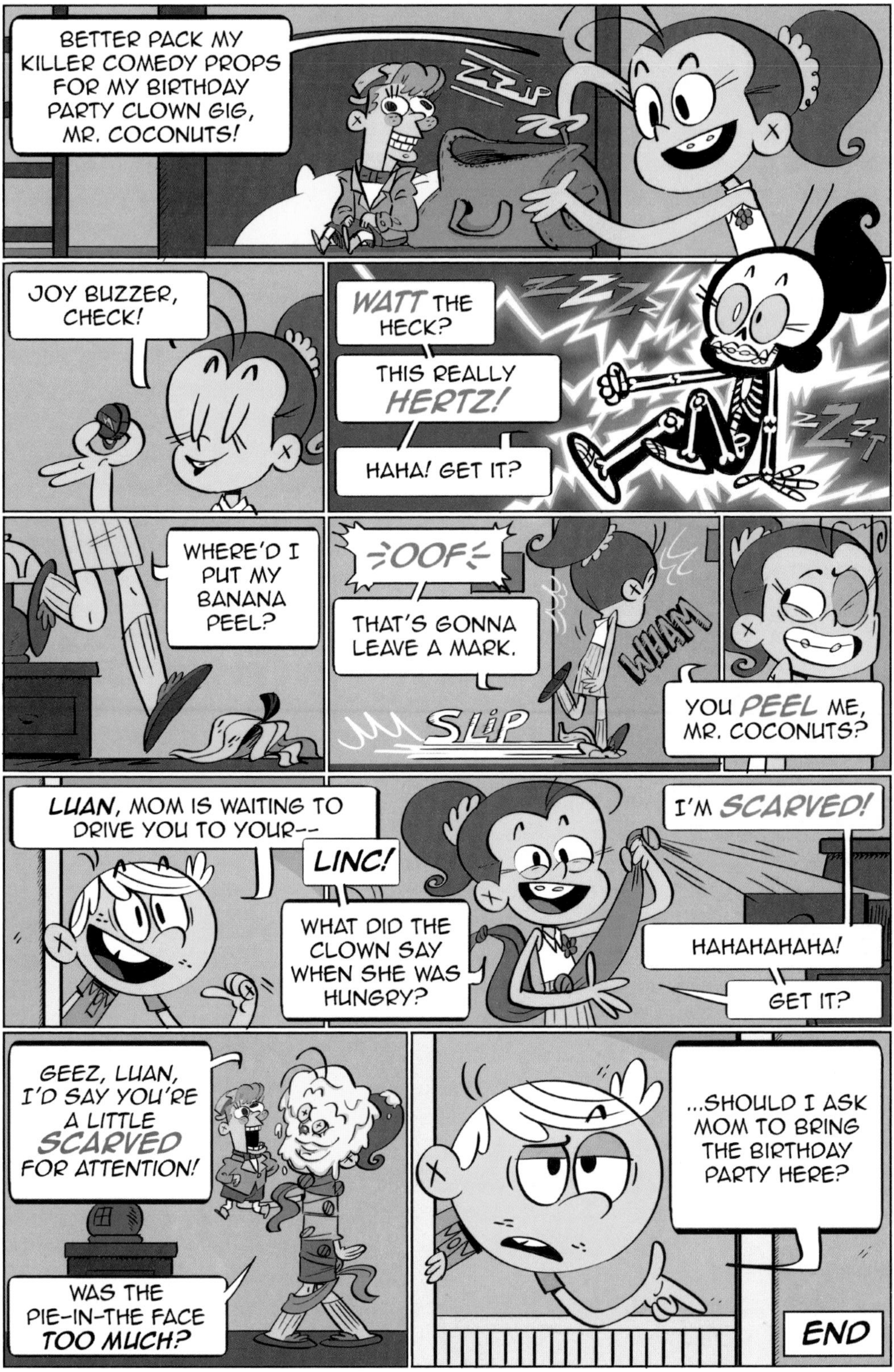

BETTER PACK MY KILLER COMEDY PROPS FOR MY BIRTHDAY PARTY CLOWN GIG, MR. COCONUTS!
ZZIP
JOY BUZZER, CHECK!
WATT THE HECK?
THIS REALLY HERTZ!
HAHA! GET IT?
WHERE'D I PUT MY BANANA PEEL?
OOF
THAT'S GONNA LEAVE A MARK.
SLIP
WHAM
YOU PEEL ME, MR. COCONUTS?
LUAN, MOM IS WAITING TO DRIVE YOU TO YOUR--
LINC!
WHAT DID THE CLOWN SAY WHEN SHE WAS HUNGRY?
I'M SCARVED!
HAHAHAHAHA!
GET IT?
GEEZ, LUAN, I'D SAY YOU'RE A LITTLE SCARVED FOR ATTENTION!
WAS THE PIE-IN-THE FACE TOO MUCH?
...SHOULD I ASK MOM TO BRING THE BIRTHDAY PARTY HERE?
END

"LOST AND FOUND"

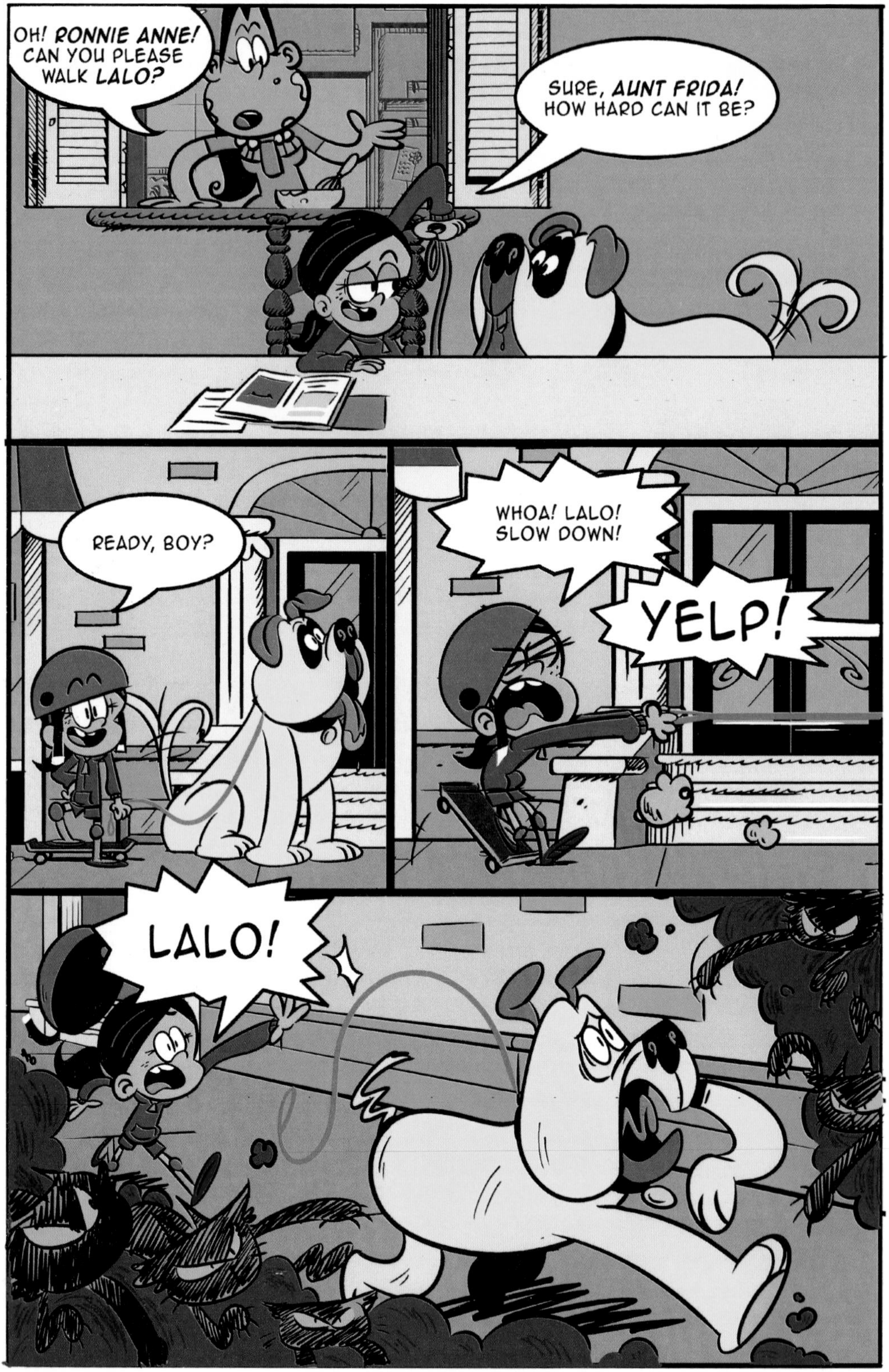

OH! RONNIE ANNE! CAN YOU PLEASE WALK LALO?
SURE, AUNT FRIDA! HOW HARD CAN IT BE?
READY, BOY?
WHOA! LALO! SLOW DOWN!
YELP!
LALO!

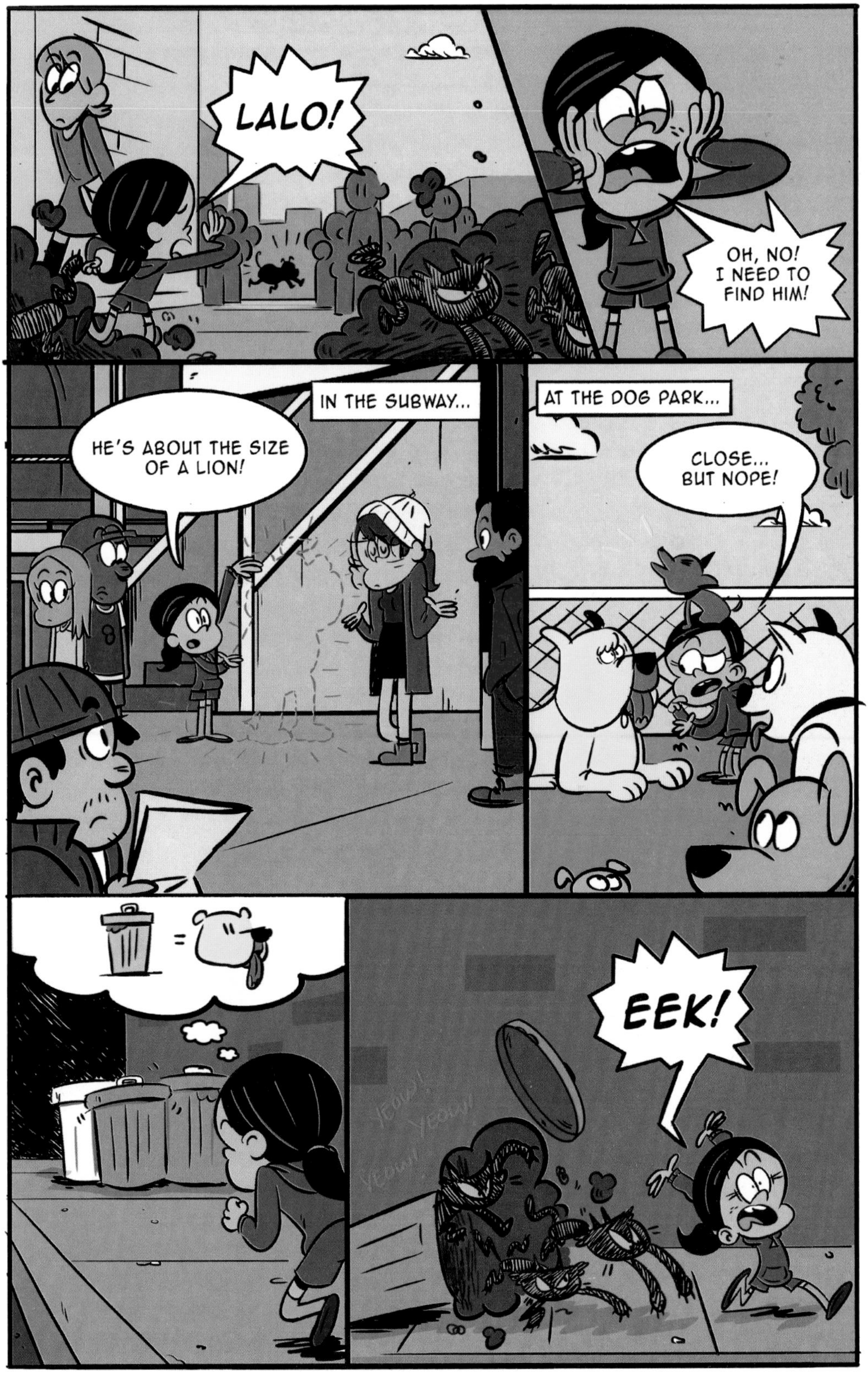
LALO!
OH, NO! I NEED TO FIND HIM!
IN THE SUBWAY...
HE'S ABOUT THE SIZE OF A LION!
AT THE DOG PARK...
CLOSE... BUT NOPE!
EEK!
YEOW! YEOW! YEOW!

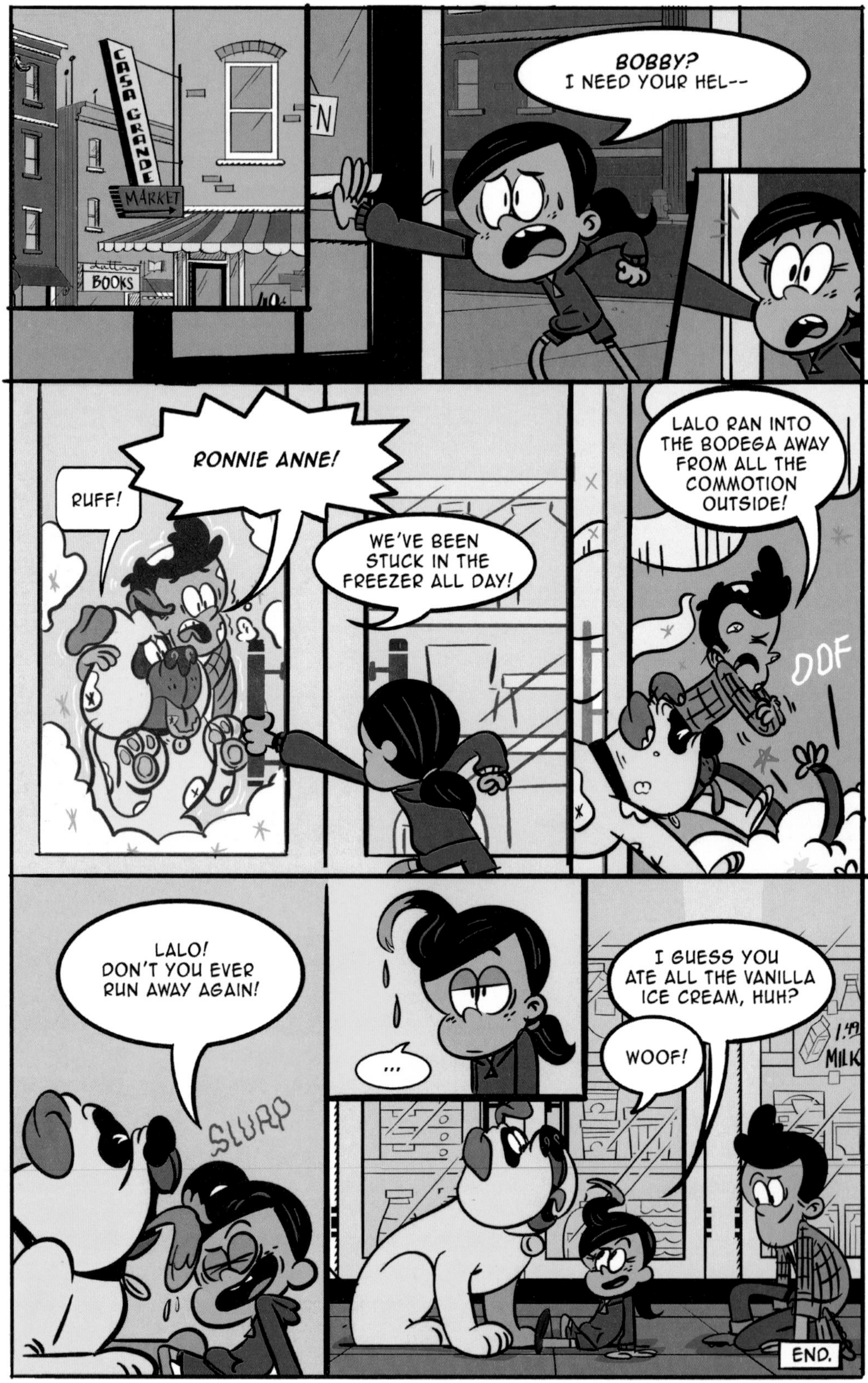
CASA GRANDE
MARKET
BOOKS
BOBBY?
I NEED YOUR HEL--
RONNIE ANNE!
RUFF!
WE'VE BEEN STUCK IN THE FREEZER ALL DAY!
LALO RAN INTO THE BODEGA AWAY FROM ALL THE COMMOTION OUTSIDE!
OOF
LALO!
DON'T YOU EVER RUN AWAY AGAIN!
SLURP
...
I GUESS YOU ATE ALL THE VANILLA ICE CREAM, HUH?
WOOF!
MILK
END.

"I SPY LASAGNA"

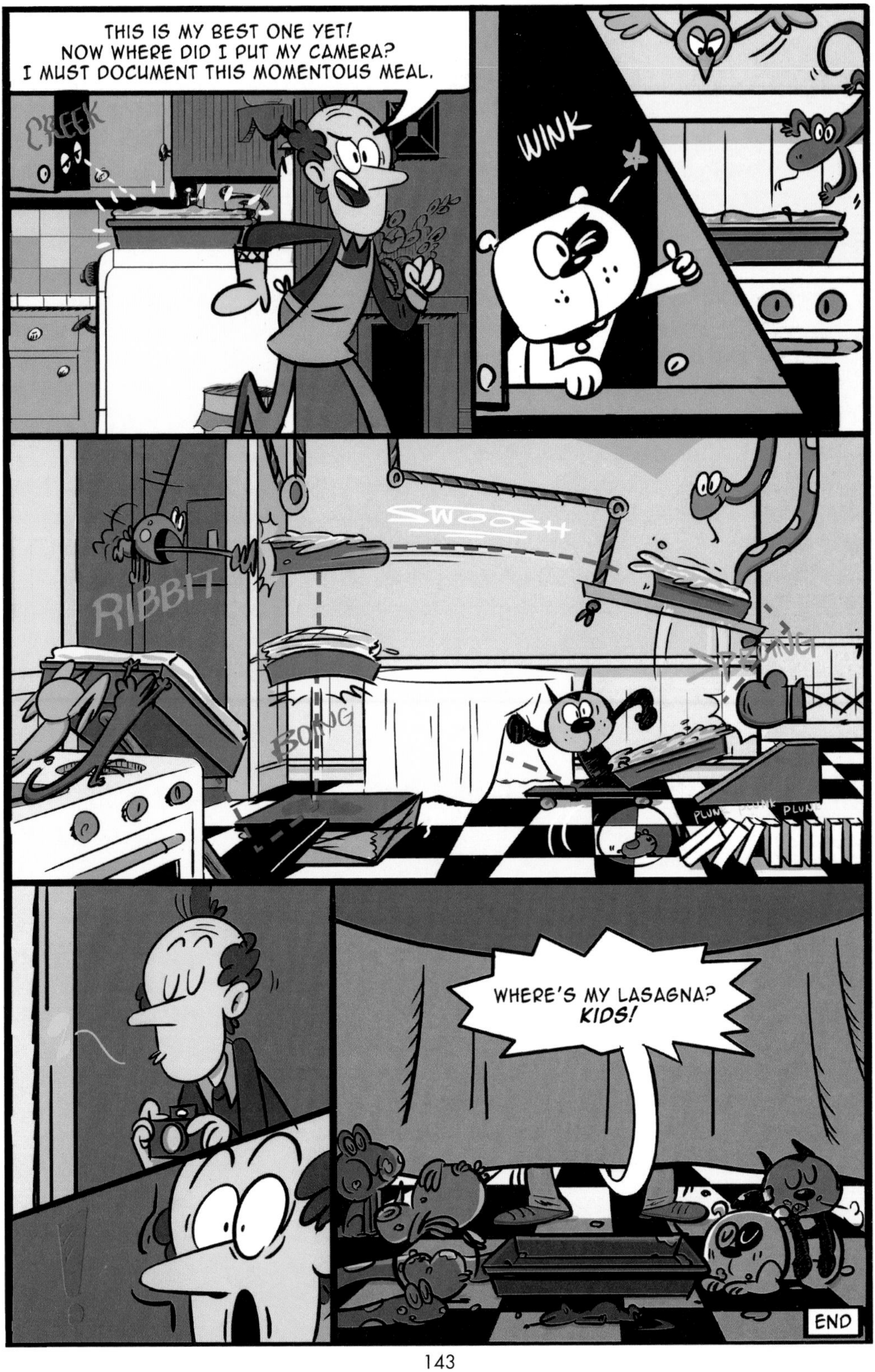
THIS IS MY BEST ONE YET!
NOW WHERE DID I PUT MY CAMERA?
I MUST DOCUMENT THIS MOMENTOUS MEAL.
CREEK
WINK
SWOOSH
RIBBIT
BONG
PLUNK PLUNK PLUNK
WHERE'S MY LASAGNA?
KIDS!
END

"SAM'S PICK"

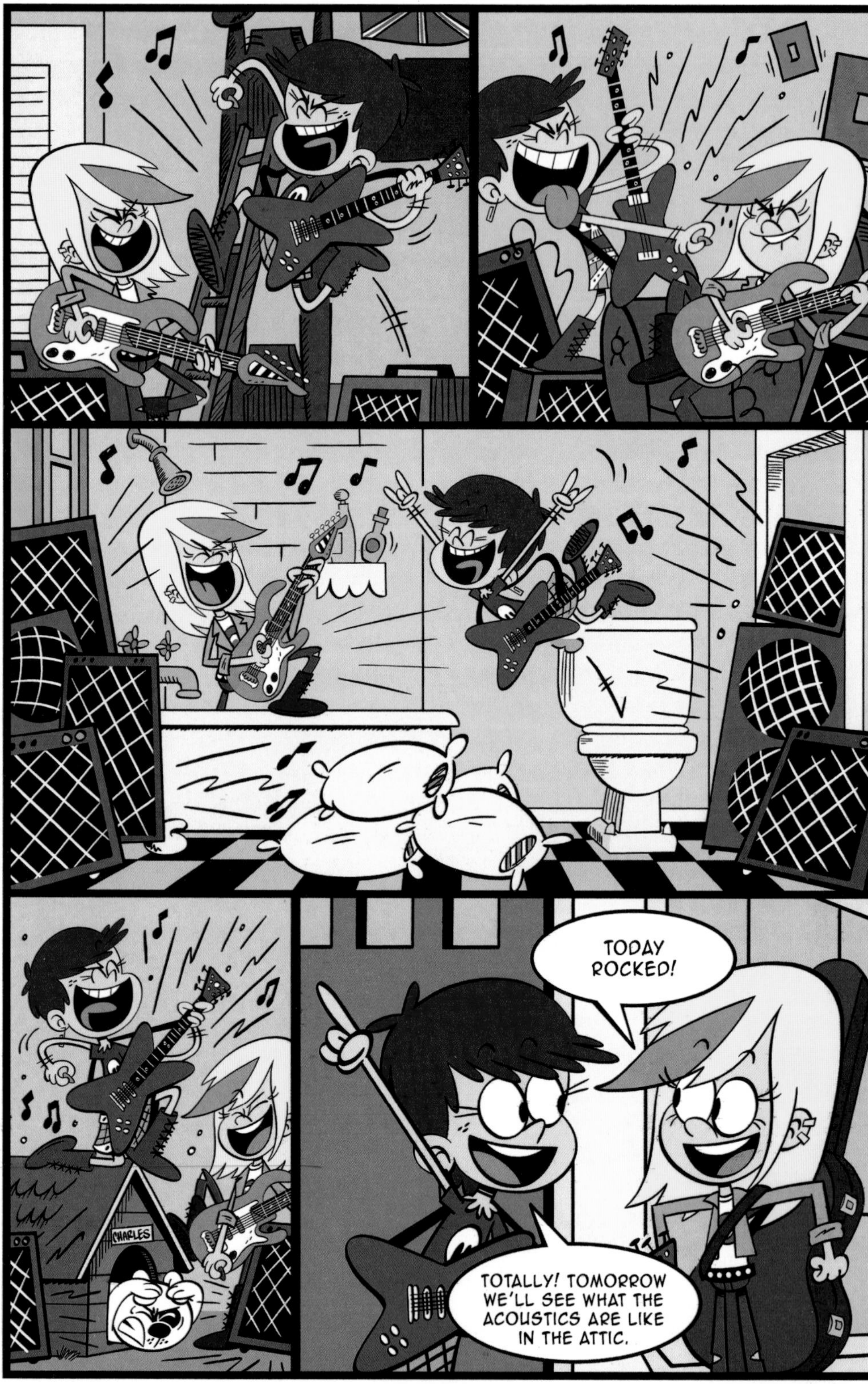
CHARLES
TODAY ROCKED!
TOTALLY! TOMORROW WE'LL SEE WHAT THE ACOUSTICS ARE LIKE IN THE ATTIC.

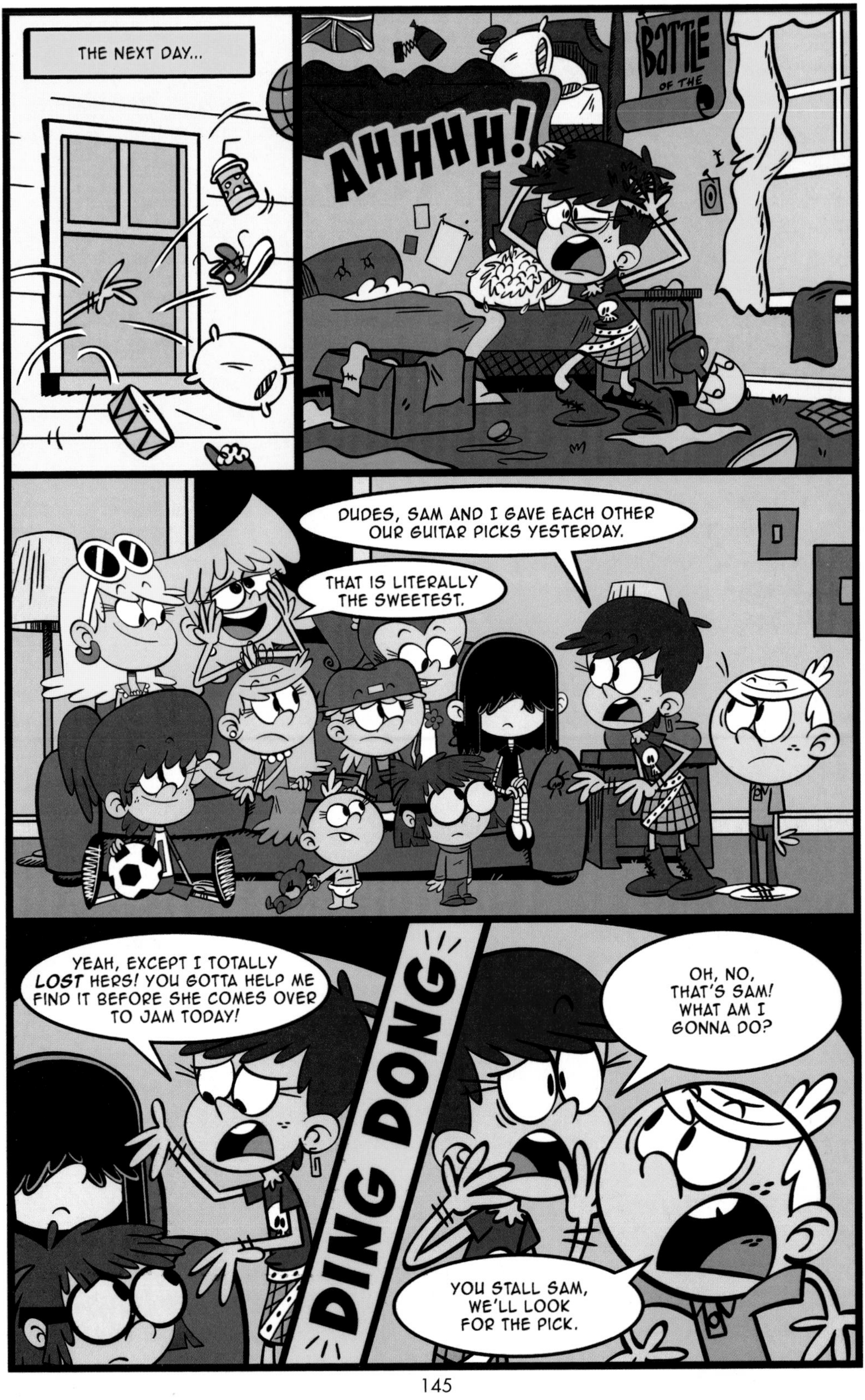
THE NEXT DAY...
BATTLE OF THE
AHHHH!
DUDES, SAM AND I GAVE EACH OTHER OUR GUITAR PICKS YESTERDAY.
THAT IS LITERALLY THE SWEETEST.
YEAH, EXCEPT I TOTALLY LOST HERS! YOU GOTTA HELP ME FIND IT BEFORE SHE COMES OVER TO JAM TODAY!
DING DONG
OH, NO, THAT'S SAM! WHAT AM I GONNA DO?
YOU STALL SAM, WE'LL LOOK FOR THE PICK.

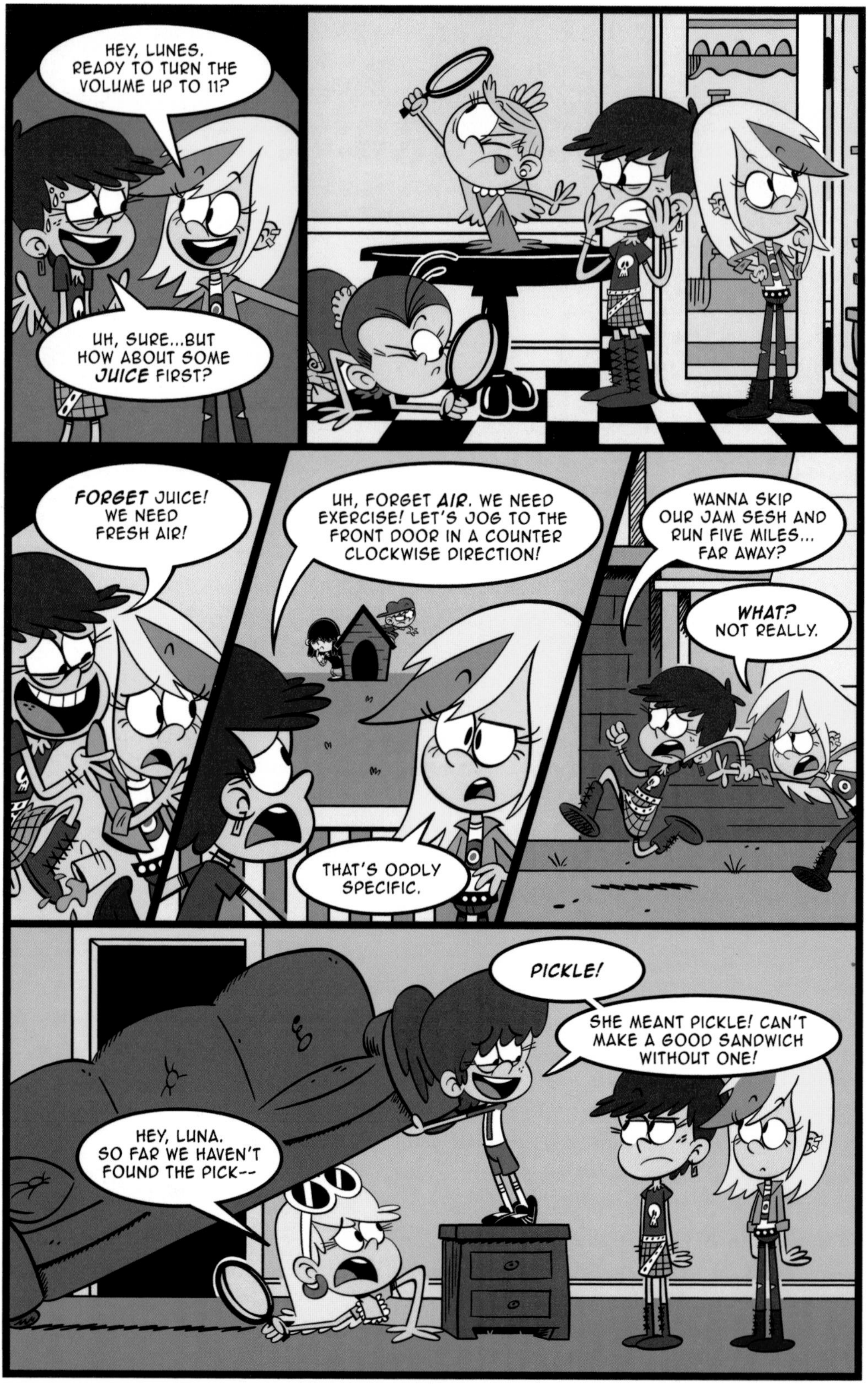
HEY, LUNES. READY TO TURN THE VOLUME UP TO 11?
UH, SURE...BUT HOW ABOUT SOME JUICE FIRST?
FORGET JUICE! WE NEED FRESH AIR!
UH, FORGET AIR. WE NEED EXERCISE! LET'S JOG TO THE FRONT DOOR IN A COUNTER CLOCKWISE DIRECTION!
THAT'S ODDLY SPECIFIC.
WANNA SKIP OUR JAM SESH AND RUN FIVE MILES... FAR AWAY?
WHAT? NOT REALLY.
HEY, LUNA. SO FAR WE HAVEN'T FOUND THE PICK--
PICKLE!
SHE MEANT PICKLE! CAN'T MAKE A GOOD SANDWICH WITHOUT ONE!

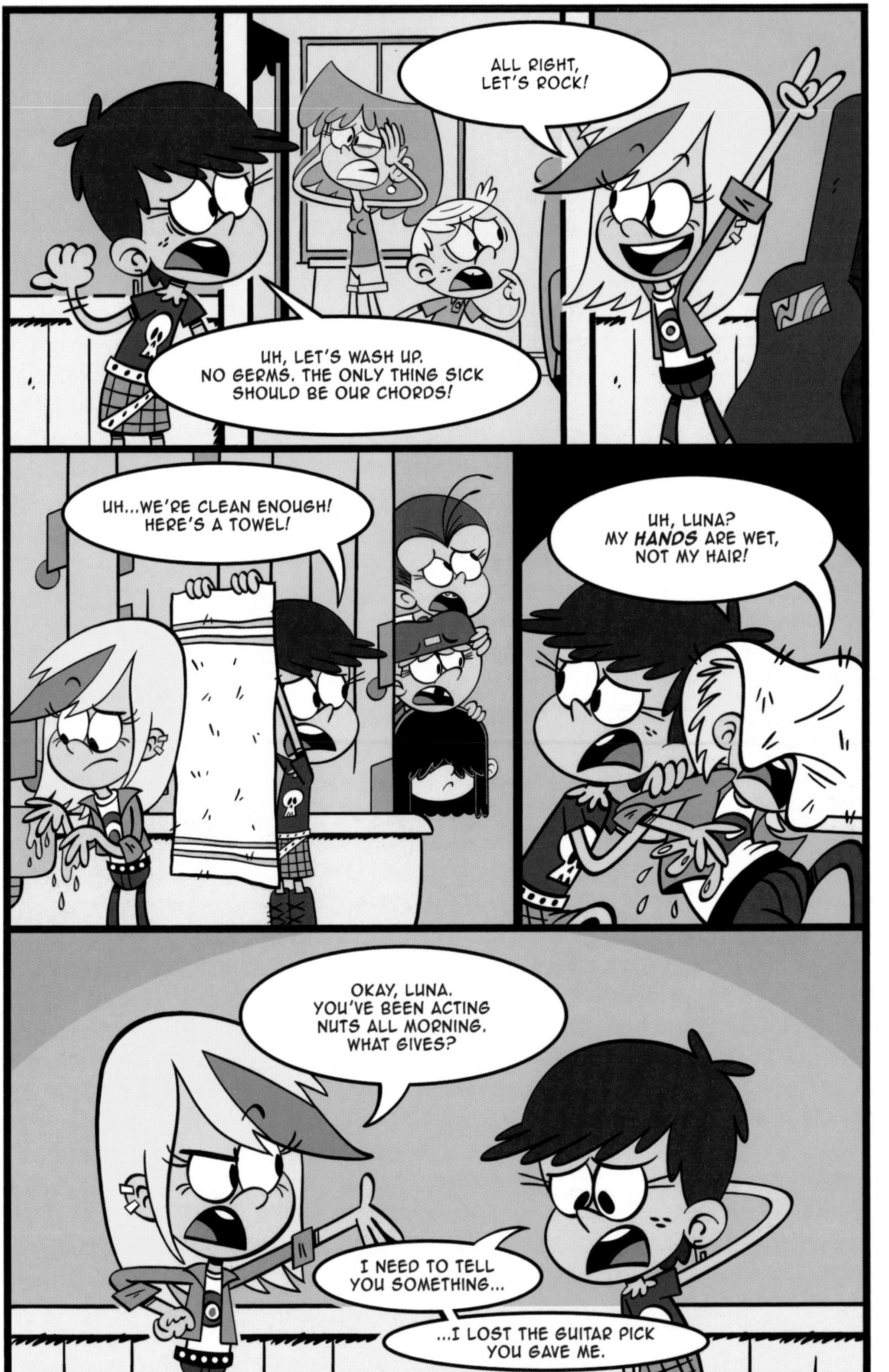
ALL RIGHT, LET'S ROCK!
UH, LET'S WASH UP. NO GERMS. THE ONLY THING SICK SHOULD BE OUR CHORDS!
UH...WE'RE CLEAN ENOUGH! HERE'S A TOWEL!
UH, LUNA? MY HANDS ARE WET, NOT MY HAIR!
OKAY, LUNA. YOU'VE BEEN ACTING NUTS ALL MORNING. WHAT GIVES?
I NEED TO TELL YOU SOMETHING...
...I LOST THE GUITAR PICK YOU GAVE ME.

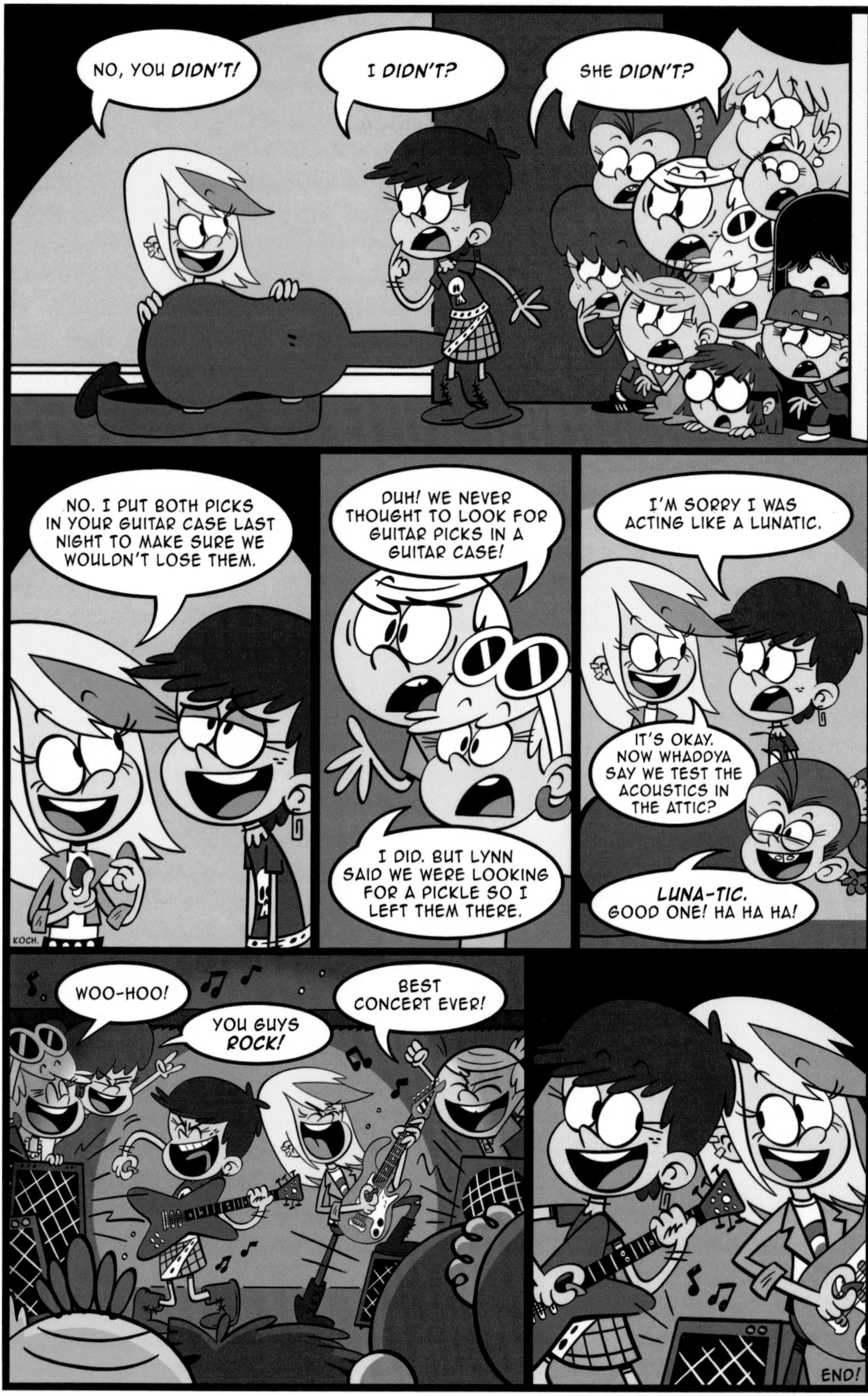
NO, YOU DIDN'T!
I DIDN'T?
SHE DIDN'T?
NO. I PUT BOTH PICKS IN YOUR GUITAR CASE LAST NIGHT TO MAKE SURE WE WOULDN'T LOSE THEM.
KOCH.
DUH! WE NEVER THOUGHT TO LOOK FOR GUITAR PICKS IN A GUITAR CASE!
I DID, BUT LYNN SAID WE WERE LOOKING FOR A PICKLE SO I LEFT THEM THERE.
I'M SORRY I WAS ACTING LIKE A LUNATIC.
IT'S OKAY. NOW WHADDYA SAY WE TEST THE ACOUSTICS IN THE ATTIC?
LUNA-TIC. GOOD ONE! HA HA HA!
WOO-HOO!
YOU GUYS ROCK!
BEST CONCERT EVER!
END!

"SHARE BEARS"

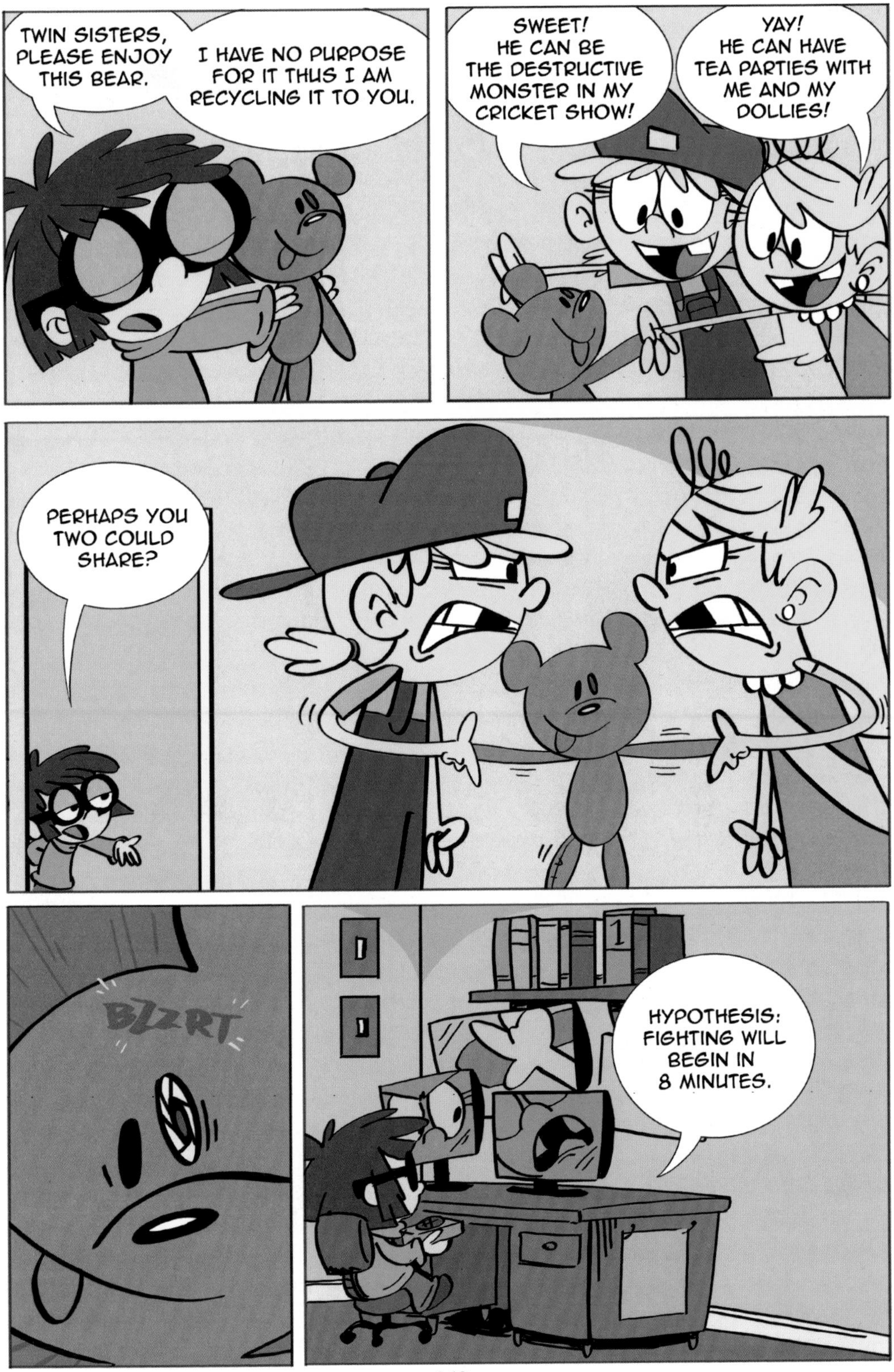
TWIN SISTERS, PLEASE ENJOY THIS BEAR.
I HAVE NO PURPOSE FOR IT THUS I AM RECYCLING IT TO YOU.
SWEET! HE CAN BE THE DESTRUCTIVE MONSTER IN MY CRICKET SHOW!
YAY! HE CAN HAVE TEA PARTIES WITH ME AND MY DOLLIES!
PERHAPS YOU TWO COULD SHARE?
BZZRT
HYPOTHESIS: FIGHTING WILL BEGIN IN 8 MINUTES.

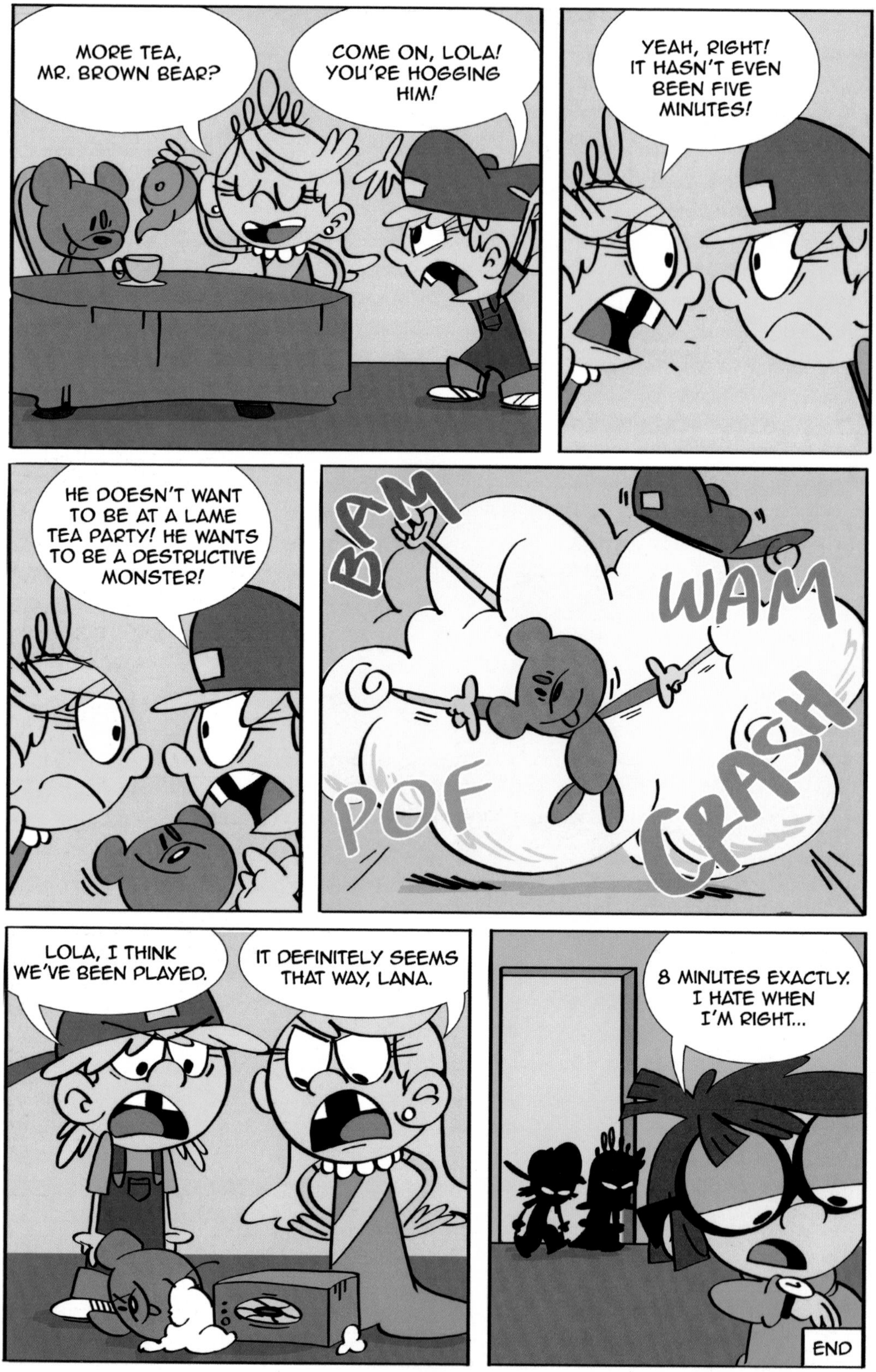
MORE TEA, MR. BROWN BEAR?
COME ON, LOLA! YOU'RE HOGGING HIM!
YEAH, RIGHT! IT HASN'T EVEN BEEN FIVE MINUTES!
HE DOESN'T WANT TO BE AT A LAME TEA PARTY! HE WANTS TO BE A DESTRUCTIVE MONSTER!
BAM
WAM
POF
CRASH
LOLA, I THINK WE'VE BEEN PLAYED.
IT DEFINITELY SEEMS THAT WAY, LANA.
8 MINUTES EXACTLY. I HATE WHEN I'M RIGHT...
END

"HELP WANTED"

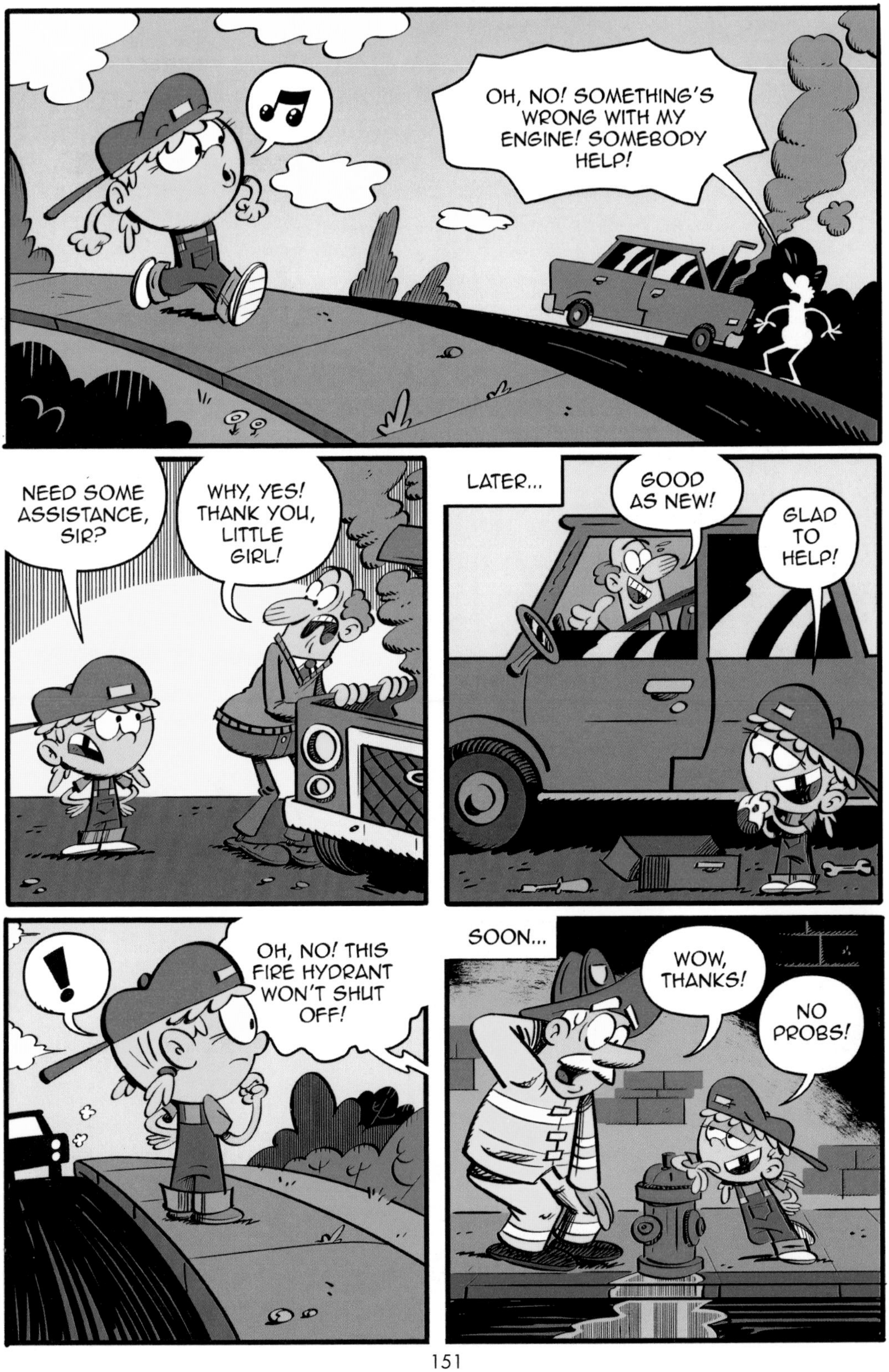

OH, NO! SOMETHING'S WRONG WITH MY ENGINE! SOMEBODY HELP!
NEED SOME ASSISTANCE, SIR?
WHY, YES! THANK YOU, LITTLE GIRL!
LATER...
GOOD AS NEW!
GLAD TO HELP!
!
OH, NO! THIS FIRE HYDRANT WON'T SHUT OFF!
SOON...
WOW, THANKS!
NO PROBS!

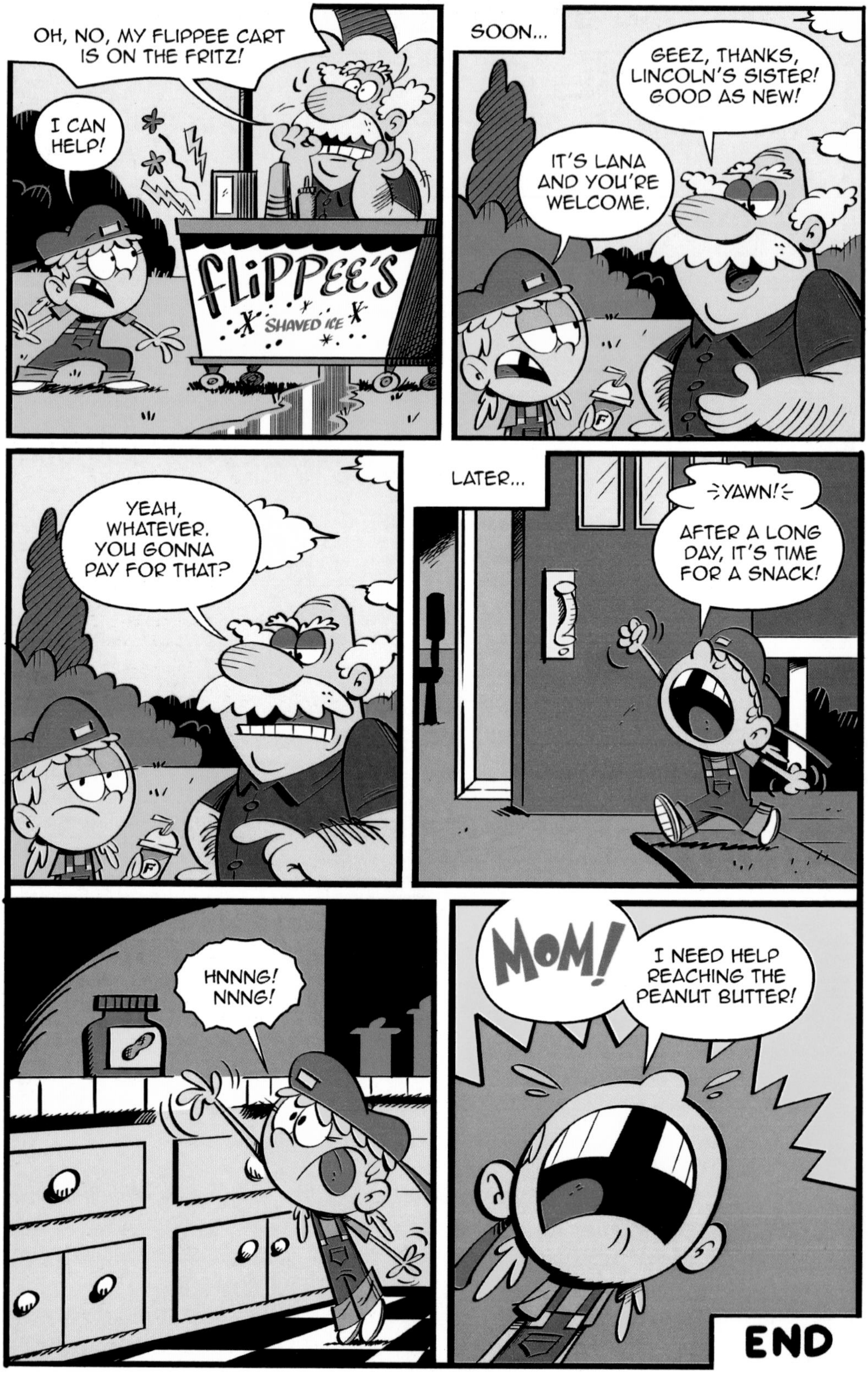
OH, NO, MY FLIPPEE CART IS ON THE FRITZ!
I CAN HELP!
FLIPPEE'S
SHAVED ICE
SOON...
GEEZ, THANKS, LINCOLN'S SISTER! GOOD AS NEW!
IT'S LANA AND YOU'RE WELCOME.
YEAH, WHATEVER. YOU GONNA PAY FOR THAT?
LATER...
YAWN!
AFTER A LONG DAY, IT'S TIME FOR A SNACK!
HNNNG! NNNG!
MOM!
I NEED HELP REACHING THE PEANUT BUTTER!
END

"ABCs OF GETTING THE LAST SLICE"

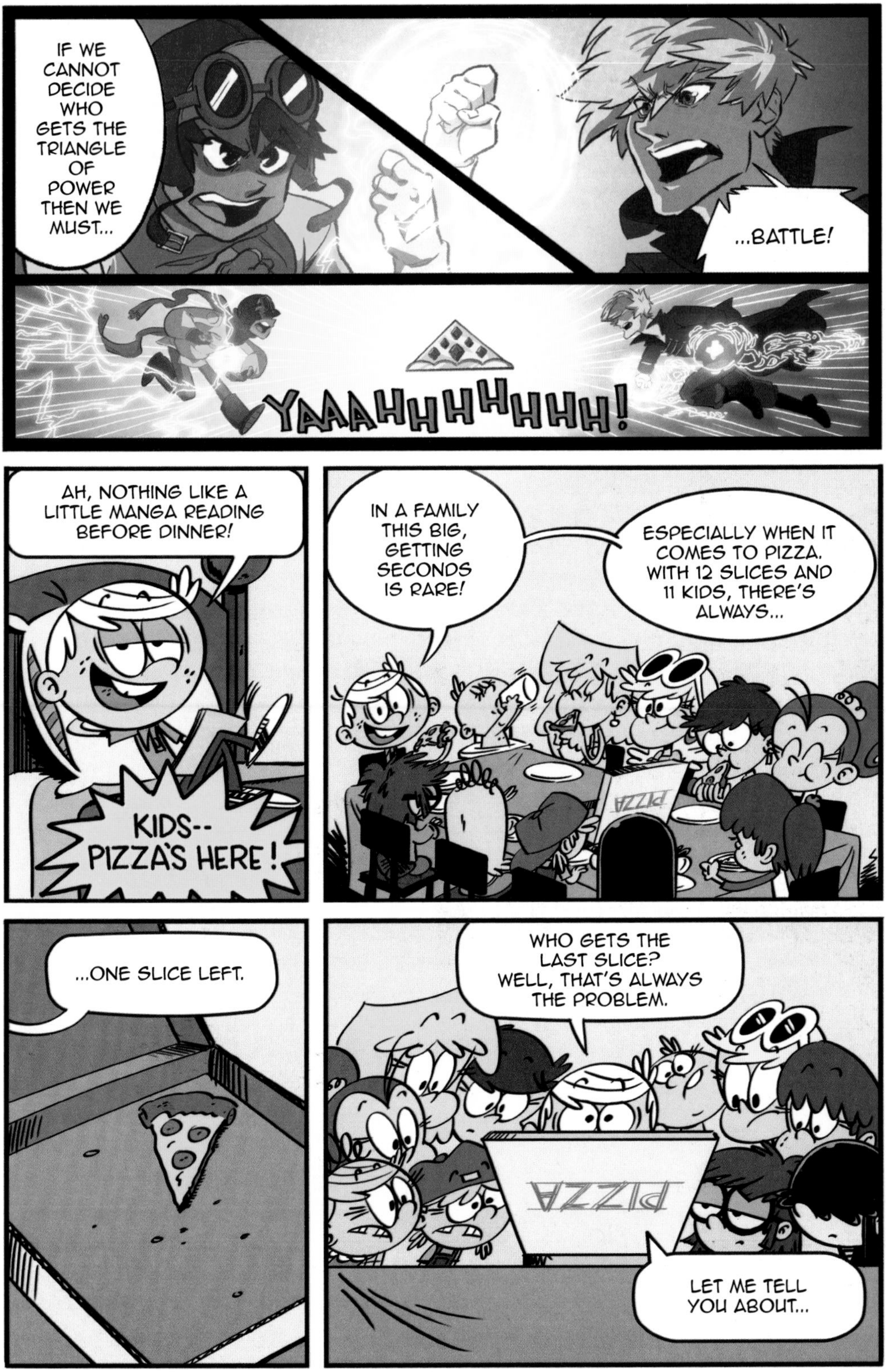
IF WE CANNOT DECIDE WHO GETS THE TRIANGLE OF POWER THEN WE MUST...
...BATTLE!
YAAAHHHHHHHH!
AH, NOTHING LIKE A LITTLE MANGA READING BEFORE DINNER!
KIDS-- PIZZA'S HERE!
IN A FAMILY THIS BIG, GETTING SECONDS IS RARE!
ESPECIALLY WHEN IT COMES TO PIZZA. WITH 12 SLICES AND 11 KIDS, THERE'S ALWAYS...
PIZZA
...ONE SLICE LEFT.
WHO GETS THE LAST SLICE? WELL, THAT'S ALWAYS THE PROBLEM.
PIZZA
LET ME TELL YOU ABOUT...

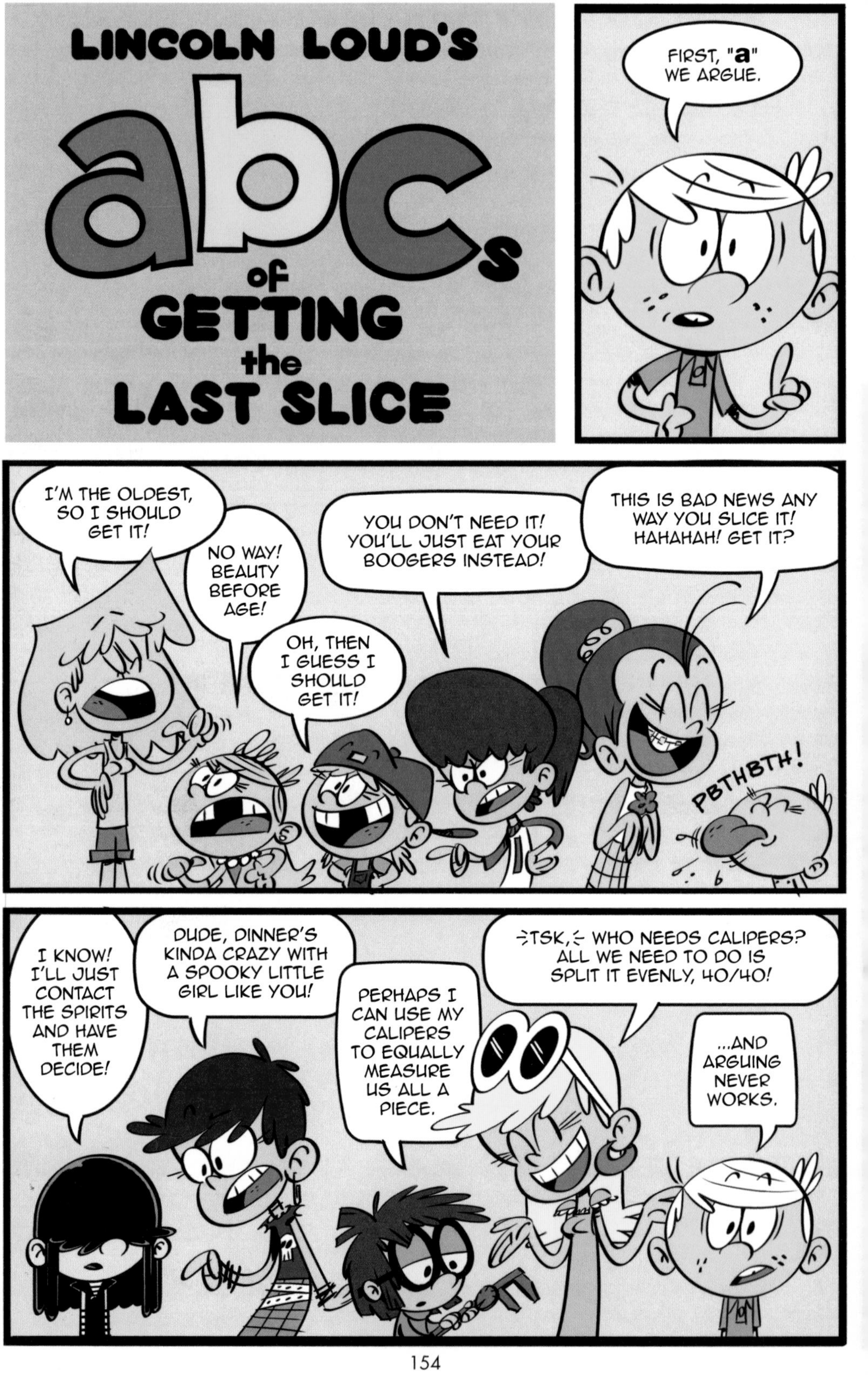
LINCOLN LOUD'S abcs of GETTING the LAST SLICE
FIRST, "a" WE ARGUE.
I'M THE OLDEST, SO I SHOULD GET IT!
NO WAY! BEAUTY BEFORE AGE!
OH, THEN I GUESS I SHOULD GET IT!
YOU DON'T NEED IT! YOU'LL JUST EAT YOUR BOOGERS INSTEAD!
THIS IS BAD NEWS ANY WAY YOU SLICE IT! HAHAHAH! GET IT?
PBTHBTH!
I KNOW! I'LL JUST CONTACT THE SPIRITS AND HAVE THEM DECIDE!
DUDE, DINNER'S KINDA CRAZY WITH A SPOOKY LITTLE GIRL LIKE YOU!
PERHAPS I CAN USE MY CALIPERS TO EQUALLY MEASURE US ALL A PIECE.
TSK, WHO NEEDS CALIPERS? ALL WE NEED TO DO IS SPLIT IT EVENLY, 40/40!
...AND ARGUING NEVER WORKS.

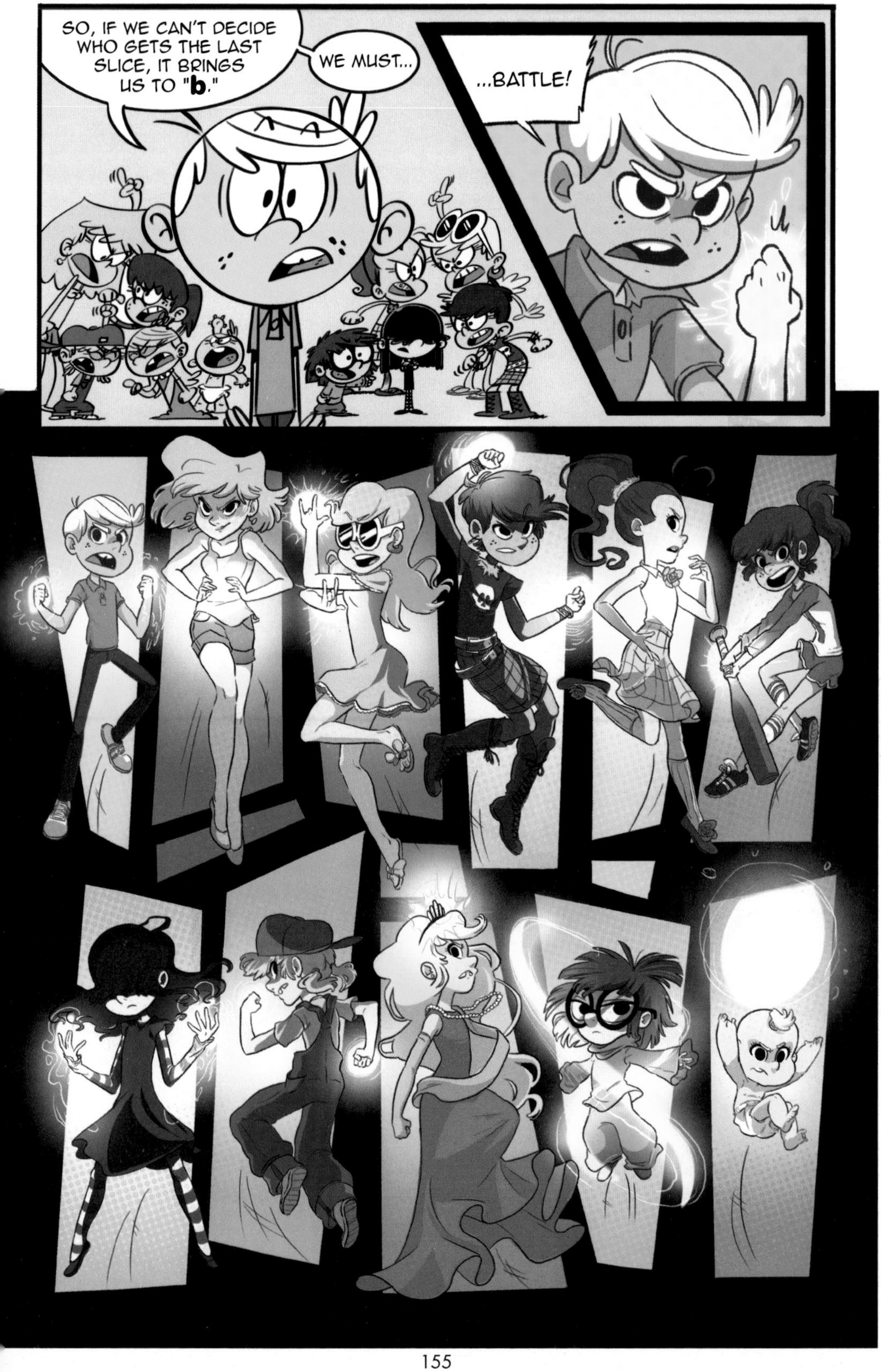
SO, IF WE CAN'T DECIDE WHO GETS THE LAST SLICE, IT BRINGS US TO "b."
WE MUST...
...BATTLE!

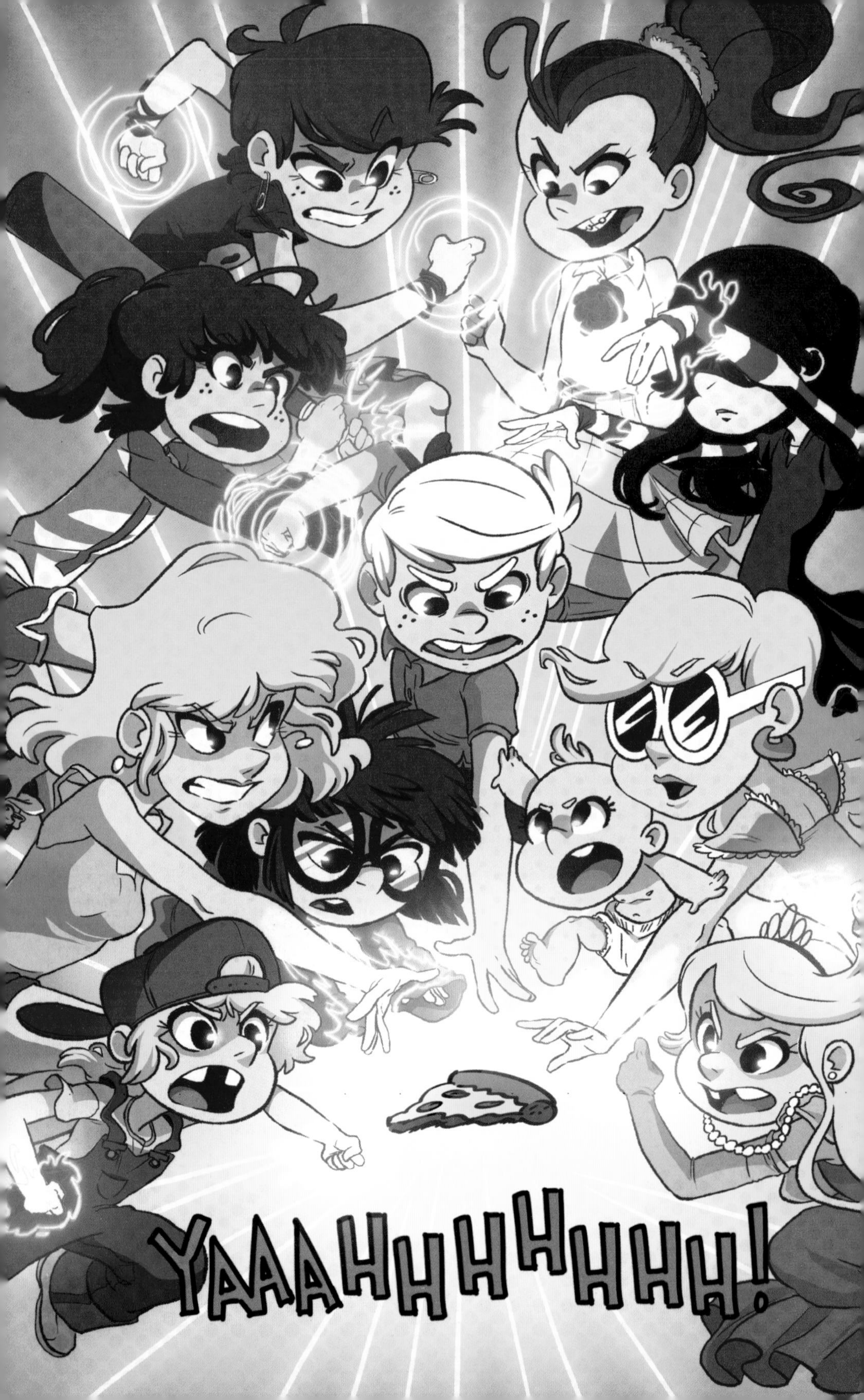
YAAAHHHHHHHH!

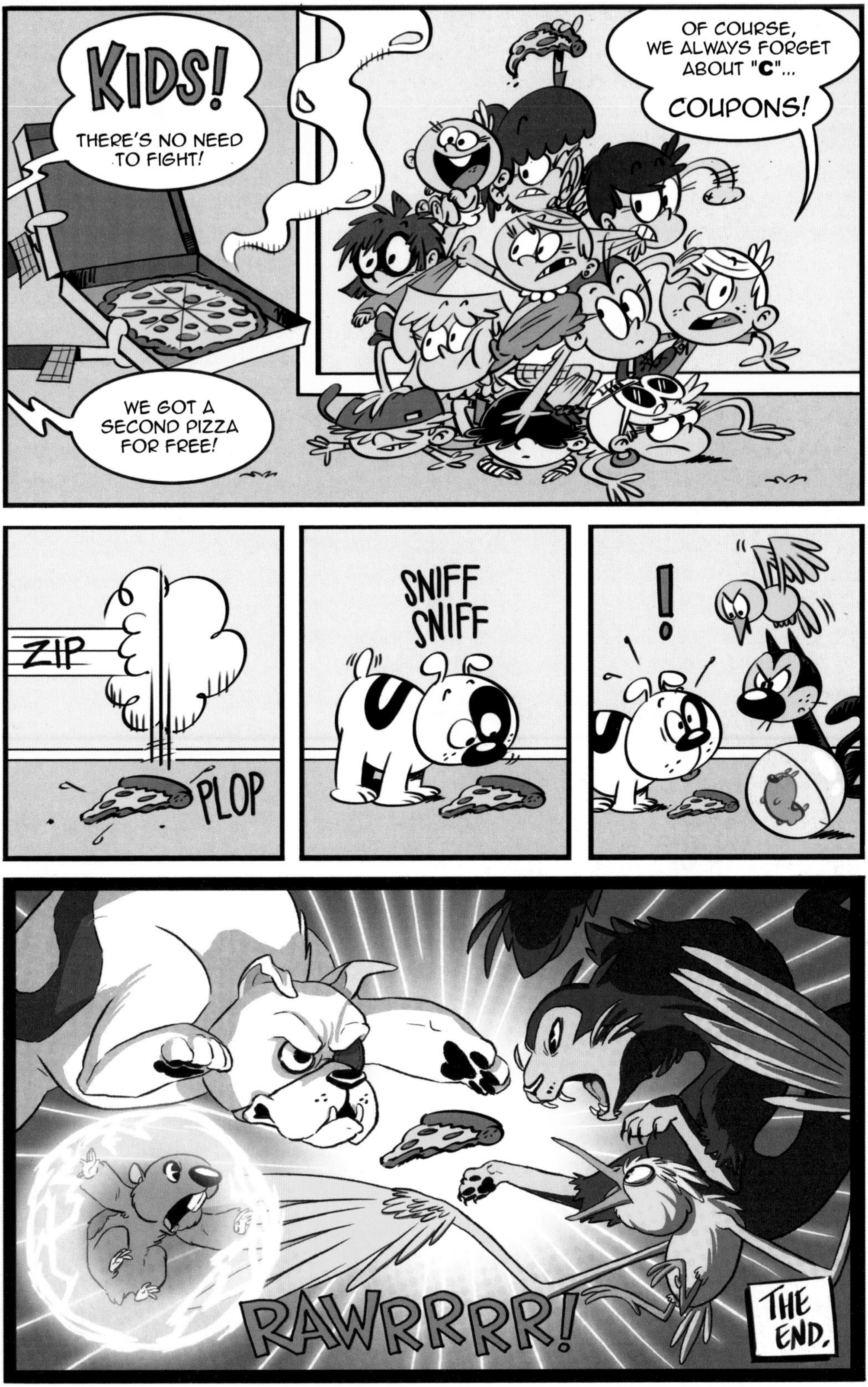

KIDS!
THERE'S NO NEED TO FIGHT!
WE GOT A SECOND PIZZA FOR FREE!
OF COURSE, WE ALWAYS FORGET ABOUT "C"...
COUPONS!
ZIP
PLOP
SNIFF SNIFF
!
RAWRRRR!
THE END.

"BEDTIME STORIES"

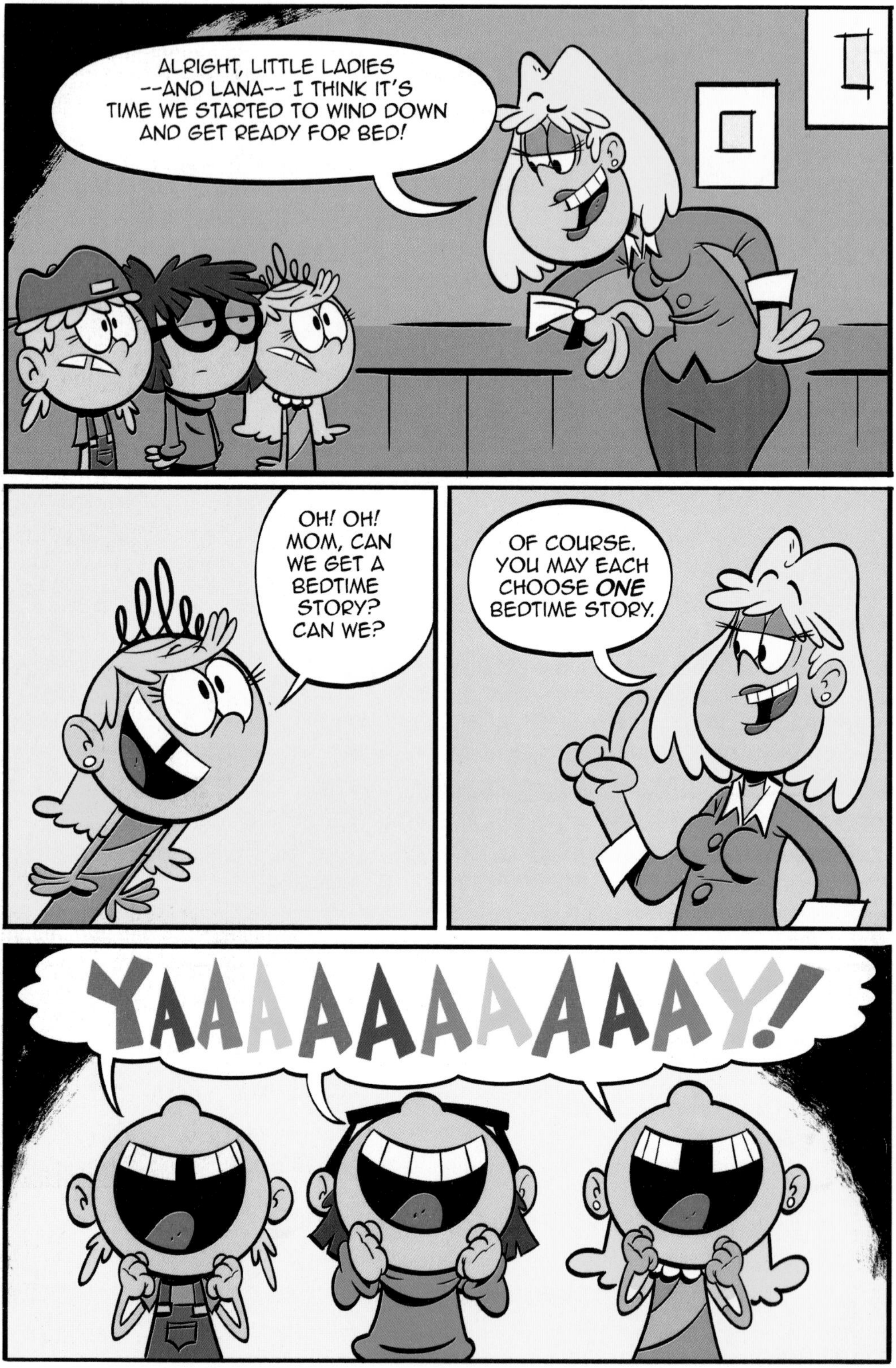
ALRIGHT, LITTLE LADIES --AND LANA-- I THINK IT'S TIME WE STARTED TO WIND DOWN AND GET READY FOR BED!
OH! OH! MOM, CAN WE GET A BEDTIME STORY? CAN WE?
OF COURSE. YOU MAY EACH CHOOSE *ONE* BEDTIME STORY.
YAAAAAAAAAY!

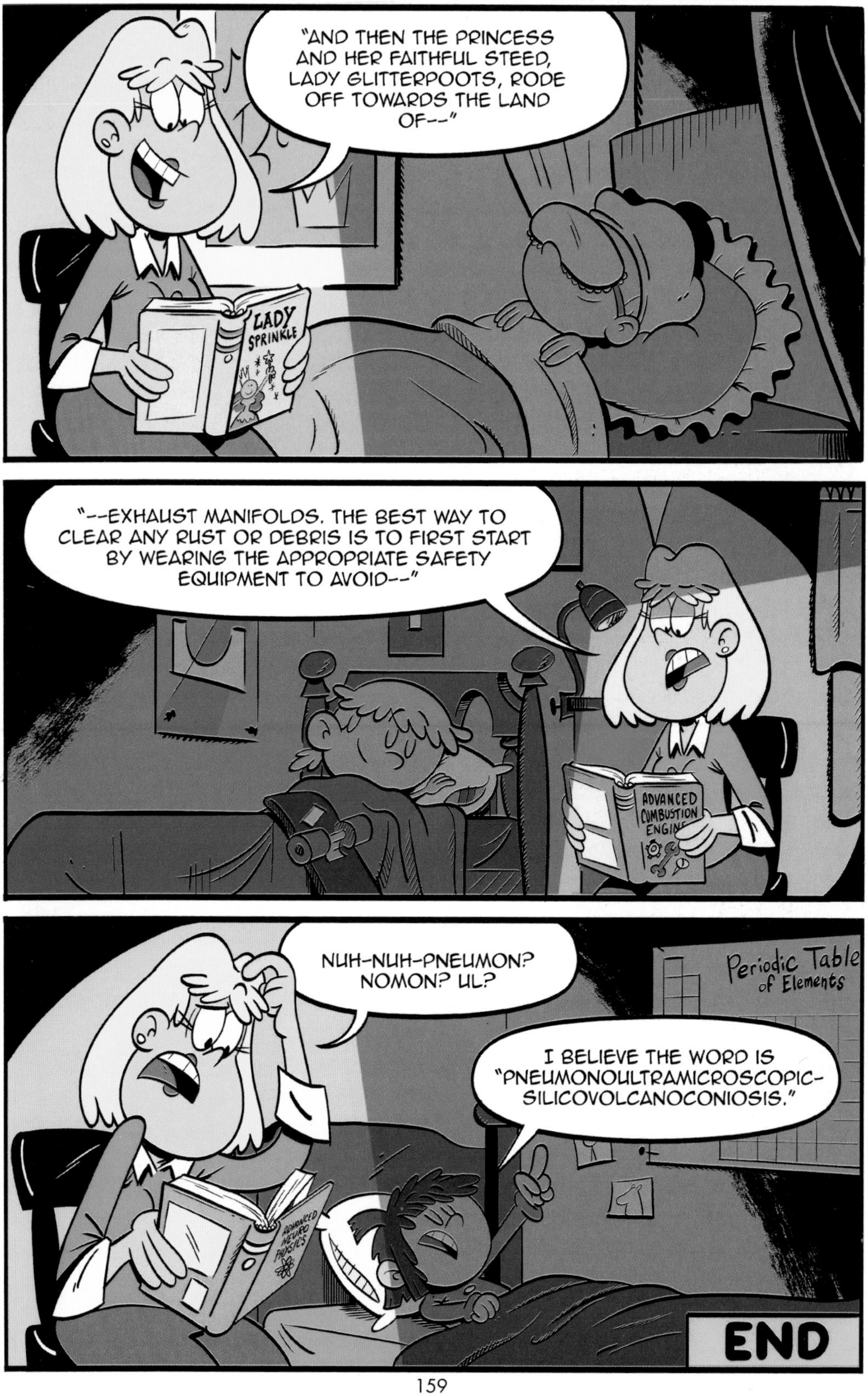
"AND THEN THE PRINCESS AND HER FAITHFUL STEED, LADY GLITTERPOOTS, RODE OFF TOWARDS THE LAND OF--"
LADY SPRINKLE
"--EXHAUST MANIFOLDS. THE BEST WAY TO CLEAR ANY RUST OR DEBRIS IS TO FIRST START BY WEARING THE APPROPRIATE SAFETY EQUIPMENT TO AVOID--"
ADVANCED COMBUSTION ENGIN
NUH-NUH-PNEUMON? NOMON? UL?
Periodic Table of Elements
I BELIEVE THE WORD IS "PNEUMONOULTRAMICROSCOPIC-SILICOVOLCANOCONIOSIS."
ADVANCED NEURO PHYSICS
END

WATCH OUT FOR PAPERCUTZ

Welcome to the first THE LOUD HOUSE 3 IN 1 graphic novel from Papercutz—those unrelated siblings dedicated to publishing great graphic novels for all ages. I'm Jim Salicrup, the Editor-in-Chief and the Unofficial Loser-of-THE LOUD HOUSE-Remote-Control.

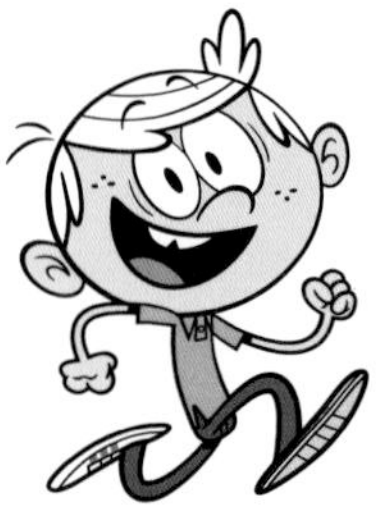

The idea here is simple — we're combining the first three THE LOUD HOUSE graphic novels into one great big graphic novel!

THE LOUD HOUSE, as if you didn't already know, is Nickelodeon's latest hit show, and THE LOUD HOUSE fans can't get enough. That's why THE LOUD HOUSE graphic novels have also been such a big hit—you want more of Lincoln Loud and his family and friends, and Papercutz is here to give it to you! Since the very first comic we've been working closely with the writers and animators of THE LOUD HOUSE to make sure these comics are as faithful to the TV series as possible. These comics are, in fact, created by the very same talented writers and animators who create the TV series. And the stories in THE LOUD HOUSE graphic novels are all-new!

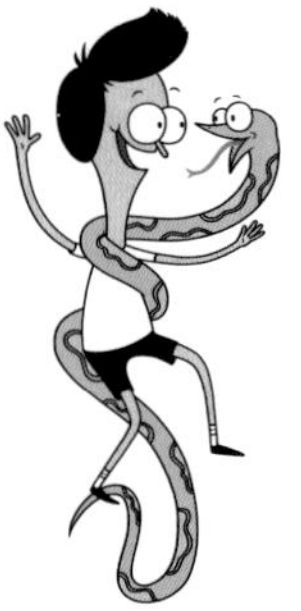

But with all the noise coming from THE LOUD HOUSE, it's easy to forget all the other Papercutz graphic novels based on popular Nickelodeon shows. For example ...

SANJAY AND CRAIG Graphic Novels #1 - 3 – If you've never watched this hilarious show or picked up the graphic novels, here's what you're missing: It's the story of two best friends. Oh, yeah, one is a snake. Sanjay is a 12 year-old boy who proves the old adage, "There's nothing you can't accomplish (or destroy) as long as your best friend is a talking snake."

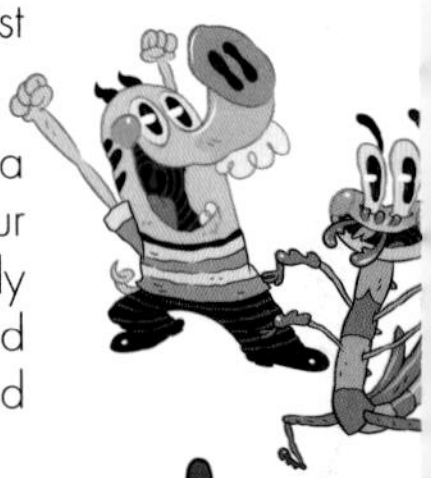

PIG GOAT BANANA CRICKET Graphic Novel #1 – What do a Pig, Goat, a Banana, and a Cricket have in common? Nothing! But that doesn't stop these four best friends from having the time of their lives in a weird and wild city where absolutely anything goes! They live together, argue with each other, stand up for each other, and even though their adventures may take them on different paths, they always start and end each day as a team.

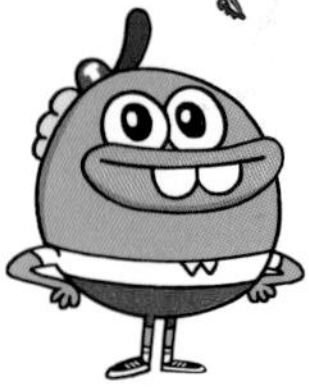

BREADWINNERS Graphic Novels #1 & 2 – SwaySway and Buhdeuce are two carefree ducks who fly around in a rocket van, delivering bread to hungry beaks everywhere. These two best buds get into all sorts of re-duck-ulous adventures together on their planet Pondgea. No matter what, nothing stops these two breadheads from shaking their tail feathers and getting a little bit QUAZY!

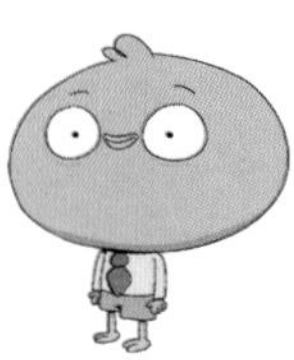

HARVEY BEAKS #1 & 2 – Harvey Beaks is the story of the unlikely friendship between Harvey, a kidwho has never broken the rules, and his two friends, Fee and Foo, who've never lived by ANY rules!

And there's NICKELODEON PANDEMONIUM! (#1-3) which is the graphic novel series that features... all of the above. That's right, you can get THE LOUD HOUSE, SANJAY AND CRAIG, PIG GOAT BANANA CRICKET, BREADWINNERS, and HARVEY BEAKS in every NICKELODEON PANDEMONIUM! graphic novel!

When it comes to great funny comics, just think Nickelodeon... and Papercutz!

STAY IN TOUCH!

EMAIL:	salicrup@papercutz.com
WEB:	papercutz.com
TWITTER:	@papercutzgn
INSTAGRAM:	@papercutzgn
FACEBOOK:	PAPERCUTZGRAPHICNOVELS
FANMAIL:	Papercutz, 160 Broadway, Suite 700, East Wing, New York, NY 10038

Thanks,

Jim